ATLANTIS
FOUND

ATLANTIS

FOUND

CLIVE CUSSLER

G.P. PUTNAM'S SONS
NEW YORK

G. P. Putnam's Sons
Publishers Since 1838
a member of
Penguin Putnam Inc.
375 Hudson Street
New York, NY 10014

Library of Congress Cataloging-in-Publication Data

Cussler, Clive.
    Atlantis found / by Clive Cussler.
       p.   cm.
    ISBN 0-399-14588-5
    I. Title
    PS3553.U75A94   1999   99-39883   CIP
    813'.54—dc21

Printed in the United States of America

10 9 8 7 6 5 4 3 2 1

This book is printed on acid-free paper. ∞

ACKNOWLEDGMENTS

I AM VERY GRATEFUL to Major Joe Andrzejewski (Retired) for his generous and valuable advice on the Special Forces.

My thanks also to K. Eric Drexler and Christine Peterson, the leading champions of nanotechnology, for their guidance, and John Stevens, who led me through the labyrinth of the Pandora Mine. Also to Colonel Howard A. Buechner, Donald Cyr, Graham Hancock, Charles Hapgood, and Plato, whose books and words were invaluable to me, and to Paul Mollar, for the loan of his incredible Skycar.

IMPACT

COMET IMPACT ON HUDSON BAY

THE INTRUDER CAME FROM beyond. A nebulous celestial body as old as the universe itself, it had been born in a vast cloud of ice, rocks, dust, and gas when the outer planets of the solar system were formed 4.6 billion years ago. Soon after its scattered particles had frozen into a solid mass one mile in diameter, it began streaking silently through the emptiness of space on an orbital voyage that carried it around a distant sun and halfway to the nearest stars again, a journey lasting many thousands of years from start to finish.

The comet's core, or nucleus, was a conglomeration of frozen water, carbon monoxide, methane gas, and jagged blocks of metallic rocks. It might accurately be described as a dirty snowball hurled through space by the hand of God. But as it whirled past the sun and swung around on its return path beyond the outer reaches of the solar system, the solar radiation reacted with its nucleus and a metamorphosis took place. The ugly duckling soon became a thing of beauty.

As it began to absorb the sun's heat and ultraviolet light, a long comma formed that slowly grew into an enormous luminous blue tail that curved and stretched out behind the nucleus for a distance of 90 million miles. A shorter, white dust tail more than one million miles wide also materialized and curled out on the sides of the larger tail like the fins of a fish.

Each time the comet passed the sun, it lost more of its ice and its nucleus diminished. Eventually, in another 200 million years, it would lose all its ice and break up into a cloud of dust and become a series of small meteorites. This comet, however, would never orbit outside the solar system or pass around the sun again. It would not be allowed a slow, cold death far out in the blackness of space. Within a few short minutes, its life would be snuffed out. But on this, its latest orbit, the comet passed within 900,000 miles of Jupiter, whose great gravitational force veered it off on a collision course with the third planet from the sun, a planet its inhabitants called Earth.

Plunging into Earth's atmosphere at 130,000 miles an hour on a forty-five-degree angle, its speed ever-increasing with the gravitational pull, the comet created a brilliant luminescent bow shock as its ten-mile-wide, four-billion-ton mass began to break into fragments due to friction from its great speed. Seven seconds later, the misshapen comet, having become a blinding fireball, smashed onto Earth's surface with horrendous effect. The immediate result from the explosive release of kinetic energy upon impact was to gouge out a massive cavity twice the size of the island of Hawaii as it vaporized and displaced a gigantic volume of water and soil.

The entire earth staggered from the seismic shock of a 12.0 earthquake. Millions of tons of water, sediment, and debris burst upward, thrown through the hole in the atmosphere above the impact site and into the stratosphere, along with a great spray of pulverized, fiery rock that was ejected into suborbital trajectories before raining back to earth as blazing meteorites. Firestorms destroyed forests throughout the world. Volcanoes that had been dormant for thousands of years suddenly erupted, sending oceans of molten lava spreading over millions of square miles, blanketing the ground a thousand or more feet deep. So much smoke and debris were hurled into the atmosphere and later blown into every corner of the land by terrible winds that they blocked out the sun for nearly a year, sending temperatures plunging below freezing, and shrouding Earth in darkness. Climatic change in every corner of the world came with incredible suddenness. Temperatures at vast ice fields and northern glaciers rose until they reached between ninety and a hundred degrees Fahrenheit, causing a rapid meltdown. Animals accustomed to tropical and temperate zones became extinct overnight. Many, such as the woolly mammoths, turned to ice where they stood in the warmth of summer, grasses and flowers still undigested in their stomachs. Trees, along with their leaves and fruit, were quick-frozen. For days, fish that were hurled upward from the impact fell from the blackened skies.

Waves five to ten miles in height were thrown against the continents, surging over shorelines with a destructive power that was awesome in magnitude. Water swept over low coastal plains and swept hundreds of miles inland, destroying everything in its path. Endless quantities of debris and sediment from the ocean floors were spread over low landmasses. Only when the great surge smashed against the base of mountains did it curl under and begin a slow retreat, but not before changing the course of rivers, filling land basins with seas where none existed before and turning large lakes into deserts.

The chain reaction seemed endless.

With a low rumble that grew to the roar of continuous thunder, the mountains began to sway like palm trees under a light breeze as avalanches swept down their sides. Deserts and grassy plains undulated as the onslaught from the oceans reared up and struck inland again. The shock from the comet's impact had caused a sudden and massive displacement in Earth's thin crust. The outer shell, less than forty miles thick, and the mantle that lay over the hot fluid core buckled and twisted, shifting crustal layers like the skin of a grapefruit that had been surgically removed and then neatly replaced so it could move around the core of fruit inside. As if controlled by an unseen hand, the entire crust then moved as a unit.

Entire continents were shoved around to new locations. Hills were thrust up to become mountains. Islands thoughout the Pacific Ocean vanished, while others emerged for the first time. Antarctica, previously west of Chile, slid over two thousand miles to the south, where it was quickly buried under growing sheets of ice. The vast ice pack that once floated in the Indian Ocean west of Australia now found itself in a temperate zone and rapidly began to melt. The same occurred with the former North Pole, which had spread throughout northern Canada. The new pole soon began to produce a thick ice mass in the middle of what once had been open ocean.

The destruction was relentless. The convulsions and holocaust went on as if they would never stop. The movement of the Earth's thin outer shell piled cataclysm upon cataclysm. The abrupt melting of the former ice packs, combined with glaciers covering the continents that had suddenly shifted into or near tropical zones, caused the seas to rise four hundred feet, drowning the already destroyed land that had been overwhelmed by tidal waves from the comet's impact. In the time span of a single day, Britain, connected to the rest of the European continent by a dry plain, was now an island, while a desert that became known as the Persian Gulf was abruptly inundated. The Nile River, having flowed into a vast fertile valley and then on toward the great ocean to the west, now ended at what had suddenly become the Mediterranean Sea.

The last great ice age had ended in the geological blink of an eye.

The dramatic change in the oceans and their circulation around the world also caused the poles to shift, drastically disturbing the earth's rotational balance. Earth's axis was temporarily thrown off by two degrees, as the North and South Poles were displaced to new geographical locations, altering the centrifugal acceleration around the outer surface of the sphere. Because they were fluid, the seas adapted before the earth made another three revolutions. But the landmass could not react as quickly. Earthquakes went on for months.

Savage storms with brutal winds swirled around the earth, shredding and disintegrating everything that stood on the ground for the next eighteen years before the poles stopped wobbling and settled into their new rotational axis. In time, sea levels stabilized, permitting new shorelines to form as bizarre climatic conditions continued to moderate. Changes became permanent. The time sequence between night and day changed as the number of days in a year decreased by two. The earth's magnetic field was also affected and moved northwest over a hundred miles.

Hundreds, perhaps thousands, of different species of animals and fish became instantly extinct. In the Americas, the one-humped camel, the mammoth, an ice age horse, and the giant sloth all disappeared. Gone also were the saber-toothed tiger, huge birds with twenty-five-foot wingspans and many other animals that weighed a hundred or more pounds, most dying by asphyxiation from the smoke and volcanic gases.

Nor did the vegetation on land escape the apocalypse. Plant life not turned to ashes by the holocaust died for lack of sunlight, along with the algae in the seas. In the end, over 85 percent of all life on Earth would die from floods, fires, storms, avalanches, poison from the atmosphere, and eventual starvation.

Human societies, many quite advanced, and a myriad of emerging cultures on the threshold of a progressive golden age were annihilated in a single horrendous day and night. Millions of Earth's men, women, and children died horribly. All vestiges of emerging civilizations were gone, and the few pathetic survivors were left with nothing but dim memories of the past. The coffin had been closed on the greatest uninterrupted advance of mankind, a ten-thousand-year journey from the simple Cro-Magnon man to kings, architects, stonemasons, artists, and warriors. Their works and their mortal remains were buried deep beneath new seas, leaving few physical examples and fragments of an ancient advanced culture. Entire nations and cities that had stood only a few hours before vanished without a trace. The cataclysm of such magnitude left almost no evidence of any prior transcendent civilizations.

Of the shockingly low number of humans who survived, almost all lived in the higher altitudes of mountain ranges and were able to hide in caves to escape the furies of the turbulence. Unlike the more advanced Bronze Age peoples who tended to cluster and build on low-lying plains near rivers and ocean shorelines, the inhabitants of the mountains were Stone Age nomads. It was as though the cream of the crop, the Leonardo da Vincis, the Picassos, and the Einsteins of their era had evaporated into nothingness, abruptly leaving the world to be taken over by primitive nomadic hunters, a phenomenon similar to what happened to the glory of Greece and Rome after it was cast aside in favor of centuries of ignorance and creative lethargy. A neolithic dark age shrouded the grave of the highly cultured civilizations that once existed in the world, a dark age that would last for two thousand years. Slowly, very slowly, did mankind finally walk from the dark and begin building and creating cities and civilizations again in Mesopotamia and Egypt.

Pitifully few of the gifted builders and creative thinkers of the lost cultures survived to reach high ground. Realizing their civilization was lost, never to rise again, they began a centuries-long quest to erect the mysterious megaliths and dolmens of huge upright stones found across Europe, Asia, the Pacific Islands, and into the lower Americas. Long after the memory of their shining legacy had dimmed and become little more than myth, their monuments commemorating the frightful destruction and loss of life still acted as warnings of the next cataclysm to future generations. But within a millennium, their descendants slowly forgot the old ways and assimilated with the nomadic tribes and ceased to exist as a race of advanced people.

For hundreds of years after the convulsion, humans were afraid to venture down from the mountains and reinhabit the lower lands and coastal shorelines. The technically superior seafaring nations were but vague thoughts of a distant past. Ship construction and sailing techniques were lost and had to be reinvented by later generations whose more accomplished ancestors were revered simply as gods.

All this death and devastation was caused by a hunk of dirty ice no larger than a small farm town in Iowa. The comet had wreaked its unholy havoc, mercilessly, viciously. The earth had not been ravaged with such vehemence since a meteor had struck 65 million years earlier in a catastrophe that had exterminated the dinosaurs.

For thousands of years after the impact, comets were associated with superstitions of catastrophic events and considered omens of future tragedies. They were blamed for everything from wars and pestilence to death and destruction. Not until recent history were comets considered nature's wonders, like the splendor of a rainbow or clouds painted gold by a setting sun.

The biblical flood and a host of other calamity legends all had ties to this one tragedy. The ancient civilizations of Olmecs, Mayans, and Aztecs of Central America had many traditions relating to an ancient cataclysmic event. The Indian tribes throughout the United States passed down stories of waters flooding over their lands. The Chinese, the Polynesians, and Africans all spoke of a cataclysm that decimated their ancestors.

But the legend that was spawned and that flourished throughout the centuries, the one that provoked the most mystery and intrigue, was that of the lost continent and civilization of Atlantis.

GHOST SHIP

ICEBOUND BRITISH INDIAMAN

ROXANNA MENDER KNEW THAT if she stopped walking she would die. She was near complete exhaustion and moving on willpower alone. The temperature was well below zero, but it was the windchill from the frigid teeth of the ice gale that was biting through her skin. The deadly drowsiness gently slipping over her was slowly draining her will to live. She moved forward, one foot groping ahead of the other, stumbling when caught off balance by a sudden break in the ice field. Her breath came in the rapid, rasping panting of a mountain climber struggling toward a peak in the Himalayas without oxygen equipment.

Her vision was nonexistent as the icy windblown particles swirled in front of her face, protected by a thick woolen scarf wrapped inside her fur-lined parka. Though she only squinted between the layers of the scarf every other minute, her eyes were sore and reddened from the onslaught of the tiny granules. Frustration gripped Roxanna when she looked up and saw the dazzling blue sky and brilliant sun above the storm. Blinding ice storms under clear skies were not an uncommon phenomenon in Antarctica.

Surprisingly, snow rarely falls in the South Polar region. It is so incredibly cold that the atmosphere cannot contain water vapor, so any snowfall is minimal. Not more than five inches falls over the continent in the course of a year. Some of the snow that is already on the ground is actually several thousand years old. The harsh sun strikes the white ice on an oblique angle and its heat is reflected back into space, contributing largely to the extraordinarily cold temperatures.

Roxanna was fortunate. The cold did not penetrate her clothing. Rather than wearing European cold-weather garb, she was dressed in clothing her husband had acquired while trading with Eskimos during his earlier whaling expeditions in the Arctic. Her inner clothing consisted of a tunic, short knee-length pants, and a socklike boot made with soft fur worn against her feet. Separate outerwear protected against extreme cold. The parka was loose-fitting to allow body heat to circulate and escape without the problem of sweat buildup. It was made from wolf fur, while the pants came from a caribou. The boots stood high and were worn over the socks, with the fur inward.

Her greatest physical danger lay in breaking an ankle or leg on the uneven surface, and if she somehow survived, there was the threat of frostbite. Though her body was protected, it was her face that worried her. At the least tingle on either her cheek or nose, she vigorously rubbed the skin to restart circulation. She had already watched six of her husband's crew develop frostbite, two of them losing toes and one his ears.

Thankfully, the icy gale began to die away and lose its violence, and her progress became easier than it had been for the past hour she had been wandering lost. The howling wind faded from her ears, and she could hear the squeak of the ice crystals beneath her feet.

She reached a hill about fifteen feet high from base to ridge formed by the restless sea ice grinding and forcing the floe upward into what was called a hummock. Most formed an uneven surface, but this one was weathered until its sides were smooth. Falling to her hands and knees, she clawed her way upward, sliding back two feet for every three she gained.

The exertion took what little strength Roxanna had left. Without knowing how, or remembering the struggle, she pulled herself onto the ridge of the hummock half-dead from exhaustion, heart pounding, breath coming in labored gasps. She did not know how long she lay there, but she was thankful to rest her eyes from the ice-plagued wind. After a few minutes, when her heart slowed and her breath began to come evenly, Roxanna cursed herself for the predicament she had foolishly caused. Time had no reference. Without a watch, she had no idea how many hours had passed since she walked from her husband's whaling ship, the *Paloverde*.

Nearly six months earlier, the ship had become locked in the pack ice, and to endure the boredom she had begun taking daily hikes, keeping within easy view of the ship and its crew, who kept an eye on her. That morning the skies had dawned crystal clear when she left the ship, but they soon turned dark and vanished when the ice storm swept over the ice. Within minutes, the ship had disappeared and Roxanna found herself wandering lost on the ice pack.

Traditionally, most whalers never sailed with women aboard. But many wives refused to sit at home for the three to four years their husbands were gone. Roxanna Mender was not about to spend thousands of lonely hours alone. She was a hardy woman, though petite, barely reaching five feet in height and weighing less than a hundred pounds. With her light brown eyes and ready smile, she was a pretty woman who seldom complained of the hardship and boredom and who rarely became seasick. In her cramped cabin she had already given birth to a baby boy, whom she had named Samuel. And though she had yet to tell her husband, she was about two months pregnant with the next baby. She had found acceptance aboard ship with the crew, taught several to read, written letters home to their wives and families, and acted as nurse whenever there was an injury or sickness on board.

THE *Paloverde* was one of the fleet of whalers that sailed from San Francisco on the nation's west coast. She was a stout ship, especially constructed for polar operations during the whaling season. With a length of 132 feet, a beam of 30 feet, and a draft of 17 feet, her tonnage was close to 330. Her dimensions allowed for a large cargo of whale oil and accommodations for a large crew of officers and men for voyages that could last as long as three years. Her pine keel, timbers, and beams were cut from the forests of the Sierra Nevada Mountains. Once they were positioned, the three-inch planking was laid on and fastened by trunnels, a wooden nail usually cut from oak.

She was rigged as a three-masted bark, and her lines were clean, bold, and rakish. Her cabins were neatly furnished and paneled in Washington spruce. The captain's cabin was particularly well appointed because of his wife's insistence that she accompany him on the long voyage. The figurehead was a finely carved image of a paloverde tree, native to the southwest. The ship's name was spread across the stern in carved letters gilded in gold. Also adorning the stern was a spread-winged carving of the California condor.

Instead of sailing north through the Bering Sea toward the Arctic and the more established waters for whale hunting, Roxanna's husband, Captain Bradford Mender, had taken the *Paloverde* south to the Antarctic. He believed that since the region was overlooked and seldom visited by the hardy whalers from New England, there was a golden opportunity to find virgin whaling grounds.

Soon after arriving near the Antarctic Circle, the crew took six whales as the ship sailed in the open water between the shore, often threading its way through a sea of icebergs. Then, in the last week of March, the Antarctic autumn, the ice built over the sea at incredible speed until it reached a thickness of nearly four feet. The *Paloverde* might still have escaped to clear water, but a sudden shift of wind became a howling gale that drove the ship back toward shore. With no avenue of escape left open, as the ice charged toward them in chunks larger than the ship itself, the crew of the *Paloverde* could only stand helpless and watch the cold trap spring shut.

The ice quickly surged around the whaler with such force as to shove her relentlessly toward the land as if caught in a giant fist. The clear water near the land was quickly filling with a sheet of ice. Mender and his crew desperately labored and finally succeeded in getting the *Paloverde*'s anchors to hold in six fathoms less than two miles from shore. But within hours, the ship was jammed tightly in the ice that continued to thicken, and soon all signs of water were replaced by a white shroud. The Antarctic winter was upon them, and the days began to shrink.

There was no hope of escaping, and mild weather with warmer temperatures was a good seven months away.

The sails were dried, rolled up, and stowed away, to be raised again in the spring, if divine providence allowed for warmer weather and permitted the ship to float free. Now, in anticipation of a long imprisonment, all food was carefully inventoried and rationed for the long months of winter. Whether the victuals stored aboard the ship could be stretched until the ice began to melt in the spring was anybody's guess. But dropping lines and hooks through holes in the ice had produced better-than-hoped-for results and a nice assortment of Antarctic fish were soon frozen in a deck larder. And then there were the comical penguins on the shore. There appeared to be millions of them. The only dilemma was that no matter how the ship's cook prepared their meat, it tasted most unpleasant.

The principal threats facing the crew of the whaler were the terrible cold and any sudden movement of the ice floe. The danger of freezing was greatly reduced by burning the oil from the whales they had harpooned before becoming locked in the ice. The hold still held more than a hundred barrels, easily enough to keep the stoves burning through the worst of the Antarctic winter.

Until now, the floe had been relatively undisturbed. But Mender knew that it was only a matter of time before the ice would buckle and shift. Then the *Paloverde* could easily find her hull crushed to splinters, her stout timbers flattened as if they were paper, by a massive migrating iceberg. He did not relish the thought of his wife and baby trying to survive on land until another ship was sighted in the summer. And the odds of that happening were a thousand to one at best.

There was also the deadly menace of disease. Seven of the men were showing signs of scurvy. The only bright area was that the vermin and rats had long before succumbed to the awful cold. The long Antarctic nights, the isolation and freezing wind, nurtured the gloom of apathy. Mender combated the restless boredom by keeping his men busy on chores, endless jobs to keep their minds and bodies active.

Mender had sat in his cabin at his desk and recalculated their odds of survival a hundred times. But no matter how he twisted the options and possibilities, the eventuality always remained the same. Their chances of floating undamaged and intact come spring were bleak indeed.

THE icy windstorm had ended as abruptly as it had arrived, and the sun returned. Peering through squinting eyes over the dazzling sparkle of the ice pack, Roxanna saw her shadow. How joyous to see her shadow again despite the endless emptiness around her. But then her heart surged as she scanned the horizon and spotted the *Paloverde* a good mile and a half away. The black hull was nearly hidden by the ice, but she could see the huge American flag flapping in the dying breeze and realized that her worried husband had hung it high in the rigging of the mainmast as a beacon. She found it hard to believe that she had strayed so far. In her numbed mind, she thought that she had remained reasonably close to the ship while wandering in circles.

The ice pack was not all empty isolation. Roxanna could see tiny specks moving across its surface, and she realized that it was her husband and his crew searching for her. She was about to stand up and wave, when suddenly she caught sight of something most unexpected—the masts of another ship looming between two giant floebergs, hummocks frozen together and grounded on the shore.

The three masts and bowsprit, along with their rigging, looked to be intact, with the sails furled. With the wind fallen to a slight breeze, she unwrapped the scarf from her face and eyes and could see that most of the ship's hull was embedded in the ice. Roxanna's father had been a sea captain who had commanded clipper ships in the tea trade to China, and as a young girl she had seen thousands of ships of all types of rigs and sails arrive and depart Boston, but the only time she had seen a ship like the one encrusted with ice was in a painting that hung in her grandfather's house.

The ghostly ship was old, very old, with a huge rounded stern bearing windows and quarter galleries that hung over the water. She had been built long, narrow, and deep. A good 140 feet in length with at least a 35-foot beam, Roxanna estimated. Like the ship she had seen in the painting. This one had to be an 800-ton British Indiaman of the late eighteenth century.

She turned from the ship and waved her scarf to attract her husband and crew. One caught the movement on the ice out of the corner of his eye and alerted the others. They quickly began running across the broken ice toward her, with Captain Mender in the lead. Twenty minutes later, the crew of the *Paloverde* had reached her, shouting joyously at finding her alive.

Usually a quiet, taciturn man, Mender showed uncharacteristic emotion when he swept Roxanne into his arms, tears frozen to his cheeks, and kissed her long and lovingly. "Oh God!" he muttered, "I thought you were dead. It's truly a miracle you survived."

A whaling master at the age of twenty-eight, Bradford Mender was thirty-six and on his tenth voyage when his ship had become locked in the Antarctic ice. A tough, resourceful New Englander, he stood six feet tall and was big all over, weighing in at close to 225 pounds. His eyes were a piercing blue and his hair was black; a beard ran from ears to chin. Stern but fair, he never had a problem with officers and crew that he couldn't handle efficiently and honestly. A superb whale-hunter and navigator, Mender was also a shrewd businessman who was not only master of his ship but its owner as well.

"If you hadn't insisted I wear the Eskimo clothing you gave me, I would have frozen to death hours ago."

He released her and turned to the six members of his crew who surrounded them, cheered that the captain's wife had been found alive. "Let us get Mrs. Mender back to the ship quickly and get some hot soup in her."

"No, not yet," she said, clutching him by the arm and pointing. "I've discovered another ship."

Every man turned, their eyes following her outstretched arm.

"An Englishman. I recognized her lines from a painting in my grandfather's parlor in Boston. It looks like a derelict."

Mender stared at the apparition, which was ghostly white under its tomb of ice. "I do believe you're right. She does have the lines of a very old merchantman from the 1770s."

"I suggest that we investigate, Captain," said the *Paloverde*'s first mate, Nathan Bigelow. "She may still contain provisions that will help us survive till spring."

"They would have to be a good eighty years old," Mender said heavily.

"But preserved by the cold," Roxanna reminded him.

He looked at her tenderly. "You've had a hard time, dear wife. I'll have one of the men escort you back to the *Paloverde.*"

"No, husband," Roxanna said resolutely, her fatigue banished, "I intend to see what there is to see." Before the captain could protest, she took off down the slope of the hummock to the pack ice and set off toward the abandoned vessel.

Mender looked at his crew and shrugged. "Far be it from me to argue with a curious woman."

"A ghost ship," murmured Bigelow. "A great pity she's forever locked in the ice, or we could sail her home and apply for salvage rights."

"She's too ancient to be worth much," said Mender.

"Why are you men standing there in the cold, babbling?" said Roxanna, turning and urging the men on impatiently. "Let us hurry before another storm sweeps in."

Making their way over the ice as fast as possible until they reached the deserted ship, they found that the ice had piled against the hull, making it easy for them to reach the upper bulwarks and climb over the gunwales. Roxanna, her husband, and the crewmen found themselves standing on the quarterdeck, which was covered by a thin layer of ice.

Mender stared around at the desolation and shook his head as if bewildered. "Amazing that her hull wasn't crushed by the ice."

"I never thought I'd be standing on the deck of an English East Indiaman," one of the crewmen muttered, his eyes reflecting apprehension. "Certainly not one built before my grandfather was born."

"She's a good-sized ship," said Mender slowly. "About nine hundred tons, I'd guess. A hundred and fifty feet long with a forty-foot beam."

Laid and fitted out in a Thames River shipyard, the workhorse of the late-eighteenth-century British merchant fleet, the Indiaman was a crossbreed among ships. She was built mainly as a cargo carrier, but those were still the days of pirates and marauding warships from England's enemies, so she was armed with twenty-eight eighteen-pound cannon. Besides being built to transport goods and merchandise, she was also fitted out with cabins to carry passengers. Everything on the deck was standing, encased in ice, as if awaiting a phantom crew. The guns sat silently at their ports, the lifeboats were still lashed atop the spare spars, and all hatches were neatly in place.

There was an eerie and dreadful strangeness about the old ship, a curious grimness that belonged not of earth but of another world. A mindless fear gripped the crewmen who stood on the deck that some hoary, gruesome creature was waiting to receive them. Sailors are a superstitious lot, and there were none, except for Roxanna, who was in the innocent throes of almost girlish enthusiasm, who did not feel a deep sense of apprehension.

"Odd," said Bigelow. "It's as if the crew abandoned the ship before it became trapped in the ice."

"I doubt that," said Mender grimly. "The lifeboats are still stowed."

"God only knows what we'll find belowdecks."

"Then let's go see," Roxanna said excitedly.

"Not you, my dear. I think it best if you remain here."

She gave her husband a proud look and slowly shook her head. "I'll not wait alone while there are ghosts walking about."

"If there are any ghosts," said Bigelow, "they'd have frozen solid by now."

Mender gave orders to his men. "We'll divide into two search parties. Mr. Bigelow, take three men and look about the crew's quarters and the cargo hold. The rest of us will go aft and search the passenger and officers' quarters."

Bigelow nodded. "Aye, Captain."

Snow and ice had built up into a small mountain around the door leading into the stern cabins, so Mender led Roxanna and his men up and onto the poop deck, where they put their muscles to work and lifted the after hatch cover over a companionway that had frozen closed. Casting it aside, they cautiously dropped down the stair inside. Roxanna was directly behind Mender, clutching the belt around his heavy coat. The normally white complexion of her face was flushed red with a mixture of excitement and suspense.

She did not suspect that she was about to enter a frozen nightmare.

At the door to the captain's cabin, they found a huge German shepherd dog, curled upon a small rug. To Roxanna, the dog appeared to be asleep. But Mender nudged it with the toe of his boot, and the slight thud told them that the dog was frozen solid.

"Literally hard as a rock," said Mender.

"Poor thing," Roxanna murmured sadly.

Mender nodded at a closed door toward the aft end of the passageway. "The captain's cabin. I shudder to think what we may find in there."

"Maybe nothing," said one of the crewmen nervously. "Everybody probably fled the ship and trekked off along the coast northward."

Roxanna shook her head. "I can't imagine anyone leaving such a beautiful animal to die on board alone."

The men forced open the door to the captain's cabin and entered, to a gruesome sight. A woman dressed in clothing from the mid to late seventeen hundreds sat in a chair, her dark eyes open and staring with great sadness at the form of a small child lying in a crib. She had frozen to death while in deep sorrow at losing what appeared to be her young daughter. In her lap was an open Bible turned to the Psalms.

The tragic sight numbed Roxanna and the crew of the *Paloverde*. Her enthusiasm at exploring the unknown had suddenly evaporated into a feeling of anguish. She stood there with the others in silence, their hushed breath misting in that crypt of a cabin.

Mender turned and walked into an adjoining cabin and found the captain of the ship, who he rightly assumed was the dead woman's husband. The man was seated at a desk, slumped in a chair. His red hair was coated by ice and his face was dead white. One hand was still clutching a quill pen. A sheet of paper lay before him on the desk. Mender brushed away the frost and read the wording.

August 26, 1779

It has been five months since we were trapped in this accursed place after that storm drove us far off our course to the south. Food gone. No one has eaten for ten days. Most of the crew and passengers dead. My little daughter died yesterday, my poor wife only an hour ago. Whoever should find our bodies, please notify the directors of the Skylar Croft Trading Company of Liverpool of our fate. All is at an end. I shall soon join my beloved wife and daughter.

Leigh Hunt
Master of the *Madras*

The leather-bound logbook of the *Madras* lay to one side of Captain Hunt on the desk. Mender carefully dislodged it from the ice that froze the rear cover to the wooden desktop and placed the book inside his heavy coat. Then he stepped from the cabin and closed the door.

"What did you find?" asked Roxanna.

"The body of the captain."

"It's all so terrible."

"I imagine there is worse to see."

The words were prophetic. They divided up and went from cabin to cabin. The more exquisite passengers' accommodations were in the roundhouse, an expansive space with quarter galleries and windows partitioned into various-sized cabins in the stern below the poop deck. Passengers booked empty space. They had to furnish their cabin themselves, providing couches, beds, and chairs, all lashed down in anticipation of heavy weather. Wealthy passengers often brought such personal possessions as bureaus, bookshelves, and musical instruments, including pianos and harps. Here the searchers found nearly thirty bodies in various positions of death. Some died sitting upright, some lay in bed, while others were sprawled on the deck. All looked as if they had peacefully dozed off.

Roxanna was unsettled by those whose eyes were open. The color of their irises seemed enhanced by the pure white faces surrounding them. She cringed when one of the *Paloverde*'s crewmen reached out and touched the hair of one of the ladies. The frozen hair made a strange crackling noise and broke off in the crewman's hand.

The great cabin on the deck below the more elegant roundhouse staterooms looked like a morgue after a disaster. Mender saw any number of dead, mostly men, many of them British military officers in uniform. Forward was the steerage cabin, which was also filled with frozen corpses in hammocks slung over ship's supplies and luggage in the steerage compartment.

Everyone aboard the *Madras* had died peacefully. There was no sign of chaos. Nothing was in disarray. All articles and goods were stowed neatly. But for the final narrative by Captain Hunt, it seemed that time had stopped and they had all peacefully died as they lived. What Roxanna and Mender saw was not grotesque or terrifying but simply an overwhelming misfortune. These people had been dead for seventy-nine years and been forgotten by the passing world. Even those who had wondered about and mourned their disappearance were long since gone.

"I don't understand," said Roxanna. "How did they all die?"

"Those who didn't starve, froze," answered her husband.

"But they could have fished through the ice and shot penguin the same as we did, and burned parts of the ship to stay warm."

"The captain's last words say his ship was driven far off their course to the south. My guess is they were trapped in the ice much farther from shore than we were, and the captain, believing they would eventually drift free, followed the rules of good seamanship and forbid fires on board his ship for fear of an accidental conflagration, until it was too late."

"So, one by one, they died."

"Then, when spring came and the ice melted, instead of being carried by the current out into the South Pacific as a derelict, contrary winds drove the ship ashore, where it has lain since the last century."

"I think you're right, Captain," said first mate Bigelow, approaching from the forward part of the ship. "Judging from the clothing on the bodies, the poor devils did not expect a voyage that would take them into frigid waters. Most all appear better dressed for a tropical climate. They must have been sailing from India to England."

"A great tragedy," Roxanna sighed, "that nothing could have saved these unfortunate people."

"Only God," muttered Mender, "only God." He turned to Bigelow. "What cargo was she carrying?"

"No gold or silver that I could find, but a general cargo of tea, Chinese porcelain in tightly packed wooden crates, and bales of silk, along with a variety of rattan, spices, and camphor. And, oh yes, I found a small storeroom, locked with heavy chains, directly below the captain's cabin."

"Did you search it?" asked Mender.

Bigelow shook his head. "No, sir. I thought it only proper that you should be present. I left my men to work at breaking the chains."

"Maybe the room contains treasure," said Roxanna, a tinge of red returning to her cheeks.

"We'll soon find out." Mender nodded at Bigelow. "Mr. Bigelow, will you lead the way?"

The first mate led them down a ladder into the aft main steerage hold. The storeroom stood opposite an eighteen-pound cannon whose port was frozen shut. Two of the *Paloverde*'s crew were attacking the heavy padlock securing the chains that were bolted into the door. Using a sledgehammer and chisel found in the carpenters' workshop, they furiously hammered away at the lock's shackle until it snapped apart. Then they twisted the heavy door latch until it sprang free and the door could be pushed inward.

The interior was dimly lit by a small port in the bulwarks. Wooden crates were stacked from bulkhead to bulkhead, but the contents appeared to have been packed haphazardly. Mender stepped over to a large crate and easily lifted one end of the lid.

"These chests were not carefully packed and loaded aboard in port by commercial traders," he said quietly. "It looks to me like they were sloppily crated by the crew sometime during the voyage and placed under lock and key by the captain."

"Don't just stand there, husband," ordered Roxanna, mesmerized by curiosity. "Open them."

While the crew stood outside the storage room, Mender and Bigelow began prying open the wooden chests. No one seemed to notice the bitter cold. They were spellbound in anticipation of finding some great treasure in gold and gemstones. But when Mender held up one of the pieces of the contents from a chest, their hopes were quickly shattered.

"A copper urn," he said, passing it to Roxanna, who held it up in the brighter light of the steerage compartment. "Beautifully sculpted. Greek or Roman, if I'm any judge of antiquity."

Bigelow removed and passed several more artifacts through the open door. Most of them were small copper sculptures of strange-looking animals with black opal eyes. "They're beautiful," whispered Roxanna, admiring the designs that had been sculpted and etched into the copper. "They're nothing like anything I've seen in books."

"They do look unusual," agreed Mender.

"Are they of any value?" asked Bigelow.

"To a collector of antiquities or a museum maybe," answered Mender. "But I seriously doubt any of us could get rich off them. . . ." He paused as he held up a life-size human skull that gleamed black in the veiled light. "Good Lord, will you look at this?"

"It's frightening," muttered Bigelow.

"Looks like it was carved by Satan himself," murmured a crewman in awe.

Totally unintimidated, Roxanna held it up and stared into the empty eye sockets. "It has the appearance of ebony glass. And see the dragon coming out between its teeth."

"My guess, it's obsidian," observed Mender, "but I couldn't begin to presume how it was carved—" Mender was interrupted by a loud crackling sound, as the ice around the stern of the ship heaved and grumbled.

One of the crew dropped down the stairway from the upper deck, shouting, his voice high-pitched and harsh. "Captain, we must leave quickly! A great crack is spreading across the ice and pools of water are forming! I fear if we don't hurry, we'll be trapped here!"

Mender wasted no time in questions. "Get back to the ship!" he ordered. "Quickly!"

Roxanna wrapped the skull in her scarf and tucked it under one arm.

"No time for souvenirs," Mender snapped at her. But she ignored him and refused to let go of the skull.

Pushing Roxanna ahead of them, the men hurried up the stairway to the main deck and dropped down onto the ice. They were horrified to see that what had been a solid field of ice was now buckling and breaking up into ponds. Cracks turned into meandering streams and rivers as the seawater poured up through the ice onto the floe. None of them had any idea the floe could melt so fast.

Skirting the upheaved masses, some of them forty feet high, and leaping across the cracks before they widened and made crossing impossible, the crew and Roxanna ran as if all the banshees of hell were after them. The macabre, indescribable sounds of the ice grinding against itself struck terror in their minds. The going was exhausting; at every step their feet sank six inches into the blanket of snow that had accumulated on the level stretches of the floe.

The wind began to pick up again, and incredibly it felt warm, the warmest air they had felt since the ship had become jammed in the ice. After running a mile and a half, everyone was ready to collapse from exhaustion. The shouts of their shipmates on the *Paloverde,* begging them to hurry, urged them to greater efforts. Then, abruptly, it seemed that their struggle to gain the ship had ended in vain. The last crack in the ice before they could reach the safety of the *Paloverde* nearly defeated them. It had widened to twenty feet, too far for them to leap over, and was spreading at a rate of a foot every thirty seconds.

Seeing their predicament, the *Paloverde*'s second mate, Asa Knight, ordered the men on board to lower a whaleboat over the side, and they manhandled it across the ice to the fissure, which had now increased to nearly thirty feet. Heaving and pulling the heavy boat, the crew struggled to save the captain and his wife and their shipmates before it was too late. After a herculean effort, they reached the opposite edge of the fissure. By then, Mender, Roxanna, and the others were standing knee-deep in water that was coming up through the ice.

The boat was quickly pushed into the freezing water, and the men rowed it across the rapidly expanding river in the ice, to the vast relief of those minutes away from death on the other side. Roxanna was lifted over the side first, followed by the rest of the crew and Mender.

"We owe you a great debt, Mr. Knight," said Mender, shaking his second mate's hand. "Your daring initiative saved our lives. I especially thank you on behalf of my wife."

"And child," Roxanna added, as two crewmen wrapped her in blankets.

He looked at her. "Our child is safe on the ship."

"I wasn't talking about Samuel," she said, through chattering teeth.

Mender stared at her. "Are you telling me you're with child again, woman?"

"I think about two months."

Mender was appalled. "You went out on the ice in a storm knowing you were pregnant?"

"There was no storm when I set out," she said with a weak grin.

"Good Lord," he sighed, "what am I to do with you?"

"If you don't want her, Captain," said Bigelow jovially, "I'll be happy to have her."

Despite the fact that he was chilled to the bone, Mender laughed as he hugged his wife, nearly crushing the breath out of her. "Do not tempt me, Mr. Bigelow, do not tempt me."

HALF an hour later, Roxanna was back on board the *Paloverde*, changed into dry clothing and warming her body around the big brick-and-cast-iron stove used to melt whale blubber. Her husband and crew did not spare any time for creature comforts. The sails were hurriedly removed from the hold where they had been stowed, and were carried into the rigging. Soon they were unfurled, the anchors were pulled off the bottom, and, with Mender at the helm, the *Paloverde* began to thread her way through the melting water between huge icebergs toward the open sea again.

After enduring six months of cold and near starvation, the captain and crew were free of the ice and headed home, but not before they had filled her casks with seventeen hundred barrels of sperm oil.

The strange obsidian skull that Roxanna had taken from the frozen *Madras* went on the family mantel of their home in San Francisco. Mender dutifully corresponded with the current owners of the Skylar Croft Trade Company of Liverpool, who were operating under a new name, and sent off the logbook, giving the position where they had found the derelict ship on the shore of the Bellingshausen Sea.

The sinister and dead relic of the past remained in frigid isolation. An expedition consisting of two ships was mounted from Liverpool in 1862 to recover the *Madras*'s cargo, but neither ship was ever seen again and were presumed lost in the great ice floe around Antarctica.

Another 144 years would pass before men were to rediscover and set foot on the decks of the *Madras* again.

PART ONE

AS CLOSE TO HELL AS YOU CAN GET

AMENES ALPHABETIC AND NUMERIC INSCRIPTIONS

1

THE WANING STARS IN the early-morning sky blazed like a theater marquee when seen from 9,000 feet above sea level. But it was the moon that had a ghostly look about it as Luis Marquez stepped from his little wooden frame house. It wore a curious orange halo that he had never seen before. He peered at the odd phenomenon for a few moments before walking across the yard to his 1973 Chevy Cheyenne 4×4 pickup truck.

He had dressed in his work clothes and slipped quietly out of the house so as not to wake his wife and two daughters. His wife, Lisa, would have gladly gotten up and fixed breakfast and a sandwich for his lunch pail, but he insisted that 4:00 A.M. was too early for anyone but a mental case to be roaming around in the dark.

Marquez and his family lived simply. With his own hands, he had remodeled the house that had been built in 1882. His children went to school in nearby Telluride, and what he and Lisa couldn't buy in the booming resort ski town, they brought home during monthly shopping trips to the larger ranch community of Montrose, sixty-seven miles to the north.

His routine was never complete until he lingered over his coffee and stared around what was now a ghost town. Under the spectral light from the moon, the few buildings that still stood looked like tombstones in a cemetery.

Following the discovery of gold-bearing rock in 1874, miners poured into the San Miguel Valley and built a town they called Pandora, after the Greek fairy tale about a beautiful girl and her box full of mysterious spirits. A banking interest in Boston bought up the mining claims, financed the mine's operation, and constructed a large ore-processing plant only two miles above the more famous mining town of Telluride.

They'd called the mine the Paradise, and soon Pandora became a small company town of two hundred citizens with its own post office. The houses were neatly painted, with mowed green lawns and white fences, and although Pandora was set in a box canyon with only one way in and out, it was not isolated. The road to Telluride was well maintained, and the Rio Grande Southern Railroad ran a spur line into town to haul passengers and supplies to the mine and the processed ore across the Continental Divide to Denver.

There were those who swore the mine was cursed. The human cost of extracting fifty million dollars' worth of gold over forty years was high. A total of twenty-eight hard-rock miners had died inside the damp and forbidding shafts—fourteen in one disaster alone—while close to a hundred were maimed for life because of freak accidents and cave-ins.

Before the old-timers who had moved down the road and resided in Telluride died off, they'd claimed that the ghost of one of the dead miners could be heard moaning throughout the ten miles of empty shafts that honeycombed the steep, ominous gray cliffs that rose nearly 13,000 feet into the lazy blue skies of Colorado.

By 1931, all the gold that could be profitably processed from the ore with the aid of chemicals was exhausted. Played out, the Paradise Mine was shut down. Over the next sixty-five years, it became only a memory and a slowly healing scar on the panoramic landscape. Not until 1996 had its haunted shafts and tunnels heard the tread of boots and the clang of a pickax again.

Marquez shifted his stare onto the mountain peaks. A four-day storm had come and gone the week before, adding four feet of snow to the already packed slopes. The increasing air temperatures that accompanied the spring turned the snow into the consistency of mushy mashed potatoes. It was the prime avalanche season. Conditions were extremely hazardous in the high country, and skiers were warned not to wander from the established ski runs. As far as Marquez knew, no major snowslide had ever struck the town of Pandora. He was secure in knowing his family was safe, but he ignored the risk to himself every time he made the drive up the steep icy road in winter and worked alone deep in the bowels of the mountain. With the coming of warm days, a snow slide was an event waiting to happen.

Marquez had seen an avalanche only once in his years on the mountain. The sheer magnitude of its beauty and power as it swept rocks, trees, and snow down a valley in great clouds, along with the rumbling sound of thunder, was something he had never forgotten.

Finally, he set his hard hat on his head, slipped behind the wheel of the Chevy pickup, and started the engine, letting it idle for a couple of minutes to warm. Then he began cautiously driving up the narrow, unpaved road that led to the mine that once was the leading gold producer in the state of Colorado. His tires had made deep ruts in the snow after the last storm. He drove carefully as the road wound higher up the mountain. Very quickly, the drop-off along the edge stretched several hundred feet to the base. One uncontrolled skid and rescuers would be untangling Marquez's broken body from his mangled pickup truck on the rocks far below.

Local people thought him foolish for buying up the claims to the old Paradise Mine. Any gold worth extracting was long gone. And yet, except for a Telluride banker, no one would have dreamed that Marquez's investment had made him a rich man. His profits from the mine were shrewdly invested in local real estate, and with the boom of the ski resort he had realized nearly two million dollars.

Marquez was not interested in gold. For ten years, he had prospected around the world for gemstones. In Montana, Nevada, and Colorado, he had prowled the old abandoned gold and silver mines searching for mineral crystals that could be cut into precious gems. Inside one tunnel of the Paradise Mine, he discovered a vein of rose-pink crystals in what the old miners had considered worthless rock. The gemstone in its natural state, Marquez recognized, was rhodochrosite, a spectacular crystal found in various parts of the world in shades of pink and deep red.

Rhodochrosite is seldom seen in cut or faceted form. Large crystals are in great demand by collectors, who have no desire to see them sliced to pieces. Clean, clear gems from the Paradise Mine that had been cut into flawless stones of eighteen carats were very expensive. Marquez knew he could retire and spend the rest of his life in style, but as long as the vein continued, he was determined to keep picking the stones from the granite until they petered out.

He stopped his battered old truck with its scratched and dented fenders and stepped out in front of a huge rusty iron door with four different chains attached to four different locks. Inserting keys the size of a man's palm, he unsnapped the locks and spread the chains. Then he took both hands and tugged the great door open. The moon's rays penetrated a short distance down a sloping mine shaft and revealed a pair of rails that stretched off into the darkness.

He fired up the engine mounted on a large portable generator, then pulled a lever on a junction box. The mine shaft was suddenly illuminated under a series of exposed lightbulbs that trailed down the shaft for a hundred yards before gradually growing smaller, until they became tiny glimmers in the distance. An ore cart sat on the rail tracks, attached to a cable that led to a winch. The cart was built to last, and the only sign of hard use was the rust on the sides of the bucket.

Marquez climbed into the bucket and pressed a button on a remote control. The winch began to hum and play out the cable, allowing the ore cart to roll down the rails, propelled by nothing more than gravity. Going underground was not for the fainthearted or the claustrophobic. The confining shaft barely allowed clearance for the ore bucket. Timbers bolted together like door frames, known as a cap and post, were spaced every few feet to shore up the roof against cave-ins. Many of the timbers had rotted badly, but others were as solid and sound as the day they were set in place by miners who had long since passed on. The ore car descended the sloping shaft at a rapid rate, coming to a stop 1,200 feet into the depths. At this level there was a constant trickle of water falling from the roof of the tunnel.

Taking a backpack and his lunch pail, Marquez climbed from the car and walked over to a vertical shaft that fell away into the lower reaches of the old Paradise Mine until it reached the 2,200-foot level. Down there, the main drift and crosscut tunnels spread into the granite like spokes on a wheel. According to old records and underground maps, there were almost a hundred miles of tunnels under and around Pandora.

Marquez dropped a rock into the yawning blackness. The sound of a splash came within two seconds.

Soon after the mine closed down and the pumps at the pumping station below the base of the mountain were turned off, the lower levels had flooded. Over time, water had risen to within fifteen feet of the 1,200-foot level, where Marquez worked the rhodochrosite vein. The slowly rising water, spurred on during a particularly heavy wet season in the San Juans, told him that it would be only a matter of a few weeks before it reached the top of the old shaft and spilled over into the main tunnel, spelling the end of his gemstone-mining operation.

Marquez set his mind on extracting as many stones as he could in the brief time he had left. His days became longer as he struggled to remove the red crystals with nothing but his miner's pick and a wheelbarrow to carry the ore to the bucket for the ride up to the mine's entrance.

As he walked through the tunnel, he stepped around old rusting ore cars and drills left by the miners when they had deserted the mine. There had been no market for the equipment, since nearby mines were closing down one by one at the same time. It was all simply cast aside and left where it was last used.

Seventy-five yards into the tunnel, he came to a narrow cleft in the rock just wide enough for him to slip through. Twenty feet beyond was the rhodochrosite lode he was mining. A lightbulb had burned out on the string hanging from the roof of the cleft, and he replaced it with one of several he kept in a backpack. Then he took his pick in hand and began to attack the rock that was embedded with the gemstones. A dull red in their natural state, the crystals looked like dried cherries in a muffin.

A dangerous overhang of rock protruded just above the cleft. If he was to continue to work safely without being crushed by a rockfall, Marquez had no choice but to blast it away. Using a portable pneumatic drill, he bored a hole into the rock. Then he inserted a small charge of dynamite and wired it to a handheld detonator. After moving around the corner of the cleft and into the main tunnel, he pushed down on the plunger. A dull thump echoed through the mine, followed by the sound of tumbling rock and a blanket of dust that rolled into the main tunnel.

Marquez waited a few minutes for the dust to settle before carefully entering the natural cleft. The overhang was gone. It had become a pile of rocks on the narrow floor. He retrieved the wheelbarrow and began removing the debris, dumping it a short distance up the tunnel. When the cleft was finally cleared, he looked up to make certain that no threatening section of the overhang remained.

He stared in wonder at a hole that had suddenly appeared in the roof above the crystal lode. He aimed the light atop his hard hat upward. The beam continued through the hole into what appeared to be a chamber beyond. Suddenly consumed by curiosity, he ran back up the tunnel for fifty yards, where he found the rusty remains of a six-foot iron ladder among the abandoned mining equipment. Returning inside the cleft, he propped up the ladder, climbed the rungs, and pried loose several rocks from the rim of the hole, widening it until he could squeeze through. Then he thrust his upper torso inside the chamber and twisted his head from shoulder to shoulder, sweeping the beam of his hard hat's light around the darkness.

Marquez found himself staring into a room hewn in the rock. It looked to be a perfect cube approximately fifteen by fifteen feet, with the same distance separating the floor and roof. Strange markings were cut into the sheer, smooth walls. This definitely was not the work of nineteenth-century miners. Then, abruptly, the beam of his hard hat's light struck a stone pedestal and glinted on the object it supported.

Marquez froze in shock at the ungodly sight of a black skull, its empty eye sockets staring directly at *him*.

2

THE PILOT BANKED THE United Airlines Beechcraft twin-engine plane around a pair of cotton-fluffed clouds and began his descent toward the short runway on a bluff above the San Miguel River. Though he had flown in and out of the little Telluride airport a hundred times, it was still a chore for him to keep his concentration on landing the aircraft and not on the incredible aerial view of the spectacular snowcapped San Juan Mountains. The serene beauty of the jagged peaks and slopes, mantled with snow under a vivid blue sky, was breathtaking.

As the plane dropped lower into the valley, the slopes of the mountains rose majestically on both sides. They appeared so close that it seemed to the passengers as if the aircraft's wings would brush the aspen trees on the rocky outcroppings. Then the landing gear dropped, and a minute later the wheels thumped and screeched as they touched the narrow asphalt runway.

The Beechcraft carried only nineteen passengers, and the unloading went quickly. Patricia O'Connell was the last one to step to the ground. Taking the advice of friends who had flown into the resort town for the skiing, she had asked for a rear seat so she could enjoy the fantastic view without its being blocked by one of the aircraft's wings.

At 9,000 feet in altitude, the air was thin but incredibly pure and refreshing. Pat inhaled deeply as she walked from the plane to inside the terminal building. As she passed through the door, a short, stocky man with a shaved head and a dark brown beard walked up to her.

"Dr. O'Connell?"

"Please call me Pat," she replied. "You must be Dr. Ambrose."

"Please call me Tom," he said, with a warm smile. "Did you have a good flight from Denver?"

"It was wonderful. A little rough coming over the mountains, but the beautiful scenery easily offset any discomfort."

"Telluride is a lovely spot," he said wistfully. "There are times I wish I could live here."

"I don't imagine there are many archaeological sites to study for a man of your experience."

"Not this high," he said. "The ancient Indian ruins are at much lower altitudes."

Dr. Thomas Ambrose may not have fit the stereotype of an eminent anthropologist, but he was one of the most respected people in the field. A professor emeritus at Arizona State University, he was an accomplished researcher, meticulous with written reports of his on-site investigations. Now in his late fifties—Pat guessed him to be ten years younger—he could boast of thirty years spent on the trail of early man and his cultures throughout the Southwest.

"Dr. Kidd was very mysterious over the phone. He offered almost no information at all about the discovery."

"And neither will I," said Ambrose. "It's best that you wait and see for yourself."

"How did you become involved with this find?" she asked.

"The right place at the right time. I was on a skiing vacation with an old girlfriend when I received a call from a colleague at the University of Colorado, asking if I'd take a look at the artifacts a miner reported finding. After a quick study of the site, I realized that I was in over my head."

"I find that hard to believe of a man with your reputation."

"Unfortunately, my area of expertise does not include epigraphy. And that's where you come in. The only one I know personally who specializes in deciphering ancient inscriptions is Dr. Jerry Kidd at Stanford. He wasn't available, but recommended you highly to take his place."

Ambrose turned, as the outside doors to the luggage drop were opened and the terminal ticket ladies who doubled as luggage handlers began throwing suitcases onto a sloping metal tray. "The big green one is mine," said Pat, thankful a man was there to tote her fifty-pound bag, which was packed with reference books.

Ambrose grunted but said nothing as he manhandled the heavy bag out to a Jeep Cherokee that he'd parked in the lot outside the terminal. Pat hesitated, before entering the car, to absorb the magnificent view of the pine and aspen forests ascending the slopes of Mount Wilson and Sunshine Peak across the valley. As she stood enthralled with the panoramic scene, Ambrose took a moment to study her. Pat's hair was a radiant red and cascaded to her waist. Her eyes were a sage green. She stood as if sculptured by an artist, her weight on her right leg with her left knee turned slightly inward. Her shoulders and arms suggested a build more muscular than most women's, no doubt fashioned by long hours of exercise in a gym. Ambrose guessed her height at five feet eight inches, her weight at a solid 135 pounds. She was a pretty woman, not cute or strikingly beautiful, but he imagined she'd look very desirable when dressed in something more alluring than jeans and a mannish leather jacket.

Dr. Kidd claimed there was no better person than Patricia O'Connell to decipher ancient writings. He had faxed her history, and Ambrose was impressed. Thirty-five years old, with a doctorate in ancient languages from St. Andrews College in Scotland, she taught early linguistics at the University of Pennsylvania. Pat had written three well-received books on inscriptions she had deciphered on stones found in different parts of the world. Married and divorced from an attorney, she supported a young daughter of fourteen. A confirmed diffusionist, one who embraced the theory that cultures spread from one to another without being independently created, she firmly believed ancient seafarers had visited American shores many hundreds of years before Columbus.

"I've put you up at a nice bed-and-breakfast in town," said Ambrose. "If you wish, I can drop you off for an hour or so to freshen up."

"No, thank you," Pat said, smiling. "If you don't mind, I'd like to go straight to the site."

Ambrose nodded, took a cellular phone from a coat pocket, and dialed a number. "I'll let Luis Marquez, the owner of the mine, who made the discovery, know that we're coming."

They drove in silence through the heart of Telluride. Pat stared up at the ski slopes of Mountain Village to the south and saw skiers assaulting the steep moguls on the run that dropped to the edge of town. They passed old buildings that had been preserved over the past century, restored and now housing retail stores instead of a sea of saloons. Ambrose pointed to a building on his left. "That's the spot where Butch Cassidy robbed his first bank."

"Telluride must have a rich history."

"It does," replied Ambrose. "Right there in front of the Sheridan Hotel is where William Jennings Bryan gave his famous 'cross of gold' speech. And farther up the South Fork Valley was the world's first generating plant, which produced alternating-current electricity for the mines. The plant's equipment was designed by Nikola Tesla."

Ambrose continued through the town of Telluride, busy with the invasion of skiers, and drove into the box canyon to where the paved road ended at Pandora. Pat stared in wonder at the steep cliffs surrounding the old mining town, taking in the beauty of Bridal Veil Falls, which was beginning to cascade with the runoff from the melting snow brought on by the prelude of a warm spring.

They came to a side road that led to the ruins of several old buildings. A van and a Jeep painted a bright turquoise were parked outside. A pair of men were wearing wet suits and unloading what looked to Pat like diving equipment. "What can divers possibly be doing in the middle of the mountains of Colorado?" she asked vaguely.

"I stopped and talked to them yesterday," answered Ambrose. "They're a team from the National Underwater and Marine Agency."

"A long way from the sea, aren't they?"

"I was told they're exploring a complex system of ancient water-ways that once drained the western flank of the San Juan Mountains. There is a maze of caverns that connect to the old mine tunnels."

Half a mile up the road, Ambrose passed a huge abandoned ore mill, where a large semitruck and trailer were parked beside the San Miguel River below the mouth of another old abandoned mine. Tents had been set up around the vehicles, and several men could be seen wandering about the camp. The sides of the big trailers were painted with words advertising the Geo Subterranean Science Corporation with home offices in Phoenix, Arizona.

"Another bunch of scientists," Ambrose volunteered without being asked. "A geophysical outfit, searching through the old mine shafts with fancy ground-penetrating equipment that is supposed to detect any veins of gold overlooked by the old miners."

"Think they'll find anything?" asked Pat.

Anbrose shrugged. "I doubt it. These mountains have been dug pretty deep."

A short distance later, Ambrose pulled to a stop in front of a picturesque little house and parked next to an old Chevy pickup truck. Marquez and his wife, Lisa, alerted to their coming, came out and greeted them, as Ambrose introduced them to Pat.

"I envy you," said Pat, "living amid such gorgeous scenery."

"Sad to say," said Lisa, "that after a year you don't notice it anymore."

"I don't think I could ever become immune to it."

"Can I get you folks anything? A cup of coffee? A beer?"

"I'm fine," answered Pat. "I would like to see your discovery as soon as it's convenient."

"No problem," said Marquez. "We still have five hours of daylight left. More than enough time for you to see the chamber and get back before dark."

"I'll have dinner waiting," said Lisa. "I thought you might like barbecued elk."

"Sounds wonderful," Pat said, already feeling the pangs of hunger.

Marquez nodded his head at the old truck. "You folks will have a more comfortable ride up to the mine if we take your Jeep, Doc."

Fifteen minutes later, they were sitting in the ore cart, making the descent from the portal into the old Paradise Mine. It was a new experience for Pat. She had never entered a mine shaft.

"It feels warmer," she observed, "the deeper we go."

"As a rule of thumb," explained Marquez, "the temperature increases by five degrees every hundred feet you descend into the earth. In the lower levels of the mine that are now flooded, the heat used to be over a hundred degrees."

The ore cart came to a stop. Marquez climbed out and dug into a large wooden toolbox. He handed Pat and Ambrose each a hard hat.

"For falling rock?" asked Pat.

Marquez laughed. "Mostly to keep your scalp from knocking against low timbers."

The dim yellow lights attached to the overhead timbers flickered overhead as they made their way through the damp tunnel with Marquez in the lead. When one of them spoke, the voice sounded hollow against the surrounding rock walls of the tunnel. Pat stumbled more than once on the ties holding the old rusting ore cart rails, but caught herself before falling. She hadn't realized when she'd dressed earlier in the morning, before flying to Telluride, what a wise decision it was to wear a pair of comfortable hiking shoes. After what seemed an hour but was actually only ten minutes, they reached the cleft leading to the chamber and followed Marquez through the narrow passage.

He stopped at the ladder and motioned upward to where a bright light spilled through the opening in the rock ceiling. "I strung lights inside since you visited yesterday, Dr. Ambrose. The sheer walls act as reflectors, so you shouldn't have a problem studying the writing." Then he stood aside and helped Pat up the ladder.

Not having been told what to expect, she was stunned. She felt like Howard Carter when he first viewed King Tut's tomb. Her eyes immediately locked on the black skull, and she reverently approached its pedestal and stared at the smooth surface gleaming under the lights.

"It's exquisite," she murmured admiringly, as Ambrose squeezed through the opening and stood beside her.

"A masterwork," he agreed. "Carved out of obsidian."

"I've seen the Mayan crystal skull that was found in Belize. This one is far more inspiring. The other is crude in comparison."

"They say the crystal skull emits an aura of light, and strange sounds are heard to come from it."

"It must have been lethargic the time I studied it," said Pat, smiling. "It only sat there and stared."

"I can't imagine how many years—generations most likely, without modern tools—it took to polish such an object of beauty from a mineral so brittle. One tap of a hammer and it would shatter into a thousand pieces."

"The surface is so smooth, it's flawless," Pat said softly.

Ambrose swept one hand around the chamber. "This entire chamber is a wonder. The inscriptions on the walls and ceiling must easily have taken five men a lifetime to engrave in the rock, but not before an immense effort was spent polishing the interior surfaces. This chamber alone had to have taken years to carve out of solid granite at this depth. I've measured the dimensions. The four walls, floor, and ceiling enclose a perfect cube. If the interior surfaces are out of alignment or plumb, it's less than one millimeter. Like the classic old mystery novel, we have a drama that took place in a room with no windows or doors."

"The opening in the floor?" Pat asked.

"Blasted by Luis Marquez while excavating for gemstones," replied Ambrose.

"Then how was this chamber created without an entrance and exit?"

Ambrose pointed to the ceiling. "The only hint I could find of an infinitesimal crack around the borders was in the ceiling. I can only assume that whoever constructed this cubicle burrowed down from above and placed a precisely carved slab atop the cubicle."

"For what purpose?"

Ambrose grinned. "The reason why *you're* here, to find answers."

Pat removed a notepad, a small paintbrush and a magnifying glass from a pack she carried on her belt. She moved close to one wall, gently swept away the dust of centuries from the rock, and peered at the script through the glass. She intently studied the markings for several moments before looking up and staring at the ceiling. Then she looked at Ambrose with a blank expression in her face. "The ceiling appears to be a celestial map of the stars. The symbols are . . ." She hesitated and stared at Ambrose with a blank expression. "This must be some sort of hoax perpetrated by the miners who dug the tunnel."

"What brought you to that conclusion?" inquired Ambrose.

"The symbols don't bear the slightest resemblance to any ancient writings I've ever studied."

"Can you decipher any of them?"

"All I can tell you is that they are not pictographic like hieroglyphics, or logographic signs that express individual words. Nor do the symbols suggest words or oral syllables. It appears to be alphabetic."

"Then they're a combination of single sounds," offered Ambrose.

Pat nodded in agreement. "This is either some sort of written code or an ingenious system of writing."

Ambrose looked at her intently. "Why do you think this is all a hoax?"

"The inscriptions do not fit any known pattern set down by man throughout recorded history," Pat said in a quiet, authoritative voice.

"You *did* say ingenious."

Pat handed Ambrose her magnifying glass. "See for yourself. The symbols have a remarkable simplicity. The use of geometric images in combination with single lines is a very efficient system of written communication. That's why I can't believe any of this comes from an ancient culture."

"Can the symbols be deciphered?"

"I'll know after I make tracings and run them through the computer lab at the university. Most ancient inscriptions are not nearly as definite and distinct as these. The symbols appear to have a well-defined structure. The main problem is that we have no other matching epigraphs anywhere else in the world to act as a guide. I'm treading in unknown waters until the computer can make a breakthrough."

"How you doin' up there?" Marquez shouted from the cleft below.

"All done for now," Pat answered. "Do you have a stationer's store in town?"

"Two of them."

"Good. I'll need to buy a ream of tracing paper and some transparent tape to make long sheets I can roll—" She fell silent as a faint rumble issued from the tunnel and the floor of the cubicle trembled beneath their feet.

"An earthquake?" Pat called down to Marquez.

"No," he replied through the hole. "My guess is an avalanche somewhere on the mountain. You and Dr. Ambrose go on about your business. I'll run topside and check it out."

Another tremor shook the chamber with a stronger intensity than the last one.

"Maybe we should go with you," Pat said apprehensively.

"The tunnel support timbers are old, and many are rotten," warned Marquez. "Excessive movement of the rock could cause them to collapse, produce a cave-in. It's safer if you two wait here."

"Don't be long," said Pat. "I feel a touch of claustrophobia coming on."

"Back in ten minutes," Marquez assured her.

As soon as Marquez's footsteps faded from the cleft below, Pat turned to Ambrose. "You didn't tell me your appraisal of the skull. Do you think it ancient or modern?"

Ambrose stared at the skull, a vague look in his eyes. "It would take a laboratory to determine if it was cut and polished by hand or with modern tools. The only fact we know for certain is that this room was not excavated and created by miners. There would have to be an account somewhere of such an extensive project. Marquez assures me that old Paradise Mine records and tunnel maps show nothing indicating a vertical shaft leading to an underground chamber in this particular location. So it must have been excavated prior to 1850."

"Or much later."

Ambrose shrugged his shoulders. "All mining operations were shut down in 1931. A major operation such as this could not have gone unnoticed since then. I'm reluctant to lay my reputation on the line, but I'll state without equivocation that I firmly believe this chamber and the skull are more than a thousand years old, probably much older."

"Perhaps early Indians were responsible," Pat persisted.

Ambrose shook his head. "Not possible. The early Americans built a number of complex stone structures, but an enterprise of this precise magnitude was beyond them. And then you have the inscriptions. Hardly the work of people without a written language."

"This does appear to have the hallmark of a high intelligence," she said softly, her fingertips lightly tracing the symbols in the granite.

With Ambrose at her side, Pat began copying the unusual symbols in a small notebook until she could account for a total of forty-two. Then she measured the depth of the engravings and the distance between the lines and the symbols. The more she examined the apparent wording, the more perplexed she became. There was a mysterious logic about the inscriptions that only a meticulous translation could solve. She was busily taking flash photos of the inscriptions and star symbols in the ceiling when Marquez climbed through the hole in the floor.

"Looks like we're going to be here for a while, folks," he announced. "An avalanche has covered the mine entrance."

"Oh, dear God," muttered Pat.

"Not to fret," Marquez said with a tight grin. "My wife has gone through this before. She'll be aware of our predicament and will have called for help. A rescue unit from town will soon be on its way with heavy equipment to dig us out."

"How long will we be trapped here?" asked Ambrose.

"Hard to say without knowing how much snow is blocking the shaft opening. Could be only a few hours. Might take as long as a day. But they'll work around the clock until they clear away the snow. You can bet on it."

A sense of relief settled over Pat. "Well, then, as long as your lights are still working, I suppose Dr. Ambrose and I can spend the time recording the inscriptions."

The words were barely out of her mouth when a tremendous rumble rose from somewhere deep beneath the chamber. Then the grinding sound of crashing timbers, followed by the deep growl of falling rock, reverberated from the tunnel. A violent rush of air roared through the cleft and into the chamber as they were all pitched headlong onto the rock floor.

Then the lights blinked out.

3

THE RUMBLE DEEP WITHIN the mountain echoed ominously from the hidden reaches of the tunnel and slowly faded away into a smothering silence, while unseen in the pitch blackness, dust disturbed by the concussion rolled through the tunnel, into the cleft, and up through the opening of the chamber like an invisible hand. Then came the sounds of coughing as the dust clogged noses and mouths, the grit quickly clinging to their teeth and tongues.

Ambrose was the first to gasp out coherent words. "What in God's name happened?"

"A cave-in," rasped Marquez. "The roof of the tunnel must have collapsed."

"Pat!" Ambrose shouted, feeling around in the darkness. "Are you hurt?"

"No," she managed between fits of coughing. "The breath was knocked out of me, but I'm all right."

He found her hand and helped her to her feet. "Here, take my handkerchief and hold it to your face."

Pat stood quite still as she fought to get a clean breath. "It felt as if the earth exploded beneath my feet."

"Why did the rock suddenly give way?" Ambrose asked Marquez, unable to see him.

"I don't know, but it sounded like a dynamite blast to me."

"Couldn't the aftershock of the avalanche have caused the tunnel to collapse?" asked Ambrose.

"I swear to God, it was dynamite," said Marquez. "I ought to know. I've used enough of it over the years to recognize the sound. I always use low particle-velocity dynamite to minimize ground shock. Someone set off a charge with concentrated powder in one of the tunnels beneath this one. A big one, judging from the shock."

"I thought the mine was abandoned."

"It was. Except for my wife and myself, no one has set foot in here for years."

"But how—"

"Not how, but why?" Marquez brushed by the anthropologist's legs as he crawled on all fours searching for his hard hat.

"Are you saying that someone purposely set off explosives to seal the mine?" Pat asked, bewildered.

"I'll damn well find out if we get out of here." Marquez found his hat, set it over his dust-coated hair, and switched on the little light. "There, that's better."

The little light gave but token illumination inside the chamber. The settling dust had the eerie and forbidding look of a waterfront fog. They all looked like statues under the dust, their faces and clothing the color of the surrounding gray granite.

"I don't care for the way you said 'if.' "

"Depends on which side of the cleft the tunnel collapsed. Farther into the mine, we'll be clear. But if the roof fell somewhere between here and the exit shaft, we have a problem. I'll go and take a look."

Before Pat could say another word, the miner had slipped through the hole and the chamber was thrown back into absolute darkness. Ambrose and Pat stood silent in a sea of suffocating blackness, the initial traces of terror and panic seeping into their minds. Less than five minutes had passed before Marquez returned. They could not see his face because of the beam from his hard hat light in their eyes, but they sensed that he was a man who had seen and touched doom.

"I'm afraid the news is all bad," he said slowly. "The cave-in is only a short distance down the tunnel toward the shaft. I estimate that the fall extends a good thirty yards or more. It'll take days, maybe weeks for rescuers to clear the rubble, timbering as they go."

Ambrose stared closely at the miner, searching for any expression of hope. Seeing none, he said, "But they *will* get us out before we starve?"

"Starving isn't our problem," Marquez said, unable to hide the tone of despair that had crept into his voice. "Water is rising in the tunnel. It's already flooded up to three feet."

It was then Pat saw that Marquez's pants up to his knees were soaking wet. "Then we're trapped in this hellhole with no way out?"

"I didn't say that!" the miner snapped back. "There's a good chance the water will run off into a crosscut tunnel before reaching the chamber."

"But you can't be sure," said Ambrose.

"We'll know in the next few hours," Marquez hedged.

Pat's face was pale and her breath was coming slowly through lips tainted with the dust. She became gripped with cold fear as she heard the first sounds of the water swirling outside the chamber. At first the volume had not been great, but it was increasing rapidly. Her eyes met Ambrose's gaze. He could not hide the dread that was written in his face.

"I wonder," she whispered softly, "what it's like to drown."

THE minutes passed like years and the next two hours crawled like centuries as the water rose steadily higher until it surged through the hole in the chamber floor and pooled around their feet. Paralyzed with terror, Pat pressed her back and shoulders against the wall, trying vainly to gain an extra few seconds from the relentless onslaught of the water. She silently prayed that it would miraculously stop before it climbed over their shoulders.

The horror of dying a thousand feet under the earth, smothered in black gloom, was a nightmare too ghastly to accept. She recalled reading about the bodies of cave divers who had become lost in a maze of underwater caverns and been found with their fingers rubbed raw to the bone where they had tried to claw their way through solid rock.

The men stood quiet, their mood somber from the buried solitude. Marquez was unable to believe that some unknown party had tried to murder them. There was no rhyme or reason to such an act, no motive. His conscious thoughts languished on the grief that would soon overcome his family.

Pat thought of her daughter and felt a deep sense of desolation, knowing that she would not be there to see her only child grow to womanhood. It did not seem fair that she would die deep in the bowels of the earth within a bleak and barren chamber, her body never to be found. She wanted to cry, but tears refused to fall.

All conversation died when water reached their knees. It continued rising until it reached their hips. It was ice cold and stabbed their flesh like thousands of tiny nails. Pat began to shiver, and her teeth chattered uncontrollably. Ambrose, recognizing the warning signs of hypothermia, waded over and put his arms around her. It was a kind and thoughtful act, and she felt grateful. She stared in rapt terror at the hideous black water that swirled beneath the yellow glow of Marquez's lamp, reflecting on the cold forbidding surface.

Then suddenly Pat thought she saw something, sensed it actually. "Turn off your light," she murmured to Marquez.

"What?"

"Turn off your light. I think something is down there."

The men were certain that fear had caused her to hallucinate, but Marquez nodded, reached up, and switched off the hard hat's little light. The chamber was immediately thrown into hellish blackness.

"What is it you think you see?" Ambrose asked softly.

"A glow," she murmured.

"I don't see anything," said Marquez.

"You must see it," she said excitedly. "A faint glow in the water."

Ambrose and Marquez peered into the rising water and saw nothing but stygian blackness.

"I saw it. I swear to God, I saw a light shining in the cleft below."

Ambrose held her tighter. "We're alone," he said tenderly. "There is no one else."

"There!" she gasped. "Don't you see?"

Marquez dipped his face under the surface and opened his eyes. And then he saw it, too, a very dim glow coming from the direction of the tunnel. As he held his breath in growing anticipation, it began to brighten as if it was coming closer. He raised his head free of the water and shouted, his voice tinged with horror. "Something *is* down there. The ghost. It can only be the ghost that is said to wander the mine shafts. No human could be moving through a flooded tunnel."

What strength they had left drained from their bodies. They stared transfixed as the light seemed to rise through the opening into the chamber. Marquez switched his lamp back on as they stood frozen, their eyes staring at the apparition that slowly rose above the surface of the water, wearing a black hood.

Then a hand lifted from the murk, removed a mouthpiece to an air regulator, and raised a diver's face mask over the forehead. A pair of vivid green opaline eyes were revealed under the miner's lamp as the lips spread into a wide smile that displayed an even set of white teeth.

"It would appear," a friendly voice said, "that I have arrived in the proverbial nick of time."

4

PAT COULD NOT HELP but wonder if her mind, numbed by fright and the torment to her body from the frigid water, was playing weird tricks. Ambrose and Marquez stared blankly, unable to speak. Shock was slowly replaced with an overpowering wave of relief at suddenly having company and knowing the stranger was in contact with the world above. Cold fear abruptly evaporated, to be replaced with inspired hope.

"Where in God's name did you come from?" Marquez blurted excitedly.

"The Buccaneer Mine next door," answered the stranger, shining his dive light around the walls of the chamber before focusing its beam on the obsidian skull. "What is this place, a mausoleum?"

"No," answered Pat, "an enigma."

"I recognize you," said Ambrose. "We talked earlier today. You're with the National Underwater and Marine Agency."

"Dr. Ambrose, isn't it? I wish I could say it was a pleasure meeting you again." The stranger looked at the miner. "You must be Luis Marquez, the owner of the mine. I promised your wife I'd get you home in time for dinner. He stared at Pat and grinned slyly. "And the gorgeous lady has to be Dr. O'Connell."

"You know my name?"

"Mrs. Marquez described you," he said simply.

"How in the world did you get here?" Pat asked, still dazed.

"After learning from your sheriff that your mine entrance was covered by an avalanche, my team of NUMA engineers decided to try and reach you through one of the tunnels leading from the Buccaneer Mine to the Paradise. We'd only covered a few hundred yards when an explosion shook the mountain. When we saw water rising in the shafts and flooding both mines, we knew the only way left to reach you was by a diver swimming through the tunnels."

"You swam here from the Buccaneer Mine?" asked Marquez incredulously. "That has to be nearly half a mile."

"Actually, I was able to walk much of the distance before I entered the water," explained the stranger. "Unfortunately, the surge was more than I expected. I was towing a waterproof pack containing food and medical supplies behind me on a line, but it was torn away and lost after a torrent of water swept me against an old drill rig."

"Were you injured?" asked Pat solicitously.

"Black and blue in places I care not to mention."

"It's a miracle you found your way through that maze of tunnels to our exact location," said Marquez.

The stranger held up a small monitor, whose screen glowed an unearthly green. "An underwater computer, programmed with every shaft, crosscut, and tunnel in the Telluride canyon. Because your tunnel was blocked by the cave-in, I had to detour to a lower level, circle around, and travel from the opposite direction. As I was swimming through the tunnel, I caught the dim glimmer of light from your miner's lamp. And here I am."

"Then no one aboveground knows that we were trapped by a cave-in," stated Marquez.

"They know," the diver answered him. "My NUMA team called the sheriff as soon as we realized what happened."

Ambrose's face showed an unhealthy pallor. He failed to display the enthusiasm of the others. "Is there another member of your dive team following you?" he asked slowly.

The diver gave a slight shake of his head. "I'm alone. We were down to our last two tanks of air. I felt it was too risky for more than one man to make the attempt to reach you."

"It seems a waste of time and effort for you to have made the trip. I see little that you can do to save us."

"I may surprise you," the diver said simply.

"There is no way your twin scuba tanks hold enough air to take all four of us back through a labyrinth of flooded tunnels to the world aboveground. And since we'll either drown or die of hypothermia in the next hour, you won't have time to go and bring back help."

"You've very astute, Doctor. Two people might make it back to the Buccaneer Mine, but only two."

"Then you must take the lady."

The diver smiled ironically. "That's very noble of you, my friend, but we're not loading lifeboats on the *Titanic*."

"Please," begged Marquez. "The water is still rising. Take Dr. O'Connell to safety."

"If it will make you happy," he said, with seeming insensibility. He took Pat by the hand. "Have you ever used scuba gear before?"

She shook her head.

He aimed his dive light at the men. "How about you two?"

"Does it really matter?" said Ambrose solemnly.

"It does to me."

"I'm a qualified diver."

"I guessed as much. And you?"

Marquez shrugged. "I can barely swim."

The diver turned to Pat who was carefully wrapping her camera and notebook in plastic. "You swim alongside me and we'll buddy-breathe by passing the mouthpiece on my air regulator back and forth. I'll take a breath and hand it to you. You take a breath and hand it back. As soon as we drop out of this chamber, grab hold of my weight belt and hang on."

Then he turned back to Ambrose and Marquez. "Sorry to disappoint you, fellows, but if you think you're going to die, forget it. I'll be back for you in fifteen minutes."

"Please make it less." Marquez stared back from a face as gray as the granite. "The water will be over our heads in twenty minutes."

"Then I suggest you stand on tiptoe."

Taking Pat by the hand, the man from NUMA slipped beneath the water and disappeared in the murky water.

KEEPING the beam of his dive light aimed ahead in the tunnel, the diver followed one of the illuminated lines displayed on his little computer. Looking up from the tiny monitor, he aimed his dive light ahead into the tunnel and swam toward the forbidding shadows. The water had risen to the roof of the tunnel, and the surge he'd experienced earlier had fallen off. He stroked and kicked his fins mightily through the flooded cavern, dragging Pat behind him.

Stealing a quick glance backward, he saw that her eyes were tightly closed, her hands clinging to his weight belt in a death grip. The eyes never opened, even as the mouthpiece to the air regulator was passed back and forth.

His decision to rely on a simple U.S. Divers' Scan face mask and a standard U.S. Diver's Aquarius scuba air regulator instead of his old reliable Mark II full face mask turned out to be wise. Traveling light made it easier for him to swim nearly half a mile through a maze of underground passages from the Buccaneer Mine, many partially filled with fallen rock and timbers. There were also dry galleries the flooding water had not yet reached, where he had to crawl and walk. Trudging over ore car rails and ties and fallen rock while toting bulky air tanks, buoyancy compensator, various gauges, a knife, and a belt loaded with lead weights was not an easy chore. The water was icy cold, but he stayed warm inside his DUI Norseman dry suit during the passages he was forced to swim. He had chosen the Norseman because it had greater ease of movement when he was out of the water.

The water was turbid and the beam from the dive light, cutting a swath in the liquid void, penetrated only ten feet into the murk. He counted the shoring timbers as they passed, trying to gain a perspective on how far they had traveled. At last the tunnel made a sharp turn and ended in a gallery that led to a vertical shaft. He entered the shaft and felt as if he had been swallowed by an alien monster from the depths. Two minutes later, they broke the surface, and he aimed the dive light into the black above. A horizontal tunnel leading on to the next level of the Paradise Mine beckoned forty feet above.

Pat smoothed the hair from her face and stared wide-eyed at him. It was then he saw that her eyes were a lovely shade of olive green. "We made it," she gasped, coughing and spitting water from her mouth. "You knew about this shaft?"

Holding up the directional computer, he said, "This little gem led the way." He placed her hands on the slimy rungs of a badly rusted ladder leading upward. "Do you think you can make it up to the next level on your own?"

"I'll fly if I have to," said Pat, overjoyed at being free of the hideous chamber and knowing she was still alive, with a chance, albeit a slim one, of eventually becoming a senior citizen.

"As you climb the ladder, pull yourself up with your hands on the vertical bars, and mind you don't step in the center of the rungs. They're old and probably half rusted through. So go carefully."

"I'll make it. I wouldn't dare mess up. Not after you got me this far."

He handed her a small outdoorsman butane lighter. "Take this, find some dry wood from a timber, and start a fire. You've been exposed to the cold water much too long."

As he pulled the dive mask back down over his face and prepared to duck under that water again, her hand suddenly tightened around his wrist. She felt drawn into the opaline green eyes. "You're going back after the others?"

He nodded and threw her a smile of encouragement. "I'll get them out. Don't worry. There's still time."

"You never told me who you are."

"My name is Dirk Pitt," he said. Then, the mouthpiece reinserted, he gave a brief wave and vanished into the murky water.

THE water had reached the shoulders of the men in the ancient chamber. The terror of claustrophobia seemed to rise along with the water. All barbs of panic had receded as Ambrose and Marquez quietly accepted their fate in their private Hades deep inside the earth. Marquez chose to fight to the last breath, while Ambrose silently embraced a diehard death. He steeled himself to swim down through the cleft into the tunnel and go until his lungs gave out.

"He's not coming back, is he?" Marquez mumbled.

"Doesn't look like it, or else he won't make it in time. He probably thought it best to give us false hope."

"Funny, I had a gut feeling we could trust the guy."

"Maybe we still can," said Ambrose, seeing what looked like a glowworm approaching from under the water.

"Thank God!" gasped Marquez as the beam from the halogen dive light refracted and danced off the ceiling and walls of the chamber just before Pitt's head broke water. "You came back!"

"Was there ever a doubt?" Pitt asked lightly.

"Where is Pat?" demanded Ambrose, as Pitt's eyes met his through the plate of the dive mask.

"Safe," Pitt said briefly. "There's a dry shaft about eighty feet down the tunnel."

"I know the one," acknowledged Marquez, his words barely intelligible. "It leads to the next level of the Paradise."

Identifying the obvious signs of hypothermia in the miner, the drowsiness, the confusion, Pitt elected to take him instead of Ambrose, who was in the better shape of the two. He had to be quick, because the numbing cold had tightened its grip and was draining the life out of them. "You're next, Mr. Marquez."

"I may panic and pass out when I'm submerged," Marquez moaned.

Pitt gripped him on the shoulder. "Pretend you're floating in the water off Waikiki Beach."

"Good luck," said Ambrose.

Pitt grinned and gave the anthropologist a friendly tap on the shoulder. "Don't go away."

"I'll wait right here."

Pitt nodded at Marquez. "All right, pal, let's do it."

The trip went smoothly. Pitt put all his strength into reaching the shaft as quickly as possible. He could see that unless the miner got dry soon, he would lose consciousness. For a man afraid of water, Marquez was game. He'd take a deep breath from the regulator and dutifully pass it back to Pitt without missing a beat.

When they came to the ladder, Pitt helped push Marquez up the first few rungs until he was completely out of the cold water. "Do you think you can make it up to the next tunnel on your own?"

"I'll have to," Marquez stammered, fighting the cold that had seeped into his veins. "I'm not about to give up now."

Pitt left him and returned for Ambrose, who was beginning to look cadaverous from the effects of the icy water. Hypothermia from the cold water had lowered his body temperature to ninety-two degrees. Another two-degree drop and he would be unconscious. Five more minutes and it would have been too late. The water was only inches away from the chamber's ceiling. Pitt didn't waste time in talk, but shoved the mouthpiece into the anthropologist's mouth and pulled him down into the cleft and out into the tunnel.

Fifteen minutes later, they were all grouped around a fire that Pat had managed to ignite from scraps of wood she'd found in a nearby crosscut passage. Scrounging about, Pitt soon discovered several old, fallen timbers that had remained dry over the years the mine had been abandoned. It wasn't long before the tunnel was turned into a blazing furnace and the survivors from the inundated chamber began to thaw out. Marquez began to look human again. Pat rebounded and was her old happy self as she vigorously massaged Ambrose's frozen feet.

While they treasured the warmth of the fire, Pitt busied himself with the computer, planning a circuitous route through the mine to the ground above. The Telluride valley was a virtual honeycomb of old mines. The shafts, crosscuts, drifts, and tunnels totaled more than 360 miles. Pitt marveled that the valley hadn't collapsed like a wet sponge. He allowed everyone to rest and dry out for close to an hour before he reminded them that they weren't out of the woods yet.

"If we want to see blue skies again, we'll have to follow an escape plan."

"What's the urgency?" shrugged Marquez. "All we have to do is follow this tunnel to the entrance shaft and then sit it out until rescuers dig through the avalanche."

"I hate to be the bearer of bad tidings," Pitt said, his voice grim, "but not only were rescuers finding it impossible to get their heavy equipment through twenty feet of snow up to the mine on a narrow road, they were pulled from the search because of rising air temperatures that were increasing the chances of another avalanche. There is no telling how many days or weeks it will take for them to clear a path to the mine entrance."

Marquez stared into the fire, picturing the conditions topside in his mind. "Everything is going against us," he said quietly.

"We have heat and drinking water, however silty," said Pat. "Surely, we can exist without food for as long as it takes."

Ambrose smiled faintly. "Sixty to seventy days is what it generally takes to starve to death."

"Or we could hike out while we're still healthy," offered Pitt.

Marquez shook his head. "You know better than anyone, the only tunnel that leads from the Buccaneer Mine to the Pandora is flooded. We can't get through the way you came."

"Certainly not without proper diving gear," added Ambrose.

"True," Pitt admitted. "But relying on my computerized road map, I estimate there are at least two dozen other dry tunnels and shafts on upper levels that we can use to reach the ground surface."

"That makes sense," said Marquez. "Except that most of those tunnels have collapsed over the past ninety years."

"Still," said Ambrose, "it beats sitting around playing charades for the next month."

"I'm with you," Pat agreed. "I've had my fill of old mine shafts for one day."

Her words prompted Pitt to walk over to the edge of the shaft and peer down. The flickering flames from the fire reflected off the water that had risen to within three feet of the tunnel floor. "We don't have a choice. The water will spill out of the shaft in another twenty minutes."

Marquez stepped beside him and stared at the turbid water. "It's crazy," he muttered. "After all these years, to see water flooding up to this level of the mine. It looks like my days of gemstone mining are over."

"One of the waterways that run under the mountain must have broken through into the mine during the earthquake."

"That was no earthquake," said Marquez angrily. "That was a dynamite charge."

"You're saying explosives caused the flooding and cave-in?" asked Pitt.

"I'm sure of it." He peered at Pitt, eyes suddenly narrowed. "I'd bet my claim that somebody else was in the mine."

Pitt stared at the menacing water. "If that's the case," he said pensively, "that somebody wants all three of you very dead."

5

"YOU LEAD OFF," PITT ordered Marquez. "We'll walk behind the beam of your miner's lamp until its batteries give out. Then we go the rest of the way on my dive light."

"Climbing to the upper levels through shafts will be the tough part," said the miner. "So far we've been lucky. Very few shafts had a ladder. Most of them used hoists to transport the miners and ore."

"We'll tackle that problem when we face it," said Pitt.

It was five o'clock in the afternoon when they set out through the tunnel, heading west as indicated on Pitt's dive compass. He looked odd, hiking through the tunnel in his dry suit, gloves, and Servus dive boots with steel toes. He carried only the computer, compass, underwater dive light, and the knife strapped to his right leg. He left the rest of his gear beside the dying embers of the fire.

The tunnel was clear of debris and the first hundred yards were fairly easy. Marquez led the way, followed by Pat and Ambrose, with Pitt bringing up the rear. There was enough walking room between the ore car tracks and the tunnel wall, making it unnecessary to step and stumble over the rail ties. They passed one shaft, then two, that were empty and lacking any means of climbing to the next level. They came to a small open gallery with three tunnels leading off into the darkness.

"If I remember the mine's layout correctly," said Marquez, "we take the tunnel that angles to the left."

Pitt consulted his trusty computer. "Right on the money."

Another fifty yards and they came to a rockfall. The amount of loose rock was not massive, and the men set to work digging a crawl space. An hour of effort and a quart of sweat later, they had gouged an opening big enough for all to snake through. The tunnel led to another chamber, this one with a shaft leading to an old hoist that was still in place. Pitt shined his light into the vertical passage. It was like looking into a bottomless pit upside down. The top lay far out of the range of the beam. But this shaft looked promising. A maintenance ladder was gripping one wall, and the cables that once lowered and raised the lift cages were still hanging in place.

"This is as good as it gets," said Pitt.

"I hope the ladder is sound," said Ambrose, grabbing the vertical sides and giving it a shake. It trembled like a bow from the base up until it vanished in the darkness. "My days of climbing hand over hand up old slimy cables are long gone."

"I'll go first," Pitt said, sliding a thong on the dive light's handle around his wrist.

"Mind the first step," Pat said, with a faint smile.

Pitt looked into her eyes and saw genuine concern. "The last step is the one that worries me most."

He gripped the ladder, climbed several rungs, and hesitated, not happy about the wobble. He pressed on, keeping an eye on the hoist cables hanging only an arm's length away. If the ladder gave way, he could at least reach out and stop his fall with one of the cables. He ascended slowly, one rung at a time, testing each one before giving it his full weight. He could have moved much faster, but he had to be sure the others could safely follow him.

Fifty feet above the people watching him in rapt suspense, he stopped and beamed his light up the shaft. The ladder abruptly ended only six feet ahead of him, but twelve feet below the floor of the tunnel above. Climbing two more rungs, Pitt extended an arm and grasped one of the cables. The woven strands were five-eighths of an inch thick, ideal for a good grip. He released his hold on the ladder and hauled himself hand over hand up the cable until he was four feet above the level of the tunnel floor. Then he swayed back and forth in an arc, gaining a couple of feet with each sweep before finally jumping onto solid rock.

"How is it?" shouted Marquez.

"The ladder is broken off just below the tunnel, but I can pull you the rest of the way. Send up Dr. O'Connell."

As Pat climbed toward Pitt's light, propped with its beam pointing down the shaft, she could hear him pounding something with a rock. By the time she reached the last rung, he had chiseled a pair of hand-grips into some old timber and lowered it over the edge.

"Grab hold of the center board with both hands and hold on."

She did as she was ordered without protest and was quickly dragged onto firm ground. Minutes later, Marquez and Ambrose were standing in the tunnel beside her. Pitt aimed his light up the tunnel as far as the beam could penetrate and saw that it was clear of rockfalls. Then he switched it off to conserve the batteries.

"After you, Marquez."

"I probed this tunnel three years ago. If I remember correctly, it leads straight to the Paradise entrance shaft."

"Can't get out that way because of the avalanche," said Ambrose.

"We can bypass it," Pitt said, studying the monitor of the computer. "If we take the next crosscut and go a hundred and fifty yards, it meets a tunnel from a mine called the North Star."

"What exactly is a crosscut?" asked Pat.

"Access through perpendicular veins driven at right angles to a working tunnel. They're used for ventilation and communication between digging operations," answered Marquez. He looked at Pitt doubtfully. "I've never seen such a passage, which doesn't mean it doesn't exist, but it's probably filled in."

"Then keep a sharp eye along the tunnel wall on your left," advised Pitt.

Marquez nodded silently and set off into the darkness, his miner's lamp lighting the way. The tunnel stretched on and seemed endless. At one point, Marquez stopped and asked Pitt to shine his stronger beam at a rock fill between the timbers.

"This looks like what we're looking for," he said, pointing to a hard granite arch above the loose rock.

The men immediately went to work clearing the debris. After several minutes, they had dug through. Pitt leaned in and aimed his beam into a passage barely large enough to walk through. Then he checked his compass. "It heads in the right direction. Let's clear a crawl space and keep going."

This tunnel was narrower than the others, and they were forced to step over the ties supporting the ore cart tracks, making the going slow and torturous. An hour of endless walking over the tracks in the gloom, with only the miner's lamp for illumination, sapped what little stamina they had left. Everyone caught their feet on the uneven ties and stumbled one step for every five that were unimpeded.

Another cave-in that could not be penetrated caused a seemingly endless detour that cost almost two hours. Finally, they were able to bypass through a shaft that sloped up three more levels before ending at a large gallery that contained the corroded remains of a steam hoist. They struggled up to the top and trudged past the great steam cylinders and reels still holding a mile of cable.

The strain of the past few hours was beginning to show on Marquez. He was in good shape for his age, but he was not conditioned for the exertion and emotional stress he had endured the last several hours. Ambrose, though, looked as though he were on a walk in a park. He appeared remarkably calm and unruffled for a classroom professor. The only amusement came from Pitt's mumbled curses. At his six feet three, the hard hat, loaned to him by Pat because she was several inches shorter, struck overhead timbers with frustrating regularity.

Trailing behind, Pitt could not see their faces in the dim and cavorting shadows, but he knew that each one of them possessed a stubbornness that would keep them going until they dropped, too proud to be the first to suggest a rest break. He noted that their breathing had become more labored. Though he still felt fresh, he began panting loudly so the others could hear his seemingly desperate plea.

"I'm done in. How about stopping to rest a minute?"

"Sounds good to me," said Marquez, relieved that someone else had suggested it.

Ambrose leaned against one wall. "I say we keep going until we get out of here."

"You won't get my vote," said Pat. "My legs are screaming with agony. We must have stepped over a thousand railroad ties."

It was only after they all sagged to the floor of the tunnel, while Pitt casually remained standing, that they knew they had been tricked. None of them complained, everyone happy to relax and massage sore ankles and knees.

"Any idea how much farther?" asked Pat.

Pitt consulted his computer for the hundredth time. "I can't be absolutely positive, but if we can climb two more levels and are not blocked by another cave-in, we should be out of here in another hour."

"Where do you reckon we'll come out?" asked Marquez.

"My guess is somewhere right under the main town of Telluride."

"That would be the old O'Reilly Claim. It was a shaft sunk not far from where the gondola runs up the mountain to the ski slopes at Mountain Village. You do have a problem, though."

"Another one?"

"The New Sheridan Hotel and its restaurant now sit directly on top of the old mine entrance."

Pitt grinned. "If you're right, dinner is on me."

They went silent for the next two minutes, lost in their thoughts. The only sounds came from their breathing and the steady drip of moisture from the roof of the tunnel. Despondency gave way to hope. Knowing the end was perhaps in sight, they felt symptoms of fatigue begin to wash away.

Pitt had always suspected that women had more acute hearing than men, from the times his various lady friends had visited his apartment and complained that the volume on his TV was too loud. His suspicions were confirmed when Pat said, "I think I hear a motorcycle."

"A Harley-Davidson or a Honda?" asked Marquez, laughing for the first time since leaving his house.

"No, I'm serious," Pat said firmly. "I swear it sounds like a motorcycle."

Then Pitt heard something, too. He turned and faced the tunnel from the direction they had come and cupped his hands to his ears. He made out the undeniable sound of exhaust from a high-performance off-road motorcycle. He stared soberly at Marquez. "Do the locals ride around old mine tunnels on motocross dirt bikes for a thrill?"

Marquez shook his head. "Never. They'd become lost in a maze of tunnels, if they didn't plunge down a thousand-foot shaft first. Then there's the danger of their exhaust noise causing rotted beams to collapse and a cave-in to crush them. No, sir, nobody I know is fool enough to joyride underground."

"Where did they come from?" Pat asked no one in particular.

"From another mine that's still accessible. Lord only knows how they happened to be in the same tunnel as we are."

"A peculiar coincidence," Pitt said, staring up the tunnel. He felt a sense of uneasiness. Why? He couldn't be sure. He stood without moving a muscle, listening to the rattling sound of the exhaust as it grew louder. It was a foreign sound in the old mine labyrinth. It did not belong. He stood still as the first flash of light showed far down the tunnel.

Pitt couldn't tell yet if it was one or more motorcycles coming through the tunnel. It seemed a reasonable assumption that he should treat the biker or bikers as a threat. Better safe than sorry. As ancient and hackneyed as the words sounded, they still had meaning, and his cautious nature had saved him on more than one occasion.

He turned and slowly walked past Ambrose and Marquez. Absorbed in the approach of the sound and lights, they took no notice as he slipped along one wall of the tunnel in the direction of the approaching bikers. Only Pat focused on Pitt as he unobtrusively stole into the darkness of a portal leading into a narrow bore between the timbers. One moment he was there, the next he had vanished like a wraith.

There were three bikers. The front of their machines were packed with an array of halogen lights that blinded the exhausted survivors, who shielded their eyes with their hands and turned away as the engines slowed and idled in neutral. Two of the intruders dismounted their bikes and walked closer, their bodies silhouetted by the bright lights behind them. They looked like space aliens in their black, sleek helmets and two-piece jerseys worn under chest protectors. Their boots came halfway to their knees and their hands were encased in black, ribbed gloves. The third biker remained on his machine as the other two approached and raised the shields on their helmets.

"You don't know how happy we are to see you," said Pat excitedly.

"We sure could have used your help earlier," said Ambrose wearily.

"My compliments on making it this far," said the figure on the right, in a voice deep and sinister. "We thought sure you'd drowned in the Amenes chamber."

"Amenes?" Pat repeated, puzzled.

"Where did you guys come from?" demanded Marquez.

"It doesn't matter," said the biker, as if he were brushing off a classroom student's irrational question.

"You knew we were trapped in the chamber by a rockfall and rising water?"

"Yes," the biker said coldly.

"And you did nothing?" Marquez said incredulously. "You didn't try to rescue us or go for help?"

"No."

A stimulating conversationalist, this guy, thought Pitt. If he'd been a tiny bit suspicious earlier, he was downright convinced now that these men were not local daredevils on a weekend adventure. These men were killers, and heavily armed. He didn't know why, but he knew they were not going to allow them to escape the mines alive. It was time to act, and surprise was his only advantage. He slipped his dive knife from its sheath and gripped the hilt. It was the only weapon he had, and it would have to do. He took several slow deep breaths and gave a final flex to his fingers. It was now or never.

"We came within minutes of drowning in the chamber," said Pat, wondering what Pitt was planning, if anything. She began to wonder if he was a coward and simply hiding from danger.

"We know. That was the plan."

"Plan? What plan?"

"You all were supposed to die," the biker said conversationally.

The words were greeted with a stunned, uncomprehending silence.

"Unfortunately, your will to survive overcame the cave-in and the flooding," the biker continued. "We did not foresee your perseverance. But it is of no matter. You merely prolonged the inevitable."

"The dynamite blast," muttered Marquez in shock. "That was you?"

The answer was candid. "Yes, we set the charge."

Pat began to look like a deer staring into the headlights of an approaching truck. She knew that the bikers were not aware of Pitt's presence, so she acted as if he didn't exist. Marquez and Ambrose assumed he was simply standing behind them quietly, as stunned with shock as they were.

"Why would you want to kill us?" she asked, her voice shaking. "Why would total strangers want to murder us?"

"You saw the skull and you saw the inscriptions."

Marquez looked like a man torn between fear and anger. "So what?" he growled.

"Your discovery cannot be allowed to become known outside these mines."

"We've done nothing wrong," Ambrose said, strangely calm. "We're scientists studying historic phenomena. We're not talking treasure but ancient artifacts. It's insane to be killed because of it."

The biker shrugged. "It's unfortunate, but you became involved with matters far beyond your comprehension."

"How could you possibly know about our entry into the chamber?" asked Marquez.

"We were informed. That's all you need to know."

"By who? Not more than five people knew we were there."

"We're wasting time," grunted the second biker. "Let's finish our business and throw them down the nearest shaft."

"This is madness," muttered Ambrose, with little or no feeling in his voice.

Pitt silently moved from the bore, any sounds of his footsteps covered by the soft popping from the exhaust, and crept up behind the rider still sitting on his bike, who was distracted by the conversation. Pitt was no stranger to killing, but it wasn't in him to knife another man in the back, no matter how rotten the victim might be. In the same motion, he reversed the grip on the knife and plunged the blunt hilt with all his strength against the base of the biker's neck below the helmet. It bordered on a killing blow, but it was a pound short of fatal. The biker sagged in his seat and fell back against Pitt without making so much as a soft moan. Pitt crouched low and quickly threw his arms around the body, held it for a moment, then lowered it, together with the bike, quietly onto the ore cart track with the engine still idling in neutral.

Working swiftly, he pushed aside the biker's chest protector and uncased a Para-Ordnance 10+1 round, .45-caliber automatic from a shoulder holster strapped under an armpit. He trained the sights on the back of the biker standing on his right and pulled back the hammer. He had never fired a P-10 before, but from the feel, he knew the magazine was full and that the gun possessed most of the same features as his trusty old Colt .45, which was locked inside the NUMA vehicle he'd driven to Colorado from Washington.

The headlights on the motorcycles brightly illuminated the two killers, who failed to detect the figure stealing up behind them, but as Pitt crept closer, he passed in front of the light from the third bike, which was lying on the track, and he became identifiable to Ambrose.

The anthropologist spied Pitt emerging from the bright light, pointed behind the bikers, and blurted, "How did you get back there?"

At the words, Pitt took careful aim and allowed his index finger to caress the trigger.

"Who are you talking to?" the first biker demanded.

"Little old me," Pitt said casually.

These men were top of the line in their profession. There was no hint of stunned surprise. No pointless discussion. No obvious questions. No hesitation or remote display of uncertainty. Their sixth sense worked as one. Their actions came with lightning speed. In a seemingly fused, well-practiced movement, they jerked the P-10 autos from their holsters and whirled around within a single second, the expressions on their faces frozen in cold implacability.

Pitt did not face the killers full-on, knees slightly bent, his gun gripped and extended in two hands directly in front of his nose, the way they taught in police academies or as seen in action movies. He preferred the classic stance, body turned sideways, eyes staring over one shoulder, gun stretched out in one hand. Not only did he present less of a target, but his aim was more precise. He knew that the gunslingers of the West who'd lived to a ripe old age had not necessarily been the fastest on the draw, but they were the straightest shooters, who'd taken their time to aim before pulling the trigger.

Pitt's first shot took the biker on the right in the nape of his neck. A slight, almost infinitesimal shift of the P-10 as he squeezed the trigger for the second time, and the biker on the left took a bullet in the chest at nearly the same instant his own gun was lining up on Pitt's silhouetted figure. Pitt could not believe that two men could react as one in the blink of an eye. Had they been given another two seconds to snap off a shot, it would have been Pitt whose body fell heavily across the granite floor of the mine tunnel.

The gunshots erupted like a deafening barrage of artillery fire, reverberating throughout the rock walls of the tunnel. For ten seconds, perhaps twenty—it seemed more like an hour—Pat, Ambrose, and Marquez stared unbelievingly at the dead bodies at their feet, eyes wide and glazed. Then the tentative beginnings of a dazed hope and the final realization that they were still alive broke the horror-numbed spell.

"What in God's name is going on?" Pat said, her voice low and vague. Then she looked up at Pitt. "You killed them?" It was more a statement than a question.

"Better them than you," Pitt said, putting his arm around her shoulders. "We've experienced a nasty nightmare, but it's almost over now."

Marquez stepped past the rails and leaned down over the dead killers. "Who are these people?"

"A mystery for law-enforcement authorities to solve," replied Ambrose. He thrust out a hand. "I'd like to shake your hand, Mr. . . ." He paused and looked blank. "I don't even know the name of the man who saved my life."

"It's Dirk Pitt," said Pat.

"I'm deeply in your debt," said Ambrose. He seemed more agitated than relieved.

"As am I," added Marquez, slapping Pitt's back.

"What mine do you think they entered to get here?" Pitt asked Marquez.

The miner thought a moment. "Most likely the Paradise."

"That means they purposely trapped themselves when they blew the dynamite that caused the avalanche," said Ambrose.

Pitt shook his head. "Not purposely. They knew they could make their way back to the surface by another route. Their big mistake was in using too massive a charge. They hadn't planned on the earth tremors, the collapse of the tunnel, and the opening of the underground fissures that allowed the water to rise and flood the tunnel."

"It figures," agreed Marquez. "Since they were on the opposite side of the cave-in, they could have easily ridden their bikes up the sloping shaft ahead of the flooding to the entrance. Finding it blocked with snow, they began searching connecting tunnels for a way out—"

"And after riding lost through the mines for hours, eventually came upon us," finished Ambrose.

Pitt nodded. "By riding up the Paradise's entrance shaft to this level, they saved climbing the vertical shafts we were forced to struggle through."

"It's almost as if they were looking for us," Marquez murmured.

Pitt didn't voice his thoughts to the others, but he was certain that once the bikers had ridden to the upper levels to escape the flooding, they had then followed in the footsteps of the four of them.

"It's all so crazy," said Pat, staring dazedly at the dead bikers. "What did he mean, we were 'involved with matters far beyond our comprehension'?"

Pitt shrugged. "That's for others to decide. The question in my mind is who sent them? Who do they represent? Beyond that, I'm only a marine engineer who is damp and cold and wants to find a thick Colorado prime rib medium rare and a glass of tequila."

"For a marine engineer," said Ambrose, grinning, "you're pretty handy with a gun."

"It doesn't take virtuosity to shoot a man from behind," Pitt came back cynically.

"What do we do with him?" inquired Marquez, pointing at the biker Pitt had clubbed senseless.

"We've no rope to tie him up, so we'll take his boots. He won't get far in bare feet through the mine tunnels."

"You want to leave him?"

"No sense in hauling an inert body around. Chances are, by the time we notify the sheriff and he sends his deputies down here, the killer will still be unconscious." Then Pitt paused and asked, "Have any of you ridden motorcycles?"

"I rode a Harley for ten years," answered Marquez.

"And I have an old Honda CBX Super Sport that belonged to my dad," Pat volunteered.

"Do you ride it?"

"Rode it all through college. I still hit the roads with it on weekends."

Pitt looked at Pat with newfound respect. "So you're an old leather-crotch, hard-in-the-saddle woman."

"You got it," she said proudly.

Then he turned to Ambrose. "And you, Doc?"

"Never sat on a motorcycle in my life. Why do you ask?"

"Because we've got what look like three perfectly good Suzuki RM125 supercross bikes, and I see no reason why we can't borrow them and ride out of the mine."

Marquez's teeth showed in a wide smile. "I'm with you."

"I'll wait here until the sheriff shows up," said Ambrose. "The rest of you get going. I don't want to spend any more time with a live killer and two dead men than I have to."

"I don't like leaving you here alone with this killer, Doc. I'd prefer that you ride behind me until we're out of here."

Ambrose was firm. "Those bikes don't look like they were meant to haul passengers. I'm damned if I'll ride on one. Besides, you'll be traveling over rail tracks, making it unstable as hell."

"Have it your way," said Pitt, giving in to the obstinate anthropologist.

Pitt crouched and removed the P-10 automatics from the bodies. He was anything but a born killer, but he showed little remorse. Only a minute earlier, these men had been intent on murdering three innocent people whom they had never met—an act he could never have allowed to happen under any circumstances.

He handed one of the guns to Ambrose. "Stay at least twenty feet away from our friend, and stay alert if he so much as blinks." Pitt also gave Ambrose his dive light. "The batteries should last until the sheriff comes."

"I doubt if I could bring myself to shoot another human," Ambrose protested, but his voice came with a cold edge.

"Don't look upon these guys as human. They're cold-blooded executioners who could slit a woman's throat and eat ice cream afterward. I warn you, Doc, if he looks cross-eyed at you, brain him with a rock."

The Suzukis were still idling in neutral, and it took them less than a minute to figure out the shift, brake, and throttle controls. With a farewell wave to Ambrose, Pitt roared off first. There was no room for the machines to move between the outer rails and the walls of the tunnel, not without scraping the handgrips on the rough granite. Pitt kept his wheels in the center of the rail tracks, closely followed by Pat and Marquez. Bouncing over the rail ties with rigid suspensions rattled their teeth and made for uncomfortable riding. Pat felt as if her insides were being shaken around by a Laundromat dryer. Pitt found the trick was to find the proper speed that gave the least vibration. It worked out to twenty-five miles an hour, a speed that might have seemed slow and safe on a paved road but was quite dangerous inside a narrow mine tunnel.

The hard-rock acoustics made the exhaust blast echo in their ears. The beams from the headlights hopped up and down, striking the rails and overhead timbers like strobe lights. He narrowly missed an ore car that was sitting on the tracks and partially protruding from an intersecting tunnel. After riding up the gentle grade of a lift shaft, they reached the upper level to a mine that was labeled "The Citizen" on Pitt's directional computer. Pitt rolled to a stop where the tunnel met another at a fork and consulted the tiny monitor.

"Are we lost?" Pat queried above the rattle from the exhaust pipes.

"Another two hundred yards down the tunnel on the left and we should come to the end of the mine tunnel you said comes out under the New Sheridan Hotel."

"The entrance to the O'Reilly Claim was covered over a hundred years ago," said Marquez. "We'll never get out that way."

"Never hurts to look," said Pitt, shifting gears and easing the clutch on the Suzuki. He gave the bike a burst of speed and was forced to brake hard within two minutes, when he suddenly confronted a brick wall that solidly blocked the old mine entrance. He came to an abrupt stop, leaned the bike against a timber, and studied the bricks under the headlight.

"We'll have to find another way," said Marquez, as he pulled alongside, came to a stop, and set both feet on the ground to keep the bike upright. "We've come out at the basement foundation wall of the hotel."

Pitt appeared not to have heard him. As if his mind was a thousand miles away, he slowly reached out and ran his hand over the old kiln-dried red bricks. He turned as Pat stopped her bike and turned off the ignition.

"Where do we go now?" she asked, her voice betraying near-total exhaustion.

Pitt spoke without turning. "There," he answered offhandedly, pointing in the general direction of the brick wall. "I suggest you both move your bikes to the side of the tunnel."

Pat and Marquez didn't get it. They still didn't get it after Pitt climbed on the Suzuki, revved up the engine, and spun gravel under the rear wheel as he rode back into the tunnel. After a short minute, he was heard accelerating down the tracks toward them, the Suzuki's headlight beam dancing madly off the timbers.

Marquez reckoned Pitt was doing nearly thirty miles an hour when he thrust out his legs and dug his heels onto the twin ore cart rails less than ten yards from the wall, released his grip on the hand controls, and stood up, allowing the Suzuki to speed on from under him. Slumped backward to compensate for his momentum, he actually remained upright for nearly twenty feet before his feet slipped off the rails and he folded into a ball before tumbling through the tunnel like a soccer ball.

The motorcycle stayed on its wheels, but was just starting to lie on its side when it crashed into the brick wall with a protesting screech of metal and a cloud of dust, before bursting through the old decaying bricks and vanishing into the void beyond.

Pat ran over to Pitt's body, which had skidded to a stop and was sprawled on the ground. She would have sworn he had killed himself, but he looked up at her, blood streaming from a gash on his chin, and grinned like a madman. "Let's see Evel Knievel try that one," he said.

Pat stared down at him in amazement. "I can't believe you didn't break every bone in your body."

"None broken," he muttered in pain, as he slowly rose to his feet. "But I think I bent a few."

"That was the craziest thing I ever saw," mumbled Marquez.

"Maybe, but it worked better than I expected." Pitt, clutching his right shoulder, nodded at the hole in the brick wall. He stood there, getting his breath and waiting for the pain from bruised ribs and a dislocated shoulder to ease, while Marquez began pulling away the bricks loosened by the bike's passage to enlarge the entry.

The miner peered around the fractured wall and aimed his miner's lamp inside. After a few seconds, he looked back and said, "I think we're in deep trouble."

"Why?" asked Pat. "Can't we get out that way?"

"We can get out," said Marquez, "but it's going to cost us big time."

"Cost?"

Pitt limped painfully to the opening and peered inside. "Oh, no," he groaned.

"What is it?" Pat demanded in exasperation.

"The motorcycle," said Pitt. "It crashed into the wine cellar of the hotel restaurant. There must be a hundred broken bottles of vintage wine flowing down a drain in the floor."

6

SHERIFF JAMES EAGAN, JR., was directing the rescue operation at the Paradise Mine when he received the call from his dispatcher informing him that Luis Marquez was being held in custody by the Telluride town marshal's deputies at the New Sheridan Hotel for breaking and entering. Eagan was incredulous. How was this possible? Marquez's wife had been adamant in claiming her husband and two others were trapped inside the mine by the avalanche. Against his better judgment, Eagan turned over command of the rescue operation and drove down the mountain to the hotel.

The last thing he expected to find was a mangled motorcycle sitting amid several cases of smashed bottles of wine. His astonishment broadened when he stepped into the hotel's conference room to confront the confessed culprits and found three damp, dirty, and bedraggled people, two men and one woman, one of them wearing a torn and tattered diver's wet suit. All were in handcuffs and in the custody of two deputy marshals, who stood with solemn expressions on their faces. One of them nodded at Pitt.

"This one was carrying an arsenal."

"You have his weapons?" Eagan asked officially.

The deputy nodded and held up three Para-Ordnance .45-caliber automatics.

Satisfied, Eagan turned his attention to Luis Marquez. "How in hell did you get out of the mine and wind up here?" he demanded in complete bewilderment.

"It doesn't matter!" Marquez snapped back. "You and your deputies have got to go down the tunnel. You'll find two dead bodies and a college professor, Dr. Ambrose, who we left guarding a killer."

There was a genuine feeling of skepticism, almost total disbelief, in Sheriff Jim Eagan's mind as he sat down, tipped his chair back on two legs, and pulled a notebook from the breast pocket of his shirt. "Suppose you tell me just what is going on here."

Desperately, Marquez gave a brief account of the cave-in and flooding, Pitt's fortuitous appearance, their escape from the mysterious chamber, the encounter with the three murderers, and their forced entry into the wine cellar of the hotel.

At first the details came slowly, as Marquez fought off the effects of strain and exhaustion. Then his words flowed faster as he sensed Eagan's obvious doubt. Frustration swelled and was replaced by urgency, as Marquez pleaded with Eagan to rescue Tom Ambrose. "Dammit, Jim, stop being stubborn. Get off your butt and go see for yourself."

Eagan knew Marquez and respected him as a man of integrity, but his story was too far-fetched to buy without proof. "Black obsidian skulls, indecipherable writings in a chamber carved a thousand feet into the mountain, murderers roaming mine shafts on motorcycles. If what you tell me is true, it will be the three of you who will be under suspicion for murder."

"Mr. Marquez has told you the honest truth," said Pat slowly, speaking for the first time. "Why can't you believe him?"

"And you are?"

"Patricia O'Connell," she said wearily. "I'm with the University of Pennsylvania."

"And what is your reason for being in the mine?"

"My field is ancient languages. I was asked to come to Telluride and decipher the strange inscriptions Mr. Marquez found in his mine."

Eagan studied the woman for a moment. She might have been pretty when attractively dressed and made up. He did not find it easy to believe she was a Ph.D. in ancient languages. Sitting there with her wet, stringy hair and mud-smeared face, she looked like a homeless bag lady.

"All I know for sure," said Eagan slowly, "is that you people destroyed a motorcycle, which might be stolen, and vandalized the wine cellar of the hotel."

"Forget that," pleaded Marquez. "Rescue Dr. Ambrose."

"Only when I'm sure of the facts will I send my men into the mine."

Jim Eagan had been sheriff of San Miguel County for eight years and worked in harmony with the marshals who policed the town of Telluride. Homicides were far and few between in San Miguel County. Law-enforcement problems usually centered around auto accidents, petty theft, drunken fights, vandalism, and drug arrests, usually involving young transients who passed through Telluride during the summer season and attended various affairs such as the bluegrass and jazz festivals. Eagan was respected by the citizens of his small but beautifully scenic domain. He was a congenial man, serious in his work, but quick to laugh when having a beer at one of the local watering holes. Of medium height and weight, he often wore a facial expression that could berate and intimidate. One look was generally all it took to cower any suspect he had arrested.

"May I ask you a small favor?" said the bruised and fatigued man in the torn diver's wet suit, who looked as though he been dragged through the impellers of a water pump.

At first glance, he looked to Eagan to be forty-five, but he was probably a good five years younger than the tanned and craggy face suggested. The sheriff guessed him to be about six feet three inches, weight 185 pounds, give or take. His hair was black and wavy, with a few strands of gray at the temples. The eyebrows were dark and bushy and stretched over eyes that were a vivid green. A straight and narrow nose dropped toward firm lips, with the corners turned up in a slight grin. What bothered Eagan wasn't so much the man's indifferent attitude—

he'd known many felons who displayed apathy—but his bemused kind of detached interest. It was obvious that the man across the table was not the least bit impressed with Eagan's dominating tactics.

"Depends," Eagan answered finally, his ballpoint pen poised above a page in the notebook. "Your name?"

"Dirk Pitt."

"And what is your involvement, Mr. Pitt?"

"I'm special projects director for the National Underwater and Marine Agency. I was just passing by and thought it might be fun to prospect for gold."

Inwardly, Eagan seethed at being at a disadvantage. "We can do without the humor, Mr. Pitt."

"If I give you a phone number, will you do me the courtesy of calling it?" Pitt's tone was polite, with no trace of hostility.

"You want to speak to an attorney?"

Pitt shook his head. "No, nothing like that. I thought a simple call to confirm my position and presence might be helpful."

Eagan thought a moment, then passed his pen and notebook across the table. "Okay, let's have the number."

Pitt wrote it in the sheriff's notebook and handed it back. "It's long distance. You can call collect if you wish."

"You can pay the hotel," Eagan said, with a tight smile.

"You'll be talking to Admiral James Sandecker," said Pitt. "The number is his private line. Give him my name and explain the situation."

Eagan moved to a phone on a nearby desk, asked for an outside line, and dialed the number. After a brief pause, Eagan said, "Admiral Sandecker, this is Sheriff Jim Eagan of San Miguel County, Colorado. I have a problem here concerning a man who claims to work for you. His name is Dirk Pitt." Then Eagan quickly outlined the situation, stating that Pitt would probably be placed under arrest and charged with second-degree criminal trespass, theft, and vandalism. From that point on, the conversation went downhill, as his face took on a dazed expression that lasted nearly ten minutes. As if talking to God, he repeated, "Yes, sir," several times. Finally, he hung up and stared at Pitt. "Your boss is a testy bastard."

Pitt laughed. "He strikes most people that way."

"You have a most impressive history."

"Did he offer to pay for damages?"

Eagan grinned. "He insisted it come out of your salary."

Curious, Pat asked, "What else did the admiral have to say?"

"He said, among other things," Eagan spoke slowly, "that if Mr. Pitt claimed the South won the Civil War, I was to believe him."

PITT and Marquez, with Eagan and one of his deputies trailing behind, stepped through the shattered wall of the wine cellar and began jogging through the old mine tunnel. They soon passed the old stationary ore car and continued into the yawning tube.

There was no way for Pitt to judge distance in the darkened bore. His best guess was that he had left Ambrose and the captured assassin approximately three-quarters of a mile from the hotel. He held a flashlight borrowed from a deputy and switched it off every few hundred feet, peering into the darkness ahead for a sign from the dive light he'd left with Ambrose.

After covering what he believed was the correct distance, Pitt stopped and aimed the beam of the flashlight as far up the tunnel as it would penetrate. Then he flicked it off. Only pitch blackness stretched ahead.

"We're there," Pitt said to Marquez.

"That's impossible," said the miner. "Dr. Ambrose would have heard our voices echoing off the rock and seen our lights. He would have shouted or signaled us."

"Something isn't right." Pitt threw the flashlight's beam at an opening in one wall of the tunnel. "There's the portal to the bore I hid in when the bikers approached."

Eagan came up beside him. "Why are we stopping?"

"Crazy as it sounds," Pitt answered, "they've vanished."

The sheriff shone his light in Pitt's face, searching for something in his eyes. "You sure they weren't a figment of your imagination?"

"I swear to God!" Marquez muttered. "We left two dead bodies, an unconscious killer, and Dr. Ambrose with a gun to cover him."

Pitt ignored the sheriff and dropped to his knees. He swept his light around the tunnel very slowly in a 180-degree arc, his eyes examining every inch of the ground and the ore car tracks.

Marquez started to say, "What are you—?" but Pitt threw up one hand, motioning him to silence.

In Pitt's mind, if Ambrose and the killer were gone, they had to have left some tiny indication of their presence. His original intent had been to look for the shell casings ejected from the P-10 automatic he'd used to shoot the killers. But there was no hint of a gleam from the brass casings. The back of his neck began to tingle. This was the right spot, he was certain of it. Then he sensed rather than saw an almost infinitesimal strand of black wire no more than eighteen inches away, so thin it didn't cast a shadow under his light. He trailed the beam along the wire, over the rail tracks, and up the wall to a black canvas bundle attached to one of the overhead timbers.

"Tell me, Sheriff," Pitt said in a strangely quiet voice, "have you had bomb-disposal training?"

"I teach a course in it to law enforcement," Eagan replied, eyebrows raised. "I was a demolitions expert in the Army. Why ask?"

"I do believe we were set up to enter the next world in pieces." He pointed to the wire leading from the tracks and up the timber. "Unless I miss my guess, that's an explosive booby trap."

Eagan moved until his face was inches away from the black strand. He followed it up to the canvas bundle and studied the bundle carefully. Then he turned to Pitt with a new level of respect in his eyes. "I do believe you are right, Mr. Pitt. Somebody doesn't like you."

"Include yourself, Sheriff. They must have known you and your men would have accompanied us back to Dr. Ambrose."

"Where is the professor?" wondered Marquez aloud. "Where did he and the killer go?"

"There are two possibilities," said Pitt. "The first is that the killer regained consciousness, overpowered Doc Ambrose, killed him and dumped his body down the nearest mine shaft. Then he placed the charge and escaped through another tunnel leading to the outside."

"You should write fairy tales," said Eagan.

"Then explain the booby trap."

"How do I know you didn't set it?"

"I have no motive."

"Get off it, Jim," said Marquez. "Mr. Pitt hasn't been out of my sight for the past five hours. He just saved our lives. If the blast didn't get us, the cave-in would."

"We're not certain the bundle contains explosives," Eagan said stubbornly.

"Then trip the wire and see what happens." Pitt grinned. "I, for one, am not going to hang around and find out. I'm out of here." He rose to his feet and began strolling along the ore car tracks back to the hotel.

"One moment, Mr. Pitt. I'm not through with you."

Pitt paused and turned. "What are your intentions, Sheriff?"

"Check out the sack wired to the timber, and if it's an explosive device, disarm it."

Pitt took a few steps back, his face dead serious. "I wouldn't if I were you. That's not some bomb built in the backyard of a junior terrorist. I'll bet my next paycheck it was exactingly assembled by experts and will burst at the slightest touch."

Eagan looked at him. "If you have a better idea, I'd like to hear it."

"The ore car sitting a couple of hundred yards up the track," replied Pitt. "We give it a shove and let it roll through here and trip the wire and detonate the explosives."

"The roof of the tunnel will collapse," said Marquez, "blocking it forever."

Pitt shrugged. "It's not like we're destroying the tunnel to deny access to future generations. We're the first to have passed through this section of the mine since the nineteen-thirties."

"Makes sense," Eagan finally agreed. "We can't leave explosives laying about for the next underground explorers who walk through here."

Fifteen minutes later, Pitt, Eagan, Marquez, and the deputy had pushed the ore car to within fifty yards of the trip wire. The heavy iron wheels squeaked and protested for the first fifty feet, but soon loosened and began to roll smoothly over the rusty rails as the ancient grease on their axles lubricated the roller bearings. The four sweating men finally reached the crest of a slight slope that led downward.

"The end of the line," Pitt announced. "One good shove and she should roll for a mile."

"Or until she drops into the next shaft," said Marquez.

The men heaved in unison and ran with the car, propelling it until it picked up speed and began to outrace them. They staggered to a halt and caught their breath, allowing their pounding hearts to slow. Then they held their flashlights on the ore car as it charged over the rails and disappeared around a gradual curve of the tunnel.

Less than a minute later, a tremendous detonation tore through the tunnel. The shock wave nearly knocked them off their feet. Then came a cloud of dust that swirled around and past them, followed by the deep rumble of tons of rock falling from the roof of the tunnel.

The rumble was still ringing in their ears, the echoes reverberating in the old mine, when Marquez shouted to Eagan, "That should stifle any doubts."

"In your haste to prove your point, you overlooked something," Eagan said loudly, his tone dry and provocative.

Pitt looked at him. "Which is?"

"Dr. Ambrose. He could still be alive somewhere beyond the cave-in. And even if he's dead, there will be no way of retrieving his body."

"It'll be a wasted effort," Pitt said briefly.

"You only gave us one possibility," said Eagan. "Does this have something to do with the second?"

Pitt gave a slight nod. "Dr. Ambrose," he said patiently, "is not dead."

"Are you saying the third assassin didn't kill him?" asked Marquez.

"He'd hardly murder his own boss."

"Boss?"

Pitt smiled and said firmly, "Dr. Tom Ambrose was one of the killers."

7

"FORGIVE ME FOR ARRIVING late for dinner," said Pat as she stepped through the Marquezes' front door. "But I desperately needed a hot bath, and I fear I soaked too long."

Lisa Marquez hugged Pat joyously. "You don't know how happy I am to see you again." She stepped back, and her face lit up like an angelic cherub as she saw Pitt following Pat into the house. She kissed him on both cheeks. "How can I ever thank you for bringing my husband home alive and well?"

"I cheated," Pitt said, with his trademark grin. "To save Luis I had to save myself."

"You're just being modest."

Pat was surprised to see Pitt show a hint of genuine embarrassment as he stared down at the carpet. She added, "Your husband wasn't the only life Dirk saved."

"Luis has been very closemouthed about your ordeal. You must fill me in on the details over dinner." Lisa looked elegant in a designer slacks outfit. "Here, let me take your coats."

"Do I smell elk sizzling on the barbecue?" said Pitt, extricating himself from an awkward situation.

"Luis is in the garage playing with his smoker," said Lisa. "It's too cold to eat outside, so I've set the table inside our glass-enclosed solarium on the rear porch deck. Luis installed heaters, so it's cozy warm. Help yourself to a beer as you pass through the kitchen."

Pitt retrieved a bottle of Pacifico beer from the refrigerator and joined Marquez in the garage. Marquez was hunched over a fifty-gallon drum that he had converted into a smoker. "Smells good," said Pitt. "You're not using a charcoal grill?"

"You get far better flavor from meat, chicken, or fish from a smoker," said Luis. "I shot the elk last season. Had it butchered in Montrose and frozen. Wait till you taste it with Lisa's special Mornay sauce."

A short time later, they were all seated at a pine log table Marquez had built inside the glassed-in porch, enjoying the elk steaks coated with Lisa's delicious sauce. Creamed spinach, baked potatoes, and a big bowl of salad enhanced the elk. Marquez had asked Pat and Dirk not to say too much about their harrowing experience. He didn't want to upset his wife any more than he had to. She had suffered enough during her agonizing wait until the word had come that he had exited the mine and was safe and sound. They had treated the ordeal lightly, omitting any reference to the killers and telling her that Ambrose was meeting friends and couldn't make it for dinner.

Despite the fact that they acted as if they had returned from a walk in the park, Lisa knew better, but she said nothing. After dinner, Pat helped her clear the table and returned, while Lisa busily fed her young daughters and made coffee before bringing out a carrot cake.

"Excuse me for a moment," said Pitt. He walked into the house and said a few words to Lisa before rejoining Pat and Marquez at the table.

Satisfied that his wife was out of earshot, Marquez stared directly at Pitt and said, "I can't accept your theory about Dr. Ambrose. I feel certain that he was murdered soon after we left him."

"I agree with Luis," said Pat. "To suggest that Tom was anything but a respected scientist is ridiculous."

"Had you ever met Ambrose before today?" asked Pitt.

She shook her head. "No, but I know him by reputation."

"But you've never seen him."

"No."

"Then how do you know whether the man we knew as Tom Ambrose wasn't an impostor?"

"All right," said Marquez. "Suppose he was a fake and working with those crazy bikers. How do you explain that fact that he would have surely drowned if you hadn't showed up?"

"That's right," Pat interjected quietly. "There's no way he'd be tied to a criminal conspiracy if the killers tried to murder him, too."

"His fellow assassins screwed up." There was a cold certainty in Pitt's voice. "They may have been demolitions experts, but not being professional hardrock miners like Luis, they set off an explosive charge too powerful for the job. Instead of merely causing a cave-in and blocking off the tunnel, they collapsed the rock holding back an underground river, diverting it into the lower levels of the mine. A miscalculation that fouled up their plans. The shaft and the chamber with the skull flooded before they could detour around the cave-in on their bikes to rescue their chief."

Marquez stared up at the mountain peaks surrounding Telluride that were outlined by the light of the evening stars. "Why cause the tunnel roof to collapse? What did they gain from that?"

"The perfect murder," answered Pitt. "They meant to kill the two of you by beating your brains in with rocks. Then they would have buried your bodies in the debris from the cave-in. When and if your remains were ever found, your deaths would be written off as a mining accident."

"Why kill us?" Pat asked incredulously. "For what purpose?"

"Because you posed a threat."

"Luis and I a threat?" She looked confused. "To whom?"

"To a well-financed, well-organized secret interest who didn't want the discovery of the chamber with the black skull to become public knowledge."

"Why would anyone want to cover up a major archaeological discovery?" said Pat, completely off balance.

Pitt turned up the palms of his hands in a helpless gesture. "That's where conjecture stops. But I'm willing to bet the farm that this is not an isolated incident. That a trail of bodies leads to other finds of this magnitude."

"The only other archaeological project I can think of that is surrounded in this kind of mystery was an expedition led by Dr. Jeffrey Taffet from Arizona State University. He and several students died while exploring a cave on the northern slope of Mount Lascar in Chile."

"What was the cause of their deaths?" asked Marquez

"They were found frozen to death," answered Pat. "Which was very peculiar, according to the rescue team who found the bodies. The weather had been perfect, without storms, and temperatures were barely below freezing. An investigation turned up no reason for Taffet and his students to have succumbed to hypothermia."

"What was of archaeological interest in the cave?" Pitt prompted.

"No one knows for sure. A pair of amateur mountain climbers from New York, both successful tax attorneys, discovered and explored the cave while descending from the summit of the mountain. They described ancient artifacts neatly placed about inside, shortly before they were killed."

Pitt stared at her. "They died, too?"

"Their private plane crashed on takeoff from the airport at Santiago for the flight home."

"The mystery deepens."

"Subsequent expeditions to the cave found nothing inside," Pat continued. "Either the attorneys exaggerated what they saw—"

"Or someone cleaned out the artifacts," Pitt finished.

"I wonder if the attorneys found a black skull," mused Marquez.

Pat shrugged. "No one will ever know."

"Did you manage to salvage your notes from the chamber?" Marquez asked Pat.

"The pages were soaked during our swim through the mine, but once I dried them with my hair dryer, they became quite readable. And if you have any questions about the meaning of the inscriptions, you can forget them. The symbols are from no known form of writing I've ever seen."

"I would think that written symbols cross over cultures, ancient and modern—that they would have similar markings," said Pitt thoughtfully.

"Not necessarily. There are many ancient inscriptions that stand alone without parallel symbols. Believe me when I say the signs on the walls in the chamber of the black skull are unique."

"Any chance they might be a deception?"

"I won't know until I have a chance to study them in depth."

"Take it from me," Marquez stated emphatically, "no one had entered that chamber before me in a long time. The surrounding rock showed no signs of recent digging."

Pat brushed her long red hair from her eyes. "The puzzle is who built it and why."

"And when," Pitt threw in. "Somehow the chamber and the killers are tied together."

A sudden breeze whistled up the canyon, rattling the windows of the solarium. Pat shivered. "The evening is getting cool. I think I'll get my coat."

Marquez turned toward the kitchen. "I wonder where Lisa is with the coffee and cake—"

His voice broke off as Pitt suddenly leaped to his feet. In one convulsive movement, he shoved the miner under the log table, then seized Pat and threw her to the wooden floor, covering her body with his own. Some alien wisp of movement in the shadows beside the house had tweaked the acute sense of menace that had been honed in him over the years. In the next instant, two explosions of gunfire burst from the shadows outside, coming so close together, they sounded as one.

Pitt lay there on Pat, hearing her gasp for the breath he had knocked from her chest. He rolled off her and came to his feet as he heard a familiar voice shout from the evening shadows, a voice distinct with an assured confidence.

"Got him!"

Pitt slowly helped Pat to a chair and pulled Marquez to his feet. "Those were gunshots . . . that voice?" murmured a dazed Marquez.

"Not to worry," Pitt said reassuringly. "The posse is on our side."

"Lisa, my kids," Marquez blurted, turning and starting to run into the house.

"Safe in the bathtub," said Pitt, grabbing an arm.

"How——?"

"Because that's where I told them to hide."

A stocky bull of a man materialized from the mountain undergrowth surrounding the house, wearing an Arctic white jumpsuit with a hood. He was dragging a body through the snow, dressed in a black ninja suit, its face covered by a ski mask. There was still enough light left in the sky to see the white-clad man's shag of black curly hair, dark Etruscan eyes, and lips spread in a white-toothed grin. He pulled the body along by one foot as effortlessly as if he were hauling a ten-pound bag of potatoes.

"Any problems?" asked Pitt quietly, stepping outside into the snow-covered yard.

"None," answered the stranger. "Like mugging a blind man. Despite a masterful attempt at a sneaky intrusion, the last thing he expected was an ambush."

"Underrating his intended prey is the worst miscalculation a professional killer can make."

Pat gazed at Pitt, ashen-faced. "You planned this?" she uttered mechanically.

"Of course," Pitt admitted, almost fiendishly. "The killers are . . ." He paused to look down at the man lying at his feet. "Or, rather, *were* fanatics. I can't begin to guess what lies behind their motive to kill anyone who entered that mysterious chamber. In my case, I moved to the head of their kill list when I showed up out of the blue and put a wrench in their well-oiled plan. They were also afraid I might return to the chamber and retrieve the black skull. Their fear of Pat was that she might decipher the inscriptions.

"After we escaped the tunnel and were released by Sheriff Eagan, this one stood back and watched us, waiting for the right opportunity. Because they had already made such a prolonged effort to hide the chamber discovery by eliminating all witnesses, it didn't take a class in village idiocy to figure they were not about to leave the job undone and allow any of us to leave Telluride alive. So I threw out the bait and reeled them in."

"You set us up as decoys," muttered Marquez. "We might have been killed."

"Better to take that risk now while the cards are on our side of the table than to wait until we're vulnerable."

"Shouldn't Sheriff Eagan be in on this?"

"As we speak, he should be apprehending the other killer at Pat's bed-and-breakfast."

"A gunman in my room?" Pat uttered in a shocked whisper. "While I was taking a bath?"

"No," Pitt said patiently. "He entered only after you left for the Marquez house with me."

"But he could have walked right in and murdered me."

"Not hardly." Pitt squeezed her hand. "Trust me when I say there was little danger. Didn't you notice the place was a little crowded? The sheriff arranged for a small throng of locals to roam the halls and dining rooms of the bed-and-breakfast, acting like conventioneers. It would have been awkward for a stalking killer to take his victim in a crowd. When it was advertised that you and I both were coming to the Marquezes' for dinner, the killers split the operation. One volunteered to send us all to the cemetery during dinner, while the other tossed your room for your notebook and camera."

"He doesn't look like anyone I know with the sheriff's department," said Marquez, pointing to the muscular intruder.

Pitt turned and placed his arm around the shoulders of the stranger who had just subdued the assassin. "May I present my oldest and dearest friend, Albert Giordino. Al is my assistant projects director with NUMA."

Marquez and Pat stood silently, uncertain of how to act. They studied Al with the intent of a bacterial researcher peering through a microscope at a specimen. Giordino simply released his grip on the intruder's foot, stepped forward, and shook their hands. "A pleasure to meet you both. I'm happy to have been of service."

"Who got shot?" Pitt queried.

"This guy had reactions you can't believe," said Giordino.

"Oh, yes, I can."

"He must have been psychic. He snapped off a shot in my direction the same instant I squeezed my own trigger." Giordino pointed to a slight tear along the hip of his jumpsuit. "His bullet barely bruised my skin. Mine took him in the right lung."

"You were lucky."

"Oh, I don't know," Giordino said loftily. "I aimed, he didn't."

"Is he still alive?"

"I should think so. But he won't be entering a marathon anytime soon."

Pitt leaned down and pulled the ski mask from the killer's head.

Pat gasped in horror—understandable, considering the circumstance, Pitt thought wryly. She still found it impossible to accept everything that had happened to her since stepping off the plane at the Telluride airport.

"Oh, dear God!" Her voice held a mixture of shock and distress. "It's Dr. Ambrose!"

"No, dear lady," Pitt said softly. "That is not Dr. Thomas Ambrose. As I told you before, the real Ambrose is probably dead. This lowlife probably took on the job of murdering you and me and Luis because only he could identify us with any certainty."

The truth of Pitt's words struck her with numbing cruelty. She knelt down and looked into the open eyes of the killer and demanded, "Why did you have to murder Dr. Ambrose?"

There was no flicker of emotion in the killer's eyes. The only indication of injury was the blood trickling from his mouth, a sure sign of a lung wound. "Not murdered, executed," he whispered. "He was a threat and had to die, just as you must all die."

"You have the guts to justify your actions," Pitt said, with an icy edge to his voice.

"I justify nothing. Duty to the New Destiny demands no justification."

"Who and what is the New Destiny?"

"The Fourth Empire, but you'll be dead before you see it." There was no hate, no arrogance in the killer's tone, just a simple statement of supposed fact. The killer spoke with a trace of a European accent.

"The chamber, the black skull, what is their significance?"

"A message from the past." For the first time, there was a hint of a smile. "The world's greatest secret. Which is all you'll ever know."

"You may become more cooperative after you've spent hard time in prison for murder."

There was a slight shake of the head. "I'll never stand trial."

"You'll recover."

"No, you're mistaken. There will be no opportunity to question me further. I die having the satisfaction of knowing you will soon follow, Mr. Pitt."

Before Pitt could stop him, the killer raised one hand to his mouth and inserted a capsule between his teeth. "Cyanide, Mr. Pitt. As functional and effective as it was when Hermann Göring took it sixty years ago." Then he bit down on the capsule.

Pitt quickly put his mouth to the killer's ear. He had to get in the last word before Tom Ambrose's slayer drifted into the great beyond. "I pity you, you pathetic slime. We already know about your moronic Fourth Empire." It was a nasty lie, but it gave Pitt wicked satisfaction.

The dark eyes widened, then slowly glazed and stared sightlessly as the killer died.

"Is he dead?" Pat whispered.

"As an Egyptian mummy," Pitt said coldly.

"Good riddance." Giordino shrugged indifferently. "A shame we can't donate his organs to the vultures."

Pat stared at Pitt. "You knew," she said quietly. "No one else noticed, but I saw you remove the ammo from his gun."

"He would have killed all three of us," Marquez muttered. "What put you onto him?"

"An educated guess," answered Pitt. "Nothing more. He struck me as too calculating, too cold. The bogus Dr. Ambrose didn't act like a man whose life was at risk."

The phone in the kitchen rang, and Marquez answered it, listened for a minute, spoke a few words, and hung up. "Sheriff Eagan," he reported. "Two of his deputies were seriously wounded in a gun battle at Pat's bed-and-breakfast. The unidentified armed suspect was mortally wounded and died before he could talk."

Pitt stared pensively at the body of the bogus Dr. Ambrose. "Who said dead men tell no tales?"

"Is it safe to come out?" asked Lisa Marquez in a tone slightly above a whisper, peering fearfully around the kitchen doorway and seeing the body lying on her floor.

Pitt walked over and took her by the hand. "Perfectly safe."

Marquez put a solicitous arm around her. "How are the girls?"

"They slept through most of it."

"The cave-in sealed off the tunnel for good," he said to Lisa slowly. "It looks as if our mining days are over."

"I won't lose any sleep over it," Lisa said, with a growing smile. "You're a wealthy man, Luis Marquez. It's time we embraced another lifestyle."

"It is also imperative," advised Pitt, as the shriek of the sirens on the sheriff's car and the ambulance could be heard approaching down the road. "Until we know who these people are and what their objective is," he paused to stare angrily down at the killer's body, "you and your family will have to leave Telluride and disappear."

Lisa stared at her husband with a faraway look in her eyes. "That small hotel surrounded by palm trees on the beach at Cabo San Lucas we always wanted to buy . . ."

He nodded. "I guess now is the time."

Pat touched Pitt's arm, and he turned and smiled down at her. "Where am I supposed to hide?" she asked softly. "I can't simply drop my academic career. I've worked too hard to get where I am with the university."

"You life isn't worth two cents if you return to the classroom and your research studies," said Pitt. "Not until we know what we're facing."

"But I'm an ancient language specialist, you're an underwater engineer. Hunting down murderers isn't our job."

"You're right," he agreed. "Government investigative agencies will take over from here. But your expertise will be invaluable in solving the puzzle."

"You don't think this is the end of it?"

He slowly shook his head. "Call it a complicated conspiracy or a Machiavellian plot—something is going down that goes far beyond mere murder. I don't have to possess psychic gifts to know the inscriptions and the black skull inside the chamber have far deeper consequences than we can possibly imagine."

When Sheriff Eagan arrived and began questioning Giordino, Pitt walked outside into the cold night and looked up at the great carpet in the black sky that was the Milky Way. The Marquez house was at nearly ten thousand feet of altitude, and here the stars were magnified into a sparkling sea of crystal.

He looked beyond the skies and cursed the night, cursed his helplessness, cursed the unknown murderers, cursed himself for being lost in a maelstrom of bewilderment. Who were the madmen and their crazy New Destiny? Answers were lost in the night. He couldn't see the obvious, and the inevitable became remote and distant.

He knew for certain that someone was going to pay, and pay bigtime.

He began to feel better. Beyond his anger lay an icy confidence, and beyond that a heightened lucidity. A thought was already forming in his mind, racing and developing until he saw clearly what he must do.

First thing in the morning, he was going back into the mines and bring out the black obsidian skull.

8

UNABLE TO USE THEIR original escape route because of the booby-trap explosive that had collapsed the roof of the tunnel, a team consisting of Pitt, Giordino, Eagan, Marquez, and two deputies traveled the course Pitt had taken from the Buccaneer Mine twenty-four hours earlier. Relying on Pitt's directional computer for guidance, the men quickly reached a flooded shaft that dropped to the tunnels below and led into the Paradise Mine.

Pitt stood on the edge of the shaft and stared into the black, ominous water, wondering if this was such a good idea. The flooding had risen two mine levels higher than the day before. During the night the pressure from far below had slowly diminished, until the water finally found its level.

Sheriff Eagan thought he was crazy. Pat O'Connell thought he was crazy, as did Luis and Lisa Marquez. Only Giordino refrained from calling Pitt crazy, and that was because he insisted on going along as backup in case Pitt ran into trouble.

The dive equipment was basically the same as that Pitt used before, except that now he intended to wear a dry suit. The wet suit had proven practical for movement out of water and protected him from cold during the hike through the mines, but the dry suit was more efficient in insulating the body against the frigid thermal temperatures of the underground water. For the hike back to the shaft, however, he wore warm, comfortable clothing, planning to change into the dry suit only when it came time to go under.

Luis Marquez had accompanied the expedition after recruiting three of his neighboring miner friends to help carry the dive equipment, which included rope ladders to ease the trip through vertical shafts. Sheriff Eagan firmly believed his services would be required to direct a rescue operation that he saw as inevitable.

Pitt and Giordino slipped out of their street clothes and, for added thermal protection, pulled on nylon-and-polyester inner suits that were shaped like long john underwear. Then they climbed into Viking vulcanized-rubber dry suits with attached hood, gloves, and traction-soled boots. Once they were suited up, their equipment and gauges checked, Pitt glanced into Giordino's face. The little Italian looked as unruffled and tranquil as if he were about to dive into an eight-foot-deep swimming pool. "I'll guide us with the directional computer and leave it to you to focus on the decompression tables."

Giordino held up a decompression computer strapped to his left arm. "Figuring an approximate dive time of thirty minutes in water one hundred and ten feet deep, at an altitude of ten thousand feet above sea level, took a bit of prodigious calculation for our decompression stops. But I think I can get you back to this rock garden without narcosis, an embolism, or the bends."

"I'll be eternally grateful."

Pitt pulled on a Mark II full face mask with a built-in underwater communications system. "Do you read me?" he asked Giordino.

"Like you were inside my head."

They had hauled ten air tanks into the mine. For the dive, they each carried twin tanks strapped to their backpacks, with a reserve tank clamped in between for a total of six. The remaining four were to be lowered by Marquez and his friends at predetermined depths as reckoned by Giordino's computer for the decompression stops. They carried no weapons except their dive knives.

"I guess we might as well go," said Pitt.

"After you," Giordino replied.

Pitt switched on his dive light and beamed it onto the smooth surface of the water. He kicked off from the edge and dropped five feet through the air, crashing through the liquid void in an explosion of bubbles. A second explosion quickly followed, as Giordino emerged out of the gloom beside him. He made a motion with his hand downward, doubled over, and kicked his fins, heading into the depths of the mine.

They swam down, down, their dive lights cutting the black water, revealing nothing but cold, hard rock walls. They went slowly, equalizing the increasing water pressure in their ears the deeper they dove. If they hadn't known they were diving down a vertical shaft, they'd have sworn they were swimming inside a horizontal drainpipe.

At last, the floor of the gallery at the bottom of the shaft appeared, the ore cart track rising to meet them, rails mute and cold under their thick film of rust. The turbidity created by the rushing surge after the explosion the day before had dissipated and the water was calm and clear, visibility reaching at least fifty feet. Pitt checked his depth gauge— the needle stood at 186 feet—and he waited until Giordino leveled out slightly ahead of him.

"How far from here?" asked Giordino.

"Ninety to a hundred yards," Pitt answered, pointing. "Just around that bend in the tunnel."

He pumped his fins and darted into the tunnel, his light sweeping back and forth through the timbers. They rounded the bend, moving above the curve of the ore cart tracks. Suddenly, Pitt thrust out his arm and abruptly stopped.

"Switch off your light!" he ordered Giordino.

His friend complied, casting the tunnel into smothering blackness, but not totally. A dim glow filtered through the water in front of them. "I think we have poachers," said Giordino.

"Why is it these characters materialize every time I blow my nose?" Pitt groaned.

THERE were two divers inside the chamber, both working with intent and purpose, photographing the inscriptions on the walls. A pair of underwater floodlights stood on stands, illuminating the drowned chamber as dazzlingly as a Hollywood studio stage. Pitt gazed upward through the hole on the floor of the chamber, staying in the shadows so the divers inside wouldn't spot a reflection from the glass plate in his full face mask.

He marveled at their efficiency. They were using self-contained breathing units that absorbed and eliminated the bubbles exhaled through their air regulators in order to prevent water disturbance in front of their camera lenses. He was especially careful not to allow his own exhaust bubbles to float through the opening in the chamber floor.

"They're tenacious, I'll give them that," Pitt muttered. "Whatever is in the inscriptions, they want it badly enough to kill and die for it."

"Good thing their communications system is on a different frequency, or they'd have eavesdropped on our conversations."

"Could be they've tuned in and plan on suckering us inside."

Giordino's lips curled into a tight grin behind the mask. "So do we disappoint them and cut and run?"

"Since when were we ever smart enough to take the easy way out?"

"Never, that I recall."

Giordino's bond with Pitt had never weakened in all their years of friendship—a friendship that went all the way back to the first grade. Whatever scheme Pitt devised, no matter how insane or ridiculous, Giordino was in for a penny, in for a pound, without the slightest protest. They had saved each other's life on more than one occasion, and when needed could get inside the other's head. That they worked as a close-knit team went without saying. Their adventures were legendary within NUMA.

"It'd be next to impossible for both of us to rush inside the chamber in unison before they react," said Pitt, eyeing the narrow diameter of the opening.

"We could swim inside and knife them in their respective guts," said Giordino quietly.

"If our positions were reversed," murmured Pitt, so softly that

Giordino could barely hear him, "that's what they would do to us. But the practical side of me says take them alive."

"Easier said than done."

Pitt moved as close as he dared to the opening and peered at the two divers, who were absorbed in their work. "I think I see an opportunity."

"Don't leave me in suspense," said Giordino, removing his gloves so his hands had freedom of movement.

"They're wearing their dive knives strapped to their lower legs."

Giordino's eyebrows rose questioningly under the mask. "So are we."

"Yes, but we're not about to be attacked from behind by a pair of genial and dashing rogues."

THE divers inside finished photographing the inscriptions and star symbols. While one loaded their camera equipment in a large duffel bag, the other began placing a charge of explosives in one corner of the chamber. The procedure played into Pitt and Giordino's hands. As soon as the diver with the camera gear had worked his way through the hole into the cavity below, Giordino snatched the mouthpiece of the breathing regulator from between the man's lips and cut off his air supply. In the same instant, he circled a massive arm around the man's exposed neck, choking him until he went limp from unconsciousness.

"I've got mine," Giordino muttered heavily.

Pitt didn't bother to reply. With a powerful kick of his fins, he shot into the chamber and toward the unsuspecting diver connecting a timer to the explosives. He came in from the side to avoid the air tanks on the diver's backpack. In a repeat of Giordino's performance, he tore away the mouthpiece and squeezed the diver's throat in a viselike grip. Pitt had not enjoyed the luxury of time, however, to see that he was tackling a man of giant size. It took all of two seconds for Pitt to realize he had bitten off more than he could chew. His opponent was built like a professional wrestler and had the muscles of one. He didn't react with helpless inertia, but thrashed around the narrow confines of the chamber like a crazy man in a violent fit. Pitt felt like a fox who had unwittingly leaped onto the back of a wounded bear and was holding on for dear life.

The sheer animal power as the man tried to reach over his shoulders and grasp Pitt's head was terrifying. Two huge hands managed to clutch Pitt around the head. For a few moments, Pitt thought his skull was beginning to crack in a hundred places. What saved him from having his brains turned into mush was a beefy wrist that moved beside his jaw. He spat out his mouthpiece, somehow managed to twist his head under the crushing grip, and bit the wrist as hard as his jaws could clamp. A cloud of blood billowed in the water. The hands around his head jerked free in chorus with a painful shout that came as a grotesque gurgle. Pitt held on and squeezed the great bull of a neck with every ounce of his fading strength. In desperation, he ripped the monster's face mask off.

The big man threw himself backward toward one wall in a convulsive jerk. Pitt's air tanks clanged against the rock and the breath was crushed out of him, but his choke hold did not loosen, even by a fraction. He gripped the wrist of the arm around the throat with his free hand and increased the pressure.

From behind and to the side, Pitt could not see the other man's face. Whipping his body from side to side like a dog shaking his coat wet with water, the giant tried desperately to find his air regulator and thrust it back in his mouth, but its hose was wrapped around Pitt's arm. Frantically, the man bent forward enough to grab his dive knife from the sheath strapped to his right calf. Pitt had expected the movement and was prepared for it. As the giant reached down, Pitt released the hand holding the arm around his throat, raised it, and jabbed a finger in an open eye.

The effect was what he expected, what he'd hoped. The gorilla of a man went stiff as a tree and clamped a hand to his eye. In the process, he blindly caught hold of Pitt's hand and slowly, relentlessly began to bend the index and middle fingers backward. The pain shot through Pitt like a shaft of lightning. The agony of having the bones of the fingers snapped is unlike any other. Excruciating doesn't do justice as a description. Pitt began to see fireworks behind his eyes. He was within a microsecond of releasing his stranglehold and clutching at the hand that was causing him so much torment, when he sensed an infinitesimal drop in pressure. The pain was still there, but lessening by tiny degrees.

Slowly, almost too slowly, the stabbing pain began to subside as the giant started sucking water in through his open mouth. His movements became uncoordinated and spasmodic. He entered the initial stages of blackout as he began to drown. His face suddenly contorted in fear and panic. Pitt waited several seconds after the big man went limp before he replaced the mouthpiece, forcing air down his victim's throat and lungs.

Giordino came halfway through the hole. "What took you so long?"

"The luck of the draw," Pitt gasped between breaths, his heart pounding like a piston inside a cylinder. "I always choose the wrong lane of traffic, the wrong line to stand in at the bank and the biggest guy in the world to pick a fight with. What about your man?"

"I wrapped him tighter than a silkworm with electrical cord I found on a string of overhead lights." Giordino looked down at the inert form on the floor of the chamber, and the eyes behind the dive mask widened. He stared at Pitt with growing respect. "Do the coaches of the National Football League know about this guy?"

"If they did, he'd be a number-one draft choice," Pitt said, as his heart began to slow and his breath came evenly. "Take their knives and any other weapons you can find. Then find some more electrical cable and let's bind him before he comes around and tears the mountain down. Leave their dive masks off so their vision is blurred."

Giordino hog-tied the giant diver with electrical cord and dropped him none too gently through the opening into the cleft below. He then removed one or two weights from the belts of both men, so their bodies were slightly buoyant, which made their mass easier to tow back through the tunnel. He also removed their dive knives. On the smaller man, he found a little gun that shot a shaft with a barb on one end. The shaft was propelled by compressed air from a tiny cylinder.

While Giordino was concentrating on their prisoners, Pitt removed a large nylon net bag from his weight belt and opened the metal clasp at the top. He stared at the sinister black skull that seemed to stare back through empty eye sockets. He could not help but wonder if a curse came with the skull. What cryptic secrets did it hold?

Pitt's idealistic nature was overpowered by his practical side. Though he was a daydreamer, he did not buy into myths and folktale. If an object or conception could not be seen, felt, or experienced, it did not exist for him. If he wasn't already a hundred and eighty feet under water, he would have spat in the eye of the obsidian skull. But because it was a link in a chain of enigmas, he was determined to place it in the hands of people who could properly study it.

"Sorry, my friend," he murmured so softly that Giordino didn't hear him, "but it's time you revealed yourself." He lifted the skull very carefully from its pedestal and slid it into the carry bag. At this depth he handled it easily, but once it came out of the water, he guessed it would weigh a solid forty pounds. He took one final look at the chamber, the inscriptions on the walls, the still-burning floodlights lying on the floor where they had been hurled during the struggle. Then he dove headfirst through the hole in the rock, mindful not to knock the skull against the rock and shatter it. Giordino had already pulled the two divers into the tunnel. The giant of a man had regained consciousness and was struggling violently to break free of the electrical cord that bound his ankles and pinned his arms tightly against his immense body.

"Need a hand?" Pitt asked.

"You carry the skull and the bag with the cameras. I'll tote the refuse."

"Best if you go first and I follow. That way I can watch them every inch of the way in case Big Boy starts breaking loose."

Giordino handed him the little gun with the barb. "Shoot him in his Adam's apple if he so much as wiggles a finger."

"We'll have to be very careful in our decompression stops. We may not have enough air for the four of us."

Giordino made an indifferent motion with his hands. "Sorry, I'm not in a sacrificial mood."

The return went slowly. Giordino made better time dragging the two divers and their breathing gear by walking over the ore track ties than trying to swim his way back to the shaft. Precious air was lost during the prolonged passage. Pitt kept a close eye on his air gauge; he knew that his air was seriously depleted. The gauge read just three hundred pounds. He and Giordino had used twice the amount of air they had computed before the dive, not having counted on a fight with intruders.

He curled his body and kicked around to the side of the bound divers, checking their air gauges. Both men had nearly seven hundred pounds. They must have found a shorter route through the mine to the chamber, Pitt surmised. After what seemed a year and a day, they finally reached the vertical shaft and rose to the first decompression stop. Sheriff Eagan and Luis Marquez had lowered two spare tanks on nylon line to the precise depth Giordino had calculated earlier.

Keeping a tight eye on his decompression computer, Giordino listened as Pitt read off the air pressure remaining in each tank. Only when they went beyond the safety level did he unstrap and push them aside. The prisoners did not become belligerent. They'd come to realize that to resist was to die. But Pitt didn't let down his guard for a second. He knew well they were two ticking time bombs, waiting to explode at the first opportunity that presented itself for them to escape.

Time passed as if mired in glue. They used up the last of their air and went on the reserve tanks. When the prisoner's tanks were dry, Pitt and Giordino began to buddy-breathe with them, exchanging their mouthpieces between breaths. After the prescribed wait, they lazily swam up to the next decompression stop.

They were scraping the bottom of the reserve tanks when Giordino finally gave the "surface" sign and said, "The party's over. We can go home now."

Pitt climbed the rope ladder thrown into the shaft by Marquez. He reached the rim of the tunnel floor and handed Sheriff Eagan his air tanks. Then he passed up the skull and camera bag. Next, Eagan took Pitt's outstretched hand and helped him onto firm rock. Pitt rolled over on his back, removed his full face mask, and lay there for a minute, thankfully breathing in the cool damp air of the mine.

"Welcome home," said Eagan. "What took you so long? You were due back twenty minutes ago."

"We ran into two more candidates for your jail."

Giordino surfaced, climbed up, and then knelt on his hands and knees before hauling the smaller prisoner into the tunnel. "I'll need help with the other," he said, lifting his face mask. "He weighs two of me put together."

Three minutes later, Eagan was standing over the intruders, questioning them. But they glared menacingly at him and said nothing. Pitt dropped to his knees and removed the dive hood covering the smaller man's head and chin.

"Well, well, my friend the biker. How's your neck?"

The constrained killer lifted his head and spat at Pitt's face, narrowly missing. The teeth were bared like a rabid dog's; eyes that had seen more than one death glared at Pitt.

"A testy little devil, aren't we?" said Pitt. "A zealot of the Fourth Empire. Is that it? You can dream about it while you rot in jail."

The sheriff reached down and gripped Pitt's shoulder. "I'll have to let them go free."

Pitt stared up, his green eyes suddenly blazing. "Like hell you will."

"I can't arrest them unless they've committed a crime," Eagan said helplessly.

"I'll press charges," Marquez cut in coldly.

"What charges?"

"Trespassing, claim-jumping, destroying private property, and you can throw in theft for good measure."

"What did they steal?" Eagan asked, puzzled.

"My overhead lighting system," Marquez replied indignantly, pointing down at the electrical cord binding the divers. "They've snatched it from my mine."

Pitt placed a hand on Eagan's shoulder. "Sheriff, we're also talking attempted murder here. I think it might be wise if you held them in custody for a few days, at least until a preliminary investigation can make an identification and perhaps uncover evidence of their intentions."

"Come on, Jim," said Marquez, "you can at least keep them under lock and key while you interrogate them."

"I doubt whether I'll get much out of this lot."

"I agree," said Giordino, running a small brush through his curly hair. "They don't look like happy campers."

"There's something going on here that goes far beyond San Miguel

County." Pitt peeled off his dry suit and began dressing in his street clothing. "It won't hurt to cover your bases."

Eagan looked thoughtful. "All right, I'll send a report to the Colorado Investigation Agency—"

The sheriff broke off as every head turned and stared up the tunnel. A man was shouting and running toward them as if chased by demons. A few seconds later, they could see that it was one of Eagan's deputies. He staggered to a halt and leaned over until his head was even with his hips, panting for breath, exhausted after running from the hotel wine cellar.

"What is it, Charlie?" Eagan pressed. "Spit it out!"

"The bodies . . ." Charlie the deputy gasped. "The bodies in the morgue!"

Eagan took Charlie by the shoulders and gently raised him upright. "What about the bodies?"

"They're missing."

"What are you talking about?"

"The coroner says they've disappeared. Somebody snatched them from the morgue."

Pitt looked at Eagan for a long moment of silence, then said quietly, "If I were you, Sheriff, I'd send copies of your report to the FBI and the Justice Department. This thing goes far deeper than any of us imagined."

PART TWO

IN THE
FOOTPRINTS
OF THE
ANCIENTS

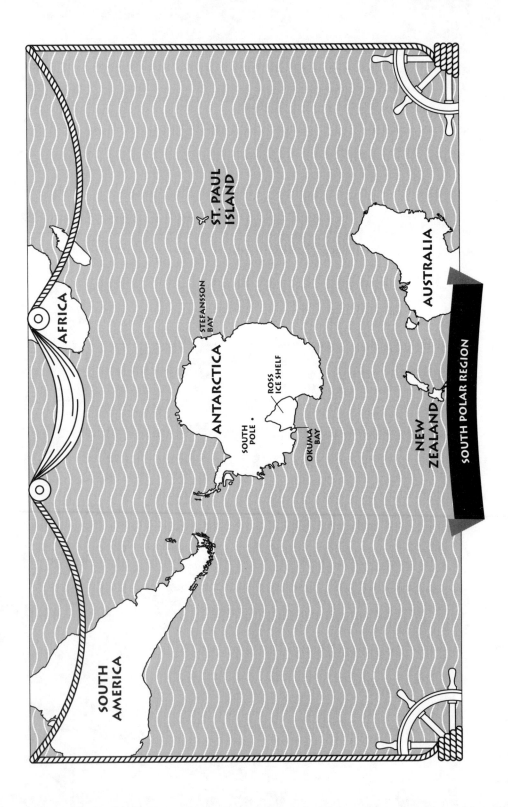

9

CAPTAIN DANIEL GILLESPIE STOOD on the huge glass-enclosed bridge of the *Polar Storm* and stared through tinted-lens binoculars at the ice that was building around the eight-thousand-ton research ice-breaker's hull. Lean as an aspen tree and prone to moments of anxiety, he studied the ice while plotting a course in his mind for the easiest passage to take the *Polar Storm*. The autumn ice had formed early in the Ross Sea. In some places, it was already two feet thick, with ridges rising to three.

The ship trembled under his feet as its great bulbous bow rammed the ice and then heaved up and over the white surface. Then the weight of the forward part of the ship crushed the pack into piano-size portions that tore at the paint on the hull as they groaned and scraped against the steel plates until they were chopped to small chunks by the ship's huge twelve-foot propellers and were left bobbing in the ship's wake. The process was repeated until they reached a part of the sea a few miles off the continent where the ice pack had been slow to thicken.

The *Polar Storm* incorporated the capabilities of both an icebreaker and a research vessel. By most maritime standards, she was an old ship, having been launched twenty years earlier, in 1981. She was also considered small alongside most icebreakers. She had an 8,000-ton displacement, a length of 145 feet, and a 27-foot beam. Her facilities supported oceanographic, meteorological, biological, and ice research, and she was capable of breaking through a minimum of three feet of level ice.

Evie Tan, who had joined the *Polar Storm* when it had stopped at Montevideo in Uruguay on its way to the Antarctic, sat in a chair and wrote in a notebook. A science and technical writer and photographer, Evie had come onboard to do a story for a national science magazine. She was a petite lady with long, silky black hair, who had been born and raised in the Philippines. She looked over at Captain Gillespie and watched him scan the ice pack ahead before asking him a question.

"Is it your plan to land a team of scientists on the pack to study the sea ice?"

Gillespie lowered his binoculars and nodded. "That's the routine. Sometimes as many as three times an Antarctic day, the glaciologists march out on the ice to take samples and readings for later study in the ship's lab. They also record the physical properties of the ice and seawater as we sail from site to site."

"Anything in particular they're looking for?"

"Joel Rogers, the expedition's chief scientist, can explain it better than I can. The primary goal of the project is to assess the impact behind the current warming trend that is shrinking the sea ice around the continent."

"Is it a scientific fact the ice is diminishing?" asked Evie.

"During the Antarctic autumn, March into May, the ocean around the continent begins to freeze and ice over. The pack once spread out from the landmass and formed a vast collar twice the size of Australia. But now the sea ice has retreated and is not as thick and extensive as it once was. The winters are simply not as cold as they were in the nineteen fifties and sixties. Because of the warming trend, a pivotal link in the Antarctic sea chain has been disrupted."

"Beginning with the single-cell algae that live on the underside of the ice pack," offered Evie, knowledgeably.

"You've done your homework." Gillespie smiled. "Without the algae to dine on, there would be no krill, the little shrimplike fellows, who in turn provide nourishment for every animal and fish in these southern waters from penguins to whales to phocids."

"By phocids, you mean seals?"

"I do."

Evie gazed out over Okuma Bay, which divided the great Ross Ice Shelf and the Edward VII Peninsula. "That range of mountains to the south," she said, "what is it called?"

"The Rockefeller Mountains," answered Gillespie. "They're anchored by Mount Frazier on this end and Mount Nilsen on the other."

"They're beautiful," said Evie, admiring the snow-covered peaks that blazed under the bright sun. "May I borrow your binoculars?"

"Certainly."

Evie focused the glasses on a complex of large buildings set around a large towerlike structure only two miles to the south in a sheltered part of Okuma Bay. She could distinguish an airfield behind the buildings and a concrete pier leading into the bay. A large cargo ship was moored to the pier, in the process of being unloaded by a high, overhead crane. "Is that a research station there at the base of Mount Frazier?"

Gillespie peered in the direction the binoculars were aimed. "No, it's a mining facility, owned and operated by a big international conglomerate based in Argentina. They're extracting minerals from the sea."

She lowered the binoculars and looked at him. "I didn't think that was economically feasible."

Gillespie shook his head. "From what I've been told by Bob Maris, our resident geologist, they've developed a new process for extracting gold and other precious minerals from seawater."

"Odd I haven't heard about it."

"Their operation is all very secret. This is as close as we can come without one of their security boats coming out and shooing us off. But it's rumored they do it through a new science called nanotechnology."

"Why in such a remote area as Antarctica? Why not on a coast or port city with easy access to transportation?"

"According to Maris, freezing water concentrates the sea brine and forces it into deeper water. The extraction process becomes more efficient when the salt is removed—" The captain broke off and studied the ice pack beyond the bow. "Excuse me, Ms. Tan, but we have an iceberg coming on dead ahead."

The iceberg loomed up from the flat ice pack like a desert plateau covered by a white sheet. Its steep walls rose well more than a hundred feet from the sea. Brilliant white under a pure radiant sun and a clear blue sky, the berg seemed pristine and unblemished by man, animals or rooted plant life. The *Polar Storm* approached the berg from the west, and Gillespie ordered the helmsman to set the ship's automated control systems on a course around the nearest tip. The helmsman expertly shifted the electronic controls on a broad console and nudged the icebreaker on a seventy-five-degree turn to port, scanning the echo sounder for any underwater spurs that might have protruded from the berg. The icebreaker's stout hull was built to withstand a hard blow from solid ice, but Gillespie saw no reason to cause even the slightest damage to its steel plates.

He skirted the berg from less than three hundred yards, a safe distance but still near enough for the crew and scientists on the outside deck to stare up at the icy cliffs towering above. It was a strange and wonderful sight. Soon the palisades slipped by, as the ship circled the huge mass and turned into the open pack beyond.

Suddenly, another vessel sailed into view, having been hidden behind the berg. Gillespie was astonished to identify the encroaching ship as a submarine. The undersea craft was sailing through an open lead in the ice and passing on a course that took it directly across the icebreaker's great bow from port to starboard.

The helmsman acted before Gillespie's orders issued across the bridge. He sized up the situation, judged the submarine's speed, and threw the icebreaker's big port diesel engine into Full Reverse. It was a wise maneuver, one that might have saved the White Star liner *Titanic*. Rather than reversing both engines in a futile effort to halt the momentum of the big icebreaker, he kept the starboard engine on Half Ahead. With one propeller thrusting the *Polar Storm* forward and the other pulling it backward, the ship began turning far more sharply than a simple rudder command. Everyone on the bridge stood mesmerized, as the big bow's direction slowly angled from the sub's hull toward the wake behind its stern.

There was no time for a warning, no time for communications between the two vessels. Gillespie hit the great horn on the icebreaker and shouted over the intercom for the crew and scientists to brace for a collision. There was a cloud of restrained frenzy on the bridge.

"Come on, baby," the helmsman pleaded. "Turn, turn!"

Evie stared enraptured for a few moments before the business and professional side of her mind shifted into gear. She quickly snatched her camera out of its case, checked the settings, and began snapping pictures. Through the range finder she saw no crew on the deck of the submarine, no officers standing in the top of the conning tower. She paused to refocus her lens, when she saw the submarine's bow slip beneath the ice pack as it began to crash dive.

The two ships closed. Gillespie was certain the massive reinforced bow of the icebreaker would crush the pressure hull of the submarine. But a sudden burst of speed from the undersea vessel, the quick action of the helmsman, and the ability of the *Polar Storm* to make sharp turns made the difference between a near miss and tragedy.

Gillespie ran out onto the starboard bridge wing and stared down, fearing the worst. The submarine had barely dipped under the surface when the icebreaker's bow swung over her stern, missing the rudder and propellers by less than the length of an ordinary dining table. Gillespie could not believe the two vessels had not collided. The strange submarine had disappeared with barely a ripple, the icy water slowly swirling in a whorl and then turning smooth, as though the submarine had never been there.

"My God, that was close!" the helmsman muttered with a thankful sigh.

"A submarine," said Evie in a vague voice, as she lowered her camera. "Where did it come from? What navy did it belong to?"

"I saw no markings," said the helmsman. "It certainly didn't look like any submarine I've ever seen."

The ship's first officer, Jake Bushey, came rushing onto the bridge. "What happened, Captain?"

"A near collision with a submarine."

"A nuclear submarine, here in Marguerite Bay? You must be joking."

"Captain Gillespie isn't joking," said Evie. "I've got a photo record to prove it."

"It wasn't a nuclear sub," said Gillespie slowly.

"She was an old model by the look of her," the helmsman said, gazing at his hands, noticing for the first time that they were shaking.

"Take the bridge," Gillespie ordered Bushey. "Keep us on a course toward that ice ridge a mile off the starboard bow. We'll drop the scientists there. I'll be in my cabin."

Evie and Jake Bushey both caught the distant, puzzled expression on the captain's face. They watched as he dropped down a companionway to the passageway on the deck below. Gillespie opened the door to his cabin and stepped inside. He was a man born to the sea and a lover of sea history. Shelves stretching around the bulkheads of his cabin were filled with books about the sea. His eyes wandered over the titles and stopped at an old ship's recognition book.

He sat in a comfortable leather chair and turned the pages, stopping at a photo in the middle of the book. There it was, a picture of the identical vessel that had suddenly appeared out of nowhere. The photo showed a large submarine cruising on the surface not far from a rocky coastline. The caption underneath read,

> Only known photo of the U-2015, one of two XXI Electro Boats to see operational service during World War II. A fast vessel that could stay submerged for indefinite periods of time and cruise nearly halfway around the world before surfacing for fuel.

The caption went on to say that the U-2015 had been last reported off the coast of Denmark and had vanished somewhere in the Atlantic and was officially listed as Fate Unknown.

Gillespie could not believe what his eyes told him. It seemed impossible, but he knew it to be true. The strange, unmarked vessel the *Polar Storm* had nearly sent to the icy bottom of the bay was a Nazi U-boat from a war that had ended fifty-six years before.

10

A FTER A LENGTHY CONFERENCE call with Admiral Sandecker, chief director of the National Underwater & Marine Agency, and Francis Ragsdale, the recently appointed director of the FBI, it was agreed that Pitt, Giordino, and Pat O'Connell would fly to Washington to brief government investigators on the strange series of events in the Paradise Mine. FBI agents were dispatched to Pat's home near the University of Pennsylvania in Philadelphia to take her daughter to a safe house just outside Washington, where they would soon be together. Agents also swooped into Telluride and hustled Luis and Lisa Marquez, along with their daughters, to a secret location in Hawaii.

Escorted by a protective ring of deputies, courtesy of Sheriff Eagan, the three of them—Pitt, Giordino, and Pat O'Connell—boarded a NUMA jet and took off for the nation's capital. As the turquoise-painted Cessna Citation Ultra V jet banked over the snow-mantled peaks of the San Juan Mountains and set a course northeast, Pat relaxed in her leather seat, reached out, and took Pitt's hand in hers.

"You're sure my daughter is safe?"

He smiled and gently squeezed her hand. "For the tenth time, she's in the capable hands of the FBI. You'll have her in your arms in a few hours."

"I can't picture us living like hunted animals the rest of our lives."

"Won't happen," Pitt assured her. "Once the lunatic nutcases of the Fourth Empire are rooted out, arrested, and convicted, we'll all be able to live normal lives again."

Pat looked over at Giordino, who had fallen asleep before the wheels lifted off the runway. "He doesn't waste any time drifting off, does he?"

"Al can sleep anywhere, anytime. He's like a cat." He held up her hand to his lips and give her fingers a light kiss. "You should get some sleep, too. You must be dead on your feet."

It was the first display of affection Pitt had offered since they'd met, and Pat felt a pleasurable warmth course through her. "My mind is too busy for me to be tired." She pulled her notebook from her case. "I'll use the flight to begin an initial analysis of the inscriptions."

"The aircraft has a computer facility in the rear cabin, if it would be of any help."

"Does it have a scanner to convert my notes onto a disk?"

"I believe so."

The fatigue seemed to ebb from her face. "That would be a great help. A pity my film was ruined after being immersed in the water."

Pitt reached down into his pants pocket, retrieved a plastic packet, and dropped it into her lap. "A complete photo survey of the chamber."

She was quite surprised as she opened the packet and found six canisters of film. "Where in the world did you get these?"

"Compliments of the Fourth Empire," he answered casually. "Al and I interrupted their photo shoot in the chamber. They were finishing up when we arrived, so I'm assuming they recorded the entire text. I'll have the rolls developed first thing in the NUMA photo lab."

"Oh, thank you," Pat said excitedly, kissing him on a cheek thick with stubble. "My notes only covered a smattering of the inscriptions." As if he were merely a passing stranger on a busy street, she turned away from him and hurried toward the aircraft's computer cabin.

Pitt eased his aching body from his seat and walked forward to the compact little galley, opened a refrigerator, and lifted out a soft drink can. Sadly, to his way of thinking, Admiral Sandecker permitted no alcoholic beverages on board NUMA ships or aircraft.

He stopped and stared down at the wooden crate that was firmly strapped in an empty seat. The black obsidian skull had not been out of his sight from the time he carried it from the chamber. He could only imagine the empty eye sockets staring at him through the wood of the crate. He sat in a seat across the aisle and raised the antenna of a Globalstar satellite telephone and punched a stored number. His call was linked to one of seventy orbiting satellites that relayed it to another satellite that relayed the signal to earth, where it was connected with a public telephone network.

Pitt gazed out the port at the passing clouds, knowing the party on the other end seldom answered before the seventh or eighth ring. Finally, on the tenth, a deep voice came through the receiver. "I'm here."

"St. Julien."

"Dirk!" St. Julien Perlmutter boomed, recognizing the voice. "If I'd known it was you, I'd have answered sooner."

"And step out of character? I don't think so."

Pitt could easily picture Perlmutter, all four hundred pounds of him in his ritual silk paisley pajamas, buried amid a mountain of nautical books in the carriage house he called home. Raconteur, gourmand, connoisseur, and acclaimed marine history authority, with a library collection of the world's rarest nautical books, private letters, papers, and plans on almost every ship ever built, he was a walking encyclopedia of man and the sea.

"Where are you, my boy?"

"Thirty-five thousand feet over the Rocky Mountains."

"You couldn't wait to call me in Washington?"

"I wanted to shift a research project into first gear at the first opportunity."

"How can I help you?"

Pitt briefly explained the mysterious chamber and the inscriptions on the walls. Perlmutter listened thoughtfully, interrupting to ask an occasional question. When Pitt finished, Perlmutter inquired, "What specifically do you have in mind?"

"You have files you've accumulated on pre-Columbian contact in the Americas."

"A whole room full of data. Material and theories on all the seafarers who visited North, Central, and South America long before Columbus."

"Do you recall any tales of ancient seafarers who traveled deep inside other continents and built underground chambers? Built them for the sole purpose of leaving a message for those who came later? Were such acts ever mentioned in recorded history?"

"I can't recall any off the top of my head. There are any number of accounts of ancient trade between the peoples of the Americas and seafarers from Europe and Africa. It's thought that extensive mining of copper and tin to make bronze took place as far back as five thousand years ago."

"Where?" asked Pitt.

"Minnesota, Michigan, Wisconsin."

"Is it true?"

"I, for one, believe so," Perlmutter continued. "There is evidence of ancient mining for lead in Kentucky, serpentine in Pennsylvania, and mica in North Carolina. The mines were worked for many centuries before Christ. Then, mysteriously, the unknown miners vanished within a very short time, leaving their tools and other artifacts of their presence right where they were dropped, not to mention stone sculptures, altars, and dolmens. Dolmens are large prehistoric horizontal stone slabs supported by two or more vertical stones."

"Couldn't they have been created by the Indians?"

"American Indians rarely produced stone sculptures and built few, if any, monuments out of stone. Mining engineers, after studying the ancient excavations, estimate that over seven hundred million pounds of copper were removed and transported away. No one believes the Indians were responsible, because the copper that has been found by archaeologists amounts to only a few hundred pounds' worth of beads and baubles. The early Indians worked very little metal."

"But no indication of underground chambers with enigmatic inscriptions?"

Perlmutter paused. "None that I'm aware of. The miners of prehistory left few signs of pottery or extensive records of inscriptions. Only some logographs and pictographs that are for the most part unreadable. We can only guess at them being, perhaps, Egyptians, Phoenicians, Norsemen, or possibly even an earlier race. There is evidence in the southwest of Celtic mines, and in Arizona it is claimed that Roman artifacts were found outside of Tucson just after the turn of the century. So who can say? Most archaeologists are unwilling to go out on a limb and sanctify pre-Columbian contact. They simply refuse to buy diffusion."

"A spread of cultural influence from one people to another through contact."

"Precisely."

"But why?" asked Pitt. "When there is so much evidence?"

"Archaeologists are a hardheaded bunch," replied Perlmutter. "They're all from Missouri. You have to show them. But because early American cultures did not find a use for the wheel, except for toys, or develop the potter's wheel, they refuse to believe in diffusion."

"There could be any number of reasons. Until the arrival of Cortez and the Spanish, there were no horses or oxen in the Americas. Even I know it took the idea of the wheelbarrow six hundred years to travel from China to Europe."

"What can I say?" Perlmutter sighed. "I'm only a marine history buff who refuses to write treatises on subjects I know little about."

"But you *will* search your library for any account of underground chambers with indecipherable inscriptions in what would have been remote corners of the world four thousand years ago?"

"I shall do my best."

"Thank you, old friend. I can't ask for more." Pitt had total faith in his old family friend who used to sit Pitt on his lap when he was a little boy and tell him sea stories.

"Is there anything else you haven't told me about this chamber of yours?" queried Perlmutter.

"Only that it came with an artifact."

"You've been holding out on me. What kind of artifact?"

"A life-size skull craved out of pure black obsidian."

Perlmutter let that sink in for a few moments. Finally, he said, "Do you know its significance?"

"None that is obvious," answered Pitt. "All I can tell you is that without modern tools and cutting equipment, the ancient people who cut and smoothed such a large chunk of obsidian must have taken ten generations to produce such an exquisitely finished product."

"You're quite right. Obsidian is a volcanic glass formed by rapid cooling of liquid lava. For many thousands of years, man used it to make arrowheads, knives, and spearheads. Obsidian is very brittle. It's a remarkable feat to have created such an object over the course of a century and a half without shattering or cracking it."

Pitt glanced over at the crate strapped in the seat. "A pity you can't be here to see it, St. Julien."

"No need for that. I already know what it looks like."

Pitt smelled a rat. Perlmutter was famous for toying with his victims when he was about to display his intellectual superiority. Pitt had no choice but to sail into the trap. "You'd have to see it with your own eyes to appreciate its beauty."

"Did I forget to tell you, dear boy," said Perlmutter, his tone dripping with mock innocence, "I know where there is another one?"

11

THE CESSNA ULTRA V touched down on the east runway of Andrews Air Force Base and taxied to the hangars leased by the Air Force to various governmental agencies. NUMA's aircraft and transportation buildings were located on the northeast part of the base. A NUMA van with two security guards was waiting to take Giordino to his condo in Alexandria, Virginia, and Pat to the safe house where her daughter waited.

Pitt carefully carried the wooden box containing the obsidian skull from the aircraft and set it on the ground. He did not accompany Pat and Giordino, but remained behind.

"You're not coming with us?" asked Pat.

"No, a friend is picking me up."

She gave him a penetrating look. "A girl friend?"

He laughed. "Would you believe my godfather?"

"No, I don't think I would," she said sarcastically. "When will I see you again?"

He gave her a light kiss on the forehead. "Sooner than you think."

Then he closed the door and watched as the van drove off toward the main gate of the base. He relaxed and sat on the ground with his back against one wheel of the landing gear, as the pilot and copilot departed. The spring air of Washington was crisp and clear, with temperatures rising unseasonably into the low sixties. He had waited only ten minutes when a very elegant two-tone green-and-silver automobile rolled whisper-quiet to a stop beside the aircraft.

The chassis of the Rolls Royce Silver Dawn had gone from the factory assembly line to the coach builders of Hooper & Company in 1955, where had been was fitted with a body designed to flow gracefully from the front fenders to the rear, with smooth sides over the fender skirts. The overhead six-cylinder, 263-cubic-inch engine could propel the stately car to a top speed of eighty-seven miles an hour, with only the sound of the rustling from the tires.

Hugo Mulholland, St. Julien Perlmutter's chauffeur, stepped from the driver's side of the car and stuck out his hand. "A pleasure to see you again, Mr. Pitt."

Pitt grinned and shook the chauffeur's hand. The greeting was given without the barest hint of cordiality, but Pitt took no offense. He'd known Hugo for more than twenty years. The chauffeur and able aide to Perlmutter was really warmhearted and considerate, but he had the stone face of a Buster Keaton, and rarely smiled or showed signs of congeniality. He took Pitt's duffel bag and laid it in the trunk of the Rolls, then stepped back as Pitt eased the wooden crate alongside the duffel bag. Then Mulholland opened the rear door and stood aside.

Pitt ducked into the car and settled into the backseat, which was two-thirds taken by Perlmutter's ample bulk. "St. Julien, you look fit as a fiddle."

"More like a bass viol." Perlmutter took Pitt's head between his two hands and kissed him on both cheeks. The huge man wore a Panama hat over his gray hair. His face was red, with a tulip nose complemented by sky-blue eyes. "It's been too long. Not since that pretty little Asian girl with the Naturalization and Immigration Service fixed dinner for us in your hangar apartment."

"Julia Marie Lee. That was about this time last year."

"What became of her?"

"Last I heard, Julia was on assignment in Hong Kong."

"They never stay long, do they?" Perlmutter mused.

"I'm not exactly the kind of guy women take home to meet their mother."

"Nonsense. You'd make a great catch if you'd ever settle down."

Pitt changed the subject. "Do I smell food?"

"When was the last time you ate?"

"I had coffee for breakfast and a soft drink for lunch."

Perlmutter lifted a picnic basket from the floor and set it in his great lap. Then he pulled down the burled walnut trays from their hiding place on the back of the front seat. "I've prepared a small repast for the drive to Fredericksburg."

"Is that where we're going?" asked Pitt, looking forward with great anticipation to the gourmet goodies inside the basket.

Perlmutter simply nodded as he held up a bottle of Yellow Label Veuve Clicquot Ponsardin Brut Champagne. "All right?"

"My favorite," Pitt acknowledged.

After Mulholland was waved through the main gate, he turned left onto the Capital Beltway and drove east across the Potomac River, until he reached Springfield, where he turned south. Inside the rear passenger compartment, Perlmutter laid out silver and china on the trays, then began passing out the various dishes, beginning with crepes filled with mushrooms and sweetbreads, grilled and breaded oysters, several pâtés and cheeses, and ending with pears poached in red wine.

"This is a real treat, St. Julien. I seldom eat this extravagantly."

"I do," said Perlmutter, patting his huge stomach. "And that's the difference between us."

The sumptuous picnic was finished off with a small thermos of espresso. "No cognac?" asked Pitt facetiously.

"It's too early in the day for a man in his sixties to partake of heavy spirits. I'd doze away the afternoon."

"Where is this second obsidian skull you mentioned?"

"In Fredericksburg."

"I assumed that."

"It belongs to a very nice old lady by the name of Christine Mender-

Husted. Her great-grandmother obtained the skull when her husband's whaling ship was trapped in winter ice in Antarctica. A gripping story. According to family history, Roxanna Mender became lost on the ice pack one day. When her husband, Captain Bradford Mender, master of the whaler *Paloverde,* and his crew rescued her, they discovered a derelict English East Indiaman sailing ship. Intrigued, they boarded and searched the ship, finding dead crew and passengers. In a storeroom, they found a black obsidian skull and other strange objects, which they had to leave behind because the ice pack began to break up and they had to rush back to their ship."

"Did they save the black skull?"

Perlmutter nodded. "Yes, Roxanna herself carried it off the derelict ship. It's been a family heirloom ever since."

Pitt stared idly through the window of the Rolls at the green, rolling countryside of Virginia. "Even if the two skulls are identical, without markings they tell us nothing of who created them or why."

"Comparing the skulls is not why I set up an appointment to meet with Mrs. Mender-Husted."

"So what's your scheme?"

"For ten years I've been trying to buy the Mender family letters pertaining to Captain Mender's whaling days. Included are the logbooks of the ships he served aboard. But the pièce de résistance of the collection, the object I'd give my few remaining teeth to get in my hands, is the log of the derelict they found in the ice."

"The Mender family has it?" Pitt asked, his curiosity rising.

"My understanding is that Captain Mender took it when they made their dash across the ice pack."

"Then you have an ulterior motive for this trip."

Perlmutter smiled like a fox. "I'm hoping that when Mrs. Mender-Husted sees your skull, she might relent and sell me hers along with the family archival collection."

"Don't you feel ashamed when you look at yourself in the mirror?"

"Yes." Perlmutter laughed diabolically. "But it soon passes."

"Is there any indication in the derelict ship's log where the skull came from?"

Perlmutter shook his head. "I've never read it. Mender-Husted keeps it locked away."

Several seconds passed, Pitt lost in his thoughts. He couldn't help wondering how many other obsidian skulls were hidden around the world.

MOVING silently along at the posted speed, the Rolls-Royce made the trip to Fredericksburg in an hour and a half. Mulholland steered the majestic car onto a circular drive that led to a picturesque colonial house on the heights of the town above the Rappahannock River, overlooking the killing field where 12,500 Union soldiers fell during one day in the Civil War. The house, built in 1848, was a gracious reminder of the past.

"Well, here we are," said Perlmutter, as Mulholland opened the door.

Pitt went around to the rear of the car, raised the trunk lid, and lifted out the crate containing the skull. "This should prove interesting," he said, as they walked up the steps and pulled a cord that rang a bell.

Christine Mender-Husted could have passed for anyone's grandmother. She was as spry as they came, white-haired, with a hospitable smile, angelic facial features, and twenty pounds on the plump side. Her movements came as quick as her sparkling hazel eyes. She greeted Perlmutter with a firm handshake and nodded when he introduced his friend.

"Please come right in," she said sweetly. "I've been expecting you. May I offer you some tea?"

Both men accepted and were led to a high-ceilinged, paneled library and motioned to sit in comfortable leather chairs. After a young girl, who was introduced as a neighbor's daughter who helped out around the house, served the tea, Christine turned to Perlmutter.

"Well, St. Julien, as I told you over the phone, I'm still not ready to sell my family's treasures."

"I admit the hope has never left my mind," said Perlmutter, "but I've brought Dirk for another reason." He turned to Pitt. "Would you like to show Mrs. Mender-Husted what you have in the box?"

"Christine," she said. "My maiden and married names together are a mouthful."

"Have you always lived in Virginia?" asked Pitt, making conversation while opening the latches on the wooden box containing the skull from the Pandora Mine.

"I come from six generations of Californians, many of whom still live in and around San Francisco. I happened to have had the good fortune of marrying a man who came from Virginia and who served under three presidents as special adviser."

Pitt went silent, his eyes captivated by a black obsidian skull that was sitting on the mantel above the flickering fire. Then slowly, as if in a trance, he opened the crate. Then he removed *his* skull, walked over, reached up, and placed it beside its double on the mantel.

"Oh my!" Christine gasped. "I never dreamed there was another one."

"Neither did I," Pitt said, studying the two black skulls. "As far as I can tell by the naked eye, they're perfect duplicates, identical in form and composition. Even the dimensions appear to be the same. It's as if they came out of the same mold."

"Tell me, Christine," said Perlmutter, a cup of tea in one hand, "what ghostly tale did your great-grandfather pass down about the skull?"

She looked at him as if he had asked a dumb question. "You know as well as I do that it was found on a ship frozen in the ice called the *Madras*. She was bound from Bombay to Liverpool with thirty-seven passengers, a crew of forty, and carrying a varied cargo of tea, silk, spices, and porcelain. My great-grandparents found the skull in a store-room filled with other ancient artifacts."

"What I meant was, did they find any indication of how the artifacts came to be onboard the *Madras?*"

"I know for a fact the skull and other oddities did not come on board the ship in Bombay. They were discovered by the crew and passengers when they stopped for water at a deserted island during the voyage. The details were in the logbook."

Pitt hesitated and, fearing the worst, repeated, "You say *were* in the log?"

"Captain Mender did not keep it. The dying wish of the *Madras*'s captain was that it be forwarded to the owners of the ship. My great-grandfather dutifully sent it by courier to Liverpool."

Pitt felt as if he had run against a brick wall in a dead-end alley. "Do you know if the *Madras*'s owners sent an expedition to find the derelict and backtrack its course to the artifacts?"

"The original ship's owners, as it turns out, sold the trading company before Captain Mender sent the log," explained Christine. "The new management sent out a two-ship expedition to find the *Madras,* but they vanished with all hands."

"Then all records are lost," Pitt said, discouraged.

Christine's eyes flashed. "I never said that."

He looked at the elderly lady, trying to read something in her eyes. "But—"

"My great-grandmother was a very sharp lady," she cut him off. "She made a handwritten copy of the *Madras*'s log before her husband sent it off to England."

To Pitt, it was as if the sun had burst through black clouds. "May I please read it?"

Christine did not immediately answer. She walked over to an antique ship captain's desk and gazed up at a painting hanging on the oak-paneled wall. It depicted a man sitting in a chair with his arms and legs crossed. But for a great beard that covered his face, he might have been handsome. He was a big man, his body and shoulders filling the chair. The woman who stood behind him with one hand on his shoulder was small in stature and stared through intense brown eyes. Both were dressed in nineteenth-century clothing.

"Captain Bradford and Roxanna Mender," she said wistfully, seemingly lost in a past she had never lived. Then she turned and looked at Perlmutter. "St. Julien, I think the time has come. I've held on to their papers and letters out of sentiment for far too long. It's better they be remembered by others who can read and benefit from the history they lived. The collection is yours at the price you quoted."

Perlmutter came out of the chair as lightly as if he had the body of an athlete, and hugged Christine. "Thank you, dear lady. I promise all will be properly preserved and stored in archives for future historians to study."

Christine came over and stood beside Pitt at the mantel. "And to you, Mr. Pitt, a gift. I place my obsidian skull in your trust. Now that you have a matching pair, what do you intend to do with them?"

"Before they go to a museum of ancient history, they'll be studied and analyzed in a laboratory to see if they can be dated and tied to a past civilization."

She looked at her skull for a long time before exhaling a long sigh. "I hate to see it go, but knowing it will be properly cared for makes it much easier. You know, people have always looked at it and thought it was a precursor of bad luck and tragic times. But from the minute Roxanna carried it over the melting ice pack to her husband's ship, it has brought nothing but good fortune and blessings to the Mender family."

ON the trip back to Washington, Pitt read the entries from the log of the *Madras* as exactingly copied in a leather-bound notebook in Roxanna Mender's delicate and flowing hand. Despite the smooth ride of the Rolls, he had to look up from time to time and gaze into the distance to keep from getting carsick.

"Find anything interesting?" Perlmutter asked, as Mulholland drove over the George Mason Bridge, which spans the Potomac River.

Pitt lifted his eyes from the notebook. "Indeed I have. Now we know the approximate location where the crew of the *Madras* discovered their skull, and much, much more."

12

THE ROLLS-ROYCE CAME to a stop at the old aircraft hangar that Pitt called home on a deserted end of Washington's International Airport. The decrepit-looking hangar, built in 1936, looked as if it had been long abandoned. Weeds surrounded its rusting corrugated walls and the windows were heavily boarded over.

No sooner had Hugo slipped from behind the wheel than two heavily armed men, dressed in camouflage fatigues, seemed to materialize out of nowhere and stand with automatic rifles at the ready. One leaned in the window, while the other stood face-to-face with Mulholland, as if daring him to make a menacing move. "One of you better be Dirk Pitt," snapped the man peering into the backseat.

"I'm Pitt."

The guard studied his face for a moment. "ID, sir." It was not a request but an order.

Pitt flashed his NUMA identification, and the guard raised his weapon and smiled. "Sorry for the inconvenience, but we're under orders to protect you and your property."

Pitt assumed the men were with a little-known federal protective security agency. Their agents were highly trained to protect government employees whose lives were threatened. "I'm grateful for your concern and dedication."

"The other two gentlemen?"

"Good friends."

The security guard handed Pitt a small remote alarm. "Please carry this with you at all times while you are in your residence. At the slightest hint of danger, press the transmit button. We'll respond within twenty seconds."

The security guard didn't offer his name, and Pitt didn't ask.

Mulholland had the trunk open, and Pitt retrieved his duffel bag. At that moment, he noticed the two security guards had vanished. He looked around the hangar grounds and scanned the empty fields off to the side of the main runway. It was as if they had never been. Pitt could only guess that they were concealed under the earth.

"I'll have Hugo drive by NUMA headquarters and drop off your obsidian heads," said Perlmutter.

Pitt placed a hand on Mulholland's shoulder. "Very gently, carry them to the lab on the sixth floor and give them to the scientist in charge. His name is Harry Matthews."

Mulholland cracked a faint grin that was equal to a wide-toothed grin from anyone else. "I'll make every effort not to drop them."

"Good-bye, St. Julien. And thank you."

"Not at all, my boy. Drop over for dinner first chance you get."

Pitt watched as the old Rolls moved over the dirt road leading to an airport security gate, trailing a wisp of dust behind its bumper. He looked up at an old worn light pole and saw a tiny security camera mounted on the top. Perhaps that would satisfy his curiosity as to where the security guards were hiding by having recorded their movements.

With a small remote, he deactivated the hangar's extensive alarm system and opened a door that appeared to have been frozen shut since World War II. He hoisted the duffel bag on his shoulder and walked inside. The interior was dustproof and dark. Not a crack of light showed anywhere. Then he closed the door and pressed a light switch, throwing the hangar into a blaze of light and a prism of color.

The floor of the hangar, painted in a gleaming white epoxy, was covered with an array of fifty antique and classic automobiles painted in a myriad of bright colors. Other displays included a German jet aircraft from World War II and a Ford trimotor aircraft from the early 1930s that was called a Tin Goose. A turn-of-the-century railroad car sat on raised rails against one wall of the hangar. As if added for conversation pieces, there was a cast-iron bathtub with an outboard motor, and a peculiar inflatable raft with a makeshift cabin and mast. The entire collection was guarded by a tall Haida Indian totem pole.

Pitt paused to sweep his eyes over the eclectic collection and scan the wording on many of the vintage signs that hung from the high arched ceiling, including the Burma Shave signs. Satisfied everything was in its place, he climbed a wrought-iron spiral staircase to his apartment above the floor of the warehouse.

The interior looked like a nautical museum. Glass-encased ship models blended with wooden-spoke helms and compass binnacles, ship's bells, and copper and brass diver's helmets. The living room, study, single bedroom with bath, and the kitchen/dining room measured no more than eleven hundred square feet.

Though he was tired beyond feeling, he unpacked the duffel bag and threw his dirty clothes on the floor of the small closet that held his washer and dryer. Then he stepped into the bathroom and took a long shower, turning the hot steaming water against one wall of the stall while he rested against the floor on his back with his legs straight up in one corner. He was relaxing with a Juan Julio silver tequila on the rocks when a ship's bell announced the presence of a visitor at the front door.

Pitt peered into one of the four TV monitors mounted between two bookshelves and recognized NUMA's deputy director, Rudi Gunn, standing on his doorstep. He pressed a switch on a remote and said, "Come on in, Rudi. I'm upstairs."

Gunn climbed the staircase and entered the apartment. A small man with thinning hair and a Roman nose, Gunn gazed through thick horn-rimmed glasses. A former commander in the Navy and first in his class at the Naval Academy, Gunn was highly intelligent and well respected among the staff at NUMA. His blue eyes were wide and magnified behind the lenses of his glasses, and he had a dazed expression on his face.

"Two guys with automatic rifles in camouflage gear scared the hell out of me until I proved I was a friend of yours from NUMA."

"Admiral Sandecker's idea."

"I knew he hired a security agency, but I had no idea they had magical powers and could appear out of nowhere. All that was missing was a puff of smoke."

"They're very efficient," said Pitt.

"I was briefed on your situation in Telluride," said Gunn, sinking into a chair. "The word circulating around town is that your life isn't worth two cents."

Pitt brought him a glass of iced tea from the kitchen. Gunn seldom drank anything with alcohol except an occasional beer. "Not to those jokers from the Fourth Empire. I suspect they'll spare no expense to inter me in a tomb."

"I took the liberty of looking under a few rocks." Gunn paused and downed half the glass of iced tea. "I met with some friends at the CIA—"

"What interest could the CIA possibly have in a domestic crime?"

"They suspect the killers you ran up against in the Pandora Mine might be part of an international crime syndicate."

"Terrorists?" asked Pitt.

Gunn shook his head. "They're not religious or cult-driven fanatics. But their agenda is still secret. CIA operatives, Interpol agents—nobody's been able to penetrate the organization yet. All the foreign intelligence agencies know is that it exists. Where it operates from or who controls it, they haven't a clue. Their killers show up, as they did in Telluride, murder their victims, and vanish."

"What crimes are they involved in, besides murder?"

"That seems to be a mystery, too."

Pitt's eyes narrowed. "Who ever heard of a crime syndicate with no motives?"

Gunn shrugged. "I know it sounds crazy, but they have yet to leave even a tiny thread."

"They've got two of the scum in Telluride to interrogate."

Gunn's eyebrows rose. "You haven't heard?"

"Heard what?"

"A Sheriff Eagan from Telluride, Colorado, called Admiral Sandecker only an hour ago. The prisoners were found dead."

"Damn!" Pitt snapped irritably. "I expressly told the sheriff to search them for cyanide pills."

"Nothing so mundane as poison. According to Eagan, a bomb was smuggled into their jail cell. They were blown to pieces, along with a deputy who was on guard nearby."

"Life is cheap to these people," Pitt said acidly.

"So I gathered."

"What's the next step?"

"The admiral is sending you on a deep-sea geological project in the middle of the Pacific, where you'll be reasonably safe from any more assassination attempts."

Pitt grinned slyly. "I won't go."

"He knew you'd say that." Gunn grinned back. "Besides, you're too important in the investigation to send off to the boondocks. As it stands, you've had more contact with this group than anyone else, and lived to tell about it. High-level investigators want to talk to you. Eight o'clock in the morning . . ." He paused to hand Pitt a slip of paper. "Here's the address. Be there. Drive your car into the open garage and wait for instructions."

"Are James Bond and Jack Ryan coming, too?"

Gunn made a wry face. "Funny." He finished off the iced tea and walked outside onto the balcony overlooking the fabulous collection below. "That's interesting."

"What?"

"You referred to the assassins as being from the Fourth Empire."

"Their words, not mine."

"The Nazis called their hideous dreamworld the Third Reich."

"Most all the old Nazis are dead, thankfully," said Pitt. "The Third Reich died with them."

"Did you ever take a course in German?" inquired Gunn.

Pitt shook his head. "The only words I know are *ja, nein,* and *auf Wiedersehen.*"

"Then you don't know that the English for 'Third Reich' is 'Third Empire.' "

Pitt went taut. "You're not suggesting they're a bunch of neo-Nazis?"

Gunn was about to reply when a great whoosh sound came, like a jet fighter using its afterburner, and was followed immediately by an ear-splitting screech of metal and a streak of orange flame that flashed across the interior of the hangar before disappearing through the far wall. Two seconds later, an explosion rattled the hangar and shook the wrought-iron balcony. Dust fell from the metal roof and settled on the shiny cars, dulling their bright paint. A weird silence trailed the fading rumble from the explosion.

Then came the rattle of prolonged gunfire, followed quickly by another, more muted explosion. Both men stood frozen, gripping the balcony railing.

Pitt found words first. "The bastards!" he hissed.

"What in God's name was that?" asked Gunn in shock.

"Damn them. They fired a missile into my hangar. The only thing that saved us from being blasted to shreds was that it didn't explode. The warhead smashed through one thin corrugated wall and out the other without the detonator in its nose striking a heavy structural beam."

The door burst open and the two security guards came running onto the floor of the hangar, pulling to a halt beneath the spiral staircase. "Are you injured?" asked one.

"I believe the word is shaken," said Pitt. "Where did it come from?"

"A handheld launcher fired from a helicopter," answered the guard. "Sorry we let it get so close. We were conned by the markings—it was supposed to be from a local television station. We did fire on it, however, and bring it down. It crashed in the river."

"Nice work," said Pitt sincerely.

"Your friends certainly don't spare any expense, do they?"

"They obviously have money to burn."

The guard turned to his partner. "We're going to have to increase our perimeter." Then he looked around the hangar. "Any damage?" he asked Pitt.

"Only a couple of holes in the walls big enough to fly kites through."

"We'll see that they're repaired immediately. Anything else?"

"Yes," Pitt said, becoming even more angered as he stared at the coating of dust on his expensive cars. "Please call in a cleaning crew."

"Maybe you should reconsider that project in the Pacific," said Gunn.

Pitt seemed not to have heard him. "Fourth Reich, Fourth Empire, whoever they are, they've made a very serious mistake."

"Oh?" said Gunn, looking curiously at his trembling hands as if they belonged to someone else. "What mistake is that?"

Pitt was staring up at the gaping, jagged holes in his hangar's walls. There was a cold malignity glaring out of his opaline green eyes, a malignity Gunn had seen on at least four other occasions, and he shivered involuntarily.

"So far, the bad guys have had all the fun," said Pitt, his mouth twisted in a crooked grin. "Now it's my turn."

13

PITT WATCHED HIS SECURITY-CAMERA tapes before going to bed and saw that the guards had done their homework. Using maps of the airport's underground drainage system, they'd found a large concrete pipe eight feet in diameter that carried away the rain and melted snow runoff from the airport's runways, taxiways, and terminal areas. The drainage pipe ran within ninety feet of Pitt's hangar. At a maintenance access, unseen in the high weeds, the guards had set up a well-camouflaged observation post.

Pitt considered walking over and offering them coffee and sandwiches, but it was only a passing thought. The last thing he needed to do was compromise their security cover.

He had just dressed and finished a quick breakfast when a truck loaded with materials to repair the holes in the hangar stopped on the road outside. An unmarked van pulled up behind the truck and several women in coveralls stepped out. The security guards did not reveal their presence, but Pitt knew they were closely observing the scene. One of the workmen walked over to him.

"Mr. Pitt?"

"Yes."

"We'll get in, make the repairs, clean up the mess and get out as fast as we can."

Pitt watched in awe as men began unloading old rusting corrugated sheets that nearly matched those on the hangar walls. "Where did you find those?" he asked, pointing.

"You'd be surprised how the government keeps track of old building materials," the foreman replied. "What you see came off the roof of an old warehouse in Capital Heights."

"Our government is more efficient than I gave them credit for."

He left them to their work and was about to slip behind the wheel of a turquoise-colored NUMA Jeep Cherokee, when a black split-window Sting Ray Corvette stopped on the road. Giordino leaned out the passenger's window and yelled, "Need a lift?"

Pitt jogged to the car and climbed in, folded his legs, and settled in the leather seat. "You didn't tell me you were coming by."

"I was told to be at the same place as you at eight o'clock. Thought we might as well share a ride."

"You're okay, Al," said Pitt cheerfully, "I don't care what they say about you."

GIORDINO turned the Corvette off Wisconsin Avenue onto a small residential side street in Glover Park near the Naval Observatory. The street, only one block in length, was shaded by century-old elm trees. Except for a single house hidden behind high hedges, the block was empty. No parked cars, no people strolling the sidewalks.

"You sure we didn't make a wrong turn?" said Giordino.

Pitt looked through the windshield and pointed. "We're on the right street, and since that's the only house in sight, this must be the place."

Giordino turned into the second entrance of a circular driveway but kept going straight, to the rear of the house, instead of stopping under the front porte cochere. Pitt studied the three-story brick structure as Giordino steered toward a detached garage at the back. The house looked to have been built for someone of importance and wealth sometime after the Civil War. The grounds and house appeared immaculately maintained, but the curtains were all drawn, as if its tenants were away for an extended length of time.

The Corvette rolled into the garage, whose double doors were spread open. The interior was vacant, except for scattered garden tools, a lawn mower, and a tool bench that looked as if it hadn't been used in decades. Giordino turned off the ignition, placed the shift lever in Park, and turned to Pitt.

"Well, what now?"

His answer came as the doors automatically closed. A few seconds later, the car began to fall slowly through the floor of the garage on an elevator. But for a barely audible hum, the ride was soundless. Pitt tried to estimate the rate of descent and distance, but it became dark. After what he guessed was a drop of nearly a hundred feet, the elevator came to a gentle stop. An array of lights flashed on and they found themselves in a fair-size concrete parking garage filled with several cars. Giordino pulled the Corvette into an empty stall between a turquoise Jeep Cherokee with "NUMA" painted on the front doors and a Chrysler limousine. The Jeep, they knew, was Admiral Sandecker's. He insisted that all NUMA transportation vehicles be four-wheel-drive suburban utility vehicles, so they could be driven in the worst weather.

A Marine guard stood at the entrance to a metal doorway. "Think the car is okay here," said Giordino impishly, "or should I lock it?"

"Just a gut feeling," answered Pitt, "but I have the feeling it's not going anywhere."

They exited the car and walked over to the uniformed guard, who wore the three stripes of a sergeant on his sleeves. He nodded and greeted them. "You must be Dirk Pitt and Albert Giordino. You're the last to arrive."

"Don't you want to see our IDs?" asked Giordino.

The guard smiled. "I've studied your photos. Knowing which is which is like comparing Joe Pesci to Clint Eastwood. You're not difficult to tell apart."

He pressed a button beside the door and it slid open, revealing a short hallway leading to another metal door. "When you reach the inner door, stand still for a moment until the guard on the other side ID's you with a security camera."

"Doesn't he trust *your* judgment?" asked Giordino.

The guard never cracked a smile. "Insurance," he said tersely.

"Aren't they overdoing the security routine?" muttered Giordino. "We could have just as easily reserved a couple booths at Taco Bell to hold a briefing."

"Bureaucrats have a fetish for secrecy," said Pitt.

"At least I could have had a burrito."

They were passed through the door into a vast carpeted room whose walls were covered with drapes to mute the acoustics. A twenty-foot-long kidney-shaped conference table dominated the room. A huge screen covered the entire far wall. The room was comfortably lit, and easy on the eyes. Several men and one woman were already seated around the table. None stood as Pitt and Giordino approached.

"You're late." This from Admiral James Sandecker, the head of NUMA. A small athletic man with flaming red hair and a Vandyke beard, he had commanding cold blue eyes that took in everything. Sandecker was as canny as a leopard sleeping in a tree with one eye open—he knew that a meal would come to him sooner or later. He was testy and irascible but ran NUMA like a benevolent dictator. He motioned now to a man sitting on his left.

"I don't believe you two know Ken Helm, special agent with the FBI."

A gray-haired man, dressed in a tailored business suit, with speculative, quiet hazel eyes that peered over reading glasses, half rose out of his chair and extended his hand. "Mr. Pitt, Mr. Giordino, I've heard a great deal about you."

Which means he's perused our personnel files, Pitt thought to himself.

Sandecker turned to the man on his right. "Ron Little. Ron has a fancy title over at Central Intelligence, but you'd never know it."

Deputy director was the title that ran through's Pitt's mind at meeting Little.

He looked through collie-brown eyes set in a deeply lined face—pious, middle-aged, a face etched with experience. He simply nodded. "Gentlemen."

"The others you know," Sandecker said, nodding down the table.

Rudi Gunn was furiously taking notes and didn't bother to look up.

Pitt stepped over and placed a hand on Pat O'Connell's shoulder and said softly, "Sooner than you thought."

"I adore a man who keeps his promises." She patted his hand, uncaring of the stares from the men around the table. "Come sit by me. I feel intimidated by all these important government officials."

"I assure you, Dr. O'Connell," said Sandecker, "that you'll leave this room with every lovely hair intact."

Pitt pulled out a chair and slid next to Pat, while Giordino took a seat next to Gunn. "Have Al and I missed anything of relevance?" Pitt asked.

"Dr. O'Connell briefed us on the skull and underground chamber," said Sandecker, "and Ken Helm was about to report on the initial results of the forensic examination on the bodies flown in from Telluride."

"Not much to tell." Helm spoke slowly. "Making a positive identification from their teeth has become difficult. Preliminary examinations suggest that their dental work came from South American dentists."

Pitt appeared dubious. "Your people can distinguish the difference in dental techniques of different countries?"

"A good forensic pathologist who specializes in identification through dental records can often name the city where the cavities were filled."

"So they *were* foreign nationals," Giordino observed.

"I *thought* their English was a bit odd," said Pitt.

Helm stared over his reading glasses. "You noticed?"

"Too perfect without an American accent, although two of them spoke with a New England twang."

Little scribbled on a yellow legal notepad. "Mr. Pitt, Commander Gunn has informed us that the murderers you apprehended in Telluride referred to themselves as members of the Fourth Empire."

"They also referred to it as the New Destiny."

"As you and Commander Gunn have already speculated, the Fourth Empire may be the successor to the Third Reich."

"Anything is possible."

Giordino pulled a gigantic cigar from his breast pocket and rolled it around in his mouth without lighting it, out of consideration for the people at the table who didn't smoke. Sandecker shot him a murderous look at seeing that the label advertised it as one from his private stock. "I'm not a smart man," Giordino said modestly. The Humble Herbert routine was an act. Giordino had been third in his class at the Air Force Academy. "For the life of me, I don't see how an organization with a worldwide army of elite killers can operate for years without the finest intelligence services in the world figuring out who they are and what they're up to."

"I'm the first to admit we're stymied," said FBI's Helm frankly. "As you know, crimes without motives are the most difficult to solve."

Little nodded in agreement. "Until your confrontation with these people in Telluride, anyone else who came in contact with them did not live to describe the event."

"Thanks to Dirk and Dr. O'Connell," said Gunn, "we now have a trail to follow."

"A few charred teeth make for a pretty faint trail," offered Sandecker.

"True," agreed Helm, "but there is the enigma of that chamber inside the Pandora Mine. If they go to such extremes to keep scientists from studying the inscriptions, slaughter innocent people, and commit suicide when apprehended—well, they must have a compelling motive."

"The inscriptions," Pitt said. "Why go to such lengths to hide their meaning?"

"They can't be overjoyed at the outcome," said Gunn. "They lost six of their professional killers and failed to secure photographs of the inscriptions."

"It's bizarre that such an ordinary archaeological discovery would cost so many lives," Sandecker said expressionlessly.

"Hardly an ordinary discovery," Pat said quickly. "If it is not a hoax perpetrated by old hard-rock miners, it could very well prove to be the archaeological find of the century."

"Have you been able to decipher any of the symbols?" asked Pitt.

"After a cursory examination of my notes, all I can tell you is that the symbols are alphabetic. That is, writing that expresses single sounds. Our alphabet, for example, uses twenty-six symbols. The symbols in the chamber suggest an alphabet of thirty, with twelve symbols representing numerals, which I managed to translate into a very advanced mathematics system. Whoever these people were, they discovered zero and calculated with the same number of symbols as modern man. Until I can program them into a computer and study them in their entirety, there is little else I can tell you."

"Sounds to me like you've done extremely well with what little you have had in such a short time," Helm complimented her.

"I'm confident we can crack the meaning of the inscriptions. Unlike the complicated logosyllabic writing systems of the Egyptians, Chinese, or Cretans, which are as yet undeciphered, this one seems unique in its simplicity."

"Do you think the black obsidian skull found in the chamber forms a link to the inscriptions?" asked Gunn.

Pat shook her head. "I can't begin to guess. Like the crystal skulls that have come out of Mexico and Tibet, its purpose could be ritual. There are some people—not accredited archaeologists, I might add—who think the crystal skulls came in a set of thirteen that can record vibrations and focus them into holographic images."

"Do you believe that?" asked Little seriously.

Pat laughed. "No, I'm pretty much of a pragmatist. I prefer hardcore proof before I advance wild theories."

Little looked at her pensively. "Do you think the obsidian skull—"

"Skulls," Pitt corrected him.

Pat gave him a queer look. "Since when do we have more than one?"

"Since yesterday afternoon. Thanks to a good friend, St. Julien Perlmutter, I obtained another one."

Sandecker looked at him intently. "Where is it now?"

"Along with the skull from Telluride, it was taken to NUMA's chemical lab for analysis. Obsidian obviously can't be dated by conventional means, but a study under instrumentation might tell us something about those who created it."

"Do you know where it came from?" asked Pat, burning with curiosity.

Without going into tedious detail, Pitt briefly described the finding of the skull inside the derelict *Madras* by the crew of the *Paloverde* in Antarctica. He then told of his meeting and conversation with Christine Mender-Husted, and how she graciously gave him the skull after accepting Perlmutter's offer for her ancestor's papers.

"Did she say where the crew and passengers of the *Madras* discovered the skull?"

Pitt tantalized her and the others seated around the table by taking his time to reply. Finally, he said, "According to the ship's log, the *Madras* was bound from Bombay to Liverpool when it was struck by a violent hurricane—"

"Cyclone," Sandecker lectured. "To a sailor, hurricanes occur only in the Atlantic and Eastern Pacific oceans. Typhoons are in the Western Pacific and cyclones in the Indian Ocean."

"I stand corrected," Pitt sighed. Admiral Sandecker loved to show off his inexhaustible reserve of sea trivia. "As I was saying, the *Madras* ran into a violent storm and heavy seas that lasted for nearly two weeks. She was battered and driven far south of her course. When the wind and waters finally calmed, it was found that their water barrels had been damaged and much of their drinking supply lost. The captain then consulted his charts and made the decision to stop at a barren chain of uninhabited islands in the subantarctic south Indian Ocean. Now known as the Crozet Islands, they form a tiny overseas territory of France. He dropped anchor off a small island called St. Paul that was very rugged, with a volcanic mountain rising in its center. While the crew repaired the water barrels and began filling them from a stream, one of the passengers, a British army colonel on his way home with his wife and two daughters after serving ten years in India, decided to go on a little hunting expedition.

"The only real game on the island were elephant seals and penguins, but the colonel in his ignorance thought the island might teem with four-legged game. After climbing nearly a thousand feet up the mountain, he and his friends came upon a footpath laid with stones worn smooth with age. They followed the path to an opening hewn in the rock in the shape of an archway. They entered and saw a passageway that led deeper into the mountain."

"I wonder if the entrance has been found and explored since then," said Gunn.

"It's possible," Pitt admitted. "Hiram Yaeger checked it out for me, and except for an unmanned meteorological station set up by the Aussies from 1978 until 1997 and monitored by satellite, the island has been totally uninhabited. If their weathermen found anything inside the mountain, they never mentioned it. All records are purely meteorological."

Little was leaning over the table, spellbound. "Then what happened?"

"The colonel sent one of his party back to the ship, and he returned with lanterns. Only then did they venture inside. They found that the passageway was smoothly carved from the rock and sloped downward for about a hundred feet, ending in a small chamber with dozens of strange and ancient-looking sculptures. They went on to describe unreadable inscriptions etched on the walls and ceiling of the chamber."

"Did they record the inscriptions?" asked Pat.

"No symbols went into the captain's log," answered Pitt. "The only drawing is a crude map to the entrance of the chamber."

"And the artifacts?" Sandecker probed.

"They're still on the *Madras*," explained Pitt. "Roxanna Mender, the wife of the captain of the whaler, mentioned them in a brief entry in her diary. She identified one as a silver urn. The others were bronze and earthenware sculptures of strange-looking animals she said she had never seen before. Under the laws of salvage, her husband and his crew intended to strip the *Madras* of anything of value, but the ice pack began to break up and they had to make a run for the whaler. They took only the obsidian skull."

"Another chamber, this one with artifacts," Pat said, staring as if seeing something beyond the room. "I wonder how many others are hidden around the world."

Sandecker eyed Giordino waspishly as the little Italian chewed on his immense cigar. "It seems we have our work cut out for us." He drew away his eyes from Giordino and trained them on Gunn. "Rudi, as soon as you can, expedite two expeditions. One to search for the *Madras* in the Antarctic. The second to check out the chamber found by the ship's passengers on St. Paul Island. Use whatever research vessels are nearest the areas in question." He turned to the men farther down the long table. "Dirk, you head up the search for the derelict. Al, you take St. Paul Island."

Giordino sat slouched in his chair. "I hope our bloodthirsty little friends didn't get to either place first."

"You'll know soon after you arrive," Gunn said, with a straight face.

"In the meantime," said Helm, "I'll keep two agents on the hunt throughout the U.S. for any leads to the organization that hired the killers."

"I must tell you, Admiral," Little said seriously to Sandecker, "this is not a priority assignment for Central Intelligence. But I'll do what I can to fill in the pieces. My people will concentrate on international corporate syndicates outside the United States that fund or search for archaeological searches. We'll also investigate any discoveries that involved murder. Your new evidence pointing to a neo-Nazi order may prove invaluable."

"Last but not least, we come to the lovely lady in our midst," Sandecker said. He wasn't being patronizing; it was the way he talked to most women.

Pat smiled in poised confidence at seeing every male eye focused on her. "My job, of course, is to attempt to decipher the inscriptions."

"The photos the killers took should be processed by now," said Gunn.

"I'll need a place to work," she said thoughtfully. "Since I am now a nonperson, I can't very well walk into my office at the University of Pennsylvania and begin an analysis program."

Sandecker smiled. "Between Ron, Ken, and myself, we have at our command what are perhaps three of the most sophisticated data-processing facilities and technicians in the world. Take your pick."

"If I may suggest, Admiral," said Pitt, making no attempt at impartiality, "because of NUMA's continued involvement with the chambers and their contents, it may be more efficient for Dr. O'Connell to work with Hiram Yaeger in our own computer facility."

Sandecker looked for some clue as to what was going on in Pitt's devious mind. Finding none, he shrugged. "It's your call, Doctor."

"I do believe Mr. Pitt is right. By working closely with NUMA, I can be in close communication with the expeditions."

"As you wish. I'll place Yaeger and Max at your disposal."

"Max?"

"Yaeger's latest toy," replied Pitt. "An artificial intelligence computer system that turns out visual holographic images."

Pat took a deep breath. "I'll need all the exotic technical help I can get."

"Not to worry," said Giordino with humorous detachment. "If the inscriptions prove ancient, they're probably nothing but a book of ancient recipes."

"Recipes for what?" inquired Helm.

"Goat," said Giordino moodily. "A thousand and one ways to serve goat."

14

"FORGIVE ME FOR ASKING, but are you Hiram Yaeger?" Fueled by enthusiasm, Pat had made her way through the vast computer network that covered the entire tenth floor of the NUMA building. She had heard computer wizards at the University of Pennsylvania talk in awe of the oceans data center of the National Underwater & Marine Agency. It was an established fact that the center processed and stored the most enormous amount of digital data on oceanography ever assembled under one roof.

The scruffy-looking man sitting at a horseshoe-shaped console pulled down his granny glasses and peered at the woman standing in the doorway of his sanctum sanctorum. "I'm Yaeger. You must be Dr. O'Connell. The admiral said to expect you this morning."

The brain behind this incredible display of information-gathering power hardly fit the image she had of him. For some reason, Pat had expected Yaeger to look like a cross between Bill Gates and Albert Einstein. He resembled neither. He was dressed in Levi's pants and jacket over a pure white T-shirt. His feet were encased in cowboy boots that looked as if they had suffered through a thousand calf-roping contests on the rodeo circuit. His hair was dark gray and long and tied back in a ponytail. His face was boyish and clean-shaven, and featured a narrow nose and gray eyes.

Pat would have also been surprised to learn that Yaeger lived in a fashionable residential section of Maryland, was married to a success-ful animal artist, and was the father of two teenage daughters who at-tended an expensive private school. His only hobby was collecting and restoring old, obsolete computers.

"I hope I'm not interrupting anything," said Pat.

"Weren't you met at the elevator and shown to my domain?"

"No, I simply wandered around until I saw somebody who didn't look like Dilbert."

Yaeger, a fan of the comic strip character by Scott Adams, laughed. "I think I'm supposed to take that as a compliment. I deeply apologize for not having someone meet and escort you."

"No bother. I took a self-guided tour. Your data empire is quite grand. Certainly nothing like the equipment I'm used to working with at the university."

"Can I get you a cup of coffee?"

"No, thank you, I'm fine," said Pat. "Shall we get to work?"

"As you wish," Yaeger replied politely.

"Do you have the photographs taken of the chamber?"

"The photo-processing lab sent them up last night. I stayed late and scanned them into Max."

"Dirk told me about Max. I'm anxious to see him in action."

Yaeger pulled up a chair next to his but didn't immediately offer it to Pat. "If you'll step around the console and stand in the middle of that open platform just in front of us, I'll demonstrate Max's unique tal-ents."

Pat walked to the platform and stood in the center, staring back at Yaeger. As she watched, the computer whiz seemed to blur before her eyes and then vanished altogether, as she found herself surrounded by what her mind swore was some kind of nebulous enclosure. Then the walls and ceiling became more distinct and she found herself standing in an exact replica of the chamber. She had to tell herself that it was a holographic illusion, but it seemed so real, especially when the inscriptions began forming on the walls in well-defined clarity.

"This is fantastic," she murmured.

"Max has all the symbols from the photographs programmed into his memory, but although we have a monitor the size of a small movie screen, I thought it would be helpful for you to read the inscription lines in their original perspective."

"Yes, yes," Pat said, becoming excited. "Being able to study the entire text in one sweep will help enormously. Thank you, and thank Max."

"Come back and meet Max," came Yaeger's voice from behind the illusionary chamber. "Then we'll get to work."

Pat was on the verge of saying "I can't," because the chamber seemed so real. But she broke the illusion by stepping through the wall as if she were a ghost, and rejoined Yaeger behind the console.

"Max," said Yaeger, "meet Dr. Pat O'Connell."

"How do you do?" came a soft feminine voice.

Pat eyed Yaeger suspiciously. "Max is a woman."

"I programmed my own voice into the original program. But I've made any number of modifications since then and decided that I'd rather listen to a female voice than that of a male."

"She's voice-activated?"

Yaeger smiled. "Max is an artificial intelligence system. No buttons to push. Just talk to her like you would a normal person."

Pat looked around. "Is there a microphone?"

"Six, but they're miniatures you can't see. You can stand anywhere within twenty feet."

Apprehensively, Pat said, "Max?"

On the huge monitor just beyond the platform, the face of a woman appeared. She stared at Pat in vivid color. Her eyes were topaz brown and her hair a shiny auburn. Her lips were spread in a smile that revealed even white teeth. Her shoulders were bare down to the tops of her breasts, which just showed above the bottom of the monitor. "Hello, Dr. O'Connell. I'm pleased to meet you."

"Please call me Pat."

"I shall from now on."

"She's lovely," said Pat admiringly.

"Thank you." Yaeger smiled. "Her real name is Elsie, and she's my wife."

"Do you work well together?" Pat asked facetiously.

"Most of the time. But if I'm not careful, she can get as testy and petulant as the original."

"Okay, here goes," Pat murmured under her breath. "Max, have you analyzed the symbols that were scanned into your system?"

"I have." Max's voice answered in tones that sounded positively human.

"Could you decipher and translate any of the symbols into the English alphabet?"

"I've only scratched the surface, but I have made progress. The inscriptions on the ceiling of the chamber appear to be a star chart."

"Explain." Yaeger ordered.

"I see it as a sophisticated coordinate system that is used in astronomy to plot the positions of celestial objects in the sky. I think it might suggest changes in the declinations of stars visible in the sky over a particular part of the world in past epochs."

"Meaning that because of deviations in the earth's rotation, the stars appear to shift positions over time."

"Yes, the scientific terms are precession and nutation," Max lectured. "Because the earth bulges around the equator from its rotation, the gravitational pull of the sun and moon is heaviest around the equator and causes a slight wobble to the earth's spinning axis. You've seen the same phenomenon in a spinning top, due to gravity. This is called precession, and it traces a circular cone in space every 25,800 years. Nutation, or nodding, is a small but irregular movement that swings the celestial pole 10 seconds away from the smooth precessional circle every 18.6 years."

"I know that sometime in the distant future," said Pat, "Polaris will no longer be the North Star."

"Exactly," Max agreed. "As Polaris drifts away, another star will move into position above the North Pole in approximately 345 years. A hundred years before the time of Christ, the vernal equinox— Excuse me, are you familiar with the vernal equinox?"

"If I remember my junior college astronomy," said Pat, "the vernal equinox is where the sun intersects the celestial equator from south to north during the spring equinox, making it a reference direction for angular distances as measured from the equator."

"Very good," Max complimented her. "Spoken like a college professor putting her class to sleep. Anyway, before Christ, the vernal equinox passed through the constellation Aries. Because of precession, the vernal equinox is now in Pisces and is advancing toward Aquarius."

"What I think you're telling us," said Pat, elation beginning to grow in her chest, "is that the starlike symbols in the ceiling in the chamber display coordinates of the star system from the past."

"That's how I read it," Max said impassively.

"Did the ancients have the scientific knowledge to make such accurate projections?"

"I'm finding that whoever carved that celestial map in the ceiling of the chamber was superior to the astronomers of only a few hundred years ago. They calculated correctly that the celestial galaxy is fixed and that the sun, the moon, and the planets revolve. The map shows the orbits of the planets, including Pluto, which was discovered only in the last century. They discovered that the stars Betelgeuse, Sirius, and Procyon remain in permanent positions, while other constellations move imperceptibly over thousands of years. Believe me, these ancient people knew their stuff when it came to stargazing."

Pat looked at Yaeger. "If Max can decipher the star coordinates as engraved in the chamber when it was built, we might be able to date its construction."

"It's worth a try."

"I deciphered a small part of the numbering system," said Pat. "Would that help you, Max?"

"You shouldn't have bothered. I have already interpreted the numbering system. I find it quite ingenious for its simplicity. I can't wait to dig my bytes into the inscriptions that spell out words."

"Max?"

"Yes, Hiram."

"Concentrate on deciphering the star symbols and put aside the alphabetic inscriptions for now."

"You'd like me to analyze the celestial map?"

"Do the best you can."

"Can you give me until five o'clock? I should be able to get a handle on it by then."

"The time is yours," Yeager responded.

"Max only requires a few hours for a project that should take months, even years?" Pat asked incredulously.

"Never underestimate Max," said Yaeger, swinging around in his chair and sipping from a cup of cold coffee. "I spent the better part of my prime years putting Max together. There isn't another computer system like her in the world. Not that she won't be obsolete in five years. But for the present, there is very little she can't do. She is unique, and she belongs heart and soul to me and NUMA."

"What about patents? Surely you must turn your rights over to the government."

"Admiral Sandecker is not your average bureaucrat. We have a verbal contract. I trust him, and he trusts me. Fifty percent of any revenue that we make on patent royalties or charges for the use of our accumulated data to private corporations or government agencies is turned over to NUMA. The other fifty percent comes to me."

"You certainly work for a fair-minded man. Any other employer would have given you a bonus, a gold watch, and a pat on the back, and taken your profits to the bank."

"I'm lucky to be surrounded by fair-minded men," said Yaeger solemnly. "The admiral, Rudi Gunn, Al Giordino, and Dirk Pitt, they're all men I'm proud to call my friends."

"You've known them for a long time."

"Close to fifteen years. We've had some wild times together and solved any number of ocean riddles."

"While we're waiting for Max to get back to us, why don't we begin analyzing the wall symbols. Perhaps we can find a clue to their meaning."

Yaeger nodded. "Sure thing."

"Can you reproduce the holographic image of the chamber?"

"Wishing will make it so," Yaeger said, as he typed a command at his keyboard and the image of the interior walls of the chamber materialized again.

"To decipher an unknown alphabetic writing, the first trick is to separate the consonants from the vowels. Since I see no indication that they represent ideas or objects, I'm assuming that the symbols are alphabetic and they record sounds of words."

"What is the origin of the first alphabet?" asked Yaeger.

"Hard evidence is scarce, but most epigraphists believe it was invented in ancient Canaan and Phoenicia somewhere between 1700 and 1500 B.C., and is labeled as North Semitic. Leading scholars disagree, of course. But they do tend to agree that early Mediterranean cultures developed the awakenings of an alphabet from prehistoric geometric symbols. Much later, the Greeks adapted and refined the alphabet, so the letters we write today are related to theirs. Further developments came from the Etruscans, followed by the Romans, who borrowed heavily to form the written language of Latin and whose later classic characters eventually formed the twenty-six-letter alphabet you and I use today."

"Where do we begin?"

"We'll be starting from scratch," said Pat, referring to her notes. "I'm unaware of any other ancient writing systems whose symbols match those inscribed in the chamber. There seems to be no influence either way, which is most unusual. The only remote similarity is to the Celtic Ogham alphabet, but there any resemblance ends."

"I almost forgot." Yaeger handed her a small batonlike shaft with a miniature camera at one end. "Max has already coded the symbols. If you want me to help you from my end with any calculations, just aim the camera at the symbol and its sequence in the inscriptions you wish to study, and I'll work at developing a decipher program."

"Sounds good," said Pat, happy to be back in the harness again. "First, let's list the different symbols and get a count on how many times each is represented. Then we can try working them into words."

"Like *the* and *and*."

"Most of the ancient script did not include words we take for granted today. I also want to see if we can detect the vowels before tackling the consonants."

They worked through the day without a break. At noon, Yaeger sent word down to the NUMA cafeteria to send up sandwiches and soft drinks. Pat was becoming increasingly frustrated. The symbols looked maddeningly simple to decipher, and yet by five o'clock she had had little or no success in untangling their definitions.

"Why is it the numbering system was so easy to break, but the alphabet so impossible?" she muttered irritably.

"Why don't we knock off until tomorrow," Yaeger suggested.

"I'm not tired."

"Neither am I," he concurred. "But we'll have a fresh outlook. I don't know about you, but my best solutions always come to me in the middle of the night. Besides, Max doesn't require sleep. I'll put her on the inscriptions during the night. By morning, she should have some ideas on the translation."

"I have no sensible argument."

"Before we knock off, I'll call up Max and see if she's made any progress with the stars."

Yaeger's fingers didn't have to play over the keyboard. He simply pressed a transmit button and said, "Max, are you there?"

Her scowling face came over the monitor. "What took you and Dr. O'Connell so long to get back to me? I've been waiting for nearly two hours."

"Sorry, Max," said Yaeger, without a deep sense of regret. "We were busy."

"You didn't spend but a few hours on the project," said Pat naively. "Did you strike out?"

"Strike out, hell," Max snapped. "I can tell you exactly what you want to know."

"Start with how you came to your conclusions," Yaeger commanded.

"You didn't think I was going to calculate movement of the stars myself, did you?"

"It *was* your project."

"Why should I strain my chips when I can get another computer to do it?"

"Please, Max, tell us what you discovered."

"Well, first of all, finding the coordinates of celestial objects in the sky takes a complicated geometric process. I won't get into boring detail on how to determine the altitude, azimuth, right ascension, and declination. My problem was to determine the sites where the coordinates engraved in the rock of the chamber were measured. I managed to calculate the original sites where the observers took their sightings within a few miles; also the stars they used to measure deviations over many, many years. The three stars in the belt of the constellation of Orion, the hunter, all move. Sirius, the dog star, who sits near the heel of Orion, is fixed. With these numbers in hand, I tapped into the astrometry computer over at the National Science Center."

"Shame on you, Max," admonished Yaeger. "You could get me into big trouble raiding another computer network."

"I think the computer over at NSC likes me. He promised to erase my inquiry."

"I hope you can take him at his word," grunted Yaeger. It was an act. Yaeger had tapped into outside computer networks for unauthorized data hundreds of times.

"Astrometry," Max continued unperturbed, "in case you don't know, is one of the oldest branches of astronomy, and deals with determining the movements of stars." Max paused. "Follow me?"

"Go on," Pat urged.

"The guy in the computer over at NSC isn't up to my standards, of course, but since this was an elementary program for him, I sweet-talked him into working out the deviation between positions of Sirius and Orion when the chamber was built with their present coordinates in the sky."

"You dated the chamber?" Pat murmured, holding her breath.

"I did."

"Is the chamber a hoax?" Yaeger asked, as if afraid of the answer.

"Not unless those old hard-rock Colorado miners you're worried about were first-class astronomers."

"Please, Max," Pat begged. "When was the chamber built and the inscriptions engraved on its walls?"

"You must remember, my time estimate is give or take a hundred years."

"It's older than a hundred years?"

"Would you believe," Max said slowly, dragging out the suspense, "a figure of nine thousand."

"What are you saying?"

"I'm saying your chamber was chiseled out of the Colorado rock sometime around 7100 B.C."

15

GIORDINO LIFTED THE BELL-BOEING 609 executive tilt-rotor aircraft straight up into a Persian blue sky outside Cape Town, South Africa, just after four in the morning. Taking off like a helicopter, its twin prop-rotor engines tilted at ninety degrees, the huge propellers beating the tropical air, the aircraft rose vertically, until the tilt-rotor was five hundred feet off the ground. Then Giordino shifted the controls of the mechanical linkage that enabled both prop rotors to swing horizontal and send the aircraft into level flight.

The 609 seated up to nine passengers, but for this trip she was empty except for a bundle of survival gear strapped to the floor. Giordino had chartered the plane in Cape Town because the nearest NUMA research ship was more than one thousand miles away from the Crozet Islands.

A helicopter could not have made the 2,400-mile round trip without refueling at least four times, and a normal multi-engine aircraft that could go the distance would have had no place to land once it reached the volcanic island. The Model 609 tilt-rotor could land any place a helicopter could and seemed the ideal craft for the job. Depending on the freakish whims of the winds, the flight should average four hours each way. The fuel would have to be monitored closely. Even with modified wing tanks, Giordino calculated that he would only have an extra hour and a half of flying time for the journey back to Cape Town. It wasn't enough to ensure a mentally soothing flight, but Giordino was never one to play a safe game.

Thirty minutes later, as he reached 12,000 feet and banked southeast over the Indian Ocean, he set the throttles at the most fuel-efficient cruise setting, watching the airspeed indicator hover at slightly under three hundred miles per hour. Then he turned to the small man sitting in the copilot's seat.

"If you have any regrets about joining this madcap venture, please be advised that it's too late to change your mind."

Rudi Gunn smiled. "I'll be in enough hot water for sneaking off with you when the admiral finds out I'm not sitting behind my desk in Washington."

"What excuse did you give for disappearing for six days?"

"I told my office to say I flew to the Baltic Sea to check on an underwater shipwreck project NUMA is surveying with Danish archaeologists."

"Is there such a project?"

"You bet your life," replied Gunn. "A fleet of Viking ships that a fisherman snagged."

Giordino passed Gunn a pair of charts. "Here, you can navigate."

"How big is St. Paul Island?"

"About two and a half square miles."

Gunn peered at Giordino through his thick glasses. "I do pray," he said placidly, "that we're not following in the footsteps of Amelia Earhart and Fred Noonan."

THREE hours into the flight, they were in good shape fuel-wise after picking up a tailwind of five knots. The Indian Ocean slowly vanished as they entered overcast skies that came from the east, bringing rain squalls and turbulence. Giordino climbed to find smooth air and blue skies again, rising above white puffy clouds that rolled beneath them like a stormy sea.

Giordino had the uncanny ability to sleep for ten minutes, then pop awake to check his instruments and make any course alteration suggested by Gunn before dozing off again. He repeated the process more times than Gunn bothered to count, never varying the routine by more or less than a minute.

Actually, there was no fear of becoming lost and missing the island. The tilt-rotor carried the latest Global Positioning System (GPS) navigation equipment. With the GPS receiver measuring the distance to a string of satellites, the precise latitude, longitude, and altitude were calculated, and the data programmed into the aircraft computer so Gunn could determine course, speed, time, and distance to their destination.

Unlike Giordino, he was an insomniac. He was also what Giordino often called him—a worrywart. Gunn couldn't have relaxed if he was lying under a palm tree on a Tahitian beach. He constantly read his watch and checked their position in between studying an aerial photo of the island.

When Giordino came awake and scanned the instrument panel, Gunn tapped him on the arm. "Don't drift off again. You should begin your descent. I make the island forty miles dead ahead."

Giordino rubbed water from a canteen on his face and eased the control column a slight inch forward. Slowly, the executive tilt-rotor began to descend, thrown about as it dropped through the turbulence from inside the clouds. With nothing to see, Giordino could have simply watched the altimeter needle swing counterclockwise, but he kept his eyes fixed on the white mist swirling past the windshield. Then, suddenly, at 5,000 feet they emerged from under the overcast and saw the ocean again for the first time in three hours.

"Nice work, Rudi," Giordino praised him. "St. Paul looks to be about five miles ahead, less than two degrees off to starboard. You as good as hit her right on the nose."

"Two degrees," Gunn said. "I really must do better next time."

With the turbulence behind them, the wingtips stopped fluttering. Giordino eased the throttles back, the roar of the engines falling to a muffled hum. The heavy rain had subsided, but rivulets of water still streaked across the windshield. Only now did he turn on the wipers, as he aimed the bow of the plane over the high cliffs that shielded the island from the relentless onslaught of the sea.

"Have you picked out a spot to set down?" asked Giordino, staring at the little island and its single mountain that seemed to rise up out of the sea like a giant cone. There was no obvious sign of a beach or open field. He saw only 360 degrees of steep rock-covered slopes.

Gunn held up a magnifying glass in front of his eyes. "I've gone over every inch of this thing, and have come to the conclusion that it's the worst piece of real estate I've ever seen. It's nothing but a rock pile, good only for supporting a gravel company."

"Don't tell me we've come all this way only to turn back," Giordino said sourly.

"I didn't say we couldn't land. The only flat area on the whole island is near the base of the mountain on the west side. Looks like little more than a ledge, maybe fifty by a hundred feet."

Giordino looked downright horrified. "Not even in the movies do they land helicopters on the sides of mountains."

Gunn pointed through the windshield. "There, on your left. It doesn't look as bad as I thought."

From Giordino's angle, the only level site to be found against the mountain looked no larger than the bed of a pickup truck. His feet finessed the rudder pedals as his hands stroked the wheel on the control column, correcting his angle and rate of descent with the elevators and ailerons. He thanked heaven that he had a head wind, even if it was only four knots. He could see the rocks scattered across his tiny landing site, but none looked large enough to cause damage to the aircraft's undercarriage. One hand came off the column and began manipulating the levers operating the prop rotors, tilting them from horizontal to vertical until the aircraft was hovering like a helicopter. The large-diameter propellers began sending small stones and dust swirling in damp clouds below the landing wheels.

Giordino was flying by feel now, head turned downward, one eye on the approaching ground, the other on the sheer side of the mountain not more than ten feet beyond the starboard wingtip. And then there was a slight bump as the tires struck the loose rock, and the tilt-rotor settled like a fat goose over her unhatched eggs. He let out a great sigh and pulled back on the throttles before shutting down the engines.

"We're home," he said thankfully.

Gunn's owlish face crinkled into a smile. "Was there ever a doubt?"

"I've got the mountain on my side. What's on yours?"

During the landing, Gunn's attention had been focused on the side of the mountain, and only now did he look out the starboard window. Not more than four feet from his exit door, the ledge dropped off at a steep angle for nearly eight hundred feet. The wingtip hung far out over empty air. The smile was gone and his face pale when he turned back to Giordino.

"It wasn't as expansive as I thought," he murmured sheepishly.

Giordino threw off his safety harness. "Do you have a route to the chamber figured out?"

Gunn held up the aerial photo and pointed to a small canyon leading up from the shore. "This is the only way a hunting party could have penetrated the island and made their way up the mountain. Pitt said that according to the ship's log, the colonel and his party climbed halfway up the mountain. We're about at that level now."

"What direction is the ravine?"

"South. And to answer your next question, we're on the west side of the mountain. With a little luck, we won't have to hike more than three-quarters of a mile, provided we can stumble onto the ancient walkway the colonel mentioned."

"Thank God for small islands," Giordino murmured. "Can you detect the old road on your photo?"

"No, I can't see any sign of it."

They proceeded to untie the straps containing the survival gear and donned their backpacks. The rain returned in sheets, so they slipped foul-weather gear on over their clothes and boots. When ready, they threw open the passenger door and stepped to the rocky ground. Beyond the ledge was the sheer drop, and beyond the drop, nothing but the Indian Ocean and gray pewter waves. As a safety precaution, they tied down the aircraft to several huge boulders.

The threatening sky made the island seem all the more drab and desolate. Gunn squinted through the rain and motioned for Giordino to lead, pointing in the direction he wanted to follow. They set off diagonally across the slope of the mountain, staying inside the larger rocks where the ground was flatter and firm beneath their feet.

They struggled across small ledges and narrow crevices, trying to walk upright without resorting to mountain-climbing gear, a skill in which neither was proficient. Giordino seemed impervious to fatigue. His thick, powerful body took the climb over the rocks in stride. Gunn had no problems, either. He was wiry and far tougher than he looked. He began to fall back from the unyielding Giordino, not from weariness but because he had to stop every twenty yards to wipe the moisture from his glasses.

About midway across the west side of the mountain, Giordino came to a halt. "If your reckoning is right, the stone walkway should be a short distance above or below us."

Gunn sat down with his back to a smooth lava rock and peered at his photo, which had become dog-eared and soggy from the damp. "Assuming the colonel took the path of least resistance from the ravine, he should have worked his way across the mountain about a hundred feet below us."

Giordino crouched, placed his hands on slightly bent knees, and stared down the slope. He seemed entranced for several moments before he turned back and looked Gunn full in the face. "I swear to God, I don't know how you do it."

"What do you mean?"

"Not thirty feet below where we sit is a narrow road paved with smooth rocks."

Gunn peered over the edge. Almost within spitting distance, he saw a road, a path really, four feet wide, laid with stones long aged by the weather. The path traveled in both directions, but landslides had carried much of it down the slope. In the cracks between the stones, a strange-looking plant was sprouting. It had lettucelike heads and grew close to the ground.

"It must be the road described by the British colonel," said Gunn.

"What's that weird stuff growing in it?" asked Giordino.

"Kerguelen cabbage. It produces a pungent oil and can be eaten as a cooked vegetable."

"Now you know why the road was indistinguishable on the photo. It was hidden by cabbages."

"Yes, I can see that now," said Gunn.

"How did it get established on such a godforsaken island?"

"Probably by its pollen that was carried across the water by the wind."

"Which direction do you want to follow the road?"

Gunn's eyes scanned the flat-laid stones as far as he could in both directions until they were lost to view. "The colonel must have stumbled onto the road down to our right. Below that point it must have been destroyed by erosion and slides. Since it makes no sense to start at the top of the mountain and work down, the chamber must be hidden farther up the slope. So we go to the left and climb."

Stepping cautiously on the loose lava rock, they quickly reached the neatly laid stones and began ascending the road. The flat passage was a welcome relief, but landslides were another matter. They had to cross two of them, each nearly thirty or more yards wide. It was slow going. The lava rock was jagged and knifelike. One slip and their bodies would tumble down the slope, gathering momentum until they bounced over the cliffs far below into the sea.

After negotiating the last hurdle, they sat and rested. Giordino idly picked a cabbage and flipped it down the hill, watching it bounce and shred on its erratic journey. He lost sight of it and did not see the splash as it shot into the water like a cannonball. Instead of lessening, the atmosphere chilled and thickened. The wind gusts strengthened and whipped the rain against their faces. Though they were protected by foul-weather gear, the water found ways of seeping in and around their collars, soaking their inner clothing.

Gunn passed him a thermos of coffee that had gone from steaming hot to lukewarm. Their lunch consisted of four granola bars. They weren't quite in the realm of miserable just yet, but they would soon enter it.

"We must be close," said Gunn, gazing through binoculars. "There is no hint of a long scar continuing across the mountain beyond that big rock just ahead."

Giordino stared at the massive boulder that protruded from the side of the slope. "The chamber better be on the other side," he grunted. "I'm not keen to be caught up here when it gets dark."

"Not to worry. We've got almost twelve hours of daylight left in this hemisphere."

"I just thought of something."

"What's that?" asked Gunn.

"We're the only two humans within two thousand miles."

"That's a cheery thought."

"What if we have an accident and injure ourselves and can't fly out of here? Even if we wanted to, I wouldn't dare take off in this wind."

"Sandecker will mount a rescue mission as soon as we notify him of our status." Gunn reached into his pocket and pulled out an Globalstar satellite phone. "He's as close as a dial tone."

"In the meantime, we'd have to subsist on these stupid cabbages. No, thank you."

Gunn shook his head in resignation. Giordino was a chronic complainer, and yet there was no better man to be with in a bad situation. Neither man had a sense of fear. Their only concern was the possibility of failure.

"Once we enter the chamber," Gunn said loudly, his voice carrying above the wind, "we'll be out of the storm and can dry out."

Giordino needed no coaxing. "Then let's move on," he said, rising to his feet. "I'm beginning to feel like a mop in a pail of dirty water."

Without waiting for Gunn, he pushed off toward the rock about fifty yards up the ancient road. The slope steepened and became a cliff towering above them. Part of the road had fallen away, and they were forced to pick their way carefully past the rock. Once around, they encountered the entrance to the chamber under a man-made archway. The opening was smaller than they thought—about six feet high by four feet wide—the same width as the road. It yawned black and portentous from inside.

"There it is, just as the colonel described it," said Gunn.

"One of us is supposed to shout 'Eureka,' " exclaimed Giordino, happy at last to get out of the wind and rain.

"I don't know about you, but I'm getting rid of my rain gear and backpack so I can be comfortable."

"I'm with you."

Within minutes, their backpacks were removed and their foul-weather gear laid out inside the tunnel for the return trip to the aircraft. They removed flashlights from their backpacks, took a final swig of coffee, and stepped deeper into the subterranean vault. The walls were smoothly carved without bumps or indentations. There was a strange-ness about the place, heightened by the eerie darkness and cavernous howl of the wind from outside the entrance.

They walked on, half curious, half uneasy, following the beams of their lights, wondering what they were going to find. The tunnel suddenly opened into a square chamber. Giordino tensed and his eyes hardened as his light traced out the skeletal bones of a foot, femur, hip, and then ribs and spinal column, attached to a skull with traces of red hair still visible. The remains of tattered and moldy clothing still clung to the bones.

"I wonder how this poor devil came to be here," said Gunn, feeling numbed.

Giordino swung his flashlight around the room, illuminating a small fire pit and various tools and furniture; all of them looked handmade from wood and lava rock. There were also the remains of seal hides and a pile of bones in the opposite corner.

"Judging from the cut of what's left of his clothes, I'd say he was a marooned sailor, a castaway on the island for God only knows how long before he died."

"Odd the colonel didn't mention him," said Gunn.

"The *Madras* made an unscheduled stop for water after being blown far off the normal sailing track in 1779. This lost soul must have arrived later. No other ship called on the island for probably another fifty or hundred years."

"I can't begin to imagine how terrible it must have been for him, alone on an ugly rain-cold pile of volcanic rock with no prospects of rescue and the threat of a lonely death hovering over him."

"He made a fire pit," said Giordino. "What do you think he used for wood? There's little but scrub brush on the island."

"He must have burned what brush he could scrounge. . . ." Gunn paused, knelt on one knee, and moved his hand through the ashes until he found something. He held up what looked like the remains of a toy chariot with two badly fire-scarred horses. "The artifacts," he said gloomily. "He must have burned the artifacts that contained wood to stay warm." Then Gunn shone his light in Giordino's direction and saw the beginnings of a smile arc across his face. "What do you find so funny?"

"I was just thinking," mused Giordino. "How many of those awful cabbages do you think the poor fellow must have eaten?"

"You won't know how they taste until you've tried one."

Giordino probed his beam on the walls, revealing the same type of inscriptions that he'd briefly seen in the Telluride chamber. A black obsidian pedestal rose from the center of the floor where the black skull had sat until removed by the British colonel. The lights also picked out a cave-in of fallen rocks that spilled down, covering the far wall of the chamber.

"I wonder what's on the other side of this rock pile."

"Another wall?"

"Maybe, maybe not." There was a vague certainty in Gunn's voice.

Giordino had learned many years before to trust the intelligence and intuitive genius of little Rudi Gunn. He looked at him. "You thinking there's another tunnel on the other side?"

"I am."

"Damn!" Giordino hissed under his breath. "Our friends from Telluride must have gotten here first."

"What makes you think that?"

Giordino played his beam over the rockfall. "Their modus operandi. They have a fetish for blowing up tunnels."

"I don't think so. This fall looks old, very old, considering the dust that has filled in among the rocks. I'll bet my Christmas bonus that this fall occurred centuries before the colonel or the old castaway stepped in here, and neither was curious and bothered to dig through and see what was on the other side." Then Gunn crawled up on the spread of rocks and played his light over the pile. "This looks natural to me. Not really a heavy fall. I think we might have a chance at getting through."

"I'm not sure my testosterone is up to this."

"Shut up and dig."

Gunn, as it turned out, was right. The rockfall was not massive. Despite his grumblings, Giordino worked like a mule. By far the stronger of the two, he tackled the heavier rocks, while Gunn worked at casting aside the smaller ones. There was a ruthless determination in his movements as he picked up and heaved hundred-pound rocks as if they were made of cork. In less than an hour, they had excavated a passage large enough for them to crawl beyond.

Because he was the smallest, Gunn went first. He paused to shine his light inside.

"What do you see?" asked Giordino.

"A short corridor leading to another chamber less than twenty feet away." Then he squirmed through. He stood up, brushed himself off, and removed several more rocks from the opposite side so Giordino, with his broad shoulders, would have an easier passage. They hesitated for a moment, beaming their combined lights into the chamber ahead, seeing strange reflections.

"I'm glad I listened to you," said Giordino, as he walked slowly forward.

"I have positive vibes. I'll bet you ten bucks nobody beat us to it."

"Skeptic that I am, you're on."

Feeling a little apprehensive now, and with a growing sense of trepidation, they stepped into the second chamber and swept their lights around the walls and floor. There were no inscriptions in here, but they froze at the astonishing sight revealed under the yellow-white beams of their flashlights, staring in almost religious awe at the twenty mummified figures that sat upright in stone chairs hewn from the rock. The two that faced the entrance sat on a raised platform. The rest were grouped to the sides in the shape of a square horseshoe.

"What is this place?" Giordino whispered, half expecting to see ghosts lurking in the shadows.

"We're in a tomb," Gunn muttered unsteadily. "Very ancient, by the look of the clothing."

The mummies and the black hair on their skulls were in a remarkable state of preservation. Their facial features were perfectly intact and their garments were complete, with red, blue, and green dyes still discernible in the fabric. The two mummies at the end sat on stone chairs elaborately carved with various species of sea life. Their finery appeared more intricately woven and colorful than the others. Copper bands with exquisite engraved designs inlaid with what Gunn recognized as gemstones of turquoise and black opal circled their foreheads. High conical caps rested on their heads. They wore long elaborate tunics with delicate seashells mixed with polished obsidian and copper disks sewn in exotic patterns from collar to hem. All the feet were encased in tooled-leather, loose-fitting boots that came halfway up the calf.

The two were obviously of higher rank and importance than the others. The skeleton on the left was larger than the one on the right. Though all the mummies had worn their hair long in life, it was a matter of simple deduction to tell the males from the females. Males have more prominent mandibles and ridges above the eyes than do females. Interestingly, their headbands or crowns were the same size, as if they had equal power. All the males sat to the right hand of the central figure in a row at an angle. All were dressed similarly, but the weaving of their garments was not as elegant. The turquoise and black opal were not as prevalent. The same configuration was represented by the females who sat to the left of the more richly adorned mummy.

A line of beautifully polished spears with obsidian heads was stacked against one wall. At the feet of each skeleton were copper bowls with drinking cups and matching spoons. Both bowls and spoons had holes with leather thongs, as if they could be slung around the neck or shoulder, indicating that these people had always carried their individual and personalized dinnerware with them. Handsome pottery, well-polished with delightful hand-painted delicate geometric designs on their surfaces, were laid out next to the stone chairs, along with large copper urns filled with withered leaves and flowers that must have been aromatic at the time the dead were interred. They looked handmade by artisans of great skill.

Gunn studied the mummies closely. He was amazed at the art of mummification. It looked technically superior to that of the Egyptians. "No sign of violent deaths. They all looked like they died in their sleep. I can't believe they all came to this place to die together, alone and forgotten."

"Somebody had to be alive to prop them up in the chairs," observed Giordino.

"That's true." Gunn made a sweeping motion around the chamber with one hand. "Notice that none are in quite the same position. Some have hands in the lap, others have hands on the arms of their chairs. The king and queen, or whatever their station in life, have their heads resting on one upraised hand as if contemplating their destiny."

"You're going theatrical on me," Giordino muttered.

"Don't you feel like Howard Carter when he first looked inside King Tut's tomb?"

"Howard was lucky. He found something we didn't."

"What's that?"

"Look around you. No gold. No silver. If these people were related to Tut, they must have been his poor relations. It looks as if copper was their prized metal."

"I wonder when they took eternal refuge here," Gunn reflected quietly.

"Better you should ask why," stated Giordino. "I'll get the camera out of my backpack so we can record this place and go home. Fooling around in sepulchral crypts upsets my delicate stomach."

For the next five hours, while Giordino recorded every square inch of the chamber with his camera, Gunn described what he saw in accurate detail into a small tape recorder. He also catalogued every artifact in a notebook. Nothing was touched, and everything was left in its place. Their effort wasn't perhaps as scientific as that of a team of archaeologists might have been, but for rank amateurs working under difficult conditions, they did a commendable job. It would be left for others, the historical experts, to solve the mysteries and identify the tomb's occupants.

When they finished, it was late afternoon. After crawling back through the opening at the cave-in and entering the room with the bones of the castaway, Gunn noticed Giordino wasn't with him. He returned to where the ceiling of the tunnel had collapsed and found Giordino furiously lifting rocks back into the hole, effectively sealing it.

"What are you doing that for?" he asked.

Giordino paused to stare at him, sweat-streaked with dust running down his face. "I'm not about to give the next guy a free ticket. Whoever wants to get into the tomb next will have to work for it the same as we did."

The two men made surprisingly good time on the return trip to the aircraft. Although the rain and wind had eased considerably and most of the trip was downhill, only the final fifty yards dictated a climb. They were only a short distance from the tilt-rotor, negotiating a narrow ledge, when suddenly an orange column of flame blossomed and streaked up into the damp air. There was no great thunderclap or ear-splitting crack. The sound of the explosion sounded more like a firecracker exploding inside a tin can. Then, as quickly as it burst, the ball of flame blinked out, leaving a pillar of smoke spiraling toward the dark clouds.

Giordino and Gunn watched helplessly and in shock as the tilt-rotor burst open like a cantaloupe dropped from a great height onto a sidewalk. Debris was hurled into the air, as the shattered and smoldering remains of the aircraft toppled over the ledge and crumpled down the slope, scattering a trail of metal scraps before plunging past the cliffs and splashing into the breakers that crashed against the island.

The tearing grind of metal being shredded against rocks died away, and the two men stood rooted, neither talking for nearly a minute. Gunn was stricken, his eyes staring in disbelief. Giordino's reaction was just the opposite. He was mad, damned mad, his hands clenched, his face white with fury.

"Impossible," Gunn mumbled at last. "There is no boat in sight, no place for another aircraft to land. It's impossible for someone to have put a bomb in the plane and escaped without us knowing."

"The bomb was placed inside the plane before we took off from Cape Town," said Giordino, his tone like ice. "Set and timed to detonate on our return trip."

Gunn stared at him blankly. "Those hours we spent examining the crypt . . ."

"Saved our lives. Whoever the killers are, they didn't count on us finding anything of great interest or spending more than an hour or two looking around, so they set their detonator four hours early."

"I can't believe anyone else has seen the chamber since the castaway."

"Certainly not our friends from Telluride, or they'd have destroyed the first chamber. Somebody leaked our flight to St. Paul Island, and we showed them the way. Now it's only a matter of time before they arrive to study the inscriptions in the first chamber."

Gunn's mind struggled to adjust to a new set of circumstances. "We've got to apprise the admiral of our predicament."

"Do it in code," Giordino suggested. "These guys are good. Ten to one they have a facility for listening in on satellite conversations. It's best that we let them think we're being eaten by fish on the bottom of the Indian Ocean."

Gunn raised his Globalstar phone and was about to dial, when a thought occurred to him. "Suppose the killers get here before the admiral's rescue party?"

"Then we'd better practice throwing rocks, because that's the only defense we have."

Almost forlornly, Gunn gazed around the rocky landscape. "Well," he said woodenly, "at least we don't have to worry about running out of ammunition."

16

THE *POLAR STORM* WITH her scientists and ship's crew had worked its way around the Antarctic Peninsula and across the Weddell Sea when Sandecker's message came in, ordering Captain Gillespie to shelve the expedition temporarily. He was to leave the ice pack immediately and sail at full speed to the Prince Olav Coast. There he was to heave to and wait off the Syowa Japanese research station until further orders. Gillespie called on his chief engineer and the engineer room crew to push the big icebreaker research ship to her maximum. They nearly achieved the impossible by gaining twenty knots out of her. Quite impressive, when Gillespie recalled that her top speed as specified by her builders twenty-two years before was eighteen knots.

He was pleased that his old ship had reached the rendezvous area eight hours earlier than expected. The water was too deep to drop anchor, so he ran the ship onto the outer edge of the ice pack before he ordered the engines shut down. Gillespie then notified Sandecker that his ship had arrived on station and was awaiting further orders.

The only reply was a succinct "Stand by to receive a passenger."

The respite gave everyone time to catch up on unfinished work. The scientists busied themselves analyzing and recording their findings into computers, while the crew went about making routine repairs to the ship.

They did not have long to wait.

On the morning of the fifth day since leaving the Weddell Sea, Gillespie was studying the sea ice through his binoculars when he saw a helicopter slowly emerge from an early-morning ice mist. It flew on a direct line toward the *Polar Storm*. He ordered his second officer to receive the aircraft at the landing pad on the stern of the ship.

The helicopter hovered for a few seconds, then descended onto the pad. A man carrying a briefcase and a small duffel bag jumped from an open cargo door and spoke to Gillespie's second officer. Then he turned and waved to the pilot who had flown him to the ship. The rotor blades increased their beat and the helicopter rose into the cold air and was heading for home when Pitt stepped onto the *Polar Storm*'s bridge.

"Hello, Dan," he greeted the captain warmly. "Good to see you."

"Dirk! Where did you drop from?"

"I was flown from Punta Arenas on the Strait of Magellan by Air Force jet to the airstrip at the nearby Japanese research station. They were kind enough to give me a lift on their helicopter to the ship."

"What brings you to the Antarctic?"

"A little search project farther down the coast."

"I knew the admiral had something up his sleeve. He was damned secretive about it. He gave me no idea you were coming."

"He has his reasons." Pitt set his briefcase on the chart table, opened it, and handed Gillespie a paper with a set of coordinates. "This is our destination."

The captain looked at the coordinates and studied the appropriate nautical chart. "Stefansson Bay," he said quietly. "It's near, on the Kemp Coast not far from the Hobbs Islands. Nothing there of interest. It's as barren a piece of property as I've ever seen. What are we looking for?"

"A shipwreck."

"A wreck under the ice?"

"No," said Pitt with a half grin. "A wreck *in* the ice."

STEFANSSON BAY looked even more desolate and remote than Gillespie had described it, especially under a sky filled with clouds as dark as charcoal and a sea sullen with menacing ice. The wind bit like the needle teeth of an eel, and Pitt began to think of the physical effort required in crossing the ice pack to reach the continent's shore. Then the adrenaline began to pump as he thought of discovering a ship whose decks hadn't been trod since 1858.

Could it still be there, he wondered, just as Roxanna Mender and her husband had found it nearly a century and a half before? Or had it been eventually crushed by the ice or bulldozed out to sea where it finally sank deep in icy waters?

Pitt found Gillespie standing on a bridge wing, peering through binoculars at an unseen object far back in the spreading wake of the icebreaker. "Looking for whales?" he asked.

"U-boats," Gillespie answered, matter-of-factly.

Pitt thought the captain was joking. "Not many wolf packs in this part of the sea."

"Just one." Gillespie kept the glasses pressed against his eyes. "The U-2015. She's been following our wake ever since we almost collided with her ten days ago."

Pitt still wasn't sure he was hearing right. "Are you serious?"

Gillespie finally lowered the glasses. "I am." Then he proceeded to tell Pitt about the meeting with the U-boat. "I identified her from an old photo I have in my maritime library. There's no doubt in my mind. She's the U-2015, all right. Don't ask me how she survived all these years or why she's tracking this ship. I don't have the answers. All I know is that she's out there."

Pitt had worked with the captain on at least four projects over the years. He knew him as one of the most trusted captains in NUMA's fleet of research ships. Dan Gillespie was not a kook or someone who told tall tales. He was a sober and decisive man who had never had a black mark on his record. No accident or serious injury ever occurred when he trod the deck.

"Who would believe after all these years . . ." Pitt's voice trailed off. He was unsure of what to say.

"I don't have to read your mind to know you think I'm ready for a straitjacket," said Gillespie earnestly, "but I can prove it. Ms. Evie Tan, who is on board writing a story on the expedition for a national magazine, took photos of the sub when we nearly rammed her."

"Do you see any sign of her now?" Pitt inquired. "Periscope or snorkel?"

"She's playing coy and staying deep," Gillespie answered.

"Then how can you be sure she's out there?"

"One of our scientists dropped his underwater acoustic microphones over the side—he uses them to record whale talk. We trailed the listening gear a quarter of a mile behind the ship. I then shut down the engines and drifted. She's not a modern nuclear attack sub that can run silent through the depths. We picked up the beat of her engines as clear as a barking dog."

"Not a bad concept, but I would have trailed a weather balloon with a magnetometer hanging from it."

Gillespie laughed. "Not a bad concept, either. We thought about sidescan, but you'd have to get your sensor alongside for a good reading, and that seemed too tricky. I was hoping that now you've come on board we might find some answers."

A warning light went off in the back of Pitt's brain. He was beginning to wonder if he hadn't entered the twilight zone. To even consider a connection between the assassins from the Fourth Empire and an antique U-boat was plain crazy. And yet nothing in the whole incredible scheme made sense.

"Brief the admiral," ordered Pitt. "Tell him we may need some help."

"Should we harass him?" said Gillespie, referring to the sub. "Double back on our track and play cat and mouse?"

Pitt gave a slight negative shake of the head. "I'm afraid our ghost will have to wait. Finding the *Madras* takes first priority."

"Was that her name?"

Pitt nodded. "An East Indiaman lost in 1779."

"And you think she's locked in the ice somewhere along the shore," Gillespie said doubtfully.

"I'm hoping she's still there."

"What's on board that's so important to NUMA?"

"Answers to an ancient riddle."

Gillespie did not require a lengthy explanation. If that was all Pitt was going to tell him, he accepted it. His responsibility was to the ship and the people on board. He would follow an order from his bosses at NUMA without question, unless it ran counter to the safety of the *Polar Storm.*

"How far into the ice pack do you want me to run the ship?"

Pitt passed the captain a slip of paper. "I'd be grateful if you could place the *Polar Storm* on top of this position."

Gillespie studied the numbers for a moment. "It's been a while since I navigated by latitude and longitude, but I'll set you as close as I can."

"Compass headings, then loran, then Global Positioning. Next they'll invent a positioning instrument that tells you where the nearest roll of toilet paper is located and how many inches away."

"May I ask where you got these numbers?"

"The log of the *Paloverde,* a whaling ship that found the East Indiaman a long time ago. Unfortunately, there is no guaranteeing how accurate they are."

"You know," Gillespie said wistfully, "I'll bet you that old whaling ship skipper could put his ship on a dime, whereas I would be hardpressed to put mine on a quarter."

THE *Polar Storm* entered the pack and plunged against the floating mantle of ice like a fullback running through a team of opposing linemen. For the first mile, the ice was no more than a foot thick and the massive reinforced bow pushed aside the frigid blanket with ease, but closer to shore, the pack began to gradually swell, reaching three to four feet thick. Then the ship would slow to a stop, move astern, and then plow into the ice again, forcing a crack and a fifty-foot path until the ice closed in and stopped her forward progress again. The performance was repeated, the bow thrusting against the resisting ice time and time again.

Gillespie was not watching the effects of the ice-ramming. He was sitting in a tall swivel chair studying the screen of the ship's depth sounder, which sent sonic signals to the seabed. The signals were bounced back and indicated the distance in feet between the ship's keel and the bottom. These were unsurveyed waters, and the bottom was unmarked on the nautical charts.

Pitt stood a few feet away, staring through Gillespie's tinted-lens binoculars, which reduced the glare of the ice. The ice cliffs just back of the shoreline soared two hundred feet high before flattening into a broad plateau. He swept the glasses along the base of the cliffs, attempting to spot some hint of the ice-locked *Madras*. No telltale sign was obvious, no stern frozen in the ice, no masts thrusting above the top of the cliffs.

"Mr. Pitt?"

He turned and faced a smiling stubby man who was a few years on the low side of forty. His face was pink and cherubic, with twinkling green eyes and a wide mouth that smiled crookedly. A small, almost delicate hand was thrust out.

"Yes" was all Pitt replied, surprised at the firmness of the hand that gripped his.

"I'm Ed Northrop, chief scientist and glaciologist. I don't think I've had the pleasure."

"Dr. Northrop. I've often heard Admiral Sandecker speak of you," said Pitt pleasantly.

"In glowing terms, I hope," Northrop said, laughing.

"As a matter of fact, he never forgave you for filling his boots with ice during an expedition north of the Bering Sea."

"Jim certainly holds a grudge. That was fifteen years ago."

"You've spent quite a number of years in the Arctic and Antarctic."

"Been studying sea ice for eighteen years. By the way, I volunteered to go with you."

"Don't think me ungrateful, but I'd rather go it alone."

Northrop nodded and held his ample stomach with both hands.

"Won't hurt to have a good man along who can read the ice, and I'm more durable than I look."

"You make a good point."

"Bottom coming up," Gillespie announced. Then he called down to the engine room. "All stop, Chief. This is as far as we go." He glanced in Pitt's direction. "We're sitting on top of the latitude and longitude you gave me."

"Thank you, Dan. Good work. This should be the approximate spot where the *Paloverde* was frozen in the ice during the Antarctic winter of 1858."

Northrop stared through the bridge windows at the ice spreading from the ship to shore. "I make it about two miles. A short hike in the brisk air will do us good."

"You have no snowmobiles on board?"

"Sorry, our work takes place within a hundred yards of the ship. We saw no need to add luxuries to the project budget."

"What temperature do you consider brisk air?"

"Five to ten degrees below zero. Relatively warm in these parts."

"I can't wait," Pitt said laconically.

"Consider yourself lucky it's autumn down here. It's much colder in spring."

"I prefer the tropics, with warm trade winds and lovely girls in sarongs swaying to the beat of a drum under the setting sun."

His eyes traveled to an attractive Asian lady who walked straight up to him. She smiled and said, "Aren't you being overdramatic?"

"It's my nature."

"I'm told you're Dirk Pitt."

He smiled cordially. "I do hope so. And you must be Evie Tan. Dan Gillespie has told me you're doing a photo story about the ice expedition."

"I read a great deal about your exploits. May I interview you when you return from whatever it is you're looking for?"

Pitt instinctively threw a questioning look at Gillespie, who shook his head. "I haven't told a soul about your target."

Pitt pressed her hand. "I'll be happy to give you an interview, but the nature of our project must be off the record."

"Does it have to do with the military?" she asked, with an innocent face.

Pitt caught her sneaky probe instantly. "Nothing to do with classified military activities, or Spanish treasure galleons, or abominable snowmen. In fact, the story is so dull, I doubt any self-respecting journalist would be interested in it." Then he addressed Gillespie. "Looks like we left the submarine at the edge of the ice floe."

"Either that," said the captain, "or else they followed us under the ice."

"They're ready for you," said First Officer Bushey to Pitt.

"On my way."

The crew lowered the gangway and brought down three sleds to the ice, one with a box of ice-cutting tools covered by a tarpaulin. The other two carried only tie-down rope to secure any artifacts they might find. Pitt stood in the feathery foot-deep snow and looked at Gillespie, who had motioned to a man who was about the size and shape of a Kodiak bear. "I'm sending my third officer with you and Doc Northrop. This is Ira Cox."

"Glad to meet y'all," said Cox, through a beard that came down to his chest. The voice seemed to rise from somewhere deep below the Mason-Dixon line. He didn't offer a hand. His immense paws were covered by equally immense Arctic gloves.

"Another volunteer?"

"My idea," offered Gillespie. "I can't allow one of Admiral Sandecker's chief directors to traipse through a field of unpredictable ice alone. I won't take the responsibility. This way, if you encounter any problems, you'll have a better chance of surviving. If you should run into a polar bear, Cox will wrestle it to death."

"There are no polar bears in the Antarctic."

Gillespie looked at Pitt and shrugged. "Why take chances?"

Pitt did not make a formal or indignant protest. Down deep, he knew that if worse came to worst, one or both of those men just might save his life.

As autumn takes over the Antarctic, the stormy seas surround the continent, but as winter arrives and temperatures drop, the water thickens into oily-appearing slicks. Then the ice fragments form floating saucers called pancake ice, which enlarge and merge together before eventually forming ice floes covered by snow. Because the ice came early this year, Pitt, Northrop, and Cox moved without incident across the uneven but fairly smooth surface. They detoured around several ice ridges and two icebergs that had drifted offshore before being frozen in the pack ice. To Pitt, the floe looked like an unkempt, lumpy bed with a white quilt thrown over it.

Trudging through a foot of feathery snow did not hinder their motion. Their pace never slackened. Northrop went first, studying the ice as he went, watchful for any deviation or crack. He walked without the burden of a sled, insisting that he required more freedom of movement to test the ice. Harnessed to a sled, Pitt followed Northrop, easily moving on cross-country skis that he had shipped from his father's lodge in Breckenridge, Colorado. Cox brought up the rear, wearing showshoes and pulling two sleds as effortlessly as if they were toys.

What began as a beautiful day with a dazzling sun in an uncluttered sky deteriorated as clouds crept over the horizon. Slowly, the blue skies went gray and the sun became a muted ball of faded orange. A light snow began to fall, reducing visibility. Pitt ignored the worsening weather, and did not allow his mind to linger on the green, frigid water only an arm's length below his feet. He kept glancing at the cliffs, which rose higher and higher above the tips of his skis the closer they came. He could see the ice-free rugged Hansen Mountains far inland, but still no sign of a shadowy shape embedded in the ice. He began to feel like an intruder in this vast, remote domain unspoiled by human habitation.

They made their crossing over the floe and reached the base of the ice cliffs in slightly over an hour. Gillespie followed their every movement until they stopped at the inner edge of the ice floe. Their turquoise NUMA arctic gear made them easily visible against the brilliant white. He checked the meteorological reports for the tenth time. The falling snow was light and there was no wind, but he knew well that could change in a matter of minutes. It was the wind that was the unknown factor. Without warning, it could turn a dazzling white landscape into a howling whiteout.

Gillespie picked up the ship's satellite phone and dialed a number. He was put through immediately to Sandecker. "They're on shore and beginning the search," he informed his boss.

"Thank you, Dan," Sandecker replied. "Report to me when they return."

"Before I ring off, Admiral, there is something else. I'm afraid we have a rather baffling situation." He then gave Sandecker a concise report on the U-boat. When he finished, there was the expected pause while the admiral tried to digest what he had just heard.

Finally, he replied tersely, "I'll take care of it."

Gillespie went back to the broad windshield of the bridge and picked up his glasses again. "All this for a shipwreck," he said under his breath. "It had better be worth it."

ON shore, Pitt was fighting off discouragement. He was well aware that any search for something lost so far back in time was a long shot. There was no way of determining how much ice had formed to enshroud the entire ship in 150 years. For all he knew, it could be a hundred yards deep within the ice. Using the *Polar Storm* as a base point, he marked off a two-mile grid below the sheer, icebound cliffs. Pitt and Cox each used small handheld GPS units the size of a cigarette pack to pinpoint their precise location at any moment. They split up, leaving the sleds at the departure point. Pitt headed to his left, making good time on his skis along the ice floe where it met the cliffs, while Cox and Northrop searched to the right. When they each reached the approximate end of a mile, they agreed to return to their starting point.

Making better time than the others, Pitt was the first to return to the sleds. Examining every foot of the lower cliffs going and coming, he was disappointed not to find the slightest clue to the *Madras*. Thirty minutes later, the glaciologist arrived and lay with his back over a small hummock of ice, legs and arms outstretched, catching his breath and resting his aching knees and ankles. He looked at Pitt through his dark bronze goggles and made a gesture of defeat.

"Sorry, Dirk, I saw nothing in the ice that resembled an old ship."

"I came up dry, too," Pitt admitted.

"I can't say without making tests, but it's a good bet the ice has broken off at one time or another and carried her out to sea."

Gillespie's muffled voice came from a pocket of Pitt's polar-fleece jacket. He pulled out a portable ship-to-shore radio and responded. "Go ahead, Dan, I have you."

"Looks like a bad storm coming up," warned Gillespie. "You should return to the ship as quickly as possible."

"No argument on that score. See you soon."

Pitt slipped the radio back into his pocket, looked over the ice floe to the north, and saw only emptiness. "Where did you leave Cox?"

Suddenly concerned, Northrop sat up and peered across the ice. "He found and entered a crevice in the cliffs. I thought he'd investigate, come out and follow me back."

"I'd better check him out."

Pitt pushed off with his ski poles and traced the footprints in the snow, two sets going, only one returning. The wind was increasing rapidly, the tiny ice particles thickening like a silken veil. Any glare was wiped out and the sun had vanished completely. He could not help but admire the courage of Roxanna Mender. He thought it a miracle she had survived the terrible cold. He found himself skiing under great icy crags that loomed over him. He had the fleeting impression the great hard mass would topple over him at any time.

He heard a muted shout not far away over the swelling sound of the wind. He stood listening, ears cocked, intent on piercing the barrier of the ice mist.

"Mr. Pitt! Over here!"

At first Pitt could see nothing but the frigid white face of the cliff. Then he caught a vague glimpse of a turquoise smear waving from a black shaft that split the cliff. Pitt dug his ski poles into the ice and pushed toward Cox. He felt like Ronald Colman in *Lost Horizon,* struggling through the Himalayan blizzard into the tunnel that took him to Shangri-la. One moment he was in the midst of swarming ice particles, the next he was in a dry, quiet, wind-free atmosphere.

He leaned forward on his poles and looked around an ice cave that measured about eight feet wide and tapered to a sharp peak twenty feet above. From the entrance, the gloom transformed from ash white to an ivory blackness. The only flash of color he could see was Cox's cold-weather gear.

"A bad storm is brewing," said Pitt, wagging a thumb through the cave entrance. "We'd best make a run for the ship."

Cox pulled up his goggles, his eyes looking at Pitt strangely. "You want to leave?"

"It's nice and comfy in here, but we can't afford to waste time."

"I thought you were looking for an old ship."

"I thought so, too," Pitt said testily.

Cox held up his gloved hand and unrolled an index finger in the up-right position. "Well?"

Pitt looked upward. There, near the peak of the crevice, a small section of a wooden stern section of an old sailing ship was protruding from the ice.

17

PITT SKIED BACK TO Northrop, and together they dragged the three sleds into the ice cave. Pitt also briefed Gillespie on their discovery and assured him that they were comfortably shielded from the foul weather outside the ice cave.

Cox immediately removed the tools and set to work attacking the ice with a hammer and chisel, chopping hand- and footholds for a ladder that would lead up to the exposed hull of the entombed ship. The upper deck had been free of ice when Roxanna and her husband, Captain Bradford Mender, had walked aboard the *Madras,* but during the passing of fourteen decades, the ice had completely covered over the wreck until the tops of her masts were buried and no longer visible.

"I'm amazed she's so well preserved," remarked Northrop. "I would have guessed she'd have been crushed to toothpicks by now."

"Just goes to show," Pitt said dryly, "glaciologists do err."

"Seriously, this bears further study. The ice cliffs on this part of the coast have built up and not broken off. Most unusual. There must be a good reason for them building higher but not moving outward."

Pitt looked up at Cox, who had chiseled a set of steps leading up to the exposed planks. "How you doing, Ira?"

"The wooden planking is frozen solid and shatters as easy as my grandma's glass eye. Ah should have a hole big enough to snake through in another hour."

"Mind you stay between the ship's timbers or you'll still be hacking next week."

"Ah know well how a ship is constructed, Mr. Pitt," said Cox, acting peeved.

"I stand rebuked," Pitt said amiably. "Put us inside in forty minutes and I'll see Captain Gillespie gives you a blue ribbon for ice carving."

Cox was not an easy man to get close to. He had few friends on board the *Polar Storm*. His first impression of Pitt had been as a snotty bureaucrat from NUMA headquarters, but he could see now that the special projects director was a down-to-earth, no-nonsense, yet humorous kind of guy. He was actually beginning to like him. The ice chips began to fly like sparks.

Thirty-four minutes later, Cox climbed down and announced in triumph. "Ah have an entrance, gentlemen."

Pitt bowed. "Thank you, Ira. General Lee would have been proud of you."

Cox bowed back. "Like Ah always said, save your Confederate money. You never know, the South might rise again."

"I believe it might at that."

Pitt climbed the footholds gouged in the ice by Cox and slipped through the hole feet first. His boots made contact with the deck four feet below the opening. He peered into the gloom and realized that he had entered the ship's aft galley.

"What do you see?" demanded Northrop excitedly.

"A frozen galley stove," answered Pitt. He leaned through the hull. "Come on up, and bring the lights with you."

Cox and Northrop quickly joined him and passed around aluminum-encased halogen lights that lit up the immediate area like a sunny day. Except for the soot on the flue atop the big cast-iron stove and oven, the galley looked as if it had never been used. Pitt pulled open the fire door of the oven but found no ashes.

"The shelves are bare," observed Cox. "They must have eaten all the paper, cans, and glass."

"Well, maybe the paper," muttered Northrop, beginning to feel distinctly uneasy.

"Let's stick together," said Pitt. "One of us may spot something the others missed."

"Anything in particular we're looking for?" asked Cox.

"A storeroom in the aft steerage hold beneath the captain's cabin."

"I say it should be two or more decks under where we stand."

"This has to be the ship's officers' and passengers' galley. The captain's cabin must be nearby. Let's find a passageway below."

Pitt stepped through a doorway and shined his light on the dining room. The table and chairs and surrounding furniture were encased in an inch-thick layer of ice. Under their halogen lights, the entire room sparkled like a crystal chandelier. A tea set rested in the center of the dining table as if waiting to be used.

"No bodies in here," said Northrop, with relief.

"They all died in their cabins," said Pitt. "Probably a combination of hypothermia, starvation, and scurvy."

"Where do we go from here?" Cox asked.

Pitt motioned his light through a doorway beyond the dining table. "Just outside, we should find a passageway that drops down to the deck below."

"How do you know your way around a two-hundred-year-old ship?"

"I studied drawings and old plans of East Indiaman merchant ships. Though I've never actually seen one until now, I know every nook and cranny by heart."

They dropped down a ladder, slipping on the ice that covered the steps but remaining on their feet. Pitt led them aft, passing old cannon that looked as new as they had the day they had left the foundry. The storeroom's door was still open, just as Roxanna and the crew of the *Paloverde* had left it.

Pitt, anticipation surging through his veins, stepped inside and swung his beam around the storeroom.

The packing crates were still stacked from deck to ceiling along the bulkheads, just as they were when last seen in 1858. Two of the wooden crates sat on the deck, their lids pried open. A copper urn was lying on its side behind the door, where it had rolled when the ship was hurriedly abandoned by Mender and his crew as the ice pack began to melt and crack apart.

Pitt knelt and began lifting the objects from the open crates with tender loving care and setting them on the icy deck. In a short time, he had collected not only a menagerie of figurines depicting common animals—dogs, cats, cattle, lions—but also sculptures of creatures he'd never seen before. Some were sculpted from copper; many were bronze. He also found figures of people, mostly females dressed in long robes, with full pleated skirts covering their legs to their strangely booted feet. The intricately grooved hair was long and braided to the waist, and the breasts were simply formed without exaggerated fullness.

Laid on the bottom of the crates, like chips on a casino craps table, were round copper disks half an inch thick and five inches in diameter. The disks were engraved on both sides with sixty symbols that Pitt recognized as similar to those in the Paradise Mine chamber. The center of the disks revealed hieroglyphs of a man on one side and a woman on the other. The man wore a long pointed hat on his head that was folded over on one side, and a flowing capelike robe over a metal breastplate and a short skirt similar to a Scottish kilt. He sat on a horse that had a single horn protruding from its head, and held a broad sword above his head that was in the act of cutting through the neck of a monstrous lizard with an open mouth full of gaping teeth.

The woman on the opposite side of the disk was dressed the same as the man, but with more ornaments about her body, strings of what looked like seashells and some kind of beads. She was also astride a horse with a horn in the center of the head. Instead of holding a sword, she was thrusting a spear into what Pitt recognized as a saber-toothed tiger, an animal extinct for thousands of years.

Pitt's mind traveled to another time, another place that was vague and nebulous, barely outlined in a gentle mist. As he held the disks in his hand, he tried to sense a contact with those who had created them. But remote viewing was not one of Pitt's skills. He was a man attuned to the here and now. He could not pass through the unseen wall separating the past from the present.

His reverie was broken by the Southern-accented voice of Ira Cox. "Do you want to start loading the sleds with these crates?"

Pitt blinked, looked up, and nodded. "Soon as I replace the lids, we'll carry them out in stages up to the next deck. Then lower them by rope through the hole you made in the hull down to the floor of the ice cave."

"I count twenty-four of them," said Northrop. He walked to a stack of crates and picked one up. His face turned four different shades of red, and his eyes bulged.

Cox, quickly sizing up the situation, took the crate from Northrop as easily as if he were handed a baby. "You'd better let me do the heavy work, Doc."

"You don't know how grateful I am, Ira," said Northrop, overjoyed at being relieved of the crate, which must have weighed close to a hundred pounds.

Cox took the most strenuous part of the job. Hoisting each crate onto one shoulder, he carried it down the ladder to Pitt, who then tied it with a sling and lowered it down to a waiting sled, where Northrop shoved it into place. When they finished, each sled held eight crates.

Pitt walked to the entrance of the cave and called the ship. "How does the storm look from your end?" he asked Gillespie.

"According to our resident meteorologist, it should blow over in a few hours."

"The sleds are loaded with the artifacts," said Pitt.

"Do you require help?"

"There must be close to eight hundred pounds per sled. Any assistance to pull them back to the *Polar Storm* will be gratefully accepted."

"Stand by until the weather clears," Gillespie said. "I'll personally lead the relief party."

"Are you sure you want to make the trip?"

"And miss walking the deck of an eighteenth-century ship? Not for all the cognac in France."

"I'll introduce you to the captain."

"You've seen the captain?" Gillespie asked curiously.

"Not yet, but if Roxanna Mender didn't exaggerate, he should be fresh as a Popsicle."

CAPTAIN Leigh Hunt still sat at the desk where he had died in 1779. Nothing had changed except for the small indentation in the ice where the ship's log had once lain on the desktop. Solemnly, they studied the child in the crib and Mrs. Hunt, two centuries of ice covering her saddened and delicate features. The dog was only a frozen mound of white.

They walked through the cabins, illuminating the long-dead passengers with their halogen lights. The shrouds of ice glittered brightly, scarcely revealing the bodies beneath. Pitt tried to visualize their final moments, but the tragedy seemed so poignant it just didn't bear thinking about. Seeing those waxen effigies in the shadowy gloom, rigid under their ice coating, made it hard to imagine them as living, breathing humans who went about their everyday lives before dying in a remote and awful part of the world. The expressions on some of the faces, distorted by the ice, were ghastly beyond description. What were their last thoughts alone, without hope of rescue?

"This is a nightmare," murmured Northrop. "But a glorious nightmare."

Pitt looked at him questioningly. "Glorious?"

"The wonder of it all. Human bodies perfectly preserved, frozen in time. Think what this means to the science of cryogenics. Think of the potential for bringing them all back to life."

The thought struck Pitt like a blow to the head. Could science make it possible someday to present the cold, dead passengers and crew of the *Madras* with a rebirth? "Think of the amazing amount of history that would be rewritten after talking to someone brought back to life after two hundred years."

Northrop threw up his hands. "Why dream? It won't happen in our lifetime."

"Probably not," said Pitt, contemplating the possibility, "but I wish I could be around to witness the reaction of these poor souls when they saw what's happened to their world since 1779."

THE storm clouds passed over and the wind died after another four hours. Cox stood outside the cave and waved the yellow tarpaulin like a flag that had covered the ice tools. A group of figures spotted the signal and began winding their way through the rugged contours of the ice toward the cave. Pitt counted ten turquoise antlike creatures approaching across the dead white floe. As they came closer, Pitt could see Gillespie was leading. He also recognized the small figure behind him as the journalist, Evie Tan.

Thirty minutes later, Gillespie walked up to Pitt and smiled. "Nice day for a walk in the park," he said cheerfully.

"Welcome to the Antarctic museum of marine antiquities," Pitt said, showing the captain inside and pointing up at the hull. "Watch your step climbing the ladder Ira so ably hacked in the ice."

While Pitt and Gillespie made a tour of the *Madras* with Evie, who shot ten rolls of film, recording every inch of the old ship's interior and its dead, Cox and Northrop helped the *Polar Storm*'s crew pull the sleds and their ancient cargo back to the icebreaker.

Pitt was amused as he watched Evie unzip her big parka, pull up the heavy wool sweater underneath, and tape rolls of film to her long john underwear. She looked at him and smiled. "Saves the film from the extreme cold."

Jake Bushey, the *Polar Storm*'s first officer, hailed Gillespie over his portable radio. The captain listened for a moment and shoved the radio back into his pocket. Pitt could tell by the expression on his face that he wasn't in a good mood. "We must get back to the ship."

"Another storm coming in?" asked Evie.

He gave a curt shake of the head. "The U-boat," he said grimly. "She's surfaced through the ice less than a mile from the *Polar Storm*."

18

As THEY NEARED THE ship and looked beyond her across the ice, they could clearly see the black whale-shaped outline of the submarine against the white floe. Closer yet and they distinguished figures standing on the conning tower, as others climbed from inside the hull and clustered around the deck gun. The U-boat had popped through the ice only a quarter of a mile from the *Polar Storm*.

Gillespie called his first officer over his portable radio. "Bushey!"

"Standing by, sir."

"Close the watertight doors and order all crew and scientists to don their life vests."

"Yes, sir," replied Bushey. "Activating watertight doors."

"That ghost ship is like a plague," muttered Gillespie. "Its bad luck is contagious."

"Be thankful for small favors," said Pitt. "There is no way a sub can fire a torpedo through the ice."

"True, but she still has a deck gun."

The sound of the alarms warning the people on board of the closing of the bulkhead doors blared through the cold air and across the ice as Pitt and the others rushed toward the ship. The snow had been packed down by the sleds and their heavy cargo, making a trail that was easy for them to follow. Several of the crew were standing in the snow around the gangway, motioning for them to hurry.

The captain called over the radio again. "Bushey. Has the U-boat attempted contact?"

"Nothing, sir. Shall I try and raise them?"

Gillespie thought a moment. "No, not yet, but keep a sharp eye for any suspicious movement."

"Did you make contact with the boat's commander during the voyage from the Peninsula?" asked Pitt.

"I made two attempts, but my requests for identification went unanswered."

Gillespie kept his eyes aimed at the sub. "What did the admiral say when you informed him?"

"All he said was, 'I'll take care of it.' "

"Whatever the admiral promises, you can take to the bank." Pitt paused reflectively. "Tell Jake to send a message to the sub, warning its commander that your research ship has dropped seismic explosive underwater devices under the ice in the exact position where he's surfaced."

"What do you expect to gain with that lie?"

"We've got to stall. Whatever scheme Sandecker is cooking up, he'll need time to assemble."

"They're probably listening in on everything we say over the radio."

"I'm counting on it," said Pitt, smiling.

"If they operate like they did in World War Two against isolated transport ships, they're jamming our satellite transmissions."

"I think we can count on that, too."

They still had another half mile to go to reach the ship. Gillespie pressed the transmit switch on his radio. "Bushey, listen to me carefully." He then told his first officer what to say and do, certain the sub was listening to their transmission.

Bushey did not question his senior officer's orders, nor did he show the slightest hesitation. "I understand, Captain. I will contact the vessel immediately and warn them."

"You've got a good man," said Pitt admiringly.

"The best," Gillespie agreed.

"We'll wait ten minutes, then come up with another cock-and-bull story and hope the sub's commander is gullible."

"Let's pick up the pace," urged Gillespie.

Pitt turned to Evie Tan, who was panting heavily. "Why don't you at least let me carry your camera equipment?"

She shook her head vigorously. "Photographers carry their own gear. I'll be all right. Go ahead. I'll catch up to you at the ship."

"I hate to be a cad," said Gillespie, "but I've got to be on board at the earliest possible moment."

"Push on," Pitt told him. "We'll see you on board."

The captain took off at a dead run. Pitt had insisted Evie use his skis at the ice cave, but she had indignantly refused. Now, with little coaxing, she allowed him to strap her feet into the bindings. Then he handed her the poles. "You go ahead. I want to get a closer look at the sub."

After sending Evie on her way, Pitt moved off on an angle until he was fifty yards astern of the ship. He stared across the ice floe at the submarine. He could clearly see the crew manning the deck gun and the officers leaning over the coaming of the conning tower. They did not appear to be wearing the standard Nazi *unterseeboot* crew uniforms. They were all dressed in black single-piece, tight-fitting, cold-weather coveralls.

Pitt stood where he could clearly be seen by the crew. He pressed the transmit button on his portable radio. "I am speaking to the commander of the U-2015. My name is Pitt. You can see me standing off the stern of the *Polar Storm*." He let that sink in for a moment before continuing. "I am fully aware of who you are. Do you understand?"

Static rasped out of the radio, then was replaced by a friendly voice. "Yes, Mr. Pitt. This is the commander of the U-2015 speaking. How may I help you?"

"You have my name, Commander. What's yours?"

"You need not know."

"Yes," Pitt said calmly, "that figures. Your cronies from the New Destiny, or should I say Fourth Empire, have a mania for secrecy. But not to worry, I promise not to whisper a word about your slimy band of killers, provided you take your geriatric pile of junk from nostalgia land and be on your way."

It was a long shot, pure guesswork at best, but the long silence told Pitt he had struck a chord. A full minute passed before the U-boat commander's voice came over the little radio.

"So you are the ubiquitous Dirk Pitt."

"I am," Pitt answered, feeling a sense of triumph at pressing the right button. "I didn't know my fame traveled so quickly."

"I see you wasted no time in arriving in the Antarctic from Colorado."

"I would have been here sooner, but I had several of your buddies' bodies to dispose of."

"Are you testing my patience, Mr. Pitt?"

The conversation was becoming inane, but Pitt egged on the U-boat commander to gain time. "No, I only wish for you to explain your weird behavior. Instead of attacking a helpless unarmed ocean research ship, you should be in the North Atlantic torpedoing impotent merchant ships."

"We ceased hostilities in April of 1945."

Pitt did not like the look of the machine gun mounted on the forward section of the conning tower and pointing in his direction. He knew time was running out and was certain the U-boat meant to destroy the *Polar Storm* and everybody on it. "And when did you launch the Fourth Reich?"

"I see no reason to carry this conversation any further, Mr. Pitt." The voice came as tonelessly as a newscaster giving a weather report in Cheyenne, Wyoming. "Goodbye."

Pitt didn't need to be poked by a sharp stick in the eye to know what was coming. He dove behind an ice hummock in the same instant the machine gun on the conning tower opened up. Bullets buzzed through the air and made strange hissing sounds as they struck the ice. He lay in a slight depression behind the hummock, unable to move. Only now did he regret wearing the NUMA turquoise Arctic gear. The bright color against the white ice made him an ideal target on which to train their sights.

From where he lay, he could look up at the superstructure of the *Polar Storm*. So close, yet so far. He began wiggling out of his Arctic suit, stripping it away until he was down to a wool sweater and woolen pants. The boots would prove too clumsy to run in, so he removed them, down to his thermal socks. The hail of bullets stopped, the gunner probably wondering if his fire had struck Pitt.

He rubbed snow on his head so his black hair would not be obvious against the white. Then he peered over a lip of the hummock. The gunner was leaning against his weapon, but the U-boat commander was looking through binoculars in Pitt's direction. After several moments, he could see the commander turn and point toward the ship. The gunner swung his weapon in the direction his captain motioned.

Pitt inhaled a deep breath and took off, sprinting across the ice, pumping his legs and zigzagging with almost the same agility he'd used many years before when playing quarterback for the Air Force Academy, only this time there was no Al Giordino to run interference for him. The ice slashed his socks and cut into his feet, but he shook off the pain.

He had dashed thirty yards before the crew of the U-boat woke up and began firing again. But their shells went high and behind him. Before they corrected and began to lead him, it was too late. He had curled around the rudder of the *Polar Storm* a second before bullets smashed into the steel, chipping the paint like angry bees.

Safe on the side of the ship away from the submarine, he slowed and caught his breath. The gangway had been pulled up and Gillespie had ordered the ship into a 180-degree turn at Full Ahead, but a rope ladder was thrown over the side. Pitt thankfully jogged along the ship as it increased speed, grasping the ladder and hoisting himself up, just as the jagged ice chunks thrown aside by the bow slid past under his stocking feet.

As soon as he reached the railing, Cox lifted him over and stood him on the deck. "Welcome back," he said, with a broad smile.

"Thank you, Ira," Pitt gasped.

"The captain would like you on the bridge."

Pitt simply nodded and padded across the deck to the ladder leading up to the ship's bridge.

"Mr. Pitt."

Turning, he said, "Yes?"

Cox nodded at the bloody footprints Pitt left on the deck. "You might ask the ship's doctor to take a look at your feet."

"I'll make an appointment first thing."

Standing out on the bridge wing, Gillespie was studying the U-boat, her black hull floating rigid amid the ice where she had surfaced. He turned as Pitt hobbled up the ladder. "You had a nasty encounter."

"It must have been something I said."

"Yes, I heard your little exchange."

"Has the commander contacted you?"

Gillespie gave a curt shake of his head. "Not a word."

"Can you get through to the outside world?"

"No. As we suspected, he's effectively jammed all satellite communications."

Pitt stared at the sub. "I wonder what's he's waiting for."

"If I were him, I'd wait until the *Polar Storm* swings around and heads toward the open sea. Then he'll have us in position for an easy beam shot."

"If that's the case," said Pitt grimly, "it won't be long now."

As if reading the U-boat commander's mind, he saw a puff of smoke from the barrel of the deck gun, instantly followed by an explosion that erupted in the ice immediately behind the icebreaker's big stern. "That was close," said Bushey, standing in front of the control console.

Evie, who was standing in the door to the bridge, had a dazed expression on her face. "Why are they shooting as us?"

"Get below!" Gillespie bellowed at her. "I want all nonessential crew, scientists, and passengers to stay below on the port side away from the sub."

Rebelliously, she snapped several shots of the U-boat with her camera before heading below to a safer part of the ship. Another explosion erupted, but with a different sound. The shell struck the helicopter pad on the stern and blew it into a tangled mass of smoking wreckage. Soon, another shell screamed through the frigid air and smashed into

the ship's funnel with a deafening crash that ripped it like an ax striking an aluminum can. The *Polar Storm* shuddered, seemed to hesitate,
and then, straining, resumed pounding through the ice.

"We're opening the gap," Cox called.

"We have a considerable way to go before we're out of range," said
Pitt. "Even then, he can submerge and pursue us beyond the ice pack."

The sub's machine gun opened up again, and its shells stitched a
pattern across the bow of the icebreaker and up the forward superstructure until they found the glass windows of the bridge and blew
them into a thousand shards. The shells tore across the bridge, smashing into anything that rose more than three feet off the deck. Pitt, Gillespie, and Cox instinctively fell and flattened themselves to the deck, but
Bushey was two seconds too slow. A bullet tore through his shoulder,
a second creased his jaw.

The U-boat's deck gun spat again. The shell struck just aft of the
bridge in the mess room, a vicious blow that smashed in the bulkhead
with a blasting impact that made the *Polar Storm* tremble from bow to
stern. The concussion smothered and reverberated all around them.
Everyone on the bridge was hurled about across the deck like rag dolls.
Gillespie and Cox had been thrown against the chart table; Bushey, already lying on the deck, was sent rolling under the shattered remains of
the control console. Pitt wound up half in and half out of the doorway
to the bridge wing.

He pulled himself erect, not bothering to count the bruises and glass
cuts. Acrid smoke filled his nostrils, and his ears rang, cutting off all
other sounds. He staggered over to Gillespie and knelt beside him. The
explosion had smashed his chest against the chart table, breaking three,
maybe four, ribs. His eardrums were bleeding. Blood also seeped from
one pant leg. The captain's eyes were open but glassy. "My ship," he
moaned softly, "those scum are destroying my ship."

"Do not move," Pitt ordered him. "You might have internal injuries."

"What in hell is happening up there?" came the voice of the chief
engineer over the only speaker still functioning. His voice was nearly
lost in the beat and roar of the engine room.

Pitt snatched the ship's phone. "We're under attack by a submarine.

Give us every bit of power you've got. We must get out of range before we're shot to scrap."

"We have damage and injuries down here."

"You'll have a lot worse," Pitt snapped, "if you don't keep us on
Full Speed."

"Jake," groaned Gillespie. "Where's Jake?"

The first officer lay unconscious and bleeding, with Cox leaning
dazedly over him. "He's down," Pitt answered simply. "Who's your next
in command?"

"Joe Bascom was my second officer, but he returned to the States in
Montevideo because his wife was having a baby. Get Cox."

Pitt motioned to the big third officer. "Ira, the captain wants you."

"Have we come completely around?" asked Gillespie.

Cox nodded. "Yes, sir, we're heading out of the ice floe on course
zero-five-zero."

Pitt gazed at the U-boat with hypnotic captivation, waiting with unblinking eyes for the next shell from the deck gun. He didn't have to
wait long. At that moment, he saw the Angel of Death streaking across
the ice. Punching through the starboard lifeboat, a large launch capable
of carrying sixty people, the shock wave sent the ship reeling convul-
sively onto her port side. The sledgehammer blast disintegrated the
lifeboat before it exploded against the bulkhead separating the boat
deck from the galley. There was a swirl of flame and smoke amid splinters and blasted railings and boat davits. Soon, the entire length of the
starboard boat deck was afire, the flames unfolding through shredded
gashes in the deck and bulkhead.

Before anyone on the bridge could recover, another projectile left the
muzzle of the sub's deck gun and screeched toward the battered icebreaker like a hysterical banshee. Then it struck in a crescendo of eruptions that nearly tore off the bow, throwing the anchor chains into the
air like pinwheels. Still the *Polar Storm* surged on.

The ship was rapidly increasing its distance from the submarine. The
machine gun on the conning tower became ineffective and went quiet.
But the gap was not widening nearly fast enough. When it became apparent to the U-boat crew there was a slim chance the icebreaker might
escape its range, they began doubling their efforts to load and fire. The

rounds were coming every fifteen seconds, but not all struck the ship. The faster pace caused several shells to miss, one flying high enough to slice off the ship's radar and radio mast.

The attack and destruction had happened so quickly that Gillespie had no time to consider surrendering the ship and saving all on board. Only Pitt knew better. The Fourth Empire was not about to allow any of them to escape. It was their intention that all would die, their bodies entombed in the icebreaker as it plunged a thousand feet to the bottom of the cold, indifferent sea.

The ice was becoming thinner the closer *Polar Storm* came to the open sea, and the battered ship lunged though the pack, smashing it beneath her bow, her engines throbbing and her propellers thrashing the cold waters. Pitt weighed the chances of heading toward the sub and ramming her, but the distance was too great. Not only would the research ship have to suffer a barrage of shells fired at point-blank range, but the U-boat would have easily dropped safely below the surface before the *Polar Storm* could reach her.

The starboard boat was little more than a pile of smoldering splinters, with the smashed remains of its bow and stern hanging from twisted davits. Smoke was billowing ominously from the jagged shell holes, but as long as the engine room remained without a mortal hit, the *Polar Storm* would plow forward. The bridge was a field of broken debris and shattered glass, decorated in places with gleaming red blood.

"Another quarter of a mile and we should be out of range!" Pitt shouted above the din.

"Steady as she goes," ordered Gillespie, painfully rising to a sitting position on the deck, his back against the chart table.

"The electronic controls are shot away," said Cox. "The rudder is locked in place, there is no control. I fear we're making a circle back toward that damned sub."

"Casualties?" asked Gillespie.

"As far as I can tell, the scientists and most of the crew are unharmed," Pitt answered. "The part of the ship in which they're riding out the fight is still untouched."

"Some fight," muttered Cox through a bleeding lip. "We can't even throw snowballs."

The sky tore apart again. An armor-piercing shell ripped through the hull and passed through the engine room, shearing electrical cables and fuel lines before crashing out the other side without exploding. None of the engine room crew was injured, but the damage was done: the big diesel engines lost their revolutions and quietly turned to a stop.

"That last hit cut and burst the fuel lines," the chief engineer's voice shouted out over the speaker.

"Can you make repairs?" asked Cox desperately.

"I can."

"How long will you need?"

"Two, maybe three, hours."

Cox looked at Pitt, who turned and stared at the U-boat. "We've bought the farm," Cox said.

"It looks that way." Pitt's voice was grave. "They can sit there and blast away at us until there's nothing but a hole in the ice. You'd better give the order to abandon ship, Dan. Maybe some of the crew and scientists can make it across the floe to the mainland and hold out in the ice cave until help arrives."

Gillespie wiped a stream of blood from his cheek and nodded. "Ira, please hand me the ship's phone."

Pitt stepped defeatedly onto the bridge wing, which looked as if it had been mangled by a scrapyard auto crusher. He gazed astern toward the Stars and Stripes, which flew defiantly. Then he looked up at the turquoise NUMA ensign that flapped in ragged concert with the breeze. Finally, he refocused his attention on the U-boat. He saw the muzzle of the deck gun flash and heard the shell shriek between the radar mast and the demolished funnel, dropping and exploding in the ice one hundred yards beyond. It was, Pitt knew, a minor reprieve.

Then a flash out of the corner of one eye and a quick glance past the U-boat. Abruptly, he exhaled a breath as a wild wave of relief swept over him at seeing a tiny trail of white smoke and flame against a blue sky.

Ten miles away, a surface-to-surface missile burst through the ice floe, arched above the horizon, reached its zenith, and then plunged unerringly downward toward the U-boat. One moment the sub was floating in the ice. The next, it was enveloped in a tremendous burst of orange, red, and yellow flame that mushroomed high into the gray overcast. The U-boat's hull split in two, the stern and bow rising skyward independent of each other. Amidships, there was a great maelstrom of fire and smoke. There was a billowing cloud of steam as a final stab of flame gushed across the ice. Then she slid under and fell to the bottom.

It all happened so quickly, Pitt could hardly believe his eyes. "She's gone," he muttered in astonishment.

The stunned silence that followed the demise of the U-boat was broken by a voice over the speaker. *"Polar Storm,* do you read me?"

Pitt snatched up the radio phone. "We read you, Good Samaritan."

"This is Captain Evan Cunningham, commander of the United States nuclear attack boat *Tucson.* Sorry we could not have arrived sooner."

" 'Better late than never' certainly applies in this case," replied Pitt. "Can you loan us your damage-control crew? We're in a bad way."

"Are you taking on water?"

"No, but we're pretty much of a mess topside, and the engine room took a hit."

"Stand by to take on a boarding crew. We'll be alongside in twenty minutes."

"Champagne and caviar will be waiting."

"Where did they come from?" asked a stunned Cox.

"Admiral Sandecker," answered Pitt. "He must have leaned on the naval chief of staff."

"Now that the U-boat is no longer jamming . . . our satellite signals," said Gillespie haltingly, "I suggest you call the admiral. He'll want a report on our damage and casualties."

Cox was tending to Bushey, who appeared to be regaining consciousness. "I'll take care of it," Pitt assured the captain. "Rest easy until we get you to sick bay and the doctor can work on you."

"How's Bushey?"

"He'll live. He has a nasty wound, but he should be back on his feet in a couple of weeks. You suffered more than anybody on board."

"Thank God for that," Gillespie gasped bravely.

As Pitt dialed NUMA headquarters in Washington, his thoughts turned to Giordino on St. Paul Island less than fifteen hundred miles away. Lucky devil, he thought. He pictured his good buddy sitting in a fancy gourmet restaurant in Cape Town with a ravishing lady in a seductive dress, ordering a bottle of vintage South African wine.

"The luck of the draw," Pitt muttered to himself on the skeleton of what was left of the bridge. "He's warm, and I'm freezing half to death."

19

"WHY IS IT DIRK gets all the choice projects?" groused Giordino. "I'll bet as we speak, he's sleeping in a warm, comfortable cabin on board the *Polar Storm* with his arms around some gorgeous female marine biologist."

He was soaked and shivering under the wind-driven sleet as he stumbled across the rocky slope toward the cave, carrying an armload of small branches he and Gunn had cut from scattered scrub brush they'd found growing around the mountain.

"We'll be warm, too, once the wood dries enough to catch fire," said Gunn. Walking slightly ahead of Giordino with his arms loaded with straggly branches almost bare of leaves, he thankfully stepped through the archway and into the tunnel. He threw his burden on the rocky floor and collapsed in a sitting position against one wall.

"I fear all we're going to do with this stuff is make a lot of smoke," Giordino murmured, removing his dripping foul-weather gear and wiping the water that had dribbled down his neck with a small hand towel.

Gunn handed Giordino a cup of the now cold coffee from the thermos, and the last of the granola bars. "The last supper," he said solemnly.

"Did Sandecker give you any idea as to when he can get us off this rock pile?"

"Only that transportation was on the way."

Giordino examined the dial of his watch. "It's been four hours. I'd like to make Cape Town before the pubs close."

"He must not have been able to charter another tilt-rotor and a pilot, or they'd have been here by now."

Giordino tilted his head, listening. He moved through the tunnel until he was standing under the archway. The sleet had fallen off to a light sprinkling rain. The overcast was breaking up, and patches of blue sky emerged between the swiftly moving clouds. For the first time in several hours, he could see far out to sea.

It was there like a flyspeck on a frosted window. As he watched, the speck grew into a black helicopter. Another mile closer, and he identified it as a McDonnell Douglas Explorer with a twin tail and no rear rotor.

"We have company," he announced. "A helicopter flying in from the northwest. Coming fast and low over the water. Looks like he's carrying air-to-ground missiles."

Gunn came and stood beside Giordino. "A helicopter doesn't have the range to fly here from Cape Town. It must have come from a ship."

"No markings. That's odd."

"Definitely not a South African military aircraft," said Gunn.

"I do not believe they're bearing gifts," said Giordino sarcastically. "Or they would have called and said to expect them."

The sound of the helicopter's turbines and rotor blades soon broke the cold air. The pilot was no daredevil, but very cautious. Flying a safe height above the cliffs, he hovered for at least three minutes while he studied the ledge that once held the tilt-rotor. Then he dropped down slowly, feeling his way through the air currents. The landing skids touched the rocky surface and the rotor blades slowly spun to a stop.

Silence then. Without the wind, the mountain slopes went quiet. After a short time lag, the big fifty-inch sliding cabin door opened and six men in black coveralls dropped to the ground. They looked as if they were carrying enough weapons and firepower to invade a small country.

"Strange-looking rescue party," said Giordino.

Gunn was already on his Globalstar phone, dialing the admiral in Washington. When Sandecker responded, Gunn said simply, "We have armed visitors in an unmarked black helicopter."

"This seems to be my day for putting out brush fires," Sandecker said caustically. "First Pitt and now you." Then his tone betrayed earnest concern. "How long can you hide out?"

"Twenty, maybe thirty, minutes," replied Gunn.

"A U.S. missile frigate is sailing at full speed toward St. Paul Island. The minute their helicopter is within range, I'll request the captain to send it aloft."

"Any idea, Admiral, how long that will be?"

There was a heavy pause, then, "Two hours, hopefully less."

"I know you tried," said Gunn quietly, a patient understanding in his voice, "and we thank you." He knew the admiral's hard shell was about to crack. "Not to worry. Al and I will be back in the office by Monday."

"See that you are," said Sandecker somberly.

"Goodbye, sir."

"Goodbye, Rudi. God bless. And tell Al I owe him a cigar."

"I will."

"How long?" Giordino asked, seeing the disquieting expression on Gunn's face and expecting the worst.

"Two hours."

"That's just peachy," Giordino grunted. "I wish someone would explain to me how those murdering slime knew we were here."

"Good question. We were part of a select group. No more than five of us knew the location where the *Madras* passengers found the black skull."

"I'm beginning to think they have an international army of finks," said Giordino.

The search party split up. Three of the armed men spread out fifty yards apart and began sweeping their way around the mountain. The other three took off in the opposite direction. It looked evident that they were going to spiral their way up the mountain until they found the tunnel.

"An hour," murmured Gunn. "It will take them the better part of an hour to stumble on the old road."

"More like five minutes," said Giordino, gesturing toward the helicopter that rose in the air. "The pilot will lead his buddies right to our doorstep."

"Think it will do any good to parley?"

Giordino shook his head. "If these guys are tied in with the bunch Dirk and I met in Telluride, they don't shake hands, hug, or give quarter."

"Two unarmed men against six loaded for bear. We need to even the odds."

"Got a plan?" asked Giordino.

"I certainly do."

Giordino gave the little man with the academic, nerdy look a bemused stare. "Is it evil, rotten, and sneaky?"

Gunn nodded, with an impish grin. "All that, and more."

THE helicopter circled the mountain nearly four times before its pilot spotted the ancient road leading to the tunnel. Informing the two search teams, one of which was far around the other side of the mountain, he hovered over the road as a guide. The first team of three men converged on the road and advanced in a line, a good twenty yards apart. It was a classic penetration pattern—the first man concentrated on the terrain ahead as the second studied the upper slope of the mountain, while the third trained his concentration on the lower side. The helicopter then moved toward the second team to guide them along the easiest path to the road.

The first team on the road negotiated the landslides and approached the giant rock Gunn and Giordino had passed earlier just outside the tunnel entrance. The lead man moved around the rock and found himself standing outside the archway. He turned and shouted to the men behind. "I've reached a tunnel," he said in English. "I'm going in."

"Be wary of an ambush, number one," the second man in line shouted back.

"If they had weapons, they'd have used them by now."

The leader disappeared around the rock. Then two minutes later, the second man did. Out of sight to the others, the third man in line was approaching the rock, when a figure quietly rose up from the rocks where he had been buried. His concentration trained on reaching the tunnel, the searcher did not notice the soft clunk of loose rock or hear the almost silent crunch of footsteps at his back. He never knew what hit him as Gunn swung a large rock with such viciousness it fractured his skull, and he dropped without a sound.

Less than a minute later, the body was completely covered and hidden under a pile of rocks. A quick look to ensure that the helicopter was still out of sight on the other side of the mountain, and Gunn was creeping around the rock. This time, though, he was armed with an assault rifle, a nine-millimeter automatic pistol, and a combat knife, and protected by a body armor vest. He had also removed the searcher's radio. Gunn's sneaky survival plan was off to a running start.

The lead man of the search team cautiously entered the tunnel, a long flashlight tucked under his armpit, lighting his path. He stepped slowly from the tunnel into the first chamber, crouched in a firing position, and pivoted his body from right to left, swinging his flashlight as he moved. All he saw was the skeleton of the old sailor, the rotting furniture, and the seal hides that hung from one wall.

He relaxed, lowered his gun, and spoke into a radio set that was clamped around his head. "This is Number One. There is nobody in the tunnel and cave except the bones of an old seaman who must have been a castaway on the island. Do you read me?"

"I read you, Number One," came the voice of the helicopter pilot, accented by the roar of the engines above and behind him. "You're certain there is no sign of the NUMA agents?"

"Believe me. They're not in here."

"Soon as Numbers Four, Five, and Six reach you, I'll conduct a search of the sea cliffs."

Number One switched off his radio. It was the last act of his life. Giordino sprang from behind the sealskins and rammed one of the ancient obsidian-tipped spears into the man's throat. There was a ghastly coughing, gurgling sound, and then silence, as the searcher crumpled to the floor of the chamber, dead.

Giordino snatched away the assault rifle almost before the man struck the ground. Quickly, he pulled the body off to the side of the tunnel portal and removed the headset radio, placing it on his own head. Next he wadded up his foul-weather gear into a ball and pressed it against the muzzle of the rifle.

"Number One," shouted a voice from the archway tunnel entrance, "what have you found?"

Giordino cupped his mouth with one hand and shouted toward the rear of the chamber. "Only an old skeleton."

"Nothing else?" The second searcher seemed reluctant to enter the cave.

"Nothing." Giordino decided to take a risk. "Come on in and see for yourself, Number Two."

As if he were a buck sniffing the air, Number Two warily entered the chamber. Giordino switched on a flashlight with the beam aimed at the intruder's eyes and shot him once in the head between the eyes, the foul-weather gear muffling the gunfire. Gunn came rushing into the chamber, assault rifle at the ready, not knowing what he would find.

"Now it's two against three," Giordino triumphantly greeted him.

"Don't get cocky," Gunn warned him. "Once the helicopter returns, we're trapped in here."

"If they buy my act as Number One like Number Two did, maybe I can play P. T. Barnum again and sucker them inside."

THE next batch of searchers were not nearly as guileless as the first. They approached on the road leading to the cave with the same degree of wariness as a postal inspector examining a possible letter bomb. While the helicopter hovered overhead, they advanced one by one, two covering their comrade, who dropped flat before covering them in a leapfrog tactic that moved them ever closer to the archway at the tunnel entrance. They were on their guard because Giordino was staying off the radio as much as possible and not responding to their calls, for fear of their wising up to a strange voice.

Gunn and Giordino stripped one of the bodies that closely matched Giordino's shoulder and waist size. After slipping into the black coveralls that were two inches longer in the sleeves and three inches in the pants length, he simply folded them back, slung the assault rifle over one shoulder, and boldly stepped outside. He spoke out of one corner of his mouth into the headset's microphone, trying to use the same pitch as had the man he'd killed.

"What's taking you so long, Number Four?" he asked, unruffled, without looking up at the helicopter. "You're acting like old women. I told you, there is nothing inside the tunnel and cave but the rotting bones of a seaman who was a castaway on the island."

"You do not sound yourself, Number One."

Giordino knew he couldn't fool them any longer. "I've got a cold coming on. Not surprising in this intolerable weather."

"Your cold must have cost you four inches in height."

"Make jokes if you will," mumbled Giordino. "I'm getting out of the rain. I suggest you do the same."

He turned and reentered the cave, certain he would not receive a bullet in the back, not until the searchers were positive they would not be shooting one of their own men.

"They're wise," said Gunn. "I heard your exchange over the radio."

"What's plan Two-A?" Giordino asked laconically.

"We crawl back through the roof collapse in the next tunnel, and ambush them from there."

"We'll be lucky to hit one or two at the most."

"At least that will put the odds in our favor," Gunn said, almost cheerfully.

They had only a few minutes, so they worked feverishly to reopen a crawl space through the rock into the tomb vault. Despite the damp cold, they were sweating heavily by the time they dragged the two dead bodies through the narrow opening and snaked in themselves, dragging their backpacks after them. Their timing was near perfect. They had no sooner propped the rocks back in place and looked into the outer chamber through tiny peepholes than Number Four leaped into the chamber and dropped to the floor as Number Five raced in just behind, both rotating their lights and their gun muzzles in swift arcs from wall to wall.

"I told you so," Giordino whispered softly in Gunn's ear, so it would not be picked up by the microphone in front of his mouth. "They left Number Six outside as reserve."

"There is no one in here," said Number Four. "The cave is empty."

"Impossible," came the voice of the helicopter pilot. "All three were approaching the tunnel not fifteen minutes ago."

"He's right," agreed Number Five. "Numbers One, Two, and Three have disappeared."

They talked in undertones, but Gunn picked up every word over his headset radios. Still on their guard and alert for any movement, they nonetheless relaxed to a small degree when they saw no possible hiding place for anyone inside the chamber.

"Take the one standing," Giordino whispered softly. "They're wearing body armor, so aim for the head. I'll take the one on the ground."

Slipping their gun muzzles into holes no larger than an inch and a half in diameter, just enough to see over the front sight, they lined up on the men who had come to kill them and squeezed off two shots in unison that sounded like a thunderclap inside the rock-walled chamber. The man on the ground merely twitched, while the one standing threw up his hands, gasped, and folded wearily over the body at his feet.

Giordino brushed away the rocks in front of his face, extended the flashlight through the hole, and studied their handiwork. He turned to Gunn and made a slashing gesture across his throat. Gunn understood and switched off his headset radio.

"We must remain where we are," Giordino muttered.

Before he could explain, a voice burst over the radio. "What happened in there?"

No longer interested in subterfuge, Giordino replied, "No big deal. We shot a rabbit."

"Rabbit?" demanded the helicopter pilot. "What sort of nonsense is that?"

"I fear our comrades are dead," said Number Six, soberly. "Those NUMA devils must have killed them."

"Those were the rabbits I was talking about," announced Giordino, adding insult to injury.

"You will surely die," said the helicopter pilot.

"As the old gangsters used to say to the cops, come and get us."

"That won't be necessary," said the pilot.

"Duck down!" Giordino hissed to Gunn. "Here it comes."

The pilot lined up the nose of his bird with the entrance of the tunnel and fired off one of his missiles. Then came a loud whoosh, as the rocket burst out of its pod attached to the fuselage of the helicopter. The rocket did not make it through the tunnel before striking against one wall and exploding. The force of the blast inside a rock-hard contained area was deafening. The concussion felt as though a grand piano had fallen on them from the tenth floor. Pulverized rock erupted in a deadly spray that sliced every object in the chamber into shreds. Smoke and dust compressed together in the small space, seethed and whirled with hurricane force, before taking the path of least resistance and funneling out the tunnel and into the atmosphere outside. Every combustible object inside the chamber immediately burst into flame.

Incredibly, neither the roofs of the tunnel nor the chamber collapsed. The main force of the explosion was blown back through the tunnel along with the smoke and dust. Giordino and Gunn felt as though huge fists had punched the air out of their lungs. Quickly reacting, they pulled the upper half of their coveralls over their faces to filter out the dust and smoke, before retreating temporarily into the inner tomb.

"I hope to God . . . they don't send another rocket in here," Gunn said, coughing. "That will spell our end for sure."

Giordino could hardly hear him above the ringing in his ears. "I have a hunch they'll think one was enough," he rasped between hacks. Slowly recovering his numbed senses, he began pulling away the rocks and widening an opening. "I'm getting damned tired of moving rock, I'll tell you."

Once through, they groped through the smoke and dust for the extra weapons from their assailants' bodies until they had five assault rifles and an equal number of automatic pistols between them. Struggling to breathe in the nonexistent air, and working blind, Giordino lashed three of the assault rifles together with cord from his backpack. The three guns were now wrapped parallel. Then he ran a cord around the triggers and tied it under the guards.

"The last thing they'll expect is for us to rush out the tunnel shooting," he said to Gunn. "You take Number Six. I'll try for the helicopter."

Gunn wiped his soiled glasses clean on his sleeve and nodded. "Better let me go first. You won't have a chance at firing at the helicopter if Number Six isn't eliminated."

Giordino was hesitant to let the little deputy director of NUMA take on an almost suicidal job. He was about to voice a protest, when Gunn raised his weapon and disappeared into the fire and smoke.

Gunn stumbled and sprawled on his chest in the tunnel, staggered to his feet and ran forward again, fearing that bullets would cut him down the second he materialized from the residue still pouring from the tunnel entrance. But Number Six was incapable of believing anyone was still alive inside, and he had let down his guard while talking with the pilot of the helicopter.

Gunn's disadvantage was that he could hardly see, and he had no idea where Number Six might be standing in relation to the archway. His glasses filmed with soot, his eyes running, he scarcely discerned a vague figure in black standing ten yards away and to the right of the archway. He squeezed the trigger and opened fire. His bullets flew wide around Number Six without striking flesh. The searcher spun around and snapped off five shots at Gunn, two missing but one striking him in the calf of his left leg, the others pounding into the body armor and sending Gunn reeling backward. Then, unexpectedly, Giordino burst through the smoke with all three guns blazing and nearly tore the head off Number Six. Without hesitation, he swung the barrels of the three guns skyward and opened up on the belly of the helicopter, sending nearly three thousand rounds a minute tearing into the thin metal.

Stunned at what he witnessed below, seeing two men in the same uniform as the searchers' shooting at each other, the pilot hesitated before taking any action. By the time he set up to fire the machine gun mounted under the nose of the M-C Explorer, Giordino was pouring a startling volume of bullets into the unarmored helicopter. As if a sewing machine were stitching a hem, the constant stream of fire moved up the side of the fuselage and sprayed through the windshield into the cockpit. Then all went silent as the rifles' ammo magazines ran empty.

The Explorer seemed to hang suspended, then it abruptly lurched, fell out of control, crashed into the side of the mountain three hundred yards below the archway, and burst into flames. Giordino dropped his rifles and rushed to the side of Gunn, who was clutching his wounded leg.

"Stay where you are!" Giordino ordered. "Do not move."

"Merely a scratch," Gunn forced through clenched teeth.

"Scratch, hell, the bullet broke your tibia. You've got a compound fracture."

Gunn looked up at Giordino through the pain and managed a tight grin. "I can't say I think a hell of a lot about your bedside manner."

Giordino didn't pay any attention to Gunn's heroics. He pulled out a lace from his shoe and made a temporary tourniquet around the thigh above the knee.

"Can you hold that for a minute?"

"I guess I'd better if I don't want to bleed to death," Gunn groaned.

Giordino ran back into the tunnel, through the smoldering chamber, and from behind the cave-in retrieved his backpack, which contained a first-aid kit. He was back in a few minutes and worked swiftly, proficiently, disinfecting the wound and doing his best to stem the flow of blood.

"I'm not even going to think about setting it," said Giordino. "Better to let a doctor do it in Cape Town." He didn't want to move the little man, so he made him as comfortable as possible and covered him from the drizzle with a plastic sheet out of his backpack. His next chore was to call the admiral, report on Gunn's wound, and beg for a quick rescue.

When he finished his conversation with Sandecker, he put the phone in his pocket and stared at the burning helicopter on the mountain slope below.

"Insanity," he said softly to himself. "Pure, unadulterated insanity. What cause can possibly motivate so many men to kill and be killed?" He could only hope the answers would come sooner rather than later.

20

"ONE HUNDRED AND SIXTY feet to the bottom," said Ira Cox, staring into the sinister hole in the ice that marked the grave of the smashed and sunken U-boat. "Are you sure you want to do this?"

"Repairs to the *Polar Storm*'s engine room and bridge by the Navy damage-control team won't be completed for another two hours," explained Pitt. "And since the ship carried Arctic diving equipment on board, I can't pass up the opportunity to investigate inside the sub's hull."

"What do you expect to find?" asked Evie Tan, who had accompanied Pitt and a small crew from the ship.

"Logbook, papers, reports, anything with writing on it that might lead to who was in command and what hidden location she sailed from."

"Nazi Germany in 1945," Cox said with a little smile, but not trying to be clever.

Pitt sat on the ice and pulled on his swim fins. "Okay, but where has she been hiding for the last fifty-six years?"

Cox shrugged and tested Pitt's underwater communication system. "Can you hear me okay?"

"You're blasting my eardrums. Turn down the volume."

"How's that?"

"Better," Pitt's voice came over a speaker set up in an operations tent beside the opening in the ice.

"You shouldn't be going alone," said Cox.

"Another diver would only get in my way. Besides, I have more than twenty dives under Arctic ice under my belt, so it's not a new experience."

In the warmth of a generator-heater in the tent, Pitt slipped on a Divex Armadillo Hot Water Suit, with internal and external tubing that circulated warm water throughout the entire body, including the hands, feet, and head. The heated water came from a combination heater and pump that forced it through an umbilical hose into the suit's inlet manifold that enabled Pitt to regulate the flow. He wore an AGA MK-II full face mask adapted to wireless communications. He elected to carry air tanks for ease of movement rather than rely on the surface support system. A quick check of his Substrobe Ikelite underwater dive light and he was ready to go.

"Good luck," shouted Evie, to make herself heard through Pitt's hood and face mask. She then busied herself shooting photos of Pitt as he sat on the edge of the ice before dropping off into the icy water. "You sure I can't talk you into taking photos with a watertight camera down there?"

Pitt gave a brief shake of his encased head as his voice came over the speaker. "I won't have time to play photographer."

He gave a wave and rolled into the water, pushing off from the ice with his finned feet. He dove and leveled out at ten feet while he vented the air from his dry suit and waited to see if its heating element was compensating for the frigid drop in temperature. A cautious diver, in all his years of diving, Pitt had rarely encountered problems underwater. He constantly talked to himself, sharpening his mind to question and probe his surroundings, and monitoring his instrument gauges and body condition.

Beneath the ice pack, which was a little over three feet thick, he found a wildly different world. Staring upward, Pitt imagined the underside of the ice as looking like the surface of an unknown planet deep in the galaxy. Transfused by the light filtering through the ice, the flat white layer was transformed into an upside-down landscape of blue-green frozen mounds and valleys covered by rolling yellow clouds of algae that were fed on by an infinite army of krill. He paused to adjust the flow of hot water before looking down and seeing a vast green void that faded to black in the depths.

It beckoned, and he dove down to be embraced by it.

THE morbid scene slowly revealed itself as if a shadowy curtain had parted as Pitt descended to the bottom. No kelp or coral or brightly colored fish here. He glanced upward at the eerie glow drifting from the ice hole above to orient himself. Then he paused a moment to switch on his dive light and probe it into the wreckage while he equalized his ears.

The remains of the U-boat were broken and scattered. The center hull beneath the conning tower was terribly ruptured and mangled by the explosion from the missile. The tower itself had been blown off the hull and was lying on its side amid a field of debris. The stern appeared attached to the keel by only the propeller shafts. The bow section was twisted but resting upright in the silt. The soft bottom had embraced the wreckage, and Pitt was surprised to see nearly twenty percent of it already buried.

"I've reached the wreck," he announced to Cox. "She's badly broken. I'm going inside the remains."

"Take great care," Cox's disembodied voice came back in Pitt's earpiece. "Cut a hole in your suit from a sharp piece of metal and you'll freeze before you reach the surface."

"Now, there's a cheery thought."

Pitt did not attempt to enter the vessel immediately. He spent nearly ten minutes of precious bottom time swimming over the wreckage and examining the debris field. The warhead had been designed to destroy a much larger target and had left the submarine almost unrecognizable as a seagoing vessel. Pipes and valves and smashed steel plates from the hull lay as if thrown about by a giant hand. He swam over body parts, passing above the grisly remains as if he were a spirit floating over the horrendous aftermath of a terrorist bus bombing.

He kicked against the current and entered the crushed hull through the massive, torn opening below the mountings where the tower once stood. Two bodies were revealed under the dive light, wedged beneath the diving controls. Fighting the bile that rose in his throat, he searched them for identification, finding nothing of value, no wallets with credit cards or picture IDs sealed in Mylar. It seemed abnormal that members of the U-boat's crew possessed no personal items.

"Eight minutes," said Cox. "You have eight more minutes before you must ascend."

"Understood." The warnings usually came from Giordino, but Pitt was deeply grateful to the big bear of a seaman for his thoughtfulness. It saved him vital seconds when he didn't have to perpetually stop and shine the light on the orange dial of his Doxa dive watch.

Moving deeper into the black of the hull, shining his light into the mass of tangled steel and pipes, he worked down a narrow passage and began examining the rooms leading off to the sides. All were empty. Ransacking the drawers and closets, he could find no documents of any kind.

He checked the air remaining in his tanks in preparation for his ascent and the required decompression stops. Then he swam into what had been the wardroom. It was badly crushed on one side of the pressure hull. The cupboard and chairs and tables attached to the deck were smashed and broken.

"Four minutes."

"Four minutes," Pitt repeated.

He moved on and found the captain's quarters. With time running out, he frantically searched for letters or reports, even diaries. Nothing. Even the sub's logbook was nonexistent. It was almost as if the wrecked sub and its dead crew were an illusion. He began to half expect it to fade and disappear.

"Two minutes." The tone was sharp.

"On my way."

Suddenly, without warning, Pitt felt a hand on his shoulder. He froze, and his slowly beating heart abruptly accelerated and pounded like a jackhammer. The contact was not exactly a tight grip; it was more like the hand was resting between his arm and neck. Beyond shock lies fear, the paralyzing, uncontrollable terror that can carry over into madness. It is a state characterized by a complete lack of comprehension and perception. Most men go totally numb, almost as if anesthetized, and are no longer capable of rational thought.

Most men, that is, except Pitt.

Despite his initial astonishment, his mind was unnaturally clear. He was too pragmatic and skeptical to believe in ghosts and goblins, and it didn't seem possible for another diver to have appeared from nowhere. Fear and terror melted away like a falling quilt. The awareness of something unknown became an intellectual awareness. He stood like an ice carving. Then slowly, carefully, he transferred the dive light and briefcase to his left hand and removed the dive knife from its sheath with his right. Gripping the hilt in his thermal glove, he spun around and faced the menace.

The apparition before his eyes was a sight he would take with him to the grave.

21

A WOMAN, A BEAUTIFUL woman, or what had once been a beautiful woman, stared at him through wide, sightless, blue-gray eyes. The arm and hand that had tapped his shoulder were still outstretched, as if beckoning. She wore the standard Fourth Empire black jumpsuit, but its material was shredded, as though a giant cat had raked its claws across it. Tentacles of flesh strayed from the openings and wafted under the gentle current. A finely contoured breast was exposed by the torn cloth, and one arm below the elbow was missing. There were insignia badges of rank on the shoulder straps, but Pitt did not recognize their significance.

The face was strangely serene and bled white by the cold water. Her features were enhanced by a mass of blond hair that rose and floated behind her head like a halo. Her cheekbones were high and her nose slightly bobbed. Her lips were loosely open, as if she were about to speak. Her blue-gray eyes seemed to be staring directly into his opaline green eyes less than a foot away. He was in the act of pushing her away as if she were a demon from the underworld, when he thought better of it and realized what he must do.

He rapidly groped through her pockets. It came as no surprise when he came up empty of identification. Next he took a thin cable from a reel that was hooked to his weight belt and tied one end around the corpse's booted foot. Then he ascended through the huge split in the U-boat's hull and headed for the dim aura of light 160 feet above.

After his decompression stops, Pitt surfaced precisely in the center of the jagged hole in the ice and swam over to the edge where Cox and several members of the crew had gathered around. Evie Tan stood nearby, shooting pictures as Pitt and his bulky dive gear were pulled from the water onto the ice by several strong arms.

"Find what you were looking for?" asked Cox.

"Nothing we can take to the bank," Pitt replied, after his mask was removed. He passed the line to Cox that led down into the water.

"Dare I ask what's on the other end?"

"I brought along a friend from the U-boat."

Evie's eyes stared at the obscure form rising from the depths. As it surfaced, the hair fanned out and the eyes seemed to be looking directly at the sun. "Oh Lord!" she gasped, her face turning as pale as the ice floe. "It's a woman!" So shocked was Evie, she neglected to shoot photos of the strange woman before she was wrapped in a plastic sheet and loaded onto a sled.

Pitt was helped off with his air tanks and gazed at the sled with the body that was being dragged by crewmen toward the *Polar Storm*. "Unless I miss my guess, she was an officer."

"A great pity," said Cox sorrowfully. "She must have been a very attractive lady."

"Even in death," Evie said, sadly, "there was an undeniable sophistication about her. If I'm any judge of character, she was a woman of quality."

"Maybe," said Pitt, "but what was she doing on a submarine that should have been destroyed five decades ago? Hopefully, she'll provide a piece of the puzzle if an identification can be made on her body."

"I'm going to follow this story to its conclusion," she said resolutely.

Pitt removed his dive fins and pulled on a pair of fur-lined boots. "You'd better check with the Navy and Admiral Sandecker. They may not want this affair leaked to the public just yet."

Evie started to voice a protest, but Pitt was already walking in the tracks of the sled back to the ship.

PITT showered and shaved, soaking up the steam in the stall before relaxing with a small glass of Agavero Liqueur de Tequila from a bottle he'd purchased when he was on a dive trip to La Paz, Mexico. Only when he had collected his thoughts in proper order did he call Sandecker in Washington.

"A body, you say," said Sandecker, after listening to Pitt's postmortem of the events following the assault on the ship. "A female officer of the U-boat."

"Yes, sir. At the first opportunity, I'll have her flown to Washington for examination and identification."

"Not easy, if she's a foreign national."

"I'm confident her history can be tracked down."

"Were any of the artifacts from the *Madras* damaged in the attack?" asked Sandecker.

"All safe and intact."

"You and everyone on board were lucky to escape without being killed."

"It was a near thing, Admiral. If Commander Cunningham hadn't shown up in the *Tucson* when he did, it would be the *Polar Storm* lying under an icy sea instead of the U-boat."

"Yaeger ran an investigation of the U-2015 through his data files. The sub was an enigma. The records indicate that she was lost off Denmark in early April of 1945. However, some historians believe she escaped the war intact and was scuttled by her crew in the Río de la Plata between Argentina and Uruguay near the site where the *Graf Spee* was blown up, but nothing has ever been proven."

"So her ultimate fate was never established?"

"No," answered Sandecker. "All that is known for sure is that she was completed in November of 1944, sent to sea, but never entered combat duty."

"What did the German navy use her for?"

"Because she was a new generation in German electrodesign, she was considered far superior to any other submarines then in service by any nation at the time. Her lower hull, which was packed with powerful batteries, enabled her to outrun most surface vessels, remain submerged for literally months, and travel great distances underwater. What little information Yaeger was able to dig out of old German military documents was that she became part of a project known as the New Destiny Operation."

"Where have I heard that term before?" Pitt muttered.

"This was a blueprint drawn up by top Nazis, in collaboration with the Perón government in Argentina, for the flow of immense wealth accumulated by the Nazis during the war. While other submarines were still maintaining combat patrols to sink Allied shipping, the U-2015 was traveling back and forth between Germany and Argentina on a mission of transferring hundreds of millions of dollars' worth of gold and silver bullion, platinum, diamonds, and art objects stolen from the great collections of Europe. High-level Nazi officials and their families were also transported along with the treasure cargo, all discharged in absolute secrecy at a remote port on the coast of Patagonia."

"This went on before the war ended?"

"Right up to the bitter end," Sandecker answered. "The story that circulated in unconfirmed reports suggests that Operation New Destiny was the brainchild of Martin Bormann. He may have possessed a fanatical adoration of Adolf Hitler, but he was smart enough to see the Third Reich crashing and burning in flames. Smuggling the Nazi hierarchy and a staggering amount of valuables to a nation friendly to Germany was his goal even before the Allied armies crossed the Rhine. His most ambitious plan was to smuggle Hitler to a secret redoubt in the Andes, but it fell through when Hitler insisted on dying in his bunker in Berlin."

"Was the U-2015 the only U-boat transporting riches and passengers to South America?" asked Pitt.

"No, there were at least twelve others. All were accounted for after the war. A few were sunk by Allied planes and warships; the rest were either turned over in a neutral country or scuttled by their crews."

"Any clues as to what happened to the money and passengers?"

"None," Sandecker admitted. "A sailor from one of the U-boats who was interviewed long after the war—he disappeared shortly after—described heavy wooden crates loaded onto trucks sitting at a deserted dock. The passengers, dressed in civilian clothes, looked and acted as if they were important personages in the Nazi party, and were hustled off in waiting cars. What happened to them or the treasure is not known."

"Argentina was a hotbed for old Nazis. What better place to recruit and organize a new world order on the ashes of the old?"

"Probably less than a handful are still alive. Any Nazi who held a high position in the party or military would have to be ninety or older."

"The plot thickens," said Pitt. "Why would a bunch of old Nazis resurrect the U-2015 and use it to destroy a research ship?"

"For the same reasons they tried to kill you in Telluride, and Al and Rudi on St. Paul Island in the Indian Ocean."

"I'm remiss for not asking about them earlier," said Pitt regretfully. "How did they make out? Did they find a chamber with the artifacts?"

"They did," Sandecker replied. "But then they narrowly missed death when their plane was destroyed before they could take off and return to Cape Town. As near as we can figure, a cargo ship sent off a helicopter with six armed men to kill any island intruders and lay their hands on whatever artifacts the passengers from the *Madras* left after their visit in 1779. Al and Rudi killed them all, as well as shooting down the helicopter. Rudi took a bullet that badly fractured his tibia. He's stable and will mend, but he'll be wearing a cast for a long while."

"Are they still on the island?"

"Just Al. Rudi was picked up about an hour ago by helicopter from a passing British missile frigate returning to Southampton from Australia. He'll soon be on his way to Cape Town for an operation in a South African hospital."

"Six killers and a helicopter," Pitt said with admiration. "I can't wait to hear their story."

"Quite astounding, when you consider they were unarmed during the initial stage of the battle."

"The Fourth Empire's intelligence network is nothing short of amazing," said Pitt. "Before the U-boat begin blasting at the *Polar Storm,* I had a brief chat with the captain. When I gave him my name, he asked how I came to be in the Antarctic after Colorado. Beware, Admiral, it pains me to say it, but I think we may have an informer in or near your NUMA office."

"I'll look into it," said Sandecker, the thought stirring him to anger. "In the meantime, I'm sending Dr. O'Connell to St. Paul Island for an on-site study of the chamber and artifacts found by Al and Rudi. I'm arranging transportation for you to meet her and oversee the removal and transportation of the artifacts back to the States."

"What about the French? Don't they own the island?"

"What they don't know won't hurt them."

"When do *I* get back to civilization again?"

"You'll be in your own bed by the end of the week. Is there anything else on your mind?"

"Have Pat and Hiram had any luck in deciphering the inscriptions?"

"They made a breakthrough with the numbering system. According to the computer's analysis of the star positions on the chamber's ceiling, the inscriptions are nine thousand years old."

Pitt wasn't sure he had heard correctly. "Did you say nine thousand?"

"Hiram dated the construction of the chamber on or about 7100 B.C."

Pitt was stunned. "Are you saying that an advanced civilization was established four thousand years before the Sumerians or Egyptians?"

"I haven't sat through a course in ancient history since Annapolis," said Sandecker, "but as I recall, I was taught the same lesson."

"Archaeologists won't be overjoyed to rewrite the book on prehistoric civilizations."

"Yaeger and Dr. O'Connell have also made headway in deciphering the alphabetic inscriptions. It's beginning to develop as some kind of record describing an early worldwide catastrophe."

"An unknown ancient civilization wiped out by a great catastrophe. If I didn't know better, Admiral, I'd say you were talking about Atlantis."

Sandecker didn't immediately reply. Pitt swore that he could almost hear the wheels turning inside the admiral's head eight thousand miles away. Finally, Sandecker spoke slowly: "Atlantis." He repeated the name as if it were holy. "Strange as it sounds, you may be closer to the mark than you think."

PART THREE

TWENTY-FIRST-CENTURY ARK

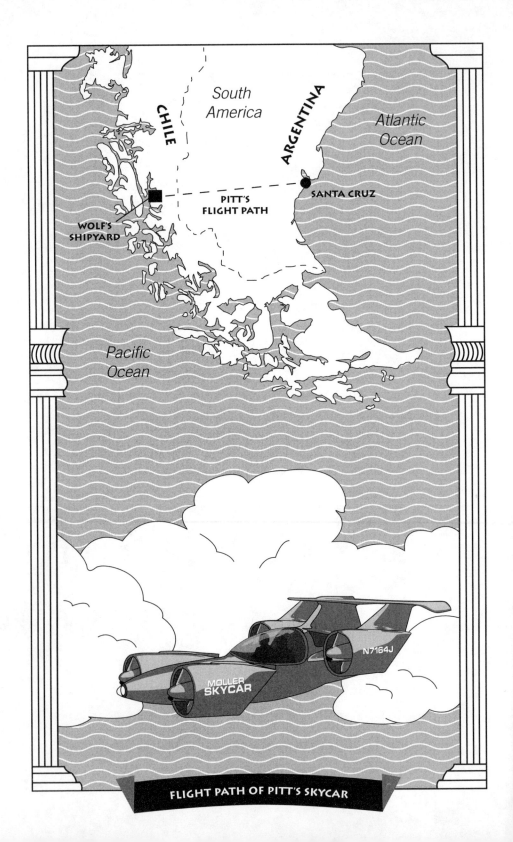

FLIGHT PATH OF PITT'S SKYCAR

22

PREMIER OPERA HOUSES THROUGHOUT the world are judged by singers and musicians for their acoustics, the quality of sound that carries from the stage to the box seats and then to the gallery far up in the stratosphere. To the opera lovers who buy the tickets, they are ranked and admired more for their elegance and flamboyance. Some are noted for their baroqueness, others for pompousness, a few for trappings and festoons. But none can hold a candle to the unmatched grandiloquence of the Teatro Colón on the Avenida 9 de Julio in Buenos Aires.

Construction began in 1890, and no expense was spared. Completed when Puccini reigned supreme in 1908, the Teatro Colón opera house stands sidewalk to sidewalk on one entire block of the city. A spellbinding blend of French art deco, Italian Renaissance, and Greek classic, its stage has felt the feet of Pavlova and Nijinsky. Toscanini conducted from its podium, and every major singer from Caruso to Callas has performed there.

The horseshoe interior is decorated on a grand scale that boggles the eye. Incredibly intricate brass molding on the upper railings, sweeping tiers with velveted chairs and gold brocaded curtains, spanned by ceilings filled with masterworks of art. On dazzling opening nights, the society elite of Argentina sweep through the foyer with its Italian marble and beautiful stained-glass dome up the magnificent stairways through the glitter to their luxuriously appointed seats.

Every seat in the house was occupied sixty seconds before the overture to the opera *The Coronation of Poppea* by Claudio Monteverdi, except for the preeminent box on the right side of the stage. That was still empty. Poppea had been the Roman emperor Nero's mistress during the glory of Rome, yet the singers wore costumes from the seventeenth century, and to rub salt in the wounds, all the male parts were sung by women. To some opera lovers, it is a genuine masterpiece; to others it is a four-hour drone.

A few seconds before the houselights dimmed, a party of one man and four women flowed unobtrusively into the remaining empty box and sat in the maroon velvet chairs. Unseen outside the curtains, two bodyguards stood alert and fashionably dressed in tuxedos. Every eye in the opera house, every pair of binoculars, every pair of opera glasses automatically turned and focused on the people entering the box.

The women were dazzlingly beautiful, not simply pretty or exotic, but shimmering beauties in the classical sense. Their matching flaxen blond hair was coiffed in long ringlets below their bare shoulders, with tightly woven braids running across a center part on top. They sat regally, delicate hands demurely laid on their laps, staring down at the orchestra pit through uniform blue-gray eyes that gleamed with the intensity of moonlight on a raven's wing. The facial features were enhanced with high cheekbones and a tanned complexion that might have come from skiing in the Andes or sunbathing on a yacht anchored off Bahía Blanca. Any one of them could have easily passed for twenty-five, although they were all thirty-five. It took no imagination to believe they were sisters; in fact, they were four of a brood of sextuplets. Enough of their body proportions could be discerned through their dresses to show that they were trim and fit from arduous exercise.

Their long, shimmering silk gowns with dyed fox trim were identical except for color. Sitting in a semicircle in the box, they radiated like yellow, blue, green, and red sapphires. They were bejeweled in a glittering display of comparable diamond chokers, earrings, and bracelets. Strikingly sensuous and sultry, they had an ethereal, untouchable goddess quality about them. It seemed unthinkable, but they were all married and each had given birth to five children. The women were attending the opening night of the opera season as a family affair, graciously nodding and smiling to the man who sat in their midst. Ramrod-straight, the male centerpiece possessed the same hair and eye color as his sisters, but there any further resemblance ended. He was as handsome as his sisters were stunning, but ruggedly so, with thin waist and hips accented by lumberjack shoulders and a weight lifter's arm and leg muscles. His face was square-cut, sporting a chin indented with a dimplelike cleft, an arrow-straight nose, and a head jungled with thick blond hair through which women dreamed of running their fingers. He was tall—at six feet six inches, he towered over his five-foot-ten-inch sisters.

When he turned and spoke to his siblings, he smiled, flashing brilliantly white teeth framed by a friendly mouth that found it impossible to turn down in a grimace. The eyes, though, showed no warmth. They stared as if they belonged to a panther gazing over the grasslands in search of prey.

Karl Wolf was a very wealthy and powerful man. The chief executive officer of a vast family-owned financial empire that stretched from China through India and across Europe over the Atlantic, and from Canada and the United States into Mexico and South America, he was stupendously rich. His personal wealth was estimated at well over a hundred billion dollars. His vast conglomerate, engaged in a multitude of scientific and high-technology programs, was known throughout the business world as Destiny Enterprises Limited. Unlike his siblings, Karl was unmarried.

Wolf and others of his family easily could have slipped into the new Argentine celebrity society. He was sophisticated, confident, and prosperous, and yet he and the other members of his family lived frugally, considering their vast fortune. But the Wolf family dynasty, consisting of, incredibly, over two hundred members, was seldom seen at fashionable restaurants or high-society functions. The Wolf women almost never made their presence known in the exclusive stores and boutiques around Buenos Aires. Except for Karl, who made a show of openness, the family remained low-profile and reclusive, and was a great mystery to Argentineans. There were no friendships with outsiders. No one, not even celebrities and high government officials, had ever cracked the Wolf family shell. The men who married the women in the family seemed to have come from nowhere and had no history. Strangely, they all took up the family name. Everyone, from the newest born to the most recently wed, carried the name of Wolf, whether male or female. They were a fraternal elite.

When Karl and his four sisters showed up on opening nights at the opera, it was a major gossip event. The overture ended and the curtains pulled open and the audience reluctantly turned their attention from the stunning and resplendent brother and sisters sitting in the premier box and gazed at the singers on the stage.

Maria Wolf, the sister sitting immediately to Karl's left, leaned over and whispered, "Why must you subject us to this terrible ordeal?"

Wolf turned to Maria and smiled. "Because, dear sister, if we didn't display the family on different occasions, the government and the public might begin to think of us as a gigantic conspiracy wrapped in an enigma. It's best to make an appearance occasionally to let them know we're not extraterrestrial aliens bent on secretly controlling the country."

"We should have waited until Heidi returned from Antarctica."

"I agree," whispered Geli, the sister on Wolf's right. "She's the only one who would have enjoyed this awful bore."

Wolf patted Geli's hand. "I'll make it up to her when *La Traviata* opens next week."

They ignored the stares of the audience, who were torn between observing the elusive Wolf family and the singing and acting on stage. The curtain for Act III had just risen when one of the bodyguards entered from the rear hall and whispered in Wolf's ear. He stiffened in his chair, the smile vanished, and his facial expression turned grave. He leaned over and spoke softly. "My dear sisters, an emergency has come up. I must go. You stay. I've reserved a private room at the Plaza Grill for a little after-show dinner. You go ahead, and I'll catch up later."

All four women turned from the opera and looked at him with controlled trepidation. "Can you tell us what it is?" asked Geli.

"We'd like to know," said Maria.

"When I know, you'll know," he promised. "Now, enjoy yourselves."

Wolf rose and left the box, accompanied by one of the bodyguards, while the other remained outside the box. He hurried out a side exit and slipped into a waiting limousine, a 1969 Mercedes-Benz 600, a car that after more than forty years still retained its reputation as the world's most luxurious limousine. The traffic was heavy, but then it was never light in Argentina. The streets were busy from late evening through to the early-morning hours. The driver steered the big Mercedes to the barrio of Recoleta, which was centered around the lush gardens of the Plaza Francia and Plaza Intendente Alvear. It was considered Buenos Aires' answer to Michigan Avenue in Chicago and Rodeo Drive in Beverly Hills, with its tree-lined boulevards featuring chic stores, exclusive hotels, and palatial residences.

The car passed the renowned Recoleta cemetery, with its narrow stone paths squeezed between more than seven thousand ornate and statued mausoleums with bands of concrete angels watching over the inhabitants. Eva Perón rests in one belonging to the Duarte family. Foreign tourists are usually amazed that her epitaph on the gate to the crypt actually reads, "Don't cry for me, Argentina. I remain quite near you."

The chauffeur turned through guarded gates, past a spectacular wrought-iron fence, and up a circular drive, stopping at the portal of a huge nineteenth-century mansion with tall colonnades and ivy-covered walls that had been the German Embassy prior to World War II. Four years after the war, the German government had moved its diplomats to a fashionable enclave known as Palermo Chico. Since then, the mansion had served as the corporate headquarters of Destiny Enterprises Limited.

Wolf exited the car and entered the mansion. The interior was anything but sumptuous. The marble floors and columns, the richly paneled walls, and the tile-inlaid ceilings were a reminder of a fabulous past, but the furnishings were sparse and any sign of elaborate decor was nonexistent. There was a white marble staircase leading to the offices above, but Wolf stepped into a small elevator concealed in one wall. The elevator rose silently and opened into a vast conference room, where ten members of the Wolf family, four women, six men, were waiting seated around a thirty-foot-long teakwood conference table.

They all stood and greeted Karl. The most astute and perceptive of his vast family, at only thirty-eight he was accepted and respected as the family's chief adviser and director.

"Forgive my tardiness, my brothers and sisters, but I came as soon as I received word of the tragedy." Then he walked over to a gray-haired man and embraced him. "Is it true, Father, the U-2015 is gone, and Heidi with it?"

Max Wolf nodded sadly. "It's true. Your sister, along with Kurt's son Eric and the entire crew, now lie on the bottom of the sea off Antarctica."

"Eric?" said Karl Wolf. "I wasn't told at the opera that he was dead, too. I did not know he was on board. Can you be certain of all this?"

"We've intercepted the National Underwater and Marine Agency's satellite transmissions to Washington," said a tall man seated across the table who could have passed for Karl's twin. Bruno Wolf's face was a mask of anger. "The transcriptions tell the story. While carrying out our plan to eliminate all witnesses to the Amenes' artifacts, our U-boat was firing on the NUMA research ship when a United States nuclear submarine arrived and launched a missile, destroying the submarine and everyone on board. There was no mention of survivors."

"A terrible loss," Karl murmured solemnly. "Two family members and the venerable old U-2015. Let us not forget that she transported our grandparents and the core of our empire from Germany after the war."

"Not forgetting the valuable service she provided over the years," added Otto Wolf, one of eight of the family's physicians. "She will be sorely missed."

The men and women at the table sat hushed. This was clearly a group who had never experienced failure. For fifty-five years, since its inception, Destiny Enterprises Limited had operated with success piled on success. Every project, every operation, was planned with detailed discipline. No contingency was overlooked. Problems were expected and dealt with. Negligence and incompetency simply did not exist. The Wolf family had reigned supreme until now. They found it nearly impossible to accept reverses beyond their control.

Wolf settled into a chair at the head of the table. "What are our losses in family and hired personnel over the past two weeks?"

Bruno Wolf, who was married to Karl's sister, Geli, opened a file and examined a column of numbers. "Seven agents in Colorado; seven on St. Paul Island, including our cousin Fritz, who directed the operation from his helicopter; forty-seven crewmen of the U-2015, plus Heidi and Eric."

"Sixty-seven of our best people and three of our family in less than ten days," spoke up Elsie Wolf. "It doesn't seem possible."

"Not when you consider the people responsible are a bunch of academic oceanographers who are little more than spineless jellyfish," Otto snarled angrily.

Karl rubbed his eyes wearily. "I might remind you, dear Otto, those spineless jellyfish killed twelve of our best agents, not including the two we were forced to eliminate to keep them from talking."

"Marine scientists and engineers are not professionnel killers," said Elsie. "Our agent working undercover at the National Underwater and Marine Agency in Washington sent me the personnel files of the men who were responsible for our dead in Colorado and on St. Paul Island. They are not ordinary men. Their exploits within NUMA read like an adventure-novel series." Elsie paused and passed several photographs around the table. "The first face you see belongs to Admiral James Sandecker, the chief director of NUMA. Sandecker is very respected among the political power elite of the United States government. After an enviable war record in Vietnam, he was personally selected to instigate and run the agency. He carries great weight among members of the American Congress."

"I met him once at an ocean sciences conference in Marseilles," said Karl. "He is not an adversary to underestimate."

"The next photo is of Rudolph Gunn, the deputy director of NUMA."

"An insignificant-looking little fellow," observed Felix Wolf, the corporate attorney for the family. "He certainly doesn't look like he has the strength to be a killer."

"He doesn't have to know how to kill with his hands," said Elsie. "As near as we can tell, he was the genius behind the loss of our search group on St. Paul Island. A graduate of the United States Naval Academy, he went on to a brilliant career in the Navy before joining NUMA and becoming Admiral Sandecker's right-hand man."

Bruno held up a third photo. "Now, this one looks like he could tear coins from your stomach and give you change."

"Albert Giordino, NUMA's assistant special projects director," explained Elsie. "A graduate of America's Air Force Academy. He served in Vietnam with distinction. Bruno is right, Giordino is known as a very tough customer. His record at NUMA is remarkable. The file on projects he has directed to successful conclusions is quite thick. He has been known to kill, and from what little information we have been able to gather, it was he, along with Gunn, who is responsible for the annihilation of our St. Paul search team."

"And the final photo," Otto prompted Elsie gently.

"His name is Dirk Pitt. Considered a legend among oceanographic circles. The special projects director for NUMA, he is known as something of a Renaissance man. Unmarried, he collects classic cars. Also a graduate of the Air Force Academy, with several decorations from Vietnam for heroism. His achievements make for heavy reading. It was he who frustrated our plans in Colorado. He was also present in the Antarctic during the sinking of the U-2015 by the American nuclear submarine."

"A great pity," said Otto in quiet anger. He looked from one face to the next around the table. "A mistake to have used *her* instead of a modern surface ship."

"A misguided attempt on all our parts," said Karl, "to confuse our enemies."

Bruno pounded the desk with his fist. "We must exact vengeance from these men. They must die."

"You ordered an assassination attempt on Pitt without the approval of the rest of us," said Karl sharply. "An attempt that failed, I might add. We cannot afford the luxury of vengeance. We have a schedule to maintain, and I do not want our attentions misdirected to petty revenge."

"I see nothing petty about it," argued Bruno. "These four men are directly accountable for the deaths of our brothers and sister. They cannot go unpunished."

Karl looked at Bruno icily. "Did it ever occur to you, dear brother, that when the New Destiny Project reaches its climax, they will all die violent deaths?"

"Karl is right," said Elsie. "We cannot afford distractions from our true purpose, regardless of how tragic they are to the family."

"The matter is settled," stated Karl firmly. "We concentrate on the work at hand and accept our grief as part of the cost."

"Now that the chambers in Colorado and St. Paul Island have been discovered by outsiders," said Otto, "I see little to be gained by continuing to expend time, money, and more lives in concealing the existence of our ancient ancestors."

"I agree," said Bruno. "With the inscriptions now in the hands of American government officials, we should stand in the shadows while they decipher the message and announce the Amenes' warning of disaster through the international news media, thereby saving us the effort."

Karl stared at the surface of the table, his expression pensive. "Our gravest concern is having the story come out too soon before the New Destiny Project is launched and the disinformation leads to our doorstep."

"Then we must muddy the waters before scientific investigators penetrate our ruse."

"Thanks to those meddling rogues from the National Underwater and Marine Agency, the world will be onto us in two weeks." Bruno gazed across the table at Karl. "Is there any chance, brother, that our people at Valhalla can move up the timetable?"

"If I explain the urgency and make them aware of the dangers arising around us, yes, I believe I can inspire them to move up the launch date to ten days from now."

"Ten days," Christa repeated heatedly. "Only ten days before the old world is destroyed and the Fourth Empire rises from the ashes."

Karl nodded solemnly. "If all goes according to the carefully laid plans of our family since 1945, we will completely alter mankind for the next ten thousand years."

23

AFTER BEING AIRLIFTED TO an ice station and flown across the western end of the Indian Ocean to Cape Town, Pitt joined Pat O'Connell, who had flown down from Washington. She was accompanied by Dr. Bradford Hatfield, a pathologist/archaeologist who specialized in the study of ancient mummies. Together, they flew to St. Paul Island by a tilt-rotor aircraft. A heavy drizzle, unleashed by hostile clouds and hurled by a stiff breeze, stung their exposed faces like pellets shot from air rifles. They were met by a team of SEALs, an elite group of fighters belonging to the United States Navy. They were big quiet men, dead set with a purpose, dressed in camouflage fatigues that matched the gray volcanic rock of the island.

"Welcome to Hell's lost acre," said a big, lanky man with a friendly smile. He was toting a huge weapon slung over one shoulder upside down. It looked like a combination automatic rifle, missile launcher, sniper rifle, and twelve-gauge shotgun. "I'm Lieutenant Miles Jacobs. I'll be your tour guide."

"Admiral Sandecker isn't taking any chances of terrorists returning," Pitt remarked, as he shook Jacobs's hand.

"He may be retired from the Navy," said Jacobs, "but he still carries a lot of weight in the upper echelons. My orders to protect you NUMA people came direct from the secretary of the Navy."

Without further conversation, Jacobs and four of his men, two in front, two bringing up the rear, led Pitt and his party up the slope of the mountain onto the ancient road leading to the tunnel. Pat was half-soaked beneath her rain gear and couldn't wait to get out of the damp. When they reached the archway, Giordino stepped out to greet them. He looked weary but swaggered as boldly as if he were the winning captain of a football team.

Pat was mildly surprised to see such rugged, staunch men greet each other with warm hugs and backslapping. There was such sentiment in their eyes, she swore they were on the verge of tears.

"Good to see you alive, pal," said Pitt happily.

"Glad you survived too," Giordino replied with a wide smile. "I hear you took on a U-boat with snowballs."

Pitt laughed. "A story greatly exaggerated. All we could do was shake our fists and call them names until the timely arrival of the Navy."

"Dr. O'Connell." Giordino bowed gallantly and kissed her gloved hand. "We needed someone like you to brighten up this dingy place."

Pitt smiled and curtsied. "My pleasure, sir."

Pitt turned and introduced the archaeologist. "Al Giordino, Dr. Brad Hatfield. Brad is here to study the mummies you and Rudi found."

"I'm told you and Commander Gunn struck an archaeological bonanza," said Hatfield. He was tall and skinny with light cork-brown eyes, a smooth narrow face, and a soft voice. He hunched over when he spoke, and peered through little round-rimmed spectacles that looked as if they had been produced in the 1920s.

"Come on in out of the rain and see for yourself."

Giordino led the way through the tunnel into the outer chamber. From fifty feet away, an overwhelming stench of smoke and charred flesh invaded their nostrils. A generator had been brought in by the SEALs, who'd laid a hose from the exhaust pipe to the archway outside to remove any fumes. Its electrical output powered an array of flood-lights.

None had expected the awesome state of devastation. The entire interior was blackened by fire and covered with soot. What few objects were lying in the chamber before the blast had been vaporized.

"What hit this place?" asked Pitt in astonishment.

"The pilot of the attacking helicopter thought it might be cute to launch a rocket through the tunnel," explained Giordino, as placidly as if he were describing how to eat an apple.

"You and Rudi couldn't have been in here."

Giordino grinned. "Of course not. There's a tunnel leading to another chamber behind this one. We were protected by a pile of rocks from an old cave-in. Rudi and I won't hear soft-spoken words for a few weeks and our lungs are congested, but we survived."

"A miracle you weren't barbecued like your friends here," said Pitt, staring down at the charred remains of the attackers.

"The SEALs are going to clean up the mess and transport the bodies back to the States for identification."

"How ghastly," murmured Pat, her face turning pale. But her professional manner quickly took over and she began running her fingers over what was left of the inscriptions on the wall. She stared in sudden sorrow at the cracked and shattered rock. "They've destroyed it," she said in a faint whisper. "Obliterated it. There isn't enough left to decipher."

"No great loss," Giordino said, unruffled. "The good stuff survived in the inner chamber without a scratch. The mummies were coated with a little dust, but other than that they're as sound as the day they were propped up."

"Propped up?" Hatfield repeated. "The mummies are not lying horizontal in burial cases?"

"No, they're sitting upright in stone chairs."

"Are they wrapped in cloth?"

"No again," replied Giordino. "They're sitting there as if they were conducting a board meeting, dressed in robes, hats, and boots."

Hatfield shook his head in wonder. "I've seen ancient burials where the bodies were wrapped tightly in gauze in coffins, in fetal positions inside clay pots, lying facedown or faceup, and in standing positions. Never have I heard of mummies sitting exposed."

"I've set up lights inside so you can examine them and the other artifacts."

During the hours Giordino was waiting for Pitt and Pat O'Connell to appear, he had enlisted the SEALs to help clear the rockfall, carry the rocks outside, and dump them down the mountain. The tunnel to the inner crypt was now open, and they could walk straight through without climbing over fallen debris. Floodlights lit the crypt even brighter than sunlight, revealing the mummies and their garments in colorful detail.

Hatfield rushed forward and began examining the first mummy's face almost nose to nose. He looked like a man lost in paradise. He went from figure to figure, examining the skin, the ears, noses, and lips. He opened a large leather folding case and removed a surgeon's metal headband that mounted a light and magnifying lens in front of the eyes. After slipping it over his head, turning on the light, and focusing the lenses, he lightly brushed the dust away from a mummy's eyelids with a soft-bristled artist's brush. The others watched in silence until he turned, lifted the headband, and spoke.

His words came as if he were giving a sermon in church. "In all my years of studying ancient cadavers," he said softly, "I have never seen bodies so well preserved. Even the eyeballs appear to be intact enough to tell the color of their irises."

"Perhaps they're only a hundred years old or less," said Giordino.

"I don't believe so. The fabric of their robes, the style of their boots, the cut and style of their head coverings and clothing is unlike any I've ever seen, certainly unlike those in historical records. Whatever their embalming methods, these people's techniques were far superior to that found in mummies I've studied in Egypt. The Egyptians mutilated the bodies to remove the internal organs of their dead, extracting the brain through the nose and removing the lungs and abdominal organs. These bodies are not disfigured inside or out. They appear virtually untouched by embalmers."

"The inscriptions we found in the mountains of Colorado were dated at nine thousand B.C.," said Pat. "Is it possible these people and their artifacts are from the same millennium?"

"Without dating technology, I can't say," replied Hatfield. "I'm out of my depth at drawing time conclusions. But I'm willing to stake my reputation that these people came from an ancient culture that is historically unknown."

"They must have been first-rate seafarers to have found this island and used it to inter their leaders," observed Pitt.

"Why here?" inquired Giordino. "Why didn't they bury their dead in a more convenient place along a continental shoreline?"

"The best guess is that they didn't want them found," answered Pat.

Pitt stared at the mummies pensively. "I'm not so sure. I think they eventually wanted them to be discovered. They left descriptive communications in other underground chambers thousands of miles apart. From what I understand, you and Hiram Yaeger have established that the inscriptions in Colorado are not messages to gods governing the land of the dead."

"That's true as far as it goes. But we have a long way to go in deciphering all the symbols and their meanings. What little we've learned until now is that the inscriptions are not of a funerary nature, but rather a warning of a future catastrophe."

"Whose future?" asked Giordino. "Maybe in the last nine thousand years, it already happened."

"We haven't determined any time projections yet," answered Pat. "Hiram and Max are still working on it." She walked over to one wall and wiped away the dust covering what looked like figures carved in the rock. Her eyes widened with excitement. "These are not the same style of symbols we found in Colorado. These are glyphs portraying human figures and animals."

Soon they were all working to remove the dust and grime of centuries from the polished rock. Beginning in the four corners of the wall, they worked toward the middle until the inscriptions were revealed in distinct detail under the bright floodlights.

"What do you make of it?" Giordino asked no one in particular.

"Definitely a harbor or a seaport," Pitt said quietly. "You can make out a fleet of ancient ships with sails and oars, surrounded by a breakwater whose ends support high towers, probably some kind of beacons or lighthouses."

"Yes," agreed Hatfield. "I can easily discern buildings around the docks where several ships are moored."

"They seem to be in the act of loading and unloading cargo," said Pat, peering through her ever-present magnifying glass. "The people are carved in meticulous detail and are wearing the same type of clothing as the mummies. One ship looks like it's unloading a herd of animals."

Giordino moved in close to Pat and squinted at the glyphs. "Unicorns," he announced. "They're unicorns. See, they only have one horn coming from the top of their heads."

"Fanciful," muttered Hatfield skeptically. "As fanciful as sculptures of nonexistent Greek gods."

"How do you know?" Pitt challenged him. "Perhaps unicorns actually existed nine thousand years ago, before they became extinct along with woolly mammoths and saber-toothed tigers."

"Yes, along with Medusas with snakes for hair and Cyclops with only one eye in their forehead."

"Don't forget gargoyles and dragons," added Giordino.

"Until bones or fossils are found that prove they existed," said Hatfield, "they'll have to remain a myth from the past."

Pitt didn't debate further with Hatfield. He turned and walked behind the stone chairs still holding the mummies and stared at a large curtain of sewn animal hides that covered the far wall. Very gently, he lifted one corner of the curtain and looked under it. His face took on a mystified expression.

"Careful," warned Hatfield. "That's very fragile."

Pitt ignored him and raised the curtain in both hands until it had curled above his head.

"You shouldn't touch that," Hatfield cautioned irritably. "It's a priceless relic and might crumble to pieces. It must be handled delicately until it can be preserved."

"What's under it is even more priceless," Pitt said in a impassive voice. He nodded at Giordino. "Grab a couple of those spears and use them to prop up the curtain."

Hatfield, his face flushed crimson, tried to stop Giordino, but he might as well have tried to halt a farm tractor. Giordino brushed him aside without so much as a sideways glance, snatched two of the ancient obsidian spears, planted their tips on the floor of the chamber, and used their butt ends to hold up the curtain. Then Pitt adjusted a pair of floodlights until their beams were concentrated on the wall.

Pat held her breath and stared at the four large circles carved into the polished wall, with strange diagrams cut within their circumferences. "They're glyphs of some kind," she said solemnly.

"They look like maps," spoke up Giordino.

"Maps of what?"

A bemused smile spread Pitt's lips. "Four different projections of the earth."

Hatfield peered through his glasses over Pat's shoulder. "Ridiculous. These glyphs don't look like any ancient maps I've ever seen. They're too detailed, and they certainly bear no resemblance to geography as I know it."

"That's because your shallow mind cannot visualize the continents and shorelines as they were nine thousand years ago."

"I must agree with Dr. Hatfield," said Pat. "All I see is a series of what might be large and small islands with jagged coastlines surrounded by wavy images suggesting a vast sea."

"My vote goes for a butterfly damaged by antiaircraft fire on a Rorschach inkblot test," Giordino muttered cynically.

"You just dropped fifty points on the gray matter scale," Pitt came back. "I thought that of all the people, I could count on you to solve the puzzle."

"What *do* you see?" Pat asked Pitt.

"I see four different views of the world as seen from the continent of Antarctica nine thousand years ago."

"All jokes aside," said Giordino, "you're right."

Pat stood back for an overall view. "Yes, I can begin to distinguish other continents now. But they're in different positions. It's almost as if the world has tilted."

"I fail to see how Antarctica fits into the picture," Hatfield insisted.

"It's right in front of your eyes."

Pat asked, "How can you be so dead sure?"

"I'd be interested in knowing how you reached that conclusion," Hatfield scoffed.

Pitt looked at Pat. "Do you have any chalk in your tote bag that you use to highlight inscriptions in rock?"

She smiled. "Chalk went out. Now we prefer talcum powder."

"Okay, let's have it, and some Kleenex. All women carry Kleenex."

She dug in her pocket and handed him a small packet of tissues. Then she fished around in her tote bag through the notebooks, camera equipment, and tools used for examining ancient symbols in rock, until she found a container of powdered talc.

Pitt spent the short wait wetting the tissue with water out of a canteen and dampening the glyphs carved on the wall so the talc would adhere in the etched stone. Then Pat passed him the talc, and he began dabbing it on the smooth surface around the ancient art. After about three minutes, he stood back and admired his handiwork.

"Ladies and gentlemen, I give you Antarctica."

All three gazed intently at the crude coating of white talc Pitt had dabbed on the polished rock and then wiped clean, outlining the etched features. It now bore a distinct similarity to the South Polar continent.

"What does all this mean?" Pat asked, confused.

"What it means," explained Pitt, gesturing toward the mummies sitting mute in their throne chairs, "is that these ancient people walked on Antarctica thousands of years before modern man. They sailed around and charted it before it was covered with ice and snow."

"Nonsense!" Hatfield snorted. "It's a scientifically proven fact that all but three percent of the continent has been covered by an ice sheet for millions of years."

Pitt didn't say anything for several seconds. He stared at the ancient figures as if they were alive, his eyes moving from one face to the next as if trying to communicate with them. Finally, he gestured toward the ancient, silent dead. "The answers," he said with steadfast conviction, "will come from them."

24

HIRAM YAEGER RETURNED TO his computer complex after lunch carrying a large cardboard box with a basset hound puppy inside that he'd saved from the city pound just hours before it was scheduled to be put to sleep. Since the family golden retriever had died from old age, Yaeger had sworn that he had buried his last family dog and refused to replace it. But his two teenage daughters had begged and pleaded for another one and even threatened to ignore their school studies if their retriever wasn't replaced. Yaeger's only consolation was that he wasn't the first father to be coerced by his children into bringing home an animal.

He had meant to find another golden retriever, but when he'd looked into the sad, soulful coffee-cup eyes of the basset and seen the ungainly body with the short legs, big feet, and ears that dragged on the floor, he'd been hooked. He laid newspapers around his desk and allowed the puppy to roam free, but it preferred to lie on a towel in the open box and stare at Yaeger, who found it next to impossible to steer his concentration away from those sad eyes.

Finally, he forced his attention on his work and called up Max. She appeared on the monitor and scowled at him. "Must you always keep me waiting?"

He reached down and held up the puppy for Max to see. "I stopped off and picked up a doggy for my daughters."

Max's face instantly softened. "He's cute. The girls should be thrilled."

"Have you made progress in deciphering the inscriptions?" he asked.

"I've pretty much unraveled the meaning of the symbols, but it takes a bit of doing to connect them into words than can be interpreted in English."

"Tell me what you have so far."

"Quite a lot, actually," Max said proudly.

"I'm listening."

"Sometime around 7000 B.C., the world suffered a massive catastrophe."

"Any idea of what it was?" inquired Yaeger.

"Yes, it was recorded in the map of the heavens on the ceiling of the Colorado chamber," explained Max. "I haven't deciphered the entire narrative yet, but it seems that not one, but two comets swept in from the far outer solar system and caused worldwide calamity."

"Are you sure they weren't asteroids? I'm no astronomer, but I've never heard of comets orbiting in parallel."

"The celestial map showed two objects with long tails traveling side by side that collide with the earth."

Yaeger lowered his hand and petted the dog as he spoke. "Two comets striking at the same time. Depending on their size, they must have caused a huge convulsion."

"Sorry, Hiram," said Max, "I didn't mean to mislead you. Only one of the comets hit the earth. The other circled past the sun and disappeared into deep space."

"Did the star map indicate where the comet fell?"

Max shook her head. "The depiction of the impact site indicated Canada, probably somewhere in the Hudson Bay area."

"I'm proud of you, Max." Yeager had lifted the basset hound onto his lap, where it promptly fell asleep. "You'd make a classic detective."

"Solving an ordinary people crime would be mere child's play for me," Max said loftily.

"All right, we have a comet crashing to the earth in a Canadian province about 7000 B.C. that caused worldwide destruction."

"Only the first act. The meat of the story comes later, with the description of the people and their civilization that existed before the cataclysm and the aftermath. Most all were annihilated. The pitiful few who survived, too weakened to rebuild their empire, saw it as their divine mission to wander the world, educate the primitive stone-age inhabitants of the era who endured in remote areas, and build monuments warning of the next cataclysm."

"Why did they expect another threat from space?"

"From what I can gather, they foresaw the return of the second comet that would finish the job of complete destruction."

Yaeger was nearly speechless. "What you're suggesting, Max, is that there really was a civilization called Atlantis?"

"I didn't say that," Max stated irritably. "I haven't determined what these ancient people called themselves. I do know that they only vaguely resembled the tale passed down from Plato, the famed Greek philosopher. His record of a conversation that took place two hundred years before his time, between his ancestor, the great Greek statesman Solon, and an Egyptian priest, is the first written account of a land called Atlantis."

"Everyone knows the legend," said Yaeger, his thoughts spinning into space. "The priest told of an island continent larger than Australia that rose in the middle of the Atlantic Ocean west of the Pillars of Hercules, or the Strait of Gibraltar, as we know it today. Several thousand years ago, it was destroyed and sank beneath the sea after a great upheaval, and vanished. A riddle that has puzzled believers, and is scoffed at by historians to this day. Personally, I tend to agree with historians that Atlantis is nothing more than an early saga of science fiction."

"Perhaps it was not a total fabrication after all."

Yaeger stared at Max, his eyebrows pinched. "There is absolutely no geological basis for a lost continent to have disappeared in the middle of the Atlantic Ocean nine thousand years ago. It never existed. Certainly not between North Africa and the Caribbean. It's now generally accepted that the legend is linked to a catastrophic earthquake and flood caused by a volcanic eruption that took place on the island of Thera, or Santorini as it is known today, and wiped out the great Minoan civilization on Crete."

"So you think Plato's portrait of Atlantis, in his works *Critias* and *Timaeus,* is an invention."

"Not portrait, Max," Yaeger lectured the computer. "He told the story in dialogue, a popular genre in ancient Greece. The story is not related in the third person by the author, but presented to the reader by two or more narrators, one who questions the other. And, yes, I believe Plato invented Atlantis, knowing with glee that future generations would swallow the con, write a thousand books on the subject, and debate it endlessly."

"You're a hard man, Yaeger," said Max. "I assume you don't believe in the predictions of Edgar Cayce, the famous psychic."

Yaeger shook his head slowly. "Cayce claimed he saw Atlantis fall and rise in the Caribbean. If an advanced civilization had ever existed in that region, the hundreds of islands would have produced clues. But to date not so much as a potsherd of an ancient culture has been found."

"And the great stone blocks that form an undersea road off Bimini?"

"A geological formation that can be found in several other parts of the seas."

"And the stone columns that were found on the seafloor off Jamaica?"

"It was proven they were barrels of dry concrete that solidified in water after the ship carrying them as cargo sank and the wooden staves eroded away. Face facts, Max. Atlantis is a myth."

"You're an old poop, Hiram. You know that?"

"Just telling it like it is," said Yaeger testily. "I prefer not to believe in an ancient advanced civilization that some dreamers believe had rocket ships and garbage disposals."

"Ah," Max said sharply, "there lies the rub. Atlantis was not one vast city populated by Leonardo da Vincis and Thomas Edisons and surrounded by canals on an island continent, as Plato described it. According to what I'm finding, the ancient people were a league of small seafaring nations who navigated and mapped the entire world four thousand years before the Egyptians raised the pyramids. They conquered the seas. They knew how to use currents, and developed a vast knowledge of astronomy and mathematics that made them master navigators. They developed a chain of coastal city-ports and built a trading empire by mining and transporting mineral ore they transformed into metals, unlike other people of the same millennium who lived at higher elevations, led a nomadic existence, and survived the disaster. The seafarers had the bad luck to be destroyed by the giant tidal waves and were lost without a trace. Whatever remains of their port cities now lies deep underwater and buried beneath a hundred feet of silt."

"You deciphered and collected all that data since yesterday?" asked Yaeger in undisguised astonishment.

"The grass," Max pontificated, "does not grow under my feet, nor, I might add, do I sit around and wait for my terminal innards to rust."

"Max, you're a virtuoso."

"It's nothing really. After all, it was you who built me."

"You've given me so much to contemplate, I can't digest it all."

"Go home, Hiram. Take your wife and daughters to a movie. Get a good night's sleep while I sizzle my chips. Then, when you sit down in the morning, I'll really have information that will curl your ponytail."

25

AFTER PAT HAD PHOTO-RECORDED the inscriptions and the strange global maps inside the burial chamber, she and Giordino were airlifted to Cape Town, where they met with Rudi Gunn in the hospital soon after his operation. Causing a scene bordering on an uproar, Gunn ignored the orders of the hospital staff and enlisted Giordino to smuggle him on an airplane out of South Africa. Giordino gladly complied, and with Pat's able assistance sneaked the tough little NUMA director past the doctors and nurses through the utility basement of the hospital and into a limousine, before speeding to the city airport, where a NUMA executive jet was waiting to fly them all back to Washington.

Pitt remained behind with Dr. Hatfield and the Navy SEAL team. Together, they carefully packed the artifacts and directed their airlift by helicopter to a NUMA deep-ocean research ship that had been detoured to St. Paul Island. Hatfield hovered over the mummies, delicately wrapping them in blankets from the ship and carefully arranging them in wooden crates for the journey to his lab at Stanford University for in-depth study.

After the last mummy had been loaded onto the NUMA helicopter,

Hatfield accompanied them and the artifacts on the short flight to the ship. Pitt turned and shook hands with Lieutenant Jacobs. "Thank you for your help, Lieutenant, and please thank your men for me. We'd have never done it without you."

"We don't often get an assignment chaperoning old mummies," Jacobs said, smiling. "I'm almost sorry the terrorists didn't try and snatch them from us."

"I don't think they were terrorists, in the strict sense of the word."

"A murderer is a murderer by any other name."

"Are you headed back to the States?"

Jacobs nodded. "We've been ordered to escort the bodies of the attackers, so ably dispatched by your friends, to Walter Reed Hospital in D.C. for examination and possible identification."

"Good luck to you," said Pitt.

Jacobs threw a brief salute. "Maybe we'll meet again somewhere."

"If there is a next time, I hope it's on a beach in Tahiti."

Pitt stood in the never-ending drizzle and watched as a Marine Osprey tilt-rotor aircraft hung in the air above the ground, and the Marines climbed on board. He was still standing there when the plane disappeared into a low cloud. He was now the only man on the island.

He walked back into the now-empty burial chamber and took one final look at the global charts etched into the far wall. The floods had been removed, and he beamed a flashlight on the ancient nautical charts.

Who were the ancient cartographers who'd drawn such incredibly accurate maps of the earth so many millennia ago? How could they have charted Antarctica when it was not buried under a massive blanket of ice? Could the southern polar continent have possessed a warmer climate several thousand years ago? Could it have been habitable for humans?

The picture of an ice-free Antarctica wasn't the only incongruity. Pitt had not mentioned it to the others, but he was disturbed by the position of the other continents and Australia. They were not where they were supposed to be. It appeared to him that the Americas, Europe, and Asia were shown almost two thousand miles farther north than they should be. Why had the ancients, who otherwise calculated the shore-

lines with such exactness, have placed the continents so far off their established locations in relation to the circumference of the earth? The
observation puzzled him.

The seafarers clearly had a scientific ability that went far beyond the
cultural races and civilizations that followed them. Their era also appeared more advanced in the art of writing and communication than
others that came thousands of years later. What message were they
trying to pass on across the constantly moving sea of time that was im-
perishably engraved in stone? A message of hope, or a warning of natural disasters to come?

The thoughts running through Pitt's mind were interrupted as the
sounds of rotor blades and engine exhaust echoed through the tunnel,
announcing the return of the helicopter that was to carry him to the research ship. With a sense of reluctance, he turned off his mind at the
same instant he switched off the flashlight and walked from the dark
chamber.

WITHOUT wasting time waiting for government transportation, Pitt
flew from Cape Town to Johannesburg, where he caught a South
African Airlines flight to Washington. He slept most of the way, taking
a short walk to stretch his legs when the plane landed in the Canary Islands to refuel. When he stepped out of the Dulles Airport terminal, it
was nearly midnight. He was pleasantly surprised to find a dazzling
1936 Ford cabriolet hot rod with the top down, waiting at the curb. The
car looked like something out of California in the 1950s. The body
and fenders were painted in metallic plum maroon that sparkled under
the lights of the terminal. The bumpers were the ribbed type from a
1936 De Soto. Ripple moon disks covered the wheel in front, while
those in the rear were hidden by teardrop skirts. The seats in front and
in the rumble seat were a biscuit-tan leather. The elegant little car was
powered by a V-8 flathead engine that had been rebuilt from top to bottom to produce 225 horsepower. The rear end was fitted with a fifty-
year-old Columbia overdrive gear system.

If the car wasn't enough to turn heads, the woman sitting behind the
wheel was equally beautiful. The long cinnamon hair was protected

from the light breeze outside the airport by a colorful scarf. She had the prominent cheekbones of a fashion model, enhanced by full lips and a short, straight nose and charismatic violet eyes. She was wearing an alpaca chunky autumn leaf brown turtleneck with taupe wool tweed pants under a taupe shearling coat that came down to her knees.

Congresswoman Loren Smith of Colorado flashed an engaging smile. "How many times have I met you like this and said, 'Welcome home, sailor'?"

"At least eight that I can think of," said Pitt, happy that his romantic love of many years had taken the time out of her busy schedule to pick him up at the airport in one of the cars from his collection.

He threw his duffel bag into the rumble seat, then slid into the passenger's seat and leaned over and kissed her, holding her in his arms for a long while. When he finally pulled back and released her, she gasped, catching her breath, "Careful, I don't want to end up like Clinton."

"The public applauds affairs by female politicians."

"That's what you think," Loren said, pressing the ignition lever on the steering column and pushing the starter button. It fired on the first rotation and emitted a mellow, throaty roar through the Smitty mufflers and dual exhaust pipes. "Where to, your hangar?"

"No, I'd like to drop by NUMA headquarters for a moment and check my computer for the latest word from Hiram Yaeger on a program we're working on."

"You must be the only single man in the country who doesn't have a computer in his apartment."

"I don't want one around the house," he said seriously. "I have too many other projects going without wasting time surfing the Internet and answering E-mail."

Loren pulled away from the curb and steered the Ford onto the broad highway leading into the city. Pitt sat silent and was still lost in thought when the Washington monument came into view, illuminated by the lights at its base. Loren knew him well enough to flow with the current. It was only a question of a few minutes before he came back down to earth.

"What's new in Congress?" he asked finally.

"As if you cared," she replied indifferently.

"Boring as that?"

"Budget debates don't exactly make a girl horny." Then her voice took on a softer tone. "I heard that Rudi Gunn was shot up pretty badly."

"The surgeon in South Africa, who specializes in bone reconstruction, did an excellent job. Rudi will be limping for a few months, but that won't stop him from directing NUMA operations from behind his desk."

"Al said you had a rough time in the Antarctic."

"Not as rough as they had it on a rock that makes Alcatraz Island look like a botanical garden."

He turned to her with a reflective look in his eyes and said, "You're on the International Trade Relations Committee?"

"I am."

"Are you familiar with any large corporations in Argentina?"

"I've traveled there on a few occasions and met with their finance and trade ministers," she answered. "Why do you ask?"

"Ever hear of an outfit calling itself the New Destiny Company or Fourth Empire Corporation?"

Loren thought a moment. "I once met the CEO of Destiny Enterprises during a trade mission in Buenos Aires. If I remember correctly, his name was Karl Wolf."

"How long ago was that?" Pitt asked.

"About four years."

"You've got a good memory for names."

"Karl Wolf was a handsome and stylish man, a real charmer. Women don't forget men like that."

"If that's the case, why do you still hang around me?"

She glanced over and gave him a provocative smile. "Women are also drawn to earthy, coarse, and carnal men."

"Coarse and carnal, that's me." Pitt put his arm around her and bit her earlobe.

She tilted her head away. "Not when I'm driving."

He gave her right knee an affectionate squeeze and relaxed in the seat, looking up at the stars that twinkled in the brisk spring night through the branches of the trees that flashed overhead, their new leaves just beginning to spread. Karl Wolf. He turned the name over in his head. A good German name, he decided. Destiny Enterprises was worth looking into, even if it might prove to be a dead end.

Loren drove smoothly, deftly passing the few cars that were still on the road that time of morning, and turned into the driveway leading to the NUMA headquarters building's underground parking. A security guard stepped out of the guardhouse, recognized Pitt, and waved him through, lingering to admire the gleaming old Ford. There were only three other cars on the main parking level. She stopped the Ford next to the elevators and turned off the lights and engine.

"Want me to come up with you?" Loren asked.

"I'll only be a few minutes," Pitt said, stepping from the car.

He took the elevator to the main lobby, where it automatically stopped and he had to sign in with the guard at the security desk, surrounded by an array of TV monitors viewing different areas of the building.

"Working late?" the guard asked pleasantly.

"Just a quick stop," Pitt remarked, fighting off a yawn.

Before taking the elevator up to his office, Pitt stepped off on the tenth floor on a hunch. True to his intuition, Hiram Yaeger was still burning the midnight oil. He looked up as Pitt entered his private domain, eyes red from lack of sleep. Max was staring out of her cyberland.

"Dirk," he muttered, rising from his chair and shaking hands. "I didn't expect you to come wandering in this time of night."

"Thought I'd see what you and Dr. O'Connell had raked from the dirt of antiquity," he said genially.

"I hate banal metaphors," said Max.

"That's enough from you," Yaeger said in mock irritation. Then he said to Pitt, "I left a printed report of our latest findings on Admiral Sandecker's desk as of ten o'clock this evening."

"I'll borrow it and return it first thing in the morning."

"Don't rush. He's meeting with the director of the National Oceanic and Atmospheric Agency until noon."

"You should be home with your wife and daughters," said Pitt.

"I was working late with Dr. O'Connell," said Yaeger, rubbing his tired eyes. "You just missed her."

"She came in and went to work without resting up after her trip?" Pitt asked in surprise.

"A truly remarkable woman. If I weren't married, I'd throw my hat in her ring."

"You always had a thing for academic women."

"Brains over beauty, I always say."

"Anything you can tell me before I wade through your report?" Pitt queried.

"An amazing story," said Yaeger, almost wistfully.

"I'll second that," Max added.

"This is a private conversation," Yaeger said testily to Max's image before he closed her down. He stood up and stretched. "What we have is an incredible story of a seafaring race of people who lived before the dawn of recorded history, and who were decimated after a comet struck the earth, causing great waves that engulfed the city ports that they had built in almost every corner of the globe. They lived and died in a forgotten age and a far different world than we know today."

"When I last talked to the admiral, he didn't rule out the legend of Atlantis."

"The lost continent in the middle of the Atlantic doesn't fit into the picture," Yaeger said seriously. "But there is no doubt that a league of maritime nations existed whose people had extensively sailed every sea and charted every continent." He paused and looked at Pitt. "The photos Pat took of the inscriptions inside the burial chamber and the map of the world are in the lab. They should be ready for me to scan into the computer first thing in the morning."

"They show placements of the continents far different than an Earth of the present," Pitt said contemplatively.

Yaeger's bloodshot eyes stared thoughtfully. "I'm beginning to sense that something more catastrophic than a comet strike took place. I've scanned the geological data my people have accumulated over the past ten years. The Ice Age ended quite abruptly in conjunction with a wild fluctuation of the sea. The sea level is over three hundred feet higher than it was nine thousand years ago."

"That would put any building or relics of the Atlanteans quite deep under the coastal waters."

"Not to mention deeply buried in silt."

"Did they call themselves Atlanteans?" asked Pitt.

"I doubt they knew what the word meant," replied Yaeger. "Atlantis is Greek and means daughter of Atlas. Because of Plato, it's become known through the ages as the world before history began, or what is called an antediluvian civilization. Today, anyone who can read, and most who don't, have a knowledge of Atlantis. Everything from resort hotels, technology and finance companies, retail stores, and swimming pool manufacturers to a thousand products including wines and food brands carry the name Atlantis. Countless articles and books have been written about the lost continent, as well as its being a subject of television and motion pictures. But until now, only those who believed in Santa Claus, UFOs, and the supernatural thought it was more than simply a fictional story created by Plato."

Pitt walked to the doorway and turned back. "I wonder what people will say," he said wistfully, "when they find out such a civilization actually existed."

Yaeger smiled. "Many of them will say I told you so."

WHEN Pitt left Yaeger and exited the elevator to the executive offices of NUMA, he couldn't help noticing that the lights in the hallway leading to Admiral Sandecker's suite were dimmed to their lowest level. It seemed strange they were still switched on, but he figured there could be any number of reasons for the faint illumination. At the end of the hallway, he pushed the glass door open into the anteroom outside the admiral's inner office and private conference room. As he stepped inside and walked past the desk occupied by Julie Wolff, the admiral's secretary, he smelled the distinctive fragrance of orange blossoms.

He paused in the doorway and groped for the light switch. In that instant, a figure leaped from the shadows and ran at Pitt, bent over at the waist. Too late, he stiffened as the intruder's head rammed square into his stomach. He stumbled backward, staying on his feet but doubling over, the breath knocked out of him. He made a grab at his assailant as they spun, but Pitt was caught by surprise, and his arm was easily knocked away.

Gasping for breath, with one arm clutching his midsection, Pitt found the light and switched it on. One quick glance at Sandecker's desk and he knew the intruder's mission. The admiral was fanatical about keeping a clean desk. Papers and files were put carefully in a drawer each evening before he left for his Watergate apartment. The surface was empty of Yaeger's report on the ancient seafarers.

His stomach feeling as if it had been tied in a huge knot, Pitt ran to the elevators. The one with the thief was going down; the other elevator was stopped on a floor below. He frantically pushed the button and waited, taking deep breaths to get back on track. The elevator doors spread and he jumped in, pressing the button for the parking lot. The elevator descended quickly without stopping. Thank God for Otis elevators, Pitt thought.

He was through the doors before they opened fully and ran to the hot rod just as a pair of red taillights vanished up the exit ramp. He threw open the driver's door, pushed Loren to one side, and started the engine.

Loren looked at him questioningly. "What's the emergency?"

"Did you see the man who just took off?" he asked, as he depressed the clutch, shifted gears, and stomped the accelerator pedal.

"Not a man, but a woman wearing an expensive fur coat over a leather pantsuit."

Loren *would* notice such things, Pitt thought, as the Ford's engine roared and the tires left twin streaks of rubber on the floor of the parking garage amid a horrendous squealing noise. Shooting up the ramp, he hit the brakes and skidded to a stop at the guardhouse. The guard was standing beside the driveway, staring off into the distance.

"Which way did they go?" Pitt shouted.

"Shot past me before I could stop them," the security guard said dazedly. "Turned south onto the parkway. Should I call the police?"

"Do that!" Pitt snapped, as he slung the car out onto the street and headed for the Washington Memorial Parkway only a block away. "What kind of car?" he tersely asked Loren.

"A black Chrysler 300M series with a three-point-five-liter, 253-horsepower engine. Zero to fifty miles an hour in eight seconds."

"You know its specifications?" he asked dumbly.

"I should," Loren answered briefly. "I own one, have you forgotten?"

"It slipped my mind in the confusion."

"What's the horsepower of this contraption?" she shouted above the roar of the flathead engine.

"About 225," Pitt replied, back-shifting and throwing the hot rod into a four-wheel drift upon entering the parkway.

"You're outclassed."

"Not when you consider we weigh almost a thousand pounds less," Pitt said calmly, as he pushed the Ford through the gears. "Our thief may have a higher top-end speed and handle tighter in the turns, but I can out-accelerate her."

The modified flathead howled as the rpms increased. The needle of the speedometer on the dashboard behind the steering wheel was approaching ninety-five when Pitt flicked the switch to the Columbia rear end and pushed the car into overdrive. The engine revolutions immediately dropped off as the car accelerated past the hundred-mph mark.

Traffic was light at one o'clock in the morning on a weekday, and Pitt soon spotted the black Chrysler 300M under the bright overhead lights of the parkway and began to overhaul it. The driver was traveling twenty miles an hour over the speed limit, but not pushing the sleek car anywhere near its potential speed. The driver moved into the empty right-hand lane, seemingly more intent on avoiding the police than worried about the possibility of a car pursuing her from the NUMA building.

When the Ford was within three hundred yards of the newer car, Pitt began to slow down, tucking in behind slower-moving cars, attempting to remain out of sight. He began to feel supremely self-confident, thinking his quarry hadn't noticed him, but then the Chrysler swung a hard turn onto the Francis Scott Key bridge. Reaching the other side of the Potomac River, it cut a tight left turn and then a right into the residential section of Georgetown, fishtailing around the corner, the tires screeching in protest.

"I think she's on to you," said Loren, shivering from the cold wind sweeping around the windshield.

"She's smart," Pitt muttered in frustration at losing the game. He gripped the old banjo-style steering wheel and swung it to its stop, throwing the Ford into a ninety-degree turn. "Instead of speeding away in a straight line, she's taking every corner in hopes of gaining enough distance until she can turn without us seeing which direction she took."

It was a cat-and-mouse game, the Chrysler pulling ahead out of the turns, the sixty-five-year-old hot rod regaining the lost yardage through its greater acceleration. Seven blocks, and still the cars were an equal distance apart, neither one gaining or closing the gap.

"This is a new twist," muttered Pitt, grimly clutching the wheel.

"What do you mean?"

He glanced at her, grinning. "For the first time I can remember, I'm the one who's doing the pursuing."

"This could go on all night," said Loren, clutching the door handle as if ready to eject in case of an accident.

"Or until one of us runs out of gas," Pitt shot back in the middle of a hard turn.

"Haven't we already circled this block once?"

"We have."

Whipping around the next corner, Pitt could see the brake lights of the Chrysler suddenly flash on as it came to an abrupt halt in front of a brick town house, one of several on the tree-lined block. He braked and skidded to a stop in the street alongside the Chrysler, just as the driver vanished through the front door.

"Good thing she gave up the chase when she did," Loren said, pointing to the steam that was rising above the hood around the radiator.

"She wouldn't have quit unless it's a setup," said Pitt, staring at the darkened town house.

"What now, Sheriff? Do we call off the posse?"

Pitt gave Loren a crafty look. "No, you're going up and knock on the door."

She looked back at him, her face aghast under the glow of a nearby streetlight. "Like hell I will."

"I thought you'd refuse." He opened the door and stepped from the car. "Here's my Globalstar phone. If I'm not back in ten minutes, call the police and then alert Admiral Sandecker. At the slightest noise or movement in the shadows, get out—and get out quick. Understand?"

"Why don't we call the police now and report a burglary?"

"Because I want to be there first."

"Are you armed?"

His lips broke into a wide grin. "Who ever heard of carrying a weapon in a hot rod?" He opened the glove box and held up a flashlight. "This will have to do." Then he leaned into the car, kissed her, and merged into the darkness surrounding the house.

Pitt didn't use the flashlight. There was enough ambient light from the city and the streetlights for him to see his way along a narrow stone sidewalk to the rear of the house. It seemed hauntingly dark and silent. From what he could see, the yard was well maintained and groomed. High brick walls covered with vines of ivy separated this house from the ones on either side. They also looked dark, their occupants blissfully sleeping in their beds.

Pitt was ninety-nine percent sure the house had a security system, but as long as there were no bloodthirsty dogs, he ignored any attempt at stealth. He was hoping the thief and her pals would show themselves. Only then would he worry about which way to jump. He came to the back door and was surprised to find it wide open. Belatedly, he realized the thief had dashed into the front of the house and out the rear. He took off running for the garage that backed onto an alley.

Abruptly, the night silence was shattered by the loud roar of a motorcycle's exhaust. Pitt tore open the door to the garage and rushed inside. The old-fashioned rear doors had been swung outward on their hinges. A figure in a black fur coat over leather pants and boots had urged the motorcycle engine into life, and was in the act of shifting it into gear and turning the throttle grip when Pitt took a running leap and threw himself on the bike rider's back, circling his arms around the neck and falling off to the side, dragging his opponent with him.

Pitt knew immediately that Loren's observations were confirmed. The body was not heavy enough for a man, nor did it feel hard. They crashed to the concrete floor of the garage, Pitt falling on top. The motorcycle dropped onto its side and raced around in a full circle, rear wheel and tire screaming against the concrete floor before the kill switch cut in and the engine stopped. The momentum carried the motorcycle against the crumpled bodies on the floor, the front tire striking the head of the rider as the handlebars impacted with Pitt's hip, breaking no bones but giving him a huge bruise that would show for weeks.

He rose painfully to his knees and found the flashlight, still beaming in the doorway where he had dropped it. He crawled over, picked it up, and swept the beam over the inert body beside the motorcycle. The rider had not had time to slip on a helmet, and a head with long blond hair was exposed. He rolled her over onto her back and beamed the light onto her face.

A knot was beginning to form above one eyebrow, but there was no mistaking the features. The front tire of the bike had knocked her senseless, but she was alive. Pitt was stunned, so much so that he nearly dropped the flashlight from a hand that had never trembled until now.

It is a proven fact in the medical profession that blood cannot run cold, not unless ice water is injected into the veins. But Pitt's felt as though his heart were working overtime to pump blood that was two degrees below freezing. He swayed on his knees in shock, the atmosphere in the garage suddenly turning heavy with a heavy sense of horror. Pitt was no stranger to the person who lay unconscious beneath him.

Without the slightest question in his mind, he was looking at the same face he had seen on the dead woman who had tapped his shoulder on the sunken hulk of the U-boat.

26

UNLIKE MOST HIGH-LEVEL government officials or corporate executive officers, Admiral James Sandecker always arrived for a meeting first. He preferred to be settled in with his data files and prepared to direct the conference in an efficient manner. It was a practice he had established when commanding fleet operations in the Navy.

Although he had a large conference room at his disposal for visiting dignitaries, scientists, and government officials, he favored a smaller workroom next to his office for private and close-knit meetings. The room was a shelter within a shelter for him, restful and mentally stimulating. A twelve-foot conference table stretched across a turquoise carpet, surrounded by plush leather chairs. The table had been crafted from a piece of the hull from a nineteenth-century schooner that had lain deep beneath the waters of Lake Erie. The richly paneled mahogany wall displayed a series of paintings depicting historic naval sea battles.

Sandecker ran NUMA like a benevolent dictator, with a firm hand, and loyal to his employees to a fault. Personally picked by a former president to form the National Underwater & Marine Agency from scratch, he had built a far-reaching operation with two thousand employees that scientifically probed into every peak and valley under the seas. NUMA was highly respected around the world for its scientific projects, and its budget requests were rarely denied by Congress.

An exercise fanatic, he maintained a sixty-two-year-old body that knew no fat. He stood a few inches over five feet and stared through hazel eyes surrounded by flaming red hair and a Vandyke beard. An occasional drinker, mostly at Washington dinner parties, his only major sin was a fondness for elegant cigars, grand and aromatic, that were personally selected and wrapped to his exacting specifications by a small family in the Dominican Republic. He never offered one to visitors, but was irritated and frustrated to extremes because he often caught Giordino smoking the exact same cigars and yet could never find any of his private stock missing.

He was sitting at the end of the table, and stood as Pitt and Pat O'Connell stepped into the room. He stepped forward and greeted Pitt like a son, shaking his hand while gripping a shoulder. "Good to see you."

"Always a pleasure to be back in the fold again," Pitt replied, beaming. The admiral was like a second father to him, and they were very close.

Sandecker turned to Pat. "Please sit down, Doctor. I'm anxious to hear what you and Hiram have for me."

Giordino and Yeager soon joined the others, followed by Dr. John Stevens, a noted historian and author of several books on the study and identification of ancient artifacts. Stevens was an academic and looked the part, complete with a sleeveless sweater under a wool sport coat that had a meerschaum pipe protruding from the breast pocket. He had a way of cocking his head like a robin listening for a worm under the sod. He carried a large plastic ice chest, which he set beside his chair on the carpet.

Sandecker set the sawed-off base of an eight-inch shell casing form a naval gun in front of him as an ashtray and lit up a cigar. He stared at Giordino, half expecting his projects specialist to light up, too. Giordino decided not to irritate his boss and did his best to look cultured.

Pitt could not help noticing that Yaeger's and Pat's faces seemed unduly strained and tired.

Sandecker opened the discussion by asking if they'd all had a chance to go over the report from Pat and Yaeger. All nodded silently, except Giordino. "I found it interesting reading," he said, "but as science fiction it doesn't measure up to Isaac Asimov or Ray Bradbury."

Yaeger gave Giordino a steady gaze. "I assure you, this is not science fiction."

"Have you discovered what this race of people called themselves?" asked Pitt. "Did their civilization have a name besides Atlantis?"

Pat opened a file on the desk in front of her and pulled out a sheet of notebook paper and peered at the writing. "As near as I can decipher and translate into English, they referred to their league of seafaring city-states as Amenes, pronounced 'Ameenees.'"

"Amenes," Pitt repeated slowly. "It sounds Greek."

"I unraveled a number of words that could well be the origins for later Greek- and Egyptian-language terms."

Sandecker gestured the end of his cigar at the historian. "Dr. Stevens, I assume you've examined the obsidian skulls?"

"I have." Stevens leaned down, opened the ice chest, lifted out one of the black skulls, and set it upright on a large silk pillow laid on the conference table. The glossy obsidian gleamed under the overhead spotlights. "A truly remarkable piece of work," he said reverently. "Amenes artisans began with a solid block of obsidian—one that was incredibly pure of imperfections—a rarity in itself. Over a period of at least ninety to a hundred years, and perhaps more, the head was shaped by hand, using what I believe was obsidian dust as a smoothing agent."

"Why not some type of hardened metal chisels tapped by a mallet?" asked Giordino.

Stevens shook his head. "No tools were wielded. There are no signs of scratches or nicks. Obsidian, though extremely hard, is very prone to fracture. One slip, one misplaced angle of a chisel, and the whole skull would have shattered. No, the shaping and polishing had to be accomplished as if a marble bust had been delicately smoothed by car polish."

"How long would it take to reproduce with modern tools?"

Stevens gave a faint grin. "Technically, it would be next to impossible to create an exact replica. The more I study it, the more I become convinced it shouldn't exist."

"Are there any markings on the base to suggest a source?" asked Sandecker.

"No markings," answered Stevens. "But let me show you something that's truly astonishing." With extreme care he slowly made a twisting motion, as he lifted the upper half of the skull until it came free. Next he removed a perfectly contoured globe from the skull cavity. Holding it devoutly in both hands, he lowered it onto a specially prepared cushioned base. "I can't begin to imagine the degree of artistic craftsmanship it took to produce such an astonishing object," he said admiringly. "Only while studying the skull under strong magnification did I see a line around the skull plate that was invisible to the naked eye."

"It's absolutely fabulous," murmured Pat in awe.

"Are there carvings on the globe?" Pitt asked Stevens.

"Yes, it's an engraved illustration of the world. If you care to view it more closely, I have a magnifying glass."

He handed the thick glass to Pitt, who peered at the lines inscribed on the globe that was about the size of a baseball. After a minute, he carefully slid the globe across the table in front of Sandecker and passed him the magnifying glass.

While the admiral was examining the globe, Stevens said, "By comparing the photographs taken inside the chamber in Colorado with those from St. Paul Island, I found that the continents perfectly match those of the obsidian globe."

"Meaning?" asked Sandecker.

"If you study the alignment of the continents, and large islands such as Greenland and Mozambique, you'll find they don't match the geography of the world today."

"I observed the differences, too," said Pitt.

"What does that prove?" asked Giordino, playing the role of skeptic. "Except that it's a primitive, inaccurate map?"

"Primitive? Yes. Inaccurate? Perhaps by modern standards. But I strongly support the theory that these ancient peoples sailed every sea on earth and charted thousands of miles of coastlines. If you look closely at the obsidian globe, you can see they even defined Australia, Japan, and the Great Lakes of North America. All this by people who lived more than nine thousand years ago."

"Unlike the Atlantis that was described by Plato as having existed on a single island or continent," Pat spoke up, "the Amenes engaged in worldwide commerce. They went far beyond the bounds of much later civilizations. They were not restricted by tradition or fear of the unknown seas. The inscriptions detail their sea routes and vast trading network that took them across the Atlantic and up the St. Lawrence River to Michigan, where they mined copper; and to Bolivia and the British Isles, where they mined tin, using advanced developments in metallurgy to create and produce bronze, thereby lifting mankind from the Stone Age to the Bronze Age."

Sandecker leaned across the table. "Surely they mined and traded in gold and silver."

"Strangely, they did not consider gold or silver useful metals, and preferred copper for their ornaments and art works. But they did journey around the world in search of turquoise and black opal, which they fashioned into jewelry. And, of course, obsidian, which was almost sacred to them. Obsidian, by the way, is still used in open-heart surgery, because it has a sharper edge that causes less tissue damage than steel."

"Both turquoise and black opal were represented on the mummies we found in the burial chamber," added Giordino.

"Which demonstrates the extent of their reach," said Pat. "The rich robin's-egg blue I saw in the chamber could only have come from the American Southwest deserts."

"And the black opal?" asked Sandecker.

"Australia."

"If nothing else," said Pitt thoughtfully, "it confirms that the Amenes had knowledge of nautical science and learned to build ships capable of sailing across the seas thousands of years ago."

"It also explains why their communities were built as port cities," Pat summed up. "And according to what was revealed by the photographs in the burial chamber, few societies in the history of man were so far-flung. I've located over twenty of their port cities in such diverse parts of the world as Mexico, Peru, India, China, Japan, and Egypt. Several of them are in the Indian Ocean and a few on islands of the Pacific."

"I can back up Dr. O'Connell's findings with my own on the globes from the skull," said Stevens.

"So their world was not based around the Mediterranean, as later civilizations were?" said the admiral.

Stevens gave a negative shake of his head. "The Mediterranean was not open to the sea during the Amenes' era. Nine thousand years ago, the Med, as we know it, was made up of fertile valleys and lakes fed by European rivers to the north and the Nile to the south, which merged and then flowed through the Straits of Gibraltar into the Atlantic. You might also be interested in knowing that the North Sea was a dry plain and the British Isles were part of Europe. The Baltic Sea was also a broad valley above sea level. The Gobi and Sahara deserts were lush tropical lands that supported huge herds of animals. The ancient ones lived on a planet very different from the one we live on."

"What happened to the Amenes?" asked Sandecker. "Why hasn't evidence of their existence come down to us before now?"

"Their civilization was utterly destroyed when a comet struck the earth around 7000 B.C. and caused a worldwide cataclysmic disaster. That's when the land bridge from Gibraltar to Morocco was breached and the Mediterranean became a sea. Shorelines were inundated and changed forever. Within the time it takes for a raindrop to fall from a cloud, the sea people, their cities, and their entire culture were erased from the earth and lost until now."

"You deciphered all that from the inscriptions?"

"That and more," Yaeger answered earnestly. "They describe the horror and suffering in vivid detail. The impact of the comet was gigantic, sudden, appalling, and deadly. The inscriptions go on to tell of mountains shaking like willows in a gale. Earthquakes shook with a magnitude that would be inconceivable today. Volcanoes exploded with the combined force of thousands of nuclear bombs, filling the sky with layers of ash a hundred miles thick. Pumice blanketed the seas as dense as ten feet. Rivers of lava buried most of what we call the Pacific Northwest. Fires spread under hurricanelike winds, creating towering clouds of smoke that blanketed the sky. Tidal waves, perhaps as much as three miles high, swept over the land. Islands vanished, buried under water for all time. Most of the people and all but a handful of animals and sea life disappeared in a time span of twenty-four hours."

Giordino put his hands behind his head and looked up at the ceiling, trying to picture in his mind the terrible devastation. "So that explains it—the sudden extinction in the Americas of the saber-toothed tiger, the humped-back camel, the musk oxen, that giant bison with a horn spread of six feet, the woolly mammoth, the small shaggy horse that once roamed the plains of North America. And the instant turning to stone of clams, soft jellyfish, oysters, and starfish—you remember we discovered them during projects coring under the sediments. These discrepancies have always been an enigma to scientists. Now maybe they can tie it to the comet's impact."

Sandecker stared at Giordino with an appraising look in his eyes. The short Etruscan possessed a brilliant mind, but worked to conceal it behind a sardonic wit.

Stevens pulled out his pipe and toyed with it. "It's well known in the scientific community that mass global extinctions of animals weighing over a hundred pounds occurred in unison with the end of the last ice age, about the same time as the comet's impact. Mastodons were found preserved by ice in Siberia, the food undigested in their stomach, establishing the fact that they died quite suddenly, almost as if sent into an instant deep freeze. The same with trees and plants that were found frozen while in leaf and in bloom."

The degree of horror could not be completely imagined by anyone sitting at the table. The scope was simply too enormous for them to conceive.

"I'm not a geophysicist," said Stevens quietly, "but I cannot believe that a comet striking the earth, even a large one, could cause such tremendous destruction on such a massive scale. It's inconceivable."

"Sixty-five million years ago, a comet or asteroid killed off the dinosaurs," Giordino reminded him.

"It must have been one enormous comet," said Sandecker.

"Comets can't be measured like asteroids or meteors that have a solid mass," Yaeger lectured. "Comets are a composite of ice, gas, and rocks."

Pat continued reciting the story of the inscriptions without reading from her notes. "Some of the inhabitants of Earth who survived lived, farmed, and hunted in the mountains and high plains. They were able to escape the aftermath of horror by going underground or hiding in caves, existing on whatever pitiful vegetation and flora that could revive and grow under unhealthy conditions, along with the few animals left to hunt. Many died of starvation or from the gaseous clouds smothering the atmosphere. Only a scant handful of the Amenes who happened to be on high ground during the tidal waves survived."

"The story of what has come down to us as the deluge," clarified Stevens, "has been recorded by Sumerian tablets dating back five thousand years in Mesopotamia—the legend of Gilgamesh and the flood predates the biblical story of Noah and the ark. Stone records of the Mayans, written records by Babylonian priests, legends handed down by every cultural race of the world, including the Indians throughout North America, all tell of a great inundation. So there is little doubt the event actually occurred."

"And now," said Yaeger, "thanks to the Amenes, we have a date of approximately 7100 B.C."

"History tells us that the more advanced the civilization," Stevens commented, "the more easily it will die and leave little or nothing of itself behind. At least ninety-nine percent of the grand total of ancient knowledge has been lost to us through natural disasters and man's destruction."

Pitt nodded in agreement. "A golden age of ocean navigation seven thousand years before Christ, but nothing to show for it but inscriptions in rock. A pity we can't have more to inherit from them."

Sandecker exhaled a cloud of blue smoke. "I sincerely hope that won't be our fate."

Pat took over from Yaeger. "Those who remained of the Amenes formed a small cult and dedicated themselves to educating the remaining Stone Age inhabitants in arts and written communication, as well as teaching them how to construct substantial buildings and ships to sail

the seas. They tried to warn future generations of another coming cataclysm, but those who came later and had not lived during the comet's
destruction and horrible aftermath could not bring themselves to accept that such a traumatic episode from the past would repeat itself. The
Amenes realized the awful truth would soon become lost in the mists
of time, recalled only in a score of myths. So they attempted to leave a
legacy by building great monuments of stone to last throughout the
centuries, engraved with their message of the past and future. The great
megalithic cult they created became widespread and lasted for four
thousand years. But time and the elements eroded the inscriptions and
erased the warnings.

"After the Amenes finally died out, centuries of paralysis set in before the Sumerians and Egyptians began to emerge from primitive cultures and gradually build new civilizations, using bits and pieces of the
knowledge from the distant past."

Pitt tapped a pencil on the table. "From what little I know on the
subject of megaliths, it would seem that later cultures, having lost the
original intent of the Amenes through the centuries, used monumen-
tal structures as temples, tombs, and stone calendars, eventually building thousands of their own."

"In studying the available data on megaliths," said Yaeger, "the very
early structures show that the Amenes had a distinct form of architecture. Their style of building was mostly circular, with triangular-shaped
stone blocks cut like interlocking pieces of a jigsaw puzzle, making
them almost impervious to any movement of the earth, regardless of
how severe."

Stevens spoke very deliberately, as he replaced the globe in its socket
inside the black skull. "Thanks to the efforts of Mr. Yaeger and Dr.
O'Connell, it's beginning to look as if elements of the Amenes culture
and ancient heritage were passed through the centuries and eventually
absorbed by the Egyptians, Sumerians, the Chinese, and Olmecs, who
preceded the Mayans, and both the Asian Indians and the American Indians. The Phoenicians, more than any other civilization, took up the
torch of deep-ocean navigation.

"Their revelations also help to explain why most of the gods and
deities from nearly every later civilization in every part of the world

came from the sea, and why all the gods setting foot in the Americas came from the east while the gods appearing in the early European cultures came from the west."

Sandecker stared at his cigar smoke spiraling to the ceiling. "An interesting point, Doctor, that answers any number of questions about our ancient ancestors that we've puzzled over for hundreds of years."

Pitt nodded at Pat. "What finally happened to the last of the Amenes?"

"Frustrated that their message would not be received and acted upon, they built chambers in different parts of the world that they hoped would not be found for thousands of years, and only then by future civilizations with the science to understand their message of danger."

"Which was?" prompted Sandecker.

"The date of the second comet's return to earth's orbit and the almost certain impact."

Stevens wagged his finger to make a point. "A recurring theme in mythology is that the cataclysm with its accompanying deluge will repeat itself."

"Hardly a cheery thought," said Giordino.

"What made them so certain there would be another devastating visitor from outer space?" wondered Sandecker.

"The inscriptions describe in great detail two comets that arrived at the same time," answered Yaeger. "One impacted. The other missed and returned to space."

"Are you suggesting the Amenes could accurately predict the date of the second comet's return?"

Pat simply nodded.

"The Amenes," said Yaeger, "were masters not only of the seas but of the heavens as well. They measured the movement of the stars with uncanny accuracy. And they did it without powerful telescopes."

"Suppose the comet does come back," said Giordino. "How could they know it wouldn't miss the earth and sail off into the great beyond again? Was their science so sophisticated they could calculate the time of impact at the exact position of the earth's orbit in space?"

"They could and did," Pat retorted. "By computing and comparing

the different positions of the stars and constellations between the ancients' star map in the Colorado chamber with present astronomical star
positions, we were able to arrive at our own date in time. It matched the
Amenes prediction within an hour.

"The Egyptians devised a double calendar that's far more intricate
than what we use today. The Mayans measured the length of the year
at 365.2420 days. Our calculation using atomic clocks is 365.2423. They
also computed incredibly accurate calendars based on the conjunctions
of Venus, Mars, Jupiter, and Saturn. The Babylonians determined the
sidereal year at 365 days, 6 hours, and 11 minutes. They were off by less
than two minutes." Pat paused for effect. "The Amenes' computation
for the earth's circuit of the sun was off by two-tenths of a second.
They based their calendar on a solar eclipse that occurred on the same
day of the year at the same site on the zodiac every 521 years. Their celestial map of the heavens, as observed and calculated nine thousand
years ago, was right on the money."

"The question on all our minds now," said Sandecker, "is at what
point in time did the Amenes predict the reappearance of the comet?"

Pat and Yaeger exchanged sober looks. Yaeger spoke first. "We
learned from a computer search of ancient archaeoastronomy files and
papers from the archives of several universities that the Amenes were
not the only ancient astronomers to predict a second doomsday. The
Mayans, the Hopi Indians, the Egyptians, the Chinese, and several other
pre-Christian civilizations all came up with dates for the end of the
world. The disturbing part is that, collectively, they arrived within a
year of each other."

"Could it be simply a coincidence or one culture borrowing from another?"

Yaeger shook his head doubtfully. "It's possible they copied what was
passed on by the Amenes, but indications are that their studies of the
stars only confirmed the impact time passed on by those they considered as ancients."

"Who do you think were the most accurate in their prediction?"
asked Pitt.

"Those of the Amenes who survived, because they were present during the actual catastrophe. They predicted not only the year but the exact day."

"Which is?" Sandecker prompted expectantly.

Pat sank in her chair as if retreating from reality. Yaeger hesitated, looking around the table from face to face. At last he said in a halting voice, "The time the Amenes predicted the comet would return and shatter the earth is May 20, in the year 2001."

Pitt frowned. "This is 2001."

Yaeger massaged his temples with both hands. "I'm well aware of that."

Sandecker hunched forward. "Are you saying doomsday is less than two months away?"

Yaeger nodded solemnly. "Yes, that's exactly what I'm saying."

27

AFTER THE MEETING, PITT returned to his office and was greeted by his longtime secretary, Zerri Pochinsky. A lovely lady with a dazzling smile, she was blessed with a body that would make a Las Vegas showgirl envious. Fawn-colored hair fell to her shoulders, and she peered at the world through captivating hazel eyes. She lived alone, with a cat named Murgatroyd, and seldom dated. Pitt was more than fond of Zerri, but exercised iron discipline in not coming on to her. As much as he often imagined her in his arms, he had a strict rule about socializing with any members of the opposite sex employed with NUMA. He had seen too many office affairs inevitably lead to disaster.

"FBI Special Agent Ken Helm called and would like you to return his call," she announced, handing him a pink slip of paper with the number of Helm's private line. "Are you in trouble with your government again?"

He grinned at her and leaned over Zerri's desk until their noses were less than an inch apart. "I'm always in trouble with my government."

Her eyes flashed mischievously. "I'm still waiting for you to sweep me off my feet and fly me to a beach in Tahiti."

He pulled back a safe distance, because the scent of her Chanel was beginning to stir unnatural feelings within him. "Why can't you find some nice, stable, home-loving male to marry, so you can stop harassing an old, unanchored, derelict beach bum?"

"Because stable home-lovers aren't any fun."

"Whoever said women are nest-oriented?" He sighed.

Pitt pulled away and stepped into his office, which looked like a trailer park after a tornado. Books, papers, nautical charts, and photographs littered every square inch of space, including the carpet. He had decorated his workplace in antiques he'd bought at auction from the American President Lines elegant passenger ship *President Cleveland*. He settled behind his desk, picked up the receiver, and dialed Helm's number.

A voice answered with a terse "Yes?"

"Mr. Helm, Dirk Pitt returning your call."

"Mr. Pitt, thank you. I just thought you'd like to know that the Bureau has identified the body you shipped from the Antarctic and also the woman you apprehended last night."

"That was fast work."

"Thanks to our new computerized photo ID department," explained Helm. "They've scanned every newspaper, magazine, TV broadcast, state motor vehicle driver's license record, company security face shot, passport photo, and police record to build the world's largest photo identification network. It consists of hundreds of millions of enhanced facial close-ups. Combined with our fingerprint and DNA files, we can now cover a vast spectrum for identifying bodies and fugitives. We had a make on both women within twenty minutes."

"What did you discover?"

"The name of the deceased from the submarine was Heidi Wolf. The woman you apprehended last night is Elsie Wolf."

"Then they *are* twin sisters."

"No, actually, they're cousins. And what is really off the wall is that they both come from a very wealthy family and are high-level executives of the same vast business conglomerate."

Pitt stared in contemplation out the window of his office, without seeing the Potomac River outside and the Capitol in the background.

"Would they happen to be related to Karl Wolf, the CEO of Destiny Enterprises out of Argentina?"

Helm paused, then said, "It seems you're two steps ahead of me, Mr. Pitt."

"Dirk."

"All right, Dirk, you're on the mark. Heidi was Karl's sister. Elsie is his cousin. And, yes, Destiny Enterprises is a privately owned business empire based in Buenos Aires. Forbes has estimated the combined family resources at two hundred and ten billion dollars."

"Not exactly living on the streets, are they?"

"And I had to marry a girl whose father was a bricklayer."

Pitt said, "I don't understand why a woman of such affluence would stoop to committing petty burglary."

"When you get the answers, I hope you'll pass them on to me."

"Where is Elsie now?" asked Pitt.

"Under guard at a private clinic run by the Bureau on W Street, across from Mount Vernon College."

"Can I talk to her?"

"I see no problem from the Bureau's end, but you'll have to go through the doctor in charge of her case. His name is Aaron Bell. I'll call and clear your visit."

"Is she lucid?"

"She's conscious. You gave her a pretty hard rap on the head. Her concussion was just short of a skull fracture."

"I didn't hit her. It was her motorcycle."

"Whatever," said Helm, the humor obvious in his tone. "You won't get much out of her. One of our best interrogators tried. She's one tough lady. She makes a clam look talkative."

"Does she know her cousin is dead?"

"She knows. She also knows that Heidi's remains are lying in the clinic's morgue."

"That should prove interesting," Pitt said slowly.

"What will prove interesting?" Helm inquired.

"The look on Elsie's face when I tell her I'm the one who recovered Heidi's body from Antarctic waters and air-shipped it to Washington."

ALMOST immediately after hanging up the phone, Pitt left the NUMA building and drove over to the unmarked clinic used exclusively by the FBI and other national security agencies. He parked the '36 Ford cabriolet in an empty stall next to the building and walked through the main entrance. He was asked for his identification, and phone calls were made before he was allowed admittance. An administrator directed him to the office of Dr. Bell.

Pitt had actually met the doctor several times, not for care or treatment but during social functions to raise money for a cancer foundation that his father, Senator George Pitt, and Bell served on as directors. Aaron Bell was in his middle sixties, a hyper character, red-faced, badly over-weight, and working under a blanket of stress. He smoked two packs of cigarettes a day and drank twenty cups of coffee. His outlook on life, as he often expressed it, was "Go like hell and go to the grave satisfied."

He emerged from behind his desk like a bear walking on its hind legs. "Dirk!" he boomed. "Good to see you. How's the senator?"

"Planning on running for another term."

"He'll never quit, and neither will I. Sit down. You're here about the woman who was brought in last night."

"Ken Helm called?"

"You wouldn't have crossed the threshold if he hadn't."

"The clinic doesn't look highly guarded."

"Stare cross-eyed at a surveillance camera and see what happens."

"Did she suffer any permanent brain damage?"

Bell shook his head vigorously. "One hundred percent after a few weeks. Incredible constitution. She's not built like most women who come through these doors."

"She *is* very attractive," said Pitt.

"No, no, I'm not talking about looks. This woman is a remarkable physical specimen, as is, or should I say was, the body of her cousin you shipped from the Antarctic."

"According to the FBI, they're cousins."

"Nonetheless, a perfect genetic match," said Bell seriously. "Too perfect."

"How so?"

"I attended the postmortem examination, then took the findings and compared the physical characteristics with the lady lying in a bed down the hall. There's more going on here than mere family similarities."

"Helm told me Heidi's body is here at the clinic."

"Yes, on a table in the basement morgue."

"Can't family members with the same genes, especially cousins, have a mirror image?" asked Pitt.

"Not impossible, but extremely rare," replied Bell.

"It's said that we all have an identical look-alike wandering somewhere in the world."

Bell smiled. "God help the guy who looks like me."

Pitt asked, "So where is this leading?"

"I can't prove it without months of examination and tests, and I'm going out on a limb with an opinion, but I'm willing to stake my reputation on the possibility that those two young ladies, one living, one dead, were developed and manufactured."

Pitt looked at him. "You can't be suggesting androids."

"No, no." Bell waved his hands. "Nothing so ridiculous."

"Cloning?"

"Not at all."

"Then what?"

"I believe they were genetically engineered."

"Is that possible?" asked Pitt, unbelieving. "Does the science and technology exist for such an achievement?"

"There are labs full of scientists working on perfecting the human body through genetics, but to my knowledge they're still in the mice-testing stage. All I can tell you is that if Elsie doesn't die in the same manner as Heidi, or fall under a truck, or get murdered by a jealous lover, she'll probably live to celebrate her hundred and twentieth birthday."

"I'm not at all sure I'd want to live that long," said Pitt thoughtfully.

"Nor I," said Bell, laughing. "Certainly not in this old bod."

"May I see Elsie now?"

Bell rose from his desk chair and motioned for Pitt to follow him out of the office and down the hall. Since entering the clinic, the only two people Pitt had seen were the administrator in the lobby and Dr. Bell. The clinic seemed incredibly clean and sterile and devoid of life.

Bell came to a door with no guard outside, inserted a card into an electronic slot, and pushed it open. A woman was sitting up in a standard hospital bed, staring through a window whose view was interrupted by a heavy screen and a series of bars. This was the first time Pitt had seen Elsie in daylight, and he was awed by the incredible resemblance to her dead cousin. The same mane of blond hair, the same blue-gray eyes. He found it hard to believe they were merely cousins.

"Ms. Wolf," said Bell, in a cheery voice, "I've brought you a visitor." He looked at Pitt and nodded. "I'll leave you two alone. Try not to take too long."

There was no warning to Pitt about communicating with the doctor in case of a problem, and though he didn't see any TV cameras, Pitt knew without a doubt that their every movement and word was being monitored and recorded.

He pulled up a chair beside her bed and sat down, saying nothing for nearly a minute, staring into the eyes that seemed to peer through his head at a lithograph of the Grand Canyon hanging on the wall beyond. At last, he said, "My name is Dirk Pitt. I don't know if the name means anything to you, but it seemed to register with the commander of the U-2015 when we communicated with each other on an ice floe."

Her eyes narrowed ever so slightly, but she remained silent. "I dove on the wreckage," Pitt continued, "and retrieved the body of your cousin, Heidi. Would you like me to arrange for her to be transported to Karl in Buenos Aires for proper burial in the Wolf private cemetery?"

Pitt was treading a narrow path, but he assumed that the Wolfs had a private cemetery.

This time he scored points. Her eyes went reflective as she tried to cut through his words. Finally, her lips pressed together with obvious anger, she began to tremble and move. "You!" she spat. "You are the one responsible for the deaths of our people in Colorado."

"Dr. Bell was wrong. You *do* have a tongue."

"You were also there when our submarine was sunk?" she asked, as if confused.

"I plead self-defense for my action in Colorado. And yes, I was on the *Polar Storm* when your sub went down, but I was not responsible for the incident. Blame the U.S. Navy if you must. If not for their timely intervention, your cousin and her bloody band of pirates would have sunk a harmless ocean research ship and killed more than a hundred innocent crewmen and scientists. Don't ask me to shed tears for Heidi. As far as I'm concerned, she and her crew got what they deserved."

"What have you done with her body?" she demanded.

"It's here in the clinic's morgue," he answered. "I'm told the two of you could have grown from the same pod."

"We are genetically unblemished," Elsie said arrogantly. "Unlike the rest of the human race."

"How did that come about?"

"It took three generations of selection and experimentation. My generation has physically perfect bodies and the mental capacity of geniuses. We are also exceedingly creative in the arts."

"Really?" Pitt said sarcastically. "And all this time I thought inbreeding generated imbeciles."

Elsie stared at Pitt for a long moment, then smiled coldly. "Your insults are meaningless. In a short time, you and all the other flawed individuals who walk the earth will be dead."

Pitt studied her eyes for a reaction. When he replied, it was with detached indifference. "Ah yes, the twin of the comet that destroyed the Amenes nine thousand years ago returns, strikes the earth, and decimates the human race. I already know all about that."

He almost missed it, but it was there. A brief glint in the eyes of elation mixed with rapture. The pure sense of evil about her seemed so concentrated he could reach out and touch it. It disturbed him. He felt as though she was keeping a secret far more menacing than any he could remotely conceive.

"How long did it take your experts to decipher the inscriptions?" she asked casually.

"Five or six days."

Her face grew smug. "Our people did it in three."

He was certain she was lying, so he continued to fence with her. "Is the Wolf family planning any festivities to celebrate the coming of doomsday?"

Elsie shook her head slowly. "We have no time for foolish revelry. Our labors have been spent in survival."

"Do you really think a comet will strike in the next few weeks?"

"The Amenes were very precise in their astronomical and celestial charts." There was a flick of the eyes from his face to the floor and a lack of conviction in her voice that made Pitt doubt her.

"So I've been told."

"We have . . . connections with some of the finest astronomers in Europe and the United States, who verified the Amenes' projections. All agreed that the comet's return was plotted and timed with amazing accuracy."

"So your family of uncharitable clones kept the news to themselves rather than warn the world," Pitt said nastily. "And your *connections* kept the astronomers from talking. Benevolence must not be in the Wolf dictionary."

"Why cause a worldwide panic?" she said carelessly. "What good would it do in the end? Better to let the people die unknowing and without mental anguish."

"You're all heart."

"Life is for those who are the fittest, and those who plan."

"And the magnificent Wolfs? What's to keep you from being killed along with the rest of the foul-smelling rabble?"

"We have been planning our survival for over fifty years," she said decisively. "My family will not be swept away by floods or burned by raging fires. We are prepared to weather the catastrophe and endure the aftermath."

"Fifty years," Pitt repeated. "Is that when you found a chamber with the Amenes inscriptions telling of their near extinction after the comet's impact?"

"Yes," she answered simply.

"How many chambers are there in total?"

"The Amenes told of six."

"How many did your family find?"

"One."

"And we found two. That leaves three that remain undiscovered."

"One was lost in Hawaii after a volcano spewed tons of lava into it, effectively destroying it. Another disappeared forever during a great earthquake in Tibet during A.D. 800. Only one remains unfound. It's supposed to lie somewhere on the slopes of Mount Lascar in Chile."

"If it remains unfound," said Pitt carefully, "why did you murder a group of college students who were exploring a cave on the mountain?"

She glared at him, but refused to answer.

"Okay, let me ask you the location of the Amenes chamber your family discovered?" he pressed her.

She gazed at him almost as if he were a lost soul. "The earliest inscriptions we found of the Amenes are inside a temple that stands amid the ruins of what once was one of their port cities. You need not ask more, Mr. Pitt. I have said all I'm going to say, except that I suggest you bid farewell to your friends and loved ones. Because very soon now, what is left of your torn and shattered bodies will be floating in a sea that never existed before."

That said, Elsie Wolf closed her eyes and shut herself off from Pitt and the world around her as effectively as if she had entered a deep freeze.

28

BY THE TIME PITT left the clinic it was late in the afternoon, and he decided to head for his hangar rather than return to the NUMA building. He was moving slowly through the rush-hour traffic that crawled over the Rocheambeau Bridge before finally exiting onto the Washington Memorial Parkway. He was just approaching the gate at the airport maintenance road leading to his hangar when the Globalstar phone signaled an incoming call.

"Hello."

"Hi, lover," came the sultry voice of Congresswoman Loren Smith.

"I'm always happy to hear from my favorite government representative."

"What are you doing tonight?"

"I thought I'd whip up a smoked salmon omelet, take a shower, and watch TV," Pitt answered, as the guard waved him through, staring at the '36 Ford with envy in his eyes.

"Bachelors lead dull lives," she said teasingly.

"I gave up barhopping when I turned twenty-one."

"Sure you did." She paused to answer a question from one of her aides. "Sorry about that. A constituent called to complain about pot-holes in the road in front of his house."

"Congresswomen lead dull lives," he retorted.

"Just for being testy, you're taking me to dinner at St. Cyr's."

"You have good taste," said Pitt. "That will set me back a month's wages. What's the occasion?"

"I have a rather thick report on Destiny Enterprises sitting on my desk and it's going to cost you big-time."

"Did anybody ever tell you, you're in the wrong business?"

"I've sold my soul to pass legislation more times than any hooker has sold her body to clients."

Pitt pulled to a stop at a large hangar entry door and pressed a code into a remote transmitter. "I hope you have reservations. St. Cyr's isn't known for taking commoners off the street."

"I did a favor for the chef once. Trust me, we'll have the best table in the house. Pick me up in front of my place at seven-thirty."

"Can you get me a discount on the wine?"

"You're cute," said Loren softly. "Goodbye."

PITT wasn't in the mood to wear a tie to a fancy restaurant. As he pulled the Ford up in front of Loren's town house in Alexandria, he was wearing gray slacks, a dark blue sport coat, and a saffron-colored turtle-neck sweater. Loren spotted him and the car from her fourth-story balcony, waved, and came down. Chic and glamorous, she wore a charcoal lace-and-beadwork cardigan with palazzo pants pleated in the front under a black, knee-length imitation fur coat. She carried a briefcase whose charcoal leather matched her outfit. She'd seen from the balcony that Pitt had put the top up on the Ford, and so, since she did not have to worry about windblown hair, she didn't bother to wear a hat.

Pitt stood on the sidewalk and opened the door for her. "Nice to see there are still a few gentlemen left," she said, with a flirty smile.

He leaned down and kissed her cheek. "I come from the old school."

The restaurant was only two miles away, just across the Capitol Beltway into Fairfax County, Virginia. The valet parking attendant's face lit up like a candle inside a Halloween pumpkin when he spotted the hot rod roll up in front of the elegant restaurant. The mellow tone from the exhaust pipes sent quivers up his spine.

He handed Pitt a claim check, but before he drove away, Pitt leaned in and scanned the odometer. "Something wrong, sir?" asked the parking attendant.

"Just reading the mileage," replied Pitt, giving the young man a knowing look.

His dream of taking the hot rod out for a spin while its owner was inside having dinner now suddenly dashed, the attendant drove the car slowly into the lot and parked it next to a Bentley.

St. Cyr's was an intimate dining experience. Established in an eighteenth-century colonial brick house, the owner-chef had come to Washington by way of Cannes and Paris after having been discovered by a pair of wealthy Washington developers with palates for fine food and wine. They'd bankrolled the restaurant, giving the chef a half interest. The dining room was decorated in deep blues and golds, with Moroccan-style decor and furniture. There were no more than twelve tables served by six waiters and four busboys. What Pitt especially enjoyed about St. Cyr's was the acoustics. With heavy curtains and miles of fabric on the walls, all sounds of conversation were cut to a bare minimum, unlike most restaurants, in which you couldn't hear what the person across the table was saying and the din literally ruined any enjoyment of a gourmet meal.

After being seated at a table in a small private alcove off the main dining room by the maître d', Pitt asked Loren, "Wine or champagne?"

"Why ask?" she said. "You know a good Cabernet puts me in a vulnerable mood."

Pitt ordered a bottle of Martin Ray Cabernet Sauvignon from the wine steward and settled comfortably into the leather chair. "While we're waiting to order, why don't you tell me what you've found on Destiny Enterprises?"

Loren smiled. "I should make you feed me first."

"Another politician on the take," he said satirically.

She leaned down, opened her briefcase and retrieved several file folders. She passed them discreetly under the table. "Destiny Enterprises is definitely not a corporation that delights in public relations, promotional programs, or advertising. They have never sold stock, and are wholly owned by the Wolf family, which consists of three generations. They do not produce, nor do they distribute, profit-and-loss statements or annual reports. Obviously, they could never operate with such secrecy in the U.S., Europe, or Asia, but they wield enormous clout with the Argentine government, beginning with the Peróns soon after World War Two."

Pitt was reading the opening pages of the file when the wine arrived. After the wine steward poured a small amount in his glass, he studied the color, inhaled the scent, and then took a mouthful. He did not daintily sip the Cabernet but gently swirled it around in his mouth for a few seconds before swallowing. He looked up at the wine steward and smiled. "I'm always amazed at the finesse yet the solid soul of a Martin Ray Cabernet Sauvignon."

"A very excellent choice, sir," said the wine steward. "Not many of our patrons know it exists."

Pitt indulged in another taste of the wine before continuing his study of the file. "Destiny Enterprises seems to have materialized out of nowhere in 1947."

Loren stared into the deep, fluid red in her wineglass. "I hired a researcher to examine Buenos Aires newspapers of the time. There was no mention of Wolf in the business sections. The researcher could only pass on rumors that the corporation was made up of high Nazi officials who had escaped Germany before the surrender."

"Admiral Sandecker talked about the flow of the Nazis and their stolen wealth by U-boat to Argentina during the final months of the war. The operation was orchestrated by Martin Bormann."

"Wasn't he killed trying to escape during the battle of Berlin?" asked Loren.

"I don't believe it was ever proven the bones they found many years later were his."

"I read somewhere that the greatest unsolved mystery of the war was the total disappearance of the German treasury. Not one Deutschmark or scrap of gold was ever found. Could it be Bormann survived and smuggled the country's stolen wealth to South America?"

"He heads the list of suspects," answered Pitt. He began sifting through the papers in the files, but found little of interest. Most were merely newspaper articles reporting business dealings of Destiny Enterprises that were too large to keep confidential. The most detailed analysis came from a CIA report. It listed the various activities and projects the corporation was involved in, but few if any details of their operations.

"They seem quite diversified," said Pitt. "Vast mining operations for recovering gemstones, gold, platinum, and other rare minerals. Their computer software development and publishing division is the fourth largest in the world behind Microsoft. They're heavily into oil field development. They're also a world leader in nanotechnology."

"I'm not sure what that is," said Loren.

Before Pitt could answer, the waiter approached the table for their order. "What catches your fancy?" he asked her.

"I trust your taste," she said softly. "You order for me."

Pitt did not attempt to pronounce the menu courses in French. He held to straight English. "For the hors d'oeuvres, we'll have your house pâté with truffles, followed by vichyssoise. For the main course, the lady will have the rabbit stewed in white wine sauce, while I'll try the sweetbreads in brown butter sauce."

"How can you eat sweetbreads?" Loren asked, with an expression of distaste.

"I've always had a craving for good sweetbreads," Pitt replied simply. "Where were we? Oh yes, nanotechnology. From what little I know on the subject, nanotechnology is a new science that attempts to control the arrangement of atoms, enabling the construction of virtually anything possible under natural law. Molecular repairs inside human bodies will be possible and manufacturing will be revolutionized. Nothing will be impossible to produce cheaply and with quality. Incredibly tiny machines that can reproduce themselves will be programmed to create new fuels, drugs, metals, and building products that would not be possible with normal techniques. I've heard that mainframe computers can be built with a volume as small as a cubic micron. Nanotechnology has to be the wave of the future."

"I can't begin to imagine how it works."

"It's my understanding the goal is to create what nanotechnology experts call an assembler, a submicroscopic robot with articulated arms that are operated by computers. Supposedly they could construct large, atomically precise objects by controlled chemical reactions, molecule by molecule. The assemblers can even be designed to replicate themselves. Theoretically, you could program your assemblers to build you a new custom set of golf clubs out of metals yet to be developed, a television set of a particular shape to fit a cabinet, even an automobile or an airplane, including special fuel to run them."

"Sounds fantastic."

"The advances over the next thirty years should prove mind-boggling."

"That explains the file on Destiny's project in Antarctica," said Loren, pausing to sip her wine. "You'll find it in file 5-A."

"Yes, I see it," acknowledged Pitt. "An extensive facility for mining minerals from the sea. They have to be the first to have ever profitably exploited seawater for valuable minerals."

"It seems Destiny's engineers and scientists have developed a molecular device capable of separating minerals such as gold from seawater."

"I assume the program is successful?"

"Very," said Loren. "According to Swiss depository records obtained covertly by the CIA—I swore to them on a thousand Bibles that this information would remain strictly confidential—Destiny's deposits of gold into Swiss vaults come close to matching the hoard at Fort Knox."

"Their retrieval of gold would have to be held on a select level, or world gold prices would plummet."

"According to my sources, Destiny's management has yet to sell so much as an ounce."

"For what purpose would they squirrel such an enormous hoard away?"

Loren shrugged. "I have no idea."

"Maybe they've slowly and discreetly sold to keep market prices up. If they suddenly flooded the market with tons of gold, their profits would go down the toilet."

The waiter arrived with their pâté with truffles. Loren took a dainty forkful into her mouth and made a gratified expression. "This is wonderful."

"Yes, it is good," Pitt agreed.

They relished the pâté in silence, finishing the last morsel before Loren resumed the conversation. "Although the CIA has accumulated a mass of data on a neo-Nazi movement after the war, they did not find evidence of an underground conspiracy involving Destiny Enterprises or the Wolf family."

"Yet according to this," said Pitt, holding up a stapled file of papers, "it was no secret that the loot stolen by the Nazis from the treasures of Austria, Belgium, Norway, France, and the Netherlands, plus much of the gold and financial assets of the Jews, were slipped into Argentina by U-boats after the war."

Loren nodded. "Most of the gold and other hard assets were converted to currency and then diverted through central banks."

"And the holder of the funds?"

"Who else? Destiny Enterprises, soon after it was organized in 1947. What's strange is that there is no record of a Wolf on their board of directors in the early years."

"They must have taken control later," said Pitt. "I wonder how the family shoved aside the old Nazi who fled Germany in 1945?"

"Good question," Loren agreed. "Over the past fifty-four years, the Destiny empire has grown to where their power influences world banks and governments to an unimaginable degree. They literally own Argentina. One of my aides has an informant who claims a significant amount of money goes into campaign funds for members of our own Congress. That's probably the reason why no government investigation of Destiny Enterprises ever got off the ground."

"Their tentacles also reach into the pockets of our honored senators and House representatives, and many of the people who have served in the White House."

Loren held up both hands. "Don't look at me. I never knowingly got a dime under the table from Destiny for my campaign funds."

Pitt threw her a foxlike look. "Really?"

She kicked him under the table. "Stop that. You know perfectly well

I've never been on the take. I happen to be one of the most respected members of Congress."

"Maybe the prettiest, but your esteemed colleagues don't know you like I do."

"You're not funny."

The bowls of vichyssoise were set before them and they savored the taste, enhanced by an occasional sip of the Martin Ray Cabernet. The wine didn't take long to course through their veins and mellow their minds, and the attentive waiter was always nearby to refill their glasses.

"It's beginning to look like what the Nazis couldn't achieve by mass slaughter, destruction, and warfare, they're accomplishing through economic power," said Loren.

"World domination is passé," Pitt disagreed. "The Chinese leaders might have it in the back of their heads, but as their economy builds the country into a superpower, they'll come to realize that a war will only bring it crashing down. Since Communist Russia fell, the major wars of the future will be economic. The Wolfs understand that economic power ultimately leads to political power. They have the resources to buy whatever and whoever they want. The only question is what direction are they headed in."

"Did you get anything out of the woman you apprehended last night?"

"Only that doomsday is just around the corner, and the entire human race, with the exception of the Wolf family, of course, will be wiped out when a comet strikes the earth."

"You don't buy that?" asked Loren.

"Do you?" Pitt said cynically. "A thousand doomsdays have come and gone with little more upheaval than a passing rain shower. Why the Wolfs are disseminating such a myth is a mystery to me."

"What do they base their reasoning on?"

"The predictions of the ancient race of people known as the Amenes."

"You can't be serious," she said, bewildered. "A family as affluent and shrewd as the Wolfs buying a myth from a race that died out thousands of years ago?"

"That's what the inscriptions said in the chambers we found in the Indian Ocean and Colorado."

"Admiral Sandecker briefly mentioned your discoveries in our phone conversation before I picked you up at the airport, but you've yet to tell me about your discoveries."

Pitt made a helpless gesture with his hands. "I haven't had a chance."

"Maybe I should begin putting my affairs in order."

"Before you prepare to meet your maker, wait until we run it by astronomers who track asteroids and comets."

The soup dishes were removed and their entrées were placed on the table. The chef's presentations of both the stewed rabbit and the sweetbreads were works of art. Pitt and Loren admired the sight in anticipation of the taste. They were not disappointed.

"The rabbit was an excellent choice," she said between mouthfuls. "It's delicious."

Pitt had an expression of ecstasy on his face. "When I'm served sweetbreads from a master chef, I hear bells with every bite. The sauce is a triumph."

"Try my rabbit," said Loren, holding up her plate.

"Care to try my sweetbreads?" queried Pitt.

"No, thank you," she said, wrinkling her nose. "I'm not keen on internal organs."

Fortunately, the portions were not as large as dishes served in lesser restaurants, and they did not feel stuffed when it was time for dessert. Pitt ordered the peaches cardinal: poached peaches with raspberry puree. Later, over Rémy Martin brandy, they resumed their discussion.

"None of what I've seen or heard about the Wolfs makes sense," said Pitt. "Why amass a fortune if they think their financial empire will go up in smoke after the comet's impact?"

Loren swirled the brandy in her glass, staring at the golden sparkle of the liquid in front of the light from the table's candle. "Perhaps they intend to survive the catastrophe."

"I've heard *that* from Elsie Wolf and one of their assassins in Colorado," said Pitt. "But how can they survive a worldwide disaster better than anyone else?"

"Did you read file eighteen?" Loren asked.

Pitt did not immediately answer, but sifted through the folders until he found the file marked "eighteen." He opened it and read. After two or three minutes, he looked up and stared into Loren's violet eyes. "Is this verified?"

She nodded. "It's as though Noah built an entire fleet of arks."

"Four colossal ships," Pitt said slowly. "One passenger liner, actually a floating community, six thousand feet in length by fifteen hundred feet wide, thirty-two stories high, displacing three and a half million tons." He looked up, his brow furrowed. "A fanciful concept, but hardly practical."

"Read the rest of it," said Loren. "It gets better."

"The gigantic oceangoing vessel has a large hospital, schools, enter-tainment centers, state-of-the-art engineering technologies. An airport with an extensive runway on the upper deck will house and maintain a small fleet of jet aircraft and helicopters, and living quarters and office facilities will accommodate five thousand passengers and crew." Pitt shook his head in disbelief. "A huge vessel like that should hold at least fifty thousand people."

"Actually, twice that number."

"Check out the other three vessels."

Pitt continued reading. "They also have the same mammoth dimen-sions. One is a cargo and maintenance vessel, housing machinery and manufacturing facilities with an immense cargo of vehicles, construction machinery, and building materials. The second is a veritable zoo—"

"See," Loren interrupted. "There is an ark."

"The last vessel is a supertanker built to carry tremendous amounts of oil, natural gas, and various other fuels." Pitt closed the folder and gazed at Loren. "I heard such vessels were on the drawing boards, but I had no idea they were actually built, and certainly not by Destiny En-terprises."

"The hulls were built in sections and then towed to a secluded ship-yard owned by Destiny Enterprises on an isolated fjord on the south-ern tip of Chile. There, the exterior superstructure and the interior build-out was completed, and the ships furnished and loaded. Estimates state the passengers and crews of the fleet should be self-sufficient, with enough food and supplies to last them twenty or more years."

"Haven't outsiders visited the vessels? Hasn't the news media written articles on what has to be the world's largest seagoing vessels?"

"Read the CIA's report on the shipyard," explained Loren. "The area is heavily restricted and patrolled by a small army of security guards. No outsiders get in or get out. The shipyard workers and their families are housed in a small community ashore without ever leaving the ships or the yard. Surrounded by the Andes, a hundred mountainous islands, and two peninsulas, the only way in and out of the fjord is by sea or aircraft."

"The investigation by the CIA seems cursory. They haven't studied the Destiny Enterprises project in depth."

Loren finished the last sip of her brandy. "An agent assigned to brief my office claimed the agency did not conduct a major investigation because they saw no threat to United States security or interests."

Pitt stared thoughtfully beyond the walls of the restaurant. "Al Giordino and I were in a Chilean fjord several years ago during a search for a liner hijacked by terrorists. The hijackers had hidden the ship near a glacier. From what I recall of the islands and waterways north of the Straits of Magellan, there are no channels wide and deep enough to permit passage of such gargantuan vessels."

"Maybe they were not intended to sail the seven seas," suggested Loren. "Maybe they were built simply to ride out the predicted cataclysm."

"As fantastic as it seems," said Pitt, attempting to accept the incredible concept, "you're close to the truth. The Wolfs must have spent billions betting on the end of the world."

Pitt became quiet, and Loren could see he was absorbed in his thoughts. She rose from the table and walked to the ladies' room, allowing him time to sift through the conceptions running through his head. Although he found it difficult to accept, he began to see why the later generations of the Wolf family were genetically engineered.

The old Nazis who'd fled Germany were long gone, but they had left in their place a family of superpeople who would be strong enough to survive the coming cataclysm and then take over what was left of the civilized world and rebuild it into a new one, controlled and directed under their exacting standards of superiority.

29

THE GRAY GRANITE CLIFFS of the gorge rose like giant shadows before they were blotted out by the night sky. Below, the blue-white ice of the glacier glittered and flashed from the glow of a three-quarter moon. The 11,800-foot snow-mantled peak of Cerro Murallón, starlit and cloud-free, soared above the western slopes of the southern Andes before dropping steeply toward the sea, as its chasms became filled with age-old glaciers from a distant past. The night was clear and sharp and the sky ablaze. Revealed from the light of the Milky Way, a small vehicle darted through the menacing walls of the gorge like a bat scanning a desert canyon for food.

It was fall in the Southern Hemisphere, and light snow had already fallen on the upper elevations. Tall conifers marched up the rugged slopes before stopping at the timberline, where the barren rocks took over and rose to the sharp and jagged mountain summits. There wasn't a man-made light to be seen in any direction. Pitt imagined that the scene in daylight would have been one of majestic beauty, but at ten o'clock at night, the steep cliffs and rocky crags became dark and threatening.

The Moller M400 Skycar wasn't much larger than a Jeep Cherokee, but it was as stable in flight as a much larger aircraft, and capable of being piloted down city streets and parked in a residential garage. The aerodynamic design, with its sloping, conical bow, gave it a look somewhere between a General Motors car of the future and a rocket fighter out of *Star Wars*. The four lift/thrust nacelles each held two counterrotating engines, enabling the Moller to lift off the ground like a helicopter and move horizontally like a conventional aircraft at a cruising speed of three hundred miles an hour, with an operational ceiling of 30,000 feet. Lose an engine or two and it could still land safely without discomfort to the passengers. Even if it suffered a catastrophic component failure, dual airframe parachutes would be deployed to lower the Skycar and its occupants to the ground, undamaged and unhurt.

Sensors and fail-safe systems protected against all errors in the flight mechanisms or computers. The vehicle's four computers constantly monitored all systems, and maintained automatic control on a preset flight path directed by Global Positioning System satellites that guided it over rivers and mountains and through valleys and canyons. The enormously efficient guidance system eliminated the need for a pilot.

Pitt's view of the environment outside the cockpit was limited. He seldom bothered to stare through the canopy. He didn't care to see the plane's shadow under the dim light from the moon whisking over the uneven rocks below, flitting over the tops of the trees, lifting over sharp rises before they could be seen ahead. He especially wasn't interested in seeing how the plane and its shadow almost blended into one. He could watch the flight's path through the virtual reality topographical display, while the automatic navigation equipment flew the Skycar to its preprogrammed destination. Turbulence was dampened by the quick, automatic reaction of the vanes below the engines commanded by the automatic stabilization system.

Pitt found it disconcerting to sit with his arms crossed while the aircraft swept in and around mountains in the dead of night without the slightest assistance from a human brain and hands. He had little choice but to put his trust in the computer guidance system and let it do the flying. If Giordino, seated next to him, was unduly concerned about the computer failing to avoid collision with the side of a mountain, no trace of it showed in his face. Giordino calmly read an adventure novel under a cockpit light, while Pitt turned his attention to a nautical chart showing the underwater depths of the fjord leading to the Wolf shipyard.

There was no plan to fly at safe heights above the tallest of the peaks. This was a stealth mission. The powerful, efficient rotary thrusters were taking them to their destination well out of sight of radar and laser detection.

Both men's bodies were sweating up a storm inside their DUI CF200 series dry suits, which were worn over radiant insulating underwear, but neither of them complained. By dressing for cold-water diving before the flight, they saved time changing after touchdown.

Pitt punched in a code and read the numbers on the box. "Two hundred and twelve miles since we lifted off the ship at Punta Entrada outside of Santa Cruz."

"How much farther?" asked Giordino without looking up from the pages of his novel.

"A little less than fifty miles and another fifteen minutes should put us in the hills above the Wolf shipyard." The exact landing site had been programmed into the computer from an enhanced photo taken from a spy satellite.

"Just enough time to knock out another chapter."

"What's so interesting that you can't tear yourself away from the book?"

"I'm just to the part where the hero is about to rescue the gorgeous heroine who is within seconds of being ravished by the evil terrorists."

"I've read that plot before," Pitt said wearily. He refocused his eyes on the virtual reality display that pictured the terrain ahead in extreme detail through a powerful night-vision scope mounted in the nose of the M400. It was like traveling inside a pinball machine. The mountainous landscape approached and flashed past in a blur. A box in the corner displayed speed, altitude, fuel range, and distance to their destination in red and orange digital numbers. Pitt recalled using a similar system on the aircraft they had flown searching for the hijacked cruise ship over an area of the Chilean fjords not more than a hundred miles south of their present position.

Pitt looked out the bubble canopy at the glacier below. He breathed a sigh of relief at seeing the worst of the mountains fall behind. The moon's rays reflected on a smooth glacier with irregular crevasses slicing through its surface every half mile. The ice spread wider as it flowed toward its rendezvous with the fjord before melting and emptying into the sea.

They were through the worst of the mountains now, and Pitt could discern lights on the horizon beyond the glacier. He knew they were not stars, because they were clustered and twinkling at too low an altitude. He also knew that because of the crisp atmosphere, the lights were much farther away than they looked. Then gradually, almost imperceptibly, he became aware of other light clusters against a plain of pure black. Another five minutes and they were solidly, unmistakably there, the lights of four monstrous ships that blazed like small cities in the night.

"Our objective is in sight," he said evenly, without emotion.

"Damn!" muttered Giordino. "Just when I was coming to the exciting climax."

"Relax. You have another ten minutes to finish it. Besides, I already know how it comes out."

Giordino looked over at him. "You do?"

Pitt nodded seriously. "The butler did it."

Giordino gave a menacing Fu Manchu squint to his eyes and went back to his book.

The Moller M400 did not fly directly over the lights of the shipyard and the great ships nearby in the fjord. Instead, as if it had a mind of its own, which it did, it banked on a course southwest. Pitt could do little but gaze at the blaze of lights rising on the starboard side of the aircraft.

"Finished." Giordino sighed. "And in case you're interested, it wasn't the butler who killed ten thousand people, it was a mad scientist." He stared out the canopy at the thousands of lights. "Won't they pick us up on their detection systems?"

"A slim possibility at best. The Moller M400 is so small, it's invisible to all but the most sophisticated military radar."

"I hope you're right," said Giordino, stretching. "I'm very modest when it comes to welcome committees."

Pitt beamed a little penlight on his chart. "At this point the computer is giving us a choice between swimming underwater for two miles or walking four miles across a glacier to reach the shipyard."

"Hiking across a glacier in the dark doesn't sound inviting," said Giordino. "What if Mrs. Giordino's little boy falls down a crevasse and isn't found for ten thousand years?"

"Somehow I can't picture you lying in a display case in a museum, being stared at by thousands of people."

"I see nothing wrong with being a star attraction from another time," Giordino said pompously.

"Did it ever occur to you that you'd probably be viewed in the nude? You'd hardly set an example as a manly specimen from the twenty-first century."

"I'll have you know I can hold my own with the best of them."

All further conversation came to an end as the Moller's ground speed began to fall away and it lost altitude. Pitt elected to make their approach underwater, and he programmed the computer, instructing it to land at a preplanned site near the shoreline that had been pinpointed by satellite photo analysts at the CIA. Minutes later, the M400's cascade vane systems on the engines altered their thrust through the duct exits and the craft came to a complete stop, hovering in the air in preparation for setting down. All Pitt could see in the darkness was that they were about thirty feet over a narrow ravine. Then the Moller descended and lightly touched the hard-rock ground. Seconds later, the engines ceased their revolutions and the systems shut down. The navigation readout proclaimed that it had landed only four inches off its programmed mark.

"I've never felt so useless in my life," said Pitt.

"It does tend to make one feel redundant," Giordino added. Only then did he peer out of the canopy. "Where are we?"

"In a ravine about fifty yards from the fjord."

Pitt unlatched the canopy, raised it, and stepped out of the flying vehicle onto the hard ground. The night was not silent. The sounds of shipyard machinery working around the clock could be heard over the water. He opened the rear seat and storage section and began passing the dive gear to Giordino, who laid the air tanks, back-mounted buoyancy compensators, weight belts, fins, and masks in a parallel row. They both pulled on their boots and hoods, slipped into the compensators, and hoisted the twin air tanks onto each other's back. Both carried chest packs, containing handguns, lights, and Pitt's trusty Globalstar phone. The final items of equipment they removed from the M400 were two Torpedo 2000 diver propulsion vehicles, with dual battery-powered hulls, attached in parallel, that looked like small rockets. Their top speed under water was 4.5 miles an hour, with a running time of one hour.

Pitt strapped a small directional computer, similar to the one he'd used in the Pandora Mine, on his left arm and set it to lock in on the GPS satellites. He then punched in a code that translated the data onto a tiny monitor that showed their exact position in relation to the shipyard and the fjord's channel leading to it.

Giordino adjusted a spectral imaging scope over his face mask and switched it on. The landscape suddenly materialized before his eyes, slightly fuzzy but distinct enough to see pebbles on the ground half an inch in diameter. He turned to Pitt.

"Time to go?"

Pitt nodded. "Since you can see our way on land, you lead off and I'll take over when we reach the water."

Giordino simply gave a brief nod and said nothing. Until they could safely penetrate the security defenses around the shipyard, there was nothing *to* say. Pitt did not require telepathic powers to know what was in Giordino's mind. He was mentally reliving the same thing as Pitt.

They were back six thousand miles in distance and twenty hours in time in Admiral Sandecker's office in the NUMA headquarters, talking their way into what had to be a scheme born under a cloud of madness.

"MISTAKES were made," said the admiral solemnly. "Dr. O'Connell is missing."

"I thought she was under round-the-clock surveillance by security agents," Pitt said, annoyed at Ken Helm.

"All anyone knows at this point is that she drove her daughter to get some ice cream. While the guards sat outside the store in their car, Dr.

O'Connell and her daughter went inside and never came out. It seems impossible that such a spur-of-the-moment event by O'Connell could be known in advance by the abductors."

"Meaning the Wolfs." Pitt slammed his fist on the table. "Why do we continually underestimate these people?"

"I suppose you'll be even less happy to hear the rest," Sandecker said somberly.

Pitt looked at him, his face clouded with exasperation. "Let me guess. Elsie Wolf has disappeared from the clinic, along with the body of her cousin, Heidi."

Sandecker wiped an imaginary speck from the polished surface of the conference table. "Believe me, it must have taken a magician," said FBI agent Ken Helm. "The clinic has the latest technology in security-detection equipment."

"Didn't your surveillance cameras reveal her escape?" asked Pitt irritably. "Elsie obviously didn't walk through the front door with her dead cousin thrown over her shoulder."

Helm gave a brief tilt of his head. "The cameras were fully operational, and the monitors observed every second. I'm sorry—no, shocked—to say that no trace of the breakout was recorded."

"These people must have the ability to slip through cracks," said Giordino, who had seated himself at the opposite end of the table from Sandecker. "Or else they developed a pill for invisibility."

"Neither," said Pitt. "They're shrewder than we are."

"All that we have, and it's fifty percent speculation," Helm admitted, "is that an executive jet belonging to Destiny Enterprises took off from an airport near Baltimore and set a course due south—"

"To Argentina," Pitt finished.

"Where else would they take her?" added Giordino. "Doesn't figure they'd keep her in the States, where they have little or no control over government investigative agencies."

Ron Little of the CIA cleared his throat. "The question is why? At one time we were led to believe they wanted to eliminate Mr. Pitt, Mr. Giordino, and Dr. O'Connell because of their discoveries of the chamber in Colorado and its inscriptions. But now, too many people are knowledgeable about the messages left by the ancient people. So the effort to keep it secret becomes immaterial."

"The only practical answer is that they need her expertise," suggested Helm.

"When I asked Elsie Wolf how many Chambers the Amenes had built, she claimed there was a total of six," Pitt said. "We had found two and they had found one. Of the others, two were destroyed by natural causes. Only one remains unfound, and she said it was somewhere in the Andes of Peru, but the directions were vague. I'll bet that despite all the experts in their computer software division, they couldn't crack the code giving instructions on how to find the remaining lost chamber."

"So they snatched her, thinking she could crack the code," said Sandecker.

"Makes sense," Helm said slowly.

Giordino leaned across the table. "Knowing Pat only a short time as I do, I have my doubts she'd cooperate."

Little smiled. "They also have Dr. O'Connell's fourteen-year-old daughter. All the Wolfs have to do is threaten to harm her."

"She'll talk," Helm said gravely. "She has no choice."

"So we go in and get her out," said Pitt.

Little looked at him doubtfully. "We have no way of knowing exactly where they're holding her."

"Their shipyard in Chile. The Wolfs are so maniacal about a coming doomsday that I'm betting the family has congregated on the ships in preparation for the deluge."

"I can provide you with satellite photos of the shipyard," said Little. "But I have to tell you, our analysts believe their security systems make the ships inaccessible and unapproachable by land, sea, or air."

"Then we'll go in underwater."

"You can expect underwater sensors."

"We'll find a way around that problem."

"I can't agree to this," Sandecker said quietly. "Too much is on the line for NUMA. This is a job for Special Operations Forces or a Navy SEAL team."

"Finding and rescuing Pat O'Connell and her daughter is only part of our plan," explained Pitt. "No one is better qualified than Al and I to investigate Destiny Enterprise's immense shipbuilding project. Less than a year ago, we performed a clandestine search under the hull of the former liner *United States* in a submersible at a shipyard in Hong Kong. In this circumstance, there has to be a method to the madness behind the Wolf family spending billions of dollars to build ships that can't reach the sea."

"The FBI can't help you on this one," said Helm. "It's half a world out of our territory."

Little nervously folded and unfolded his hands. "Other than providing information, I'm afraid my agency's hands are tied. The State Department would squelch any involvement by the CIA to intervene."

Pitt looked at Sandecker and smiled tightly. "It seems we're elected."

Sandecker did not smile in return. "Are you sure there is a desperate urgency to penetrate the Wolfs' operation?"

"I do," Pitt said heavily. "I also believe, and I can't tell you why, that there is a far more sinister purpose behind their undertaking. A purpose with horrible consequences."

THE narrow ravine meandered for a hundred yards before opening onto the waters of the fjord. The western shoreline sloped upward onto a peninsula with the strange name of Exmouth. The eastern coast was split by channels gouged by receding glaciers. The bright lights of the Wolf shipyard and those of the four floating cities reflected across the water on the north end of the fjord.

Giordino stopped and gestured for Pitt to stay in the shadows of a large rock. Two patrol boats running side by side on opposite sides of the channel moved across the black water, sweeping the surface and shore with searchlights. Giordino studied the patrol craft through his spectral imaging sensors, which turned darkness into a dusky daylight.

"You're the powerboat expert," said Pitt. "Can you identify them?"

"Thirty-eight-foot Dvichak Industries boat," Giordino replied easily. "Usually built as an oil spill response boat, but in this case they've loaded them with weapons. A good, tough, reliable boat. Not fast, about eighteen knots max, but the three-hundred-horsepower engine gives them enough torque to push and tow large barges. Serving as armed patrol boats is a new practice."

"Can you make out the type of guns?"

"Twin automatics, big millimeter, fore and aft," answered Giordino. "That's all I can recognize."

"Speed?"

"They seem to be loafing along at four knots, taking their time to look for intruders."

"Slow enough for our Torpedo 2000s to keep pace," said Pitt.

"What evil is swirling in your mind?"

"We wait underwater until they turn and begin sweeping back toward the shipyard," answered Pitt. "Then, when the boat passes over, we follow astern of its wake. The prop wash will screen our presence from their underwater security sensors."

"Sounds like a winner."

While the patrol boats continued their sweep to the south, Pitt and Giordino checked their equipment for a final time before slipping on dry hoods over their heads and gauntlet-style quarter-inch neoprene gloves onto their hands. Next they pulled their swim fins over the attached boots of their dry suits. They wore full face masks over their hoods, with Aquacom underwater communicators. Lastly, they each clipped a thin umbilical line to their weight belts; this line ran from one man to the other to keep them from becoming separated and losing one another in the pitch-black water.

After purging the air from his dry suit, Giordino gave a thumbs-up sign to indicate that he was ready. Pitt returned a brief wave and entered the water. The bottom near the shore was rocky and slippery with slimy growth. Loaded down by their equipment, they had to walk carefully to maintain their balance until the water rose to their waists and they could launch themselves forward and swim just beneath the surface. The bottom quickly fell away and Pitt descended to ten feet, where he paused and vented the last of the air out of his suit. He was breathing shallowly, and his descent gathered momentum until the water pressure compressed the suit and he added a small amount of air to maintain near-neutral buoyancy so he could hover motionlessly.

After he had moved fifty yards from shore, Pitt surfaced and looked south. The patrol boats had reached the end of their circuit and were turning to come back. "Our escort is heading our way," he spoke through the communicator. "I hope you're right about them doing four knots. That's about as fast as our propulsion vehicles can pull us."

Giordino's head slipped from the black water beside him. "It will be close, but I think we can hang with them. Let's hope they have no infrared underwater cameras."

"The fjord is at least half a mile wide—too large an area to be effectively covered by cameras." Pitt swung around and gazed at the lights to the north. "With three shifts working twenty-four hours, the Wolfs must be paying a king's treasury in wages."

"What do you bet they don't tolerate employee unions?"

"What do you figure the patrol boat's draft at?"

"Less than two feet, but it's the prop we worry about. It's probably almost three feet in diameter."

They watched closely as the patrol boat on their side of the fjord approached. Estimating its course, they swam out another ten yards and then curled over and swam down to twelve feet, before the searchlight could catch their heads protruding above the surface. Underwater, the boat's engine and thrashing propeller sounded four times louder than they did in the air. They rolled onto their backs and waited. They stared at the fjord's surface from below, watching the searchlight beams come closer at they danced over the icy water.

And then the boat's shadowed hull swept overhead, propelled by the big screw that churned past in a cyclone of froth and frenzied bubbles. Almost instantly, Pitt and Giordino pressed the magnetic speed switches against their stops, gripped the handles, and merged into the seething wake of the patrol boat.

At four knots, the prop wash was not as extreme as it would have been if the boat had been speeding along at its maximum of eighteen. They easily maintained a stabilized course behind the patrol boat without being pitched and buffeted. Their most pressing dilemma was that it was almost impossible to see where they were going. Fortunately, a bright stern light was visible to Pitt through the agitated water, so he kept his eyes locked on it, his hands gripped around the handles of the propulsion vehicle as he manhandled its torpedo-rounded bow so that it maintained a steady course through the turbulent water.

They trailed the boat for the next two miles, six feet below the cold surface water of the fjord, barely keeping pace, pushing their propulsion vehicles to their limits. They were draining the batteries at a rapid rate. Pitt could only hope they would have enough juice for the return trip to the ravine and the Skycar. His only consolation was that he and Giordino would not be easily visible so close to the surface under the brilliant lights from the shipyard. Though they were shielded by the wake and with their black dry suits blending into the freezing depths, a sharp-eyed crewman just might catch a glint of something suspicious. But no assault came. Pitt had correctly assumed that the crew had their eyes focused on the sweep of the searchlights forward.

"Can you hear me okay?" asked Pitt through the communicator inside his full face mask.

"Every syllable," replied Giordino.

"My monitor shows we've covered almost two miles. The boat should be ready to begin a turn for its next pass down the fjord. The second we feel the wake cut either left or right, we head down to a safe depth for a few minutes before surfacing to get sight bearings."

"I'll tag along," said Giordino, as calmly as if he were waiting for a bus to come around the corner.

In less than three minutes, the patrol boat began a wide 180-degree turn. Sensing the wake begin to curve, Pitt and Giordino dove to twenty feet and hung in the water until the searchlight faded into the distance and could no longer be seen from underwater. Slowly, cautiously, they kicked their fins and ascended, not knowing exactly where they would surface in the shipyard.

Both heads inched above the water surface, both pair of eyes scanning the surrounding water. They found themselves drifting only seventy-five yards from the first of four enormous docks that extended over a mile into the fjord. A colossal floating city was moored along the nearest dock, while the three other immense ships were tied beside parallel docks. They presented a dazzling sight as they glittered under the night sky. To Pitt and Giordino, staring up at the colossus from the water, its size was inconceivable. They could not conceive that such an unbelievable mass not only floated but could cruise the world's seas under its own power.

"Can it be real?" Giordino murmured in awe.

"Stupendous comes to mind," Pitt said, barely above a whisper.

"Where does one begin?"

"Forget the ships for now. We've got to find a place to get out of our dive gear before we hunt down the shipyard offices."

"You think Pat is kept there?"

"I don't know, but that's as good a place as any to start."

"We can move beneath the dock until we reach the rocks along the shore," said Giordino, holding up a hand to gesture at the water between the great dock pilings. "There are some darkened sheds off to the right. Hopefully, we can gain entry and change into our work clothes."

The work clothes were orange coveralls, similar to American prison uniforms, that had been custom-made from blown-up, enhanced photos of the workers. The pictures had been recorded by a spy satellite and given to Admiral Sandecker, along with detailed maps of the shipyard and a photo-analysis identification of the many buildings.

Punching a program into his direction finder, Pitt then held the monitor against his face mask and saw the pilings of the dock materialize before his eyes as if he were standing on dry land under a bright sun. He felt as if he were swimming through an underwater corridor with shimmering lights filtering down from above.

They moved over large pipes and electrical conduits that led from the shore to the end of the dock. Visibility had increased to over a hundred feet beneath the reflection of thousands of lights so bright it was as if they were along the Las Vegas strip.

Pitt swam, with Giordino at his side and slightly behind, over a bottom layered with smooth rocks. Gradually, the rock-strewn bottom began to rise until the divers were pulling themselves along by hand. Stopping and lying in the shallows, they saw steps leading up from a small concrete quay not far from the dock pilings. A single light globe cast its paltry glow over the quay, in contrast to the galaxy of lights illuminating from the shipyard, lighting up the front of small buildings that Pitt had memorized from the satellite photo as toolsheds. Only the side walls away from the bright lights were lost in the shadows.

"How does it look?" asked Giordino.

"Deserted," Pitt answered. "But there is no way of telling if anyone is lurking out there in the dark." He had no sooner spoken than Giordino, who was peering through his spectral image scope, spotted movement along the side of the nearest toolshed. He gripped Pitt's shoulder as a warning, as a uniformed guard with an automatic weapon slung over one shoulder emerged into the light and briefly glanced down at the quay. They lay unmoving and half submerged, partially hidden by the dock pilings.

As Pitt half expected, the guard looked bored, since he had never seen any suspicious person attempting to sneak into the shipyard. No burglar, thief, or vandal would have bothered to rob a facility over a hundred miles from the nearest town, and especially not one that was on the other side of several glaciers and the Andes Mountains. He soon turned and walked back into the gloom along the row of toolsheds.

Even before the guard faded into the darkness, Pitt and Giordino were on the quay, fins in hand, propulsion vehicles under their arms, stealing up the steps and moving hurriedly out from under the glare of the lights. The door to the first shed was unlocked, and they thankfully stepped inside. Pitt closed the door.

"Home at last," Giordino said blissfully.

Pitt found a painter's canvas tarpaulin and hung it over the only window, stuffing the edges into any cracks. Then he switched on his dive light and beamed it around the shed. It was filled with marine hardware: bins heaped with brass and chrome nuts, bolts and screws; shelves neatly arranged with electrical supplies consisting of coils and bales of wire; cabinets stacked with gallon cans of marine paint—all precisely organized and labeled.

"They certainly have a fetish for neatness."

"It carries down from their German ancestry."

Swiftly, they removed their dive equipment and dry suits. The orange uniforms were pulled from their chest packs and slipped on over their insulated underwear. Next, they removed their boots and replaced them with sneakers.

"I just had a thought," said Giordino apprehensively.

"Yes?"

"What if the Wolf personnel have names or some kind of advertising on their overalls the satellite photos didn't pick up?"

"That's not half our problem."

"What can be worse?"

"We're in South America," said Pitt mildly. "Neither of us can speak enough Spanish to ask directions to a toilet."

"I may not be fluent, but I know enough to fake it."

"Good. You do the talking, and I'll act as though I have a hearing disability."

While Giordino studied the photo map of the shipyard, figuring the shortest path to the Wolf corporate offices, Pitt dialed his Globalstar phone.

THE atmosphere inside Sandecker's condominium at the Watergate was heavy with foreboding. A fire shimmered in the fireplace, a warm, restful kind of fire that looked comforting though it didn't throw off a wave of heat. Three men were seated on opposite sofas across a low glass table holding a tray of coffee cups and a half-emptied pot. Admiral Sandecker and Ron Little sat and stared spellbound at an elderly man in his middle eighties with snow-white hair, who related a story never told before.

Admiral Christian Hozafel was a former highly decorated officer in the German Kriegsmarine during World War II. He'd served as captain aboard U-boats from June 1942 until July 1945, when he'd formally surrendered his boat in Veracruz, Mexico. After the war, Hozafel had bought a Liberty ship from the U.S. government under the Marshall Plan and had parlayed it over the next forty years into an extremely successful commercial shipping venture, eventually selling his interest and retiring when the Hozafel Marine fleet numbered thirty-seven ships. He'd become a U.S. citizen and now lived in Seattle, Washington, on a large estate on Whidbey Island, where he kept a two-hundred-foot brigantine that he and his wife sailed throughout the world.

"What you're saying," said Little, "is that the Russians did not find the scorched remains of Hitler's body outside his bunker in Berlin."

"No," Hozafel answered firmly. "There were no scorched remains. Adolf Hitler's and Eva Braun's bodies were burned over a period of five hours. Gallons of gasoline siphoned from wrecked vehicles around the Reich Chancellery were used to douse the bodies, which were lying in a crater that had been blown in the ground outside the bunker by a Soviet shell. The fire had been kept blazing until there were only ashes and a few tiny bits of bones. Loyal SS officers had then placed the ashes and bones in a bronze box. Nothing was left. Every bit of ash and every scrap of bone was carefully swept up and deposited in the box. Then the SS officers had placed the badly charred and unrecognizable bodies of a man and woman who had been killed during an air raid in the crater, where they were buried along with Hitler's dog Blondi, who had been forced to test the cyanide capsules later used by Hitler and Eva Braun."

Sandecker's eyes were fixed on Hozafel's face. "These were the bodies found by the Russians," Sandecker said.

The old former U-boat commander nodded. "They later claimed that dental records firmly established the identities of Hitler and Braun, but they knew better. For fifty years, the Russians carried out the hoax, while Stalin and other high Soviet officials thought Hitler had escaped to either Spain or Argentina."

"What became of the ashes?" asked Little.

"A light airplane landed near the bunker amid the flames and bursting Soviet shell fire as Russian armies closed in on the core of the city. The minute the pilot had swung his aircraft around for a fast takeoff, SS officers rushed forward and placed the bronze box in the cargo compartment. Without a word of conversation, the pilot gunned the engine and the plane raced down the runway, quickly vanishing in the pall of smoke rising above the city. The pilot refueled in Denmark and flew across the North Sea to Bergen, Norway. There he landed and turned over the bronze box to Captain Edmund Mauer, who in turn had the box carried aboard the U-621. Numerous other crates and boxes containing precious relics of the Nazi party, including the Holy Lance and the sacred Blood Flag and other prized art treasures of the Third Reich, were loaded aboard another submarine, the U-2015, under the command of Commander Rudolph Harger."

"This was all part of the plan conceived by Martin Bormann and given the code name of New Destiny," said Sandecker.

Hozafel looked at the admiral respectfully. "You are very well informed, sir."

"The Holy Lance and the Blood Flag," Sandecker pressed on. "They were included in the cargo of the U-2015?"

"Are you familiar with the Lance?" Hozafel inquired.

"I studied and wrote of the Lance as a class project at Annapolis," replied Sandecker. "Legends handed down from the Bible claim that a metalsmith by the name of Tubal Cain, a direct descendent of Cain, the son of Adam, forged the Lance from the iron found in a meteorite that was sent by God. This was sometime before 3000 B.C. The sacred lance was passed down from Tubal Cain to Saul, then to David and Solomon and other kings of Judea. Eventually, it came into the hands of the Roman conqueror Julius Caesar, who carried it in battle against his enemies. Before he was assassinated, he gave it to a centurion who had saved his life during the war with the Gauls. The son of the centurion passed it on to his son, who gave it to his son, who also served in the Roman legions as a centurion. It was he who stood on the hill and watched as Christ was crucified. The law of the land required that all crucified criminals be declared dead before the sun fell so they would not defile the coming Sabbath. The thieves on the crosses beside Jesus had their legs broken to speed up their demise. But when it was Jesus' turn, they found that he was already dead. The centurion, for reasons he took to the grave, pierced Jesus' side with his lance, causing an inexplicable stream of blood and water. As the holy blood spewed forth, the stained lance instantly became the most sacred relic in Christendom, next to the True Cross and the Holy Grail.

"The Holy Lance, as it became known, came down to King Charlemagne and was inherited by each of the following Holy Roman emperors over the next thousand years, before ending up in the hands of the Hapsburg emperors and being placed on display in the royal palace in Vienna."

"You must also know the fable behind the lance's power," said Hozafel, "the fable that drove Hitler to possess it."

" 'Whosoever possesses this Holy Lance, and understands the powers it serves, holds in his hand the destiny of the world for good and evil,' " quoted Sandecker. "That's why Hitler stole the lance from Austria and held it until his dying day. He imagined that it would give him mastery of the world. If Hitler had never heard of the lance, it would be interesting to speculate if he might not have sought the path of power toward world domination. His final request was that it be hidden from his enemies."

"You mentioned a Blood Flag," said Little. "I'm not familiar with that relic, either."

"In 1923," Hozafel clarified, "Hitler attempted a coup against the existing German government in Munich. It was a disaster. The army fired into the crowd and several people were killed. Hitler escaped but was later tried and sentenced to jail, where he spent nine months writing *Mein Kampf.* The coup forever became known as the Munich Putsch. One of the early swastika Nazi flags was carried by one of the would-be revolutionaries, who was shot and was splattered with his blood. Naturally, it became the bloodstained symbol of a Nazi martyr. This Blood Flag was then used in ceremonies to consecrate future Nazi flags at party rallies by holding it against them as a blessing."

"And so the Nazi treasures were smuggled out of Germany, never to be seen again," said Little meditatively. "According to old CIA archive records, no trace of the lance and other Nazi hoards, including stolen art treasures and the loot from banks and national treasuries, was ever discovered."

"Your submarine," Sandecker said evenly, "was the U-699."

"Yes, I was her captain," Hozafel admitted. "Shortly after a number of influential Nazi military officers, high party officials, and Hitler's ashes were safely loaded on board, I sailed from Bergen in the wake of the U-2015. Until now, the disappearance of Hitler has been a mystery. I am telling you the story only at the urging of Mr. Little, and because of the possibility, as I understand it, that the world will be in upheaval after a coming comet strike. If true, this makes my sworn silence irrelevant."

"We're not ready to cry doom yet," said Sandecker. "What we want to know is if the Wolf family is truly spending untold sums of money building huge arks in a fanatical belief that a cataclysm will destroy the

Earth and every living creature on it—or if they have some other motive."

"An interesting family, the Wolfs," Hozafel said pensively. "Colonel Urich Wolf was one of the most trusted men on Hitler's staff. He saw that Hitler's irrational orders and simplest wishes were carried out. The colonel was also the leader of a group of devoted Nazis who formed an elite group of SS officers dedicated to defending the faith. They called themselves the Guardians. Most of them died fighting in the final days of the war—all, that is, except Colonel Wolf and three others. He and his entire family—a wife, four sons and three daughters, two brothers, and three sisters and their families—sailed aboard the U-2015. I was told by an old naval comrade who's still living that Wolf was the last of the few Guardians and created some kind of contemporary order called the New Destiny."

"It's true. They operate as a giant conglomerate known as Destiny Enterprises," Sandecker informed Hozafel.

The old German sea dog smiled. "So they gave up their uniforms and propaganda for business suits and profit-and-loss statements."

"No longer calling themselves Nazis, they've modernized their manifesto," said Little.

"They've also created a race of superior humans," said Sandecker. "Through genetic engineering, the new generation of Wolfs not only resemble each other in appearance but their physical anatomy and characteristics are identical. They have the minds of geniuses and an extraordinary immune system that enables them to live extremely long lives."

Hozafel stiffened visibly, and his eyes took on a look of deep dread. "Genetic engineering, you say? One of the canisters that was transported aboard my U-boat was kept frozen at all times." He drew a deep breath. "It contained the sperm and tissue samples taken from Hitler the week before he killed himself."

Sandecker and Little exchanged tense looks. "Do you think it's possible Hitler's sperm was used to procreate the later generation of Wolfs?" asked Little.

"I don't know," said Hozafel nervously. "But I fear it is a distinct prospect that Colonel Wolf, working with that monster at Auschwitz known as the Angel of Death, Dr. Joseph Mengele, may have experimented with Hitler's preserved sperm to impregnate the Wolf women."

"There's an abhorrent thought if I ever heard one," muttered Little.

Suddenly a muted tone interrupted the conversation. Sandecker punched the speaker button on a phone in front of him on the coffee table.

"Is anyone home?" came Pitt's familiar voice.

"Yes," Sandecker answered tersely.

"This is the Leaning Pizza Tower. You called in an order?"

"I did."

"Did you want salami or ham on your pizza?"

"We would prefer salami."

"It's going in the oven. We will call when our delivery boy is on his way. Thank you for calling the Leaning Pizza Tower."

Then the line cut off and a dial tone came through the speaker.

Sandecker passed a hand across his face. When he looked up, his eyes were strained and grim. "They're inside the shipyard."

"God help them now," Little murmured softly.

"I don't understand," said Hozafel. "Was that some sort of code?"

"Satellite phone calls are not immune to interception by the right equipment," explained Little.

"Does this somehow have to do with the Wolfs?"

"I do believe, Admiral," Sandecker dropped his voice and answered slowly, "that it's time you heard our side of the story."

30

PITT AND GIORDINO HAD no sooner stepped through the door of the toolshed than a voice in Spanish hailed them from around the corner of the building.

Giordino calmly replied and made empty motions with his hands.

Evidently satisfied with the answer, the guard went back to walking his beat around the toolsheds. Pitt and Giordino waited a moment, then moved out onto the road that led toward the heart of the shipyard.

"What did the guard say, and what did you answer?" asked Pitt.

"He wanted a cigarette, and I told him we didn't smoke."

"And he didn't challenge you."

"He did not."

"Your Spanish must be better than I thought. Where did you learn it?"

"Haggling with the vendors on the beach at my hotel in Mazatlán," Giordino answered modestly. "And when I was in high school, I was taught a few phrases by my mother's cleaning girl."

"I'll bet that wasn't *all* she taught you," Pitt said ironically.

"That's another story," said Giordino, without missing a beat.

"From now on, we'd better lay off English when we're within earshot of the shipyard workers."

"Out of curiosity, what kind of side arm are you packing?"

"My old tried-and-true Colt .45. Why do you ask?"

"You've carried that old relic ever since I've known you. Why don't you trade it in for a more modern piece?"

"It's like an old friend," Pitt said quietly. "It's saved my tail more times than I can count." He nodded at the bulge in Giordino's coveralls. "How about you?"

"One of the Para-Ordnance 10+1s we took off those clowns at the Pandora Mine."

"At least you have good taste."

"And it was free, too," Giordino said, smiling. Then he nodded toward the main buildings of the shipyard. "Which one are we heading for?"

Pitt consulted his compact directional computer, whose monitor was programmed with the layout of the shipyard. He looked up the road running adjacent to the docks on one side and bordered on the other by giant metal warehouses. He pointed at a twenty-story building rising above the warehouses a good mile up the road. "The tall building on the right."

"I've never seen a shipbuilding facility this big," said Giordino, staring over the giant complex. "It beats anything in Japan or Hong Kong."

They stopped suddenly and stared at the nearest supership, like yokels from the boondocks, heads tilted back looking up at their first view of tall city buildings. An executive jet aircraft whined in on its approach before flaring out and touching down on the long landing deck atop the behemoth. The sounds of the engines echoed across the water, up the slopes of the mountains, and back again. The sight was staggering. Even the most sophisticated Hollywood special effects could not come close to replicating the real thing.

"None of the shipyards around the world have the capacity to build ships this grand," said Pitt, standing and gazing overwhelmed at the gargantuan ship moored along the dock, its hull seeming to stretch nearly to infinity. No single building on earth, including the twin towers of the World Trade Center in New York placed end to end, could have matched the inconceivable size of the Wolfs' ark.

Except for the great bow, the vessel did not resemble a ship. Rather, it looked like a modern skyscraper laid on its side. The entire superstructure was sided in armored and tinted glass with the strength of low-alloy steel. Gardens with trees could be seen on the other side of the glass, flourishing amid rock gardens set in large parklike atmospheres. There were no promenade or outer decks or balconies. All the decks were completely enclosed. A conventional pointed bow swept up the superstructure on a gradual angle to the landing deck in what Pitt recognized as an apparent strategy to reduce the crushing impact of a giant tidal wave.

He observed the stern of the ship with more than a passing interest. Beginning at the waterline, twenty parallel pierlike projections that Pitt reckoned to be two hundred feet in length extended astern, beneath a high roof supported with fifty-foot-high Grecian-sculpted pillars. The piers doubled as shrouds for the ship's propellers and as piers to moor fleets of powerboats, hydrofoils, and hovercraft. Wide staircases and glass elevators rose from the forward end of the piers into the main superstructure. Improbable as it seemed, the gigantic vessel had its own marina, where boats could be moored and lifted from the water between the piers when the ship was under way.

Pitt studied the thousands of workers who crowded the docks and open decks. The operation to fit out and supply the ship seemed to be in a frenzied rush. Towering cranes rolled on rails up and down the dock, lifting wooden crates into huge open cargo hatches set into the hull. The spectacle was too unreal to grasp. It seemed unbelievable that these floating cities were never meant to sail through the fjord and reach the sea. Their primary purpose was to survive great tidal waves before being carried by the backwash into deep water.

There was no slinking in the shadows, because the bright lights eliminated them. Pitt and Giordino walked leisurely along the wide road quay, waving to an occasional passing guard, who didn't give them a second look. Pitt quickly observed that most of the workers moved around the immense facility and the ships in electric golf-type carts. He began looking around for one, and soon spied several parked in front of a large warehouse.

Pitt set off toward the carts, followed by Giordino, who could not tear his eyes from the ships. "This place is too vast to cover on foot," said Pitt. "Me, I'd rather ride."

The battery-operated carts looked to be available to any worker who wanted to requisition one. Several were parked around a large charging unit, cords running to sockets beneath the front seats. Pitt pulled the plug on the first one in line. Throwing the electrical spools and paint cans in the rear cargo bed of the cart, they climbed onto the front seat. Pitt turned the ignition key and set off as though it were a procedure he had executed at the yard for years.

They drove past a long string of warehouses until they came to the tall building that held the shipyard offices. The entrance of the second dock extended from the road along the shore. The second floating leviathan that was moored alongside had a more austere appearance than the one that was expected to carry its residents into a new world. This vessel was designed to carry agricultural cargo. Various species of trees and shrubbery were hauled aboard in big trailers that were pulled up wide cargo ramps into the hull. Hundreds of long cylindrical containers, labeled "Plant Seed," were stacked on the dock waiting to be loaded aboard. A long convoy of farm equipment, trucks and tractors of different sizes, harvest combines, plows, and every other piece of machinery imaginable was driven inside the cavernous hull.

"These people mean to launch a new world order on a grand scale," Pitt said, still trying to absorb the immensity of it all.

"What do you want to bet one of the other ships is carrying two of every kind of animal?"

"I won't bet," Pitt replied curtly. "I just hope they had the foresight to leave the flies, mosquitoes, and venomous reptiles behind."

Giordino spread his lips to make some suitable comeback, thought better of it, and stepped out of the cart, as Pitt parked it beside the steps leading into the modern, glass-walled office building. Retrieving the electrical cable and paint cans, they walked inside and approached a long counter manned by two security guards. Giordino flashed his most sociable smile and spoke softly in Spanish to one of the guards.

The guard simply nodded and threw a thumb in the direction of the elevators. "What line did you feed him this time?" queried Pitt, as they stepped inside, but not before he peered with one eye around the elevator door and spied one guard pick up a phone and speak excitedly. Then he stepped back and the doors closed.

"I said we were ordered by one of the Wolfs to make electrical repairs behind a wall in the penthouse suite on the tenth floor, then mend and repaint the wall when we were finished. He didn't give me the least argument."

Pitt scanned the elevator for TV cameras but found none. It's almost as if they have no fear of covert actions, he thought. Or else they know we're here and have laid a trap. He might have been whistling in the dark, but he didn't trust the Wolfs as far as he could throw that floating monstrosity outside. He also sensed that the guards in the lobby had been expecting them.

"Time for an ingenious scheme," he said.

Giordino looked at him. "Plan C?"

"We'll stop on the fifth floor to throw off the guards who are probably monitoring our movements. But we remain inside and send the elevator up to the penthouse, while we climb through the roof and ride up the rest of the way."

"Not half bad," said Giordino, pressing the button to stop the elevator on the fifth floor.

"Okay," said Pitt. "Hold me on your shoulders while I climb through the ceiling." But Pitt made no move. Though he did not detect the presence of TV cameras, Pitt was dead sure the elevator contained listening devices. He stood quietly still and grinned darkly at Giordino.

Giordino immediately understood and pulled out his P-10 automatic. "Damn, you're heavy," he grunted.

"Give me your hand and I'll pull you up," Pitt said quietly, as he gripped the old .45 Colt in his right hand. Remaining inside the elevator, they stood on opposite sides of the doors and pressed themselves into the corners.

The doors opened, and three guards, wearing identical coveralls, black with matching stocking caps on their heads, rushed inside, handguns drawn, eyes staring up at the open maintenance door in the ceiling. Pitt stuck out his leg and tripped the third man, who fell against the first two, sending them all sprawling in a tangled heap on the floor. Then he punched the door-close button, waited until they descended several feet, and pressed the red emergency stop button, freezing the elevator between floors.

Giordino had expertly clubbed two of the guards on the head with the butt of his automatic before they could recover, then held the muzzle against the forehead of the third and snarled in Spanish, "Drop your gun or go brain-dead."

The guard was as tough and coldly efficient as the mercenaries they had encountered in the Pandora Mine. Pitt tensed, sensing the guard might attempt a lightning move to get in the first shot. But the man detected the cold look of composure in Pitt's eyes and recognized a deadly threat. Knowing the slightest flick of his eyes would bring a bullet smashing into his head, he wisely dropped his gun onto the elevator floor, the same model Para-Ordnance that Giordino was pressing between his eyes.

"You clowns are going nowhere!" the guard spat in English.

"Well, well," said Pitt. "What have we here? Another mercenary hit man like we met in Colorado. Karl Wolf must pay you guys handsome wages to murder and die for him."

"Give up, pal. You're the one who's going to die."

"You people have a nasty habit of repeating the same old song." Pitt pointed his old Colt an inch from the guard's left eye until it was lined up to fire across his face. "Dr. O'Connell and her daughter. Where are they held?" Pitt wasn't trying to imitate the rattle of a diamondback, but he gave a pretty good impression of it. "Talk or I pull the trigger. You'll probably live, but you won't have any eyeballs to see with. *Now, then, where are they?*"

Pitt was tough, but he wasn't sadistic. The look on his twisted face and the malice in his eyes was enough to fool the guard into thinking a madman was about to blow his eyes out. "They're confined on one of the great ships."

"Which ship?" demanded Pitt. "There are four of them."

"I don't know, I swear I don't know."

"He's lying," said Giordino, his tone cold enough to freeze oil.

"The truth," Pitt said menacingly, "or I'll blast both your eyeballs into the far wall." He pulled back the hammer of the Colt and pressed the muzzle against the edge of the guard's right eye in line with the left.

The guard's face did not transform from defiance to pure fright, but still, staring from eyes filled with loathing, he gasped, "The *Ulrich Wolf*. They're being held on the *Ulrich Wolf*."

"Which ship is that?"

"The ship-city that will carry the people of the Fourth Empire to sea after the cataclysm."

"It would take two years to search a ship that size," Pitt pressured. "Give a more exact location or go blind. Quickly!"

"Level Six, K Section. I don't know which residence."

"He's still lying," said Giordino coarsely. "Pull the trigger, but wait till I look away. I can't stand to see blood spray all over the furniture."

"Then kill me and get it over with," the guard growled.

"Where do the Wolfs find murdering scum like you?"

"Why would you care?"

"You're American. He didn't hire you off the street, so you must have come out of the military, an elite force, unless I miss my guess. Your loyalty to the Wolf family goes far beyond rationality. Why?"

"Giving my life for the Fourth Empire is an honor. I'm repaid by knowing, as we all are, that my wife and sons will be safely onboard the *Ulrich Wolf* when the rest of the world is devastated."

"So that's your insurance policy."

"He has a human family?" Giordino said in amazement. "I'd have sworn he curls up and lays eggs."

"What good is a bank account with a billion dollars when the world's population is about to perish?"

"I hate a pessimist," said Giordino, as he swung the barrel of his automatic against the nape of the mercenary's neck, dropping him unconscious onto the inert bodies of his comrades. In almost the same instant a series of alarms began to sound throughout the building. "That tears it. We'll have to shoot our way out of town."

"Style and sophistication," Pitt said, seemingly unconcerned. "Always style and sophistication."

Six minutes later, the elevator stopped at the lobby level and the door opened. On the floor of the lobby, nearly two dozen men, with automatic weapons raised and aimed into the elevator, stood and knelt in the firing position.

Two men in the black coverall uniforms of security guards, with stocking caps pulled down almost to their eyes, raised their hands and shouted with lowered heads in both English and Spanish. "Do not shoot. We have killed two of the intruders!" Then they dragged two bodies dressed in orange coveralls by the feet out onto the lobby's marble floor and unceremoniously dumped them. "There are others who were working from the inside," Giordino said excitedly. "They've barricaded themselves on the tenth floor."

"Where is Max?" inquired a guard who acted as if he was in command.

Pitt, his arm over his face as if wiping away perspiration, turned and pointed upward. Giordino said, "We had to leave him. He was wounded in the fight. Hurry, send for a doctor."

The well-trained security force rapidly broke down into two units, one heading into the elevator, the other rushing up the emergency fire stairs. Pitt and Giordino knelt over the two unconscious guards they had pulled from the elevator and made a show of examining them, until they saw an opportunity to walk quietly from the lobby through the front doors.

"I can't believe we pulled it off," said Giordino, as they commandeered a cart and sped off toward the dock where the *Ulrich Wolf* was moored.

"Luckily, they were all too focused on apprehending the evil intruders to take a good look at our faces and recognize us as strangers."

"My security uniform is too long and too tight. How about yours?"

"Too short and too loose, but we don't have time to stop off at a tailor," Pitt muttered, as he steered the cart back toward the first dock while dodging around a soaring crane that was moving ponderously over its rail track. He kept his foot flat on the pedal, but the cart had a top speed of only about twelve miles an hour and the pace seemed agonizingly slow.

They traveled alongside the stupendous floating city, avoiding the busy loading activities. The dock was packed with a milling horde of workers, many moving about in electric carts, others on bicycles, with quite a few darting in and around all obstacles on Rollerblades. Pitt had to frequently ram his foot onto the brake to keep from colliding with workers who moved carelessly into his path, absorbed in their jobs. Huge forklifts also ignored their approach and crossed in front of them to deliver their loads, moving up ramps and into the cavernous cargo holds. There were any number of raised fists and angry shouts as Pitt careened around all obstacles, humans or solid objects.

If it wasn't for the black security uniforms, stolen off the guards in the elevator, they would have surely been stopped and threatened with a beating for such reckless driving. Seeing an opportunity to board the ship without climbing long gangways, Pitt cramped the steering wheel and sent the cart into a hard right turn up a ramp empty of loading vehicles, across the main deck, and then down another ramp into the bowels of the floating city, to where the cargo was stored and all ship maintenance was performed. Inside a yawning cargo depot, with huge passageways leading in all directions through the lower warehouse bays of the ship, Pitt spotted a man in red coveralls who looked to be in charge of loading supplies and equipment. He alerted Giordino on what to ask in Spanish and came to an abrupt stop.

"Quickly, we have an emergency at Level Six, K Section," shouted Giordino. "Which is the shortest route to take?"

Recognizing the black uniform of the shipyard security guards, the man asked, "Don't you know?"

"We've just been transferred from shore security," Giordino answered vaguely, "and we're not familiar with the *Ulrich Wolf*."

Accepting the presence of security people on an emergency mission, the loading director pointed down a passageway. "Drive to the second elevator on the right. Park your cart and take the elevator up to Deck Floor Four. That will put you at Tram Station Eight. Board the Tram to K Section. Then take the corridor leading amidships to the security office and ask again, unless you know which residence you're looking for."

"The one where the American scientist and her daughter are being confined."

"I have no idea where that would be. You'll have to ask the chief security officer or the leader of K Section when you arrive."

"Muchas gracias," Giordino said over his shoulder, as Pitt sped off in the direction indicated. "So far so good, said the man on his way down to the sidewalk after jumping from the Empire State Building." Then he added, "My compliments. Swapping our orange goon suits for black security uniforms was a master stroke."

"It was the only way I could think of to get through the trap," said Pitt modestly.

"How much time do you think we have before they cut us off at the pass?"

"If you struck the guard a good clout, he won't come around anytime soon and give the show away. All they'll discover in the next ten minutes is that we drove straight to the *Ulrich Wolf* and came on board. They still don't know who we are or who we're after."

They followed the Cargo Deck leader's directions and brought the cart to a halt next to the second elevator. It was built to carry heavy freight, and it was expansive. Workers were accompanying a pallet piled with boxes of canned food. Pitt and Giordino joined them and stepped off onto Level Six, near a boarding platform raised above twin tracks that encircled the entire ship. They paced the platform impatiently for five minutes, before an electric tram with five cars painted a soft yellow outside and hyacinth violet inside approached and quietly rolled to a stop. The doors slid open with a soft hissing sound. They stepped inside the first car and found a forty-passenger vehicle that was half full of people clothed in a rainbow of coverall uniforms. As if drawn by a magnet, Giordino sat down next to an attractive woman with silver-blond hair and blue eyes whose coveralls were a soft blue-gray. Pitt tensed as he recognized the unvarying image of one of the Wolf family.

She looked at them and smiled. "You look like Americans," she said in English with a touch of a Spanish accent.

"How can you tell?" asked Pitt.

"Most all our security people were recruited from the American military," she replied.

"You are a member of the Wolf family," he said softly, as if speaking to a member of the elite.

She laughed lightheartedly. "It must look to strangers as if we all came out of the same pod."

"Your resemblance to one another is quite striking."

"What is your name?" she asked, in a tone of authority.

"My name is Dirk Pitt," he said brazenly, actually stupidly, he thought, studying her eyes for a reaction. There was none. She had not been advised of his menacing actions toward the family. "My little friend here is Al Capone."

"Rosa Wolf," she identified herself.

"A great honor, Miss Wolf," Pitt said, "to be associated with your family's great venture. The *Ulrich Wolf* is a glorious masterwork. My friend and I were recruited from the United States Marines only two weeks ago. It is indeed a privilege to serve a family that has created such an extraordinary work of genius."

"My cousin Karl was the driving force behind the construction of the *Ulrich Wolf* and our other three Fourth Empire floating cities," Rosa sermonized from pride, obviously pleased with Pitt's praise. "He assembled the world's finest naval architects and marine engineers to design and construct our vessels, from the blueprint stage to completion, under a cloak of extreme secrecy. Unlike most large cruise liners and supertankers, our ships have no single hull but employ nine hundred watertight sealed compartments. If, during the massive surge expected from the coming cataclysm, a hundred cells are damaged and flooded on any of our vessels, they will sink no more than ten inches."

"Truly astounding," said Giordino, acting enthralled. "What is the power source?"

"Ninety ten-thousand-horsepower diesel propulsion engines that are geared to push the ship through the water at twenty-five knots."

"A city of fifty thousand inhabitants capable of moving around the world," said Pitt. "It doesn't seem possible."

"Not fifty thousand, Mr. Pitt. When the time comes, this ship will carry one hundred and twenty-five thousand people. Between them, the other three vessels will carry fifty thousand people, for a total of two hundred and seventy-five thousand, all trained and educated to launch the Fourth Empire from the ashes of archaic democratic systems."

Pitt fought the urge to instigate a heated debate, but he turned his attention out the window of the train. He watched as a landscaped park of at least twenty acres unfolded along the tram tracks. He was repeatedly stunned by the impact of such an immense project. Bike and jogging paths wound through trees and ponds with swans, geese, and ducks.

Rosa noticed his captivation by the pastoral scene. "This is one of a network of parks, leisure and recreation areas, that total five hundred acres. Have you seen the sport facilities, swimming pools, and health spas yet?"

Pitt shook his head. "Our time has been limited."

"Are you married, with children?"

Recalling his conversation with the security guard, Pitt nodded. "A boy and a girl."

"We have recruited the world's finest educators to teach in and direct our schools, from the nursery level through college-level courses and postgraduate studies."

"That is very comforting to know."

"You and your wife will be able to enjoy theaters, educational seminars and conferences, libraries, and art galleries filled with historical art treasures. We also have compartments housing the great artifacts passed down from the ancient ones, so that they can be studied while we wait for the earth's environment to regenerate itself after the coming cataclysm."

"The ancient ones?" asked Pitt, playing dumb.

"The civilization our grandfathers discovered in Antarctica, called the Amenes. They were an advanced race of people who were destroyed when Earth was struck by a comet nine thousand years ago."

"I'd never heard of them," Giordino played along.

"Our scientists are studying their records so we can learn what to expect in the coming months and years."

"How long do you think it will take before we can begin our work on land?" asked Pitt.

"Five, perhaps ten, years before we can go forth and establish a new order," explained Rosa.

"Can a hundred and twenty-five thousand people subsist that long?"

"You're forgetting the other ships," she said boastfully. "The fleet will be totally self-supporting. The *Karl Wolf* has fifty thousand acres of tilled soil already planted with vegetables and fruit orchards. The *Otto Wolf* will carry thousands of animals for food as well as breeding. The final ship, the *Hermann Wolf*, was built purely for cargo. It will haul all the equipment and machinery to construct new cities, roads, ranches, and farms when we are able to walk the earth again."

Giordino pointed up to a digital sign above the doors. "K Section coming up."

"A great pleasure meeting you, Ms. Wolf," said Pitt gallantly. "I hope you will remember me to your cousin Karl."

She looked at him questioningly for a moment, then nodded. "I'm sure we'll meet again."

The train slowed to a stop, and Pitt and Giordino disembarked. They walked from the boarding platform into an antechamber with corridors leading off like wagon wheel spokes into a vast labyrinth.

"Now which way?" asked Giordino.

"We go dead amidships and follow the signs to the K Section," Pitt said, as he set off into the center corridor. "We want to avoid the security office like the plague."

Walking along what seemed to be an endless corridor, they passed numbered doors, several of them open while the rooms were being furnished. They looked in and saw spacious living quarters on a par with luxury condominiums. Pitt could understand now why the guard had referred to them as residences. The plan was for the occupants to live as comfortably as possible during the long wait before they could establish their community on what was left of the earth after the comet's collision.

Paintings were spaced every thirty feet along the walls between the doors to the residences. Giordino stopped briefly and examined a landscape in vivid colors. He leaned close and peered at the artist's scrawled name.

"No way can this be a Van Gogh," he said skeptically. "It must be a forgery or a reproduction."

"It's genuine," said Pitt, with conviction. He motioned toward the other art hanging on the walls. "These works doubtless come from the museums and the private collections of Holocaust victims that were looted by the Nazis during World War Two."

"How charitable of them to save art treasures that never belonged to them."

"The Wolfs plan to carry the great masterworks to the promised land."

How could the Wolfs be so positive that the second coming of the comet would strike the earth? Pitt wondered. Why wasn't it possible the comet would miss again, as it had nine thousand years before? There were no ready answers, but once he and Giordino could escape the shipyard with Pat and her daughter, he was determined to find solutions.

After what Giordino estimated as a quarter of a mile, they came to a large door marked "Security, Level K." They hurried past and finally came to a tastefully decorated reception area with tables, chairs, and sofas in front of a large fireplace. It could have passed for a lobby in any five-star hotel. A man and a woman dressed in green coveralls sat behind a counter beneath a large painting of Noah's Ark.

"Somebody in authority must have a color-code mania," Giordino muttered under his breath.

"Ask them where the American epigraphist, who is deciphering the ancient descriptions, is confined," Pitt instructed.

"How in hell would I know what 'epigraphist' is in Spanish?"

"Fake it."

Giordino rolled his eyes and approached the counter in front of the woman, thinking she might be more helpful.

"We've been sent to move Dr. O'Connell and her daughter to another part of the ship," he said softly, in an attempt to muffle his American accent.

The woman, attractive in a mannish sort of way, with a pale complexion and her hair swept back in a bun, looked up at Giordino and noted his security uniform. "Why wasn't I notified earlier that she was scheduled to be moved?"

"I was told only ten minutes ago myself."

"I should verify this request," said the woman in an official tone.

"Better yet, my superior is on his way. I suggest you wait and settle the matter with him."

She nodded. "Yes, I'll do that."

"Meanwhile, you might point out the residence where she is being held, so we can prepare her for the move."

"You don't know?" the woman asked, suspicion growing in her mind.

"How could we?" Giordino asked innocently, "since she is under your charge as section leader. My partner and I are simply paying you the courtesy of checking with you rather than just going in and taking her. Now, tell me where she is and we'll wait until my superior shows with the proper authority, if that will make you sleep easier."

The female section leader yielded. "You will find Dr. O'Connell locked in residence K-37. But I can't give you the key until I see a signed order."

"There's no need for us to enter just yet," Giordino said, with an indifferent shrug. "We'll stand outside and wait." He tilted his head in a gesture for Pitt to follow him, and he began walking back the way they had come. Once out of earshot, he said, "She's held in K-37. I think we passed residences numbered in the thirties on the way from the elevator."

"Is her residence guarded?" asked Pitt.

"Wearing this security outfit, I'm supposed to know if guards are posted. No, I wasn't about to bring up the subject and look like a suspicious idiot."

"We'd better be quick," said Pitt. "They must be on our tail by now."

When they reached K-37, they found a guard standing outside. Giordino walked up casually and said, "You're relieved."

The guard, a man who was a good foot taller than the short Etruscan, stared down with a questioning look on his face. "I have another two hours left on my shift."

"Aren't you lucky we were sent early."

"You don't look familiar," said the guard uneasily.

"Neither do you." Then Giordino made as if to turn away. "Forget it. My partner and I will wait in the dining room until your shift ends."

The guard suddenly changed his tune. "No, no, I could use the extra time to get some sleep." Without further procrastination, he began walking swiftly toward the elevator.

"A productive performance," said Pitt.

"I have a persuasive personality," Giordino said, grinning.

As soon as the guard stepped into the elevator at the end of the long corridor, Pitt kicked his foot hard against the door near the latch and smashed it open. They charged into the residence almost before the door thumped against its stop. A young girl was standing in the kitchen, wearing blue coveralls and in the act of drinking a glass of milk. In fright, she dropped the glass in her hand onto the carpet. Pat came running out of the bedroom, also dressed in blue coveralls, her long red hair spread behind her like a fan. She stopped frozen in the doorway and stared unbelievingly at Pitt and Giordino, her mouth open but unable to utter words, eyes mirroring total confusion.

Pitt grabbed her by the arm as Giordino swept up the girl. "No time for hugs and kisses," he said quickly. "We've got a plane to catch."

"Where did you two beautiful men come from?" she finally mumbled, incredulous, still unable to understand.

"I don't know if I care to be described as beautiful," Pitt said, as he grabbed her around the waist and hustled her toward the shattered door.

"Wait!" she snapped, twisting out from his encircling arm. She darted back inside and reappeared in seconds, clutching a small attaché case to her breast.

The time for caution and furtive movements was gone—if either had truly existed in the men's minds. Tearing down the long corridor, rushing past workers who were putting the finishing touches on the ship, they were stared at queerly, but no one made a move to stop or question them.

If the alarm was out by now, and Pitt was certain it was, the thought of a confrontation with the merciless Wolfs spurred him on. Getting off the ship, reaching the end of the dock, and disappearing into the old water of the fjord for a two-mile swim was only half his problem. Though pulled faster than they could swim by the diver propulsion vehicles, Pat and her daughter would probably die of hypothermia before they could reach the ravine and the Skycar.

His fears suddenly mushroomed when the eerie sounds of high-pitched alarms began sounding throughout the shipyard just as they reached the nearest elevator.

Luck was with them this far. The elevator was stopped on Level Six with the doors open. Three men in red coveralls were in the act of unloading office furniture. Without a word of explanation, Pitt and Giordino muscled the startled movers into the foyer, pushed Pat and her daughter inside, and sent the elevator moving downward in the space of fifteen seconds.

While they temporarily caught their breath, Pitt smiled at Pat's daughter, a pretty young girl with hair the color of shimmering topaz and Capri-blue eyes. "What's your name, dear heart?"

"Megan," she said, her eyes wide with fear.

"Take a deep breath and relax," he said softly. "My name is Dirk, and my burly little munchkin friend is Al. We're going to take you safely home."

His words had a soothing effect, and her expression of dire anxiety slowly altered to simple uneasiness. She placed her explicit trust in him, and Pitt began to dread for the second time that night what he might find when they reached their stop and the elevator doors opened. They could not shoot their way out, not with the women beside them.

His fears were groundless, as it turned out. There was no army of guards with drawn guns waiting on the cargo level. "I am totally lost," he said, looking at a labyrinth of corridors.

Giordino grinned ruefully. "Too bad we didn't pick up a street map."

Pitt pointed at a golf cart parked in front of a door marked "Circuit Room." "Salvation is at hand," he said, jumping into the driver's seat and twisting the ignition key. Everyone climbed in, and he punched the accelerator to the floorboard almost before their feet left the deck. Unable to use his little direction finder except for course headings, he made a lucky guess after crossing the tram tracks and found a large freight passageway that opened onto a loading ramp leading down to the dock.

The army of guards with drawn guns he was concerned about had arrived.

They were pouring out of trucks and dispersing on the dock,

weapons drawn and at the ready, as they clustered around the loading ramps. Pitt estimated that there were nearly four hundred of them, not counting a thousand already on duty aboard the ship. He instantly sized up their dilemma and shouted, "Hold on! I'm heading back toward the elevator." He slammed on the brake, spun the cart in a U-turn, and turned back into the freight passageway.

Looking behind, all Giordino could see were black coveralls swirling like ants around the dock. "I hate it when things don't go right," he said morosely.

"We'll never escape—" Pat broke off, clutching her daughter. "Not now."

Pitt looked at Giordino. "Wasn't there an old war song called 'We Did It Before, and We Can Do It Again'?"

"World War Two was before my time," said Giordino. "But I get your drift."

They quickly reached the elevator, but Pitt didn't stop. The doors were still open, and he drove the cart inside just before they began to close. He pressed the button for the sixth level, pulled out the .45 and gestured for Giordino to do the same. As soon as the doors spread open, they came face-to-face with the three furniture movers they had thrown out of the elevator earlier. Still stunned by their eviction, the movers were shouting and gesturing at a man wearing yellow coveralls, who looked to be someone in command. At seeing Pitt and Giordino come charging out of the elevator on the cart like unleashed starving German shepherds, their guns drawn and aimed, the four men froze and threw their hands into the air.

"Into the elevator!" Pitt ordered.

The four men stood blank and uncomprehending until Giordino shouted the command in Spanish.

"Sorry," said Pitt, suddenly self-conscious. "I got carried away by the drama of the moment."

"You're forgiven," Giordino absolved him.

The routine they'd hastily improvised in the office building was repeated. Six minutes later, they were all on their way again, leaving the four men in their underwear bound with duct tape and lying on the floor of the elevator. As soon as the doors opened wide, Pitt drove the cart onto the main cargo entry deck, stopped, and ran back. He sent the elevator upward and jammed the controls, leaping out before the doors closed. Then he followed the direction signs and drove toward the tram. Three of them now wore the red coveralls of interior ship workers, while the fourth—himself—was dressed in the yellow uniform of a supervisor.

Security guards were already stationed at an intersection just short of the tram station. One of them stepped forward and held up his hand. Pitt brought the cart to an unhurried stop and looked at the guard questioningly.

Not knowing that Pat and her daughter had been whisked from their quarters, the guard was not unduly disturbed at seeing two women in the uniforms of cargo loaders, since many of them had been recruited to operate forklifts and tow vehicles. Pat squeezed her daughter's arm as a warning not to speak or move. She also turned Megan's face away from the guard, so he wouldn't notice her tender age.

Pitt figured the yellow coveralls he had appropriated represented authority, and the respectful look in the guard's eyes confirmed it.

"What's going on here?" Giordino demanded, his Spanish improving with practice.

"Two intruders in security guard uniforms have infiltrated the shipyard and are believed to have boarded the *Ulrich Wolf.*"

"Intruders? Why didn't you stop them before they entered the shipyard?"

"I can't say," the guard replied. "All I know is that they killed four of our security force guards in an attempt to escape."

"Four dead," Giordino said sadly. "A great pity. I hope you catch the murdering swine. Right, group?" He turned to the others and nodded spiritedly.

"*Sí, sí,*" Pitt said, agreeing with a vigorous display of disgust.

"We have to check everyone going on or coming off each ship," the guard persisted. "I must see your identification cards."

"Do we look like trespassers in security guard uniforms?" Giordino demanded indignantly.

The guard shook his head and smiled. "No."

"Then let us pass!" Giordino's friendly voice went suddenly cold and official. "We have a cargo to load and a deadline that we won't meet sitting around the dock talking to you. I'm already late for a meeting with Karl Wolf. Unless you don't want to be left behind when the cataclysm hits, I suggest you step aside."

Properly browbeaten, the guard lowered his weapon and yielded. "I'm sorry to have detained you."

Not able to translate the exchange, Pitt stepped on the cart's accelerator pedal only after Giordino elbowed him in the ribs. Thinking it best to appear like ordinary shipyard workers on a job-related assignment, he continued toward the nearest tram station at a moderate pace, drowning an urge to run the cart at its full speed. With one hand on the steering wheel, he dialed the Globalstar phone with the other.

SANDECKER pounded the speaker button halfway through the first ring. "Yes?"

"This is the Leaning Pizza Tower calling. Your order is on its way."

"Do you think you can find the house all right?"

"The issue is in doubt whether we can arrive before the pizza gets cold."

"I hope you hurry," said Sandecker, suppressing an urgent tone in his voice. "There are hungry people here."

"Traffic is heavy. Will do my best."

"I'll leave a light on." Sandecker set down the phone and stared at Admiral Hozafel with a heavy face. "Forgive the rather silly talk, Admiral."

"I understand perfectly," said the courtly old German.

"What is their situation?" asked Little.

"Not good," replied Sandecker. "They have Dr. O'Connell and her daughter, but must be facing enormous odds in escaping the shipyard. 'Traffic is heavy' meant that they were under pursuit by Wolf security forces."

Little looked directly at Sandecker. "What do you think their odds of making a clean getaway are?"

"Odds?" Sandecker's expression seemed pained. He looked as though he had aged ten years in the past hour. "They have no odds."

31

THE TRAM MOVED SLOWLY out of the station, passing another tram going in the opposite direction. Though it picked up speed until it was gliding over the rails at nearly thirty miles an hour, Pitt felt as if the tram were crawling and he wanted to get out and help push it. Stations designated in the letters of the alphabet came and went, each one met with their expectation of security guards flooding on board and seizing them. When the tram exchanged passengers at W Station, Pitt's hopes began to rise, but at X Station, their luck ran out.

Six black uniformed security guards boarded the end car and began checking the passengers' identification tags, which Pitt only now observed were carried on bracelets around their wrists. He cursed himself for not knowing earlier so he could have stolen the bracelets from the furniture movers. Too late, it occurred to him that the guards would make a special effort to search for people without them. He also noted that they seemed to be taking extra time to check any workers wearing red or yellow coveralls.

"They're working their way closer," Giordino noted without emotion, as the guards entered the second car of the five-car tram.

"One at a time," said Pitt, "move casually to the first car."

Without a word passing between them, Giordino went first, followed by Megan and then Pat, with Pitt bringing up the rear.

"We might make the next station before they reach this car," said Giordino. "But it's going to be close."

"I doubt if we'll get off that easy," Pitt said grimly. "They'll probably be waiting there, too."

He walked forward and peered through the window of the door leading to a small control cab in the front of the car. There was a console with lights, buttons, and switches, but no driver or engineer. The tram was fully automatic. He tried the door latch, but wasn't surprised to find it locked.

He studied the symbols and markings on the console panel. One in particular struck his eye. Gripping the Colt, he rapped the barrel against the glass window and shattered it. Ignoring the startled looks of the car's passengers, he reached inside and unlocked the door. Without the slightest pause, he reached out and moved the first of five toggle switches connected to the tram's electronic couplings. Next he reset the computer that actuated the speed of the tram.

The desired effect gave him a surge of pleasure. The four rear cars detached from the lead car and began to fall back. Though each car had its own power source, their preset speed was now slower than that of the forward car. The security guards could only contact other search teams and watch helplessly as the distances between the cars rapidly widened and their quarry gained a growing lead.

Four minutes later, the car with Pitt and the others swept past Y Station without stopping, to the frustration of a team of security guards and the dumb expressions of the workers who stood on the platform. Pitt felt as if his stomach were being squeezed by a cold hand, and his mouth felt as though it were stuffed with dry leaves. He was playing a desperate gamble, with the dice loaded against him. He glanced behind him into the car and caught sight of Pat, sitting with an arm around Megan's shoulder, one arm still clutching the attaché case, her face pale and strangely sad and forlorn. He walked back and ran his hand through her streaming red hair.

"We'll get through this," he said, with an air of conviction. "Old Dirk will take you over the water and the mountains."

She looked up and managed a faint smile. "Is that a guarantee?"

"Ironclad," he said, with a growing conviction inside him.

Half a minute passed. Pitt walked back into the control cabin and saw that they were approaching the marina at the stern of the ship. Up ahead, he could see the tracks begin their curve toward the marina, where the tram, he was certain, was supposed to stop at Z Station before continuing around the ship. He didn't need mystical powers to know security guards had reached the station platform first and were waiting to blast them with an arsenal of weapons.

"I'm going to slow the car to about ten miles an hour," Pitt said. "When I give the word, we jump. The edge of the tracks is planted with vegetation, so our landing should be fairly soft. Try to roll forward when you hit. At this point we can't afford to have anybody suffer a fractured ankle or leg."

Giordino put his arm around Megan. "We'll go together. That way you'll have lots of fat to cushion your fall." It was a broad misstatement. Giordino didn't have an ounce of fat on his muscular body.

Pitt reset the controls and the car slowed abruptly. The instant the red numbers on the speed scale dropped to ten miles an hour, he yelled, "All right, everyone out!"

He hesitated, making sure they all had leaped from the tram. Then he punched up the numbers until the dial read sixty miles an hour, before running from the cab to the door and jumping as the tram car quickly accelerated toward its fastest speed. He struck soft earth feet first before rolling with the momentum of a cannonball into a bed of ornamental bonsai trees, crushing their distorted branches and mashing them into the soil with his weight. He staggered to his feet; one knee protested in pain, but he was still capable of active movement.

Giordino was beside him, helping him regain his balance. He was relieved to see Pat and Megan, their faces clear of expressions of pain. They seemed more concerned with brushing the soil and pine needles from their hair. The tram had disappeared around the bend, but the stairway leading to the first pier was no more than fifty feet away, and no guards were nearby.

"Where are we going?" Pat asked, regaining a small measure of composure.

"Before we catch our plane," answered Pitt, "we have to take a little boat trip."

He caught her by the arm and dragged her behind him, as Giordino hustled Megan along. They ran along the track until they reached the stairs leading down to Pier Number One. As Pitt suspected, the security guards had encircled the station at Z Section two hundred yards farther up the track in the center of the marina. Confusion reigned, as the tram car shot past the station and around the next bend on its way along the port side of the ship. The guards, completely deluded into thinking their prey was still hiding in the speeding car, hurriedly launched a pursuit, as the security director in command ordered the power circuits for the tram system to be closed down.

Pitt figured it would take them another seven minutes before the guards could reach the stopped car and realize that it was empty. If he and the others weren't off the ship by then, capture was a foregone conclusion.

None of the workers on the pier paid any attention to them as they calmly strolled down the steps and onto the pier. There were three boats moored between the first and second piers, a small twenty-four-foot sailboat, a vessel that Pitt recognized as a forty-two-foot Grand Banks cabin cruiser, and a twenty-four-foot classic runabout. "Climb aboard the big powerboat," said Pitt, walking placidly across the pier.

"I guess we're not going to retrieve our dive gear," said Giordino.

"Pat and Megan could never make it back alive in the water. Better we take our chances on the surface."

"The runabout is faster," Giordino pointed out.

"True," Pitt agreed, "but the security force will be suspicious of a fast boat speeding away from the shipyard. The Grand Banks powerboat, cruising calmly across the water, won't create near the attention."

There was a dockhand hosing down the deck when Pitt walked up and stopped at the gangway. "Nice boat," he said, smiling.

"Heh?" The dockhand looked at him, unable to understand English.

Pitt moved up the gangway and gestured at the no-nonsense lines of the Grand Banks 42. "She's a nice boat," he repeated, boldly stepping into the bridge cabin.

The dockhand followed him inside, protesting his trespass on the boat, but once they were out of sight of other workers on the pier, Pitt lashed out with his fist and decked him with a solid blow to the jaw. Then he leaned out the doorway and announced, "Al, cast off the lines. You ladies, all aboard."

Pitt stood for a moment and studied the instruments on the console. He turned the key and hit the twin starter buttons. Down below in the engine compartment, a pair of big marine diesel engines turned over, the fuel inside their firing chambers compressing and igniting to the tune of high-pitched clacking. He slid open the starboard window and peered out. Giordino had untied the fore and aft lines and was climbing on board.

Pitt engaged the reverse drive and very slowly began edging the boat away from the pier and backing it toward the open water twenty yards astern. He passed two dockworkers installing a railing around the pier, and waved. They waved back. It's so much easier to be sneaky, he thought, than to burst out of the corral like a wild bull.

The boat passed the end of the pier into open water. Now the stern of the great ship soared above them. Pitt moved the shift lever into Forward and steered the Grand Banks on a course along the *Ulrich Wolf.* To reach the fjord and escape the shipyard, they had to cruise entirely around the floating titan. Pitt set the throttles until the speed instruments read eight knots, a pace that he hoped would not arouse suspicions. So far, there had been no shouts, no bells or whistles, no signs of a chase or searchlights pinning them against the dark water.

At this speed, it would take fifteen minutes to pass the entire length of the supership and turn the bow until they could move a safe distance away and out from under the glare of the lights from the shipyard. Fifteen agonizing minutes that would seem like fifteen years. That was only the first hurdle. They still had the patrol boats to contend with, and by then there was every possibility their crews would have been alerted to the fugitives' escape in the Grand Banks cabin cruiser.

There was nothing they could do except remain inside the main cabin out of sight and stare up at the immense monster as they crept alongside. From bow to stern, the great mass of glass was a blaze of light inside and out, giving it the effect of a baseball stadium during a night game. The famous classic liners of their time, *Titanic, Lusitania, Queen Mary, Queen Elizabeth,* and *Normandy,* if anchored in a row, would still have come up short next to the *Ulrich Wolf.*

"I could use a hamburger about now," said Giordino, trying to relieve the tension.

"Me, too," said Megan. "All they fed us was yucky nutritional stuff."

Pat smiled, though her face looked strained. "It won't be long, honey, and you'll get your hamburger."

Pitt turned from the helm. "Were you treated badly?"

"No abuse," answered Pat, "but I've never been ordered around by so many nasty and arrogant people. They worked me twenty hours a day."

"Deciphering Amenes inscriptions from another chamber?"

"They weren't from another chamber. They were photos taken of inscriptions they found at a lost city in the Antarctic."

Pitt looked at her curiously. "The Antarctic?"

She nodded solemnly. "Frozen in the ice. The Nazis discovered it before the war."

"Elsie Wolf told me they'd found evidence the Amenes built six chambers."

"I can't say," admitted Pat. "All I can tell you is that I got the impression they're using the ice city for some purpose. What, I didn't find out."

"Did you learn anything new from the inscriptions they forced you to decipher?"

As she talked, Pat no longer looked sad and forlorn. "I was barely into the project when you burst through the door. They were extremely interested in what *we* deciphered in the Colorado and St. Paul chambers. It appeared that the Wolfs were desperate to study the accounts passed down by the Amenes describing the effects of the cataclysm."

"That's because any inscriptions they found inside the lost city came before the cataclysm." He paused and nodded toward her briefcase.

"Is that what's in there?"

She held it up. "The photos from the Antarctic chamber. I couldn't bring myself to leave them behind."

He looked at her steadily. "They don't make women like you anymore."

Pitt might have said more, but a boat was crossing his bow about a hundred yards ahead. It looked to be a workboat, and its course remained steady as it turned and passed on the Grand Bank's port side. The crew seemed intent on their labors and didn't pay the slightest attention to the cabin cruiser.

Relaxing a bit as they neared the forward section of the *Ulrich Wolf* without any sign of pursuit, Pitt asked, "You said they're studying what conditions will be like in the aftermath of the cataclysm?"

"In a big way. I assume they want every bit of data they can glean for their survival."

"I'm still at a loss as to why the Wolfs are so positive a comet is going to return and collide with Earth within days of the prediction made by the Amenes nine thousand years ago," Pitt said.

Pat shook her head slowly. "I have no answers to that."

Still crawling along at eight knots, Pitt gently turned the wheel, sending the Grand Banks on a wide arc around the bow of the *Ulrich Wolf* and passing the end of the dock, now swarming with shipyard workers and security guards checking the identification of every man and woman in red coveralls. He passed a small powerboat running with no lights that ominously swung around in a 180-degree turn and began following in their wake. He set his directional computer on the frame of the windshield and studied the readings that would lead him through the darkness to the ravine that held the Skycar.

Three miles to the ravine, three miles over water in a boat that offered no protection from probing lights or automatic weapons and heavy machine guns. All they carried were a pair of handguns. And there were the patrol boats that surely must have been alerted by now of a stolen powerboat carrying intruders attempting to escape the shipyard. His only consolation was that the patrol boats were at the far end of the fjord, giving them an extra few minutes of time. A slim consolation at best. With their superior speed, the patrol boats could easily intercept the Grand Banks before they could reach the mouth of the ravine.

"Al!"

Giordino was at his side immediately. "Aye, aye."

"Find some bottles. There must be some on board. Empty, then fill them with whatever you can find that's highly inflammable. Diesel fuel is too slow-burning. Look for gas or solvent."

"Molotov cocktails," said Giordino, grinning like a demon. "I haven't thrown one of those since kindergarten." Two steps, and he was dropping down a ladder to the engine compartment.

Pitt brushed aside an urge to shove the throttles to their stops, judging that it was more productive to play out a passive role. He stared over one shoulder at the twenty-five-foot runabout behind them, its big, powerful outboard motor clamped to its transom; it had increased speed and was drawing alongside. The lights from the shipyard revealed only two men in black uniforms, one steering the boat, the other standing in the stern gripping an automatic rifle. The one at the helm was motioning at his ear. Pitt understood the message and turned on the radio, leaving it on the frequency it was set.

A voice crackled over the speaker in Spanish, with an indisputable inflection that Pitt knew was a command to lay to. He picked up the microphone and answered: *"No habla español."*

"Alto, alto!" the voice shouted.

"Get down below and lay flat on the deck," he ordered Pat and Megan. They silently complied and hurried down the ladder to the main cabin.

Pitt slowed the boat and stood in the doorway, his Colt cocked and stuffed under his belt. The guard in the stern of the runabout crouched in readiness to jump on board the Grand Banks.

Pitt then pulled back the throttles but kept a slight headway, measuring the distance between the two boats and moving at just enough parallel speed so that the boarder would come over the railing almost in line with the doorway to the bridge. His timing would have to be exactly on the mark. He waited patiently, like a hunter in a blind watching the skies for a passing duck.

At the precise moment the security guard crouched to leap between the two boats, he shoved the twin throttles forward in a brief burst of speed, before abruptly pulling them back again. The sudden movement threw off the balance of the guard, and he landed sprawling on the narrow port deck of the Grand Banks.

Pitt smoothly stepped through the cabin door, jammed the heel of his right foot into the guard's neck, bent down and snatched up his automatic rifle, a Bushmaster M17S, and clubbed him behind the neck with the butt end. He leveled it at the guard at the helm of the outboard and fired. He missed, as the guard dropped to his knees, cramped the wheel over, hit the throttle, and turned the outboard on a sharp angle away from the Grand Banks. With a loud roar from the motor, the boat leaped away in a cloud of spray and churning water. Without waiting to see more, Pitt stepped back into the cabin and pushed the throttles as far as they would go. The stern of the Grand Banks dug down in the water, the bow lifted, and soon it was rushing across the black waters at nearly twenty knots.

Now Pitt focused on the patrol boats that had swung around on a course back up the fjord, coming at full speed, the searchlights playing the water in ever-closer sweeps toward the Grand Banks. It was a given that the guard driving the outboard had radioed a report. The lead boat was a good half mile ahead of its escort. From Pitt's view through the windshield, it was impossible to predict when the nearest patrol boat would meet the Grand Banks on a converging course. The only certainty was that it would cross his bows before they reached the mouth of the ravine. Another six or seven minutes would spell the difference between survival and death.

They were well clear of the shipyard now, with less than two miles to go.

The outboard cruiser was less than a hundred yards off and slightly behind. The only reason the remaining security guard had not opened up with his own Bushmaster rifle was that he was afraid of hitting his partner.

Giordino returned to the cabin, carrying an armload of four bottles filled with solvent from a can used to clean oil and grease within the engine compartment. Thin strips of rags were stuffed in the bottle necks.

He carefully set the bottles on the cushions of a bench. The beefy Italian was nursing a large bruise on his forehead.

"What happened to you?" Pitt asked.

"Some guy I know can't drive a boat. I was thrown all over the engine compartment and bounced my head off a water pipe during a series of wild gyrations." Then Giordino spotted the unconscious body of the security guard lying partially in the door. "My sincerest apologies. You had a social caller."

"He failed to produce an invitation."

Giordino moved beside Pitt and stared through the windshield at the rapidly approaching patrol boat. "No warning shot across the bow with this crew. They're armed to the teeth and looking for any excuse to blow us out of the water."

"Maybe not," said Pitt. "They still need the expertise of Pat to decipher their inscriptions. They might rough her up and slap Megan around, but they won't kill them. You and I will be history. I plan on giving them a bit of a surprise. If we can suck them in close enough, we might give them a bonfire to enjoy."

Giordino stared Pitt in the eyes. Most men would have reflected inevitable defeat, but Giordino saw no such reflection. What he saw was calculated determination and a faint gleam of anticipation. "I wonder how John Paul Jones would see it."

Pitt nodded. "You'll be busy with your toys. Lend me your piece. Then lay low on the far side of the bridge until you hear shooting."

"You or them?"

Pitt gave Giordino a dour look. "It doesn't matter who."

Giordino handed over his Para-Ordnance automatic without question, as Pitt pushed against the throttles in a fruitless attempt to goad a few more revolutions out of the engines. The Grand Banks was giving everything it had, but it was a boat built for comfortable cruising, not speed.

The commander of the patrol boat had no reservations about closing in on the Grand Banks. He had no reason to believe that anyone on board was crazy enough to take on a boat armed with twin machine guns plus the weapons held by men who were trained to kill at the slightest provocation. He studied the Grand Banks through night glasses, saw only one man standing at the helm on the bridge, and made the ultimate mistake of an aggressor—he profoundly underestimated his adversary. The searchlights were trained on the Grand Banks, illuminating the boat in a blinding glare.

The bone of foam cut by the bow fell away as the thirty-eight-foot patrol boat edged closer to the Grand Banks and gradually pulled alongside, until it was less than twenty feet away. From his position on the bridge, Pitt squinted his eyes against the bright light and made out a man behind each machine gun, pointing the barrels directly at him in the bridge cabin. Three other men stood shoulder to shoulder on the open deck aft of the cabin, armed with Bushmaster automatic rifles. Pitt was unable to see Giordino crouched on the opposite side of the cabin, but he knew that his friend was poised with either a match or a lighter to ignite the wicks on the bottles filled with the solvent. It was a nerve-prickling moment, but not one of total hopelessness, certainly not in Pitt's mind.

He had no burning desire to execute anyone, not even the species of hardened killers whom he was looking at across the water, and whose mercenary comrades he'd met in Colorado. It was no mystery that his life and that of Giordino weren't worth two cents if they were captured. He watched as the commander of the patrol boat raised a loudspeaker to his mouth.

Pitt recognized that the word *alto* meant "stop," and he could only assume the words that followed were a threat that if he didn't do what he was ordered, the security guards would open fire. He waved that he understood, took one more look at the distance separating him from the ravine, now down to less than half a mile, and a quick glance at the second patrol boat to estimate when it would arrive to back up its escort— five to six minutes. Next he checked to make sure the two automatics were snug under the belt behind his back. Only then did he pull back the throttles to the idle position, but he kept the boat in gear so that it still maintained very slow headway.

He moved to the doorway of the cabin, no farther, raised his hands, and stood properly subdued in the dazzling beam of the light. He didn't bother using his limited Spanish vocabulary. He shouted back in English. "What do you want?"

"Do not resist," ordered the commander, now close enough to dispense with the loudspeaker. "I am sending men to board you."

"How can I possibly resist?" Pitt offered helplessly. "I have no machine guns like you."

"Tell the others to come on deck!"

Pitt kept his hands in the air, turned, and made as if he were relaying the commander's orders. "They are afraid you will shoot them."

"We're not going to shoot anyone," the commander answered, in a tone that was about as slimy as an eel.

"Please turn the light out," Pitt begged. "You are blinding me and frightening the women."

"Stand where you are and do not move," the commander shouted in exasperation.

In a few moments, the patrol boat slowed its engines to a slow throb and angled toward the Grand Banks. A few feet away, two of the guards laid down their rifles and began dropping bumpers over the rail of the patrol boat. It was the opportunity Pitt had been waiting for. Even the men behind the machine guns had relaxed. Sensing no sign of trouble, one lit a cigarette. The crew and their commander, their wariness sharply diminished at seeing not the slightest hint of a threat, felt they had the situation firmly under their control.

Their attitude was exactly what Pitt had hoped for. Coldly, precisely, he dropped his hands, whipped out the two automatics, aimed the one in his right hand at the man standing at the forward machine gun, and in the same moment in time lined up the left muzzle at the gunner in the stern, pulling both triggers as fast as his fingers could curl. At a range of fifteen feet, he couldn't miss. The machine gunner in the bow sank to his knees on the deck with a bullet in his shoulder. The gunner in the stern threw his hands in the air, stumbled backward, and fell over the gunwale into the water.

Almost simultaneously, flaming bottles of fuel soared over and past the Grand Banks' bridge like a meteor shower and dropped onto the cabin and decks of the patrol boat, erupting in a roar of flames as the glass shattered and the contents ignited. The fiery liquid pooled and spread across the patrol boat, turning it into a blazing funeral pyre. Virtually the whole open stern deck and half the cabin erupted into flame.

Tongues of fire soon poked from every port. Finding themselves about to burn alive, the crew unhesitatingly hurled their bodies into the cold water. The wounded gunner on the bow also staggered across the deck through the flames and leaped overboard. His clothing afire, the commander ignored the flames and stared scathingly at Pitt, before shaking his fist and leaping over the side.

Truculent jerk, Pitt thought.

He didn't waste so much as a second. He rushed to the bridge console and thrust the throttles full forward again, sending the Grand Banks on its interrupted journey toward the ravine. Only then did he spare the time to turn and stare at the patrol boat. The entire craft was engulfed with contorted flames that danced high into the night sky. Black smoke curled and twisted upward, blotting out the stars. In another minute, the fuel tanks exploded, throwing burning debris into the air like a fireworks display. She began to sink by the stern, sliding backward with a hissing sound as the icy water met the blistering flames. Then, with a great sigh, as if she had a soul, the patrol boat sank out of sight.

Giordino came around the cabin and stood at the door, looking at the bits and pieces of burning debris and oil that floated on the surface. "Nice shooting," he said quietly.

"Good pitching."

Giordino inclined his head toward the second patrol boat that was hurtling across the fjord. Then he turned slightly and stared toward the shore. "It's going to be close," he said objectively.

"They won't fall for a sucker play like their buddies. They'll stand off at a safe distance and try and disable us by shooting at our engines."

"Pat and Megan are down there," Giordino reminded him.

"Bring them up," said Pitt, his eyes reading the numbers on the directional computer. He made a slight adjustment and swung the Grand Banks another five degrees to the southwest. Four hundred yards remained. The gap was rapidly narrowing. "Tell them to get ready to abandon the boat the instant we hit shore."

"You're going to hit the rocks at full throttle?"

"We don't have time to tie up to a rock and step ashore with confetti and bands playing."

"On my way," Giordino acknowledged with a brief wave.

The second patrol boat was driving directly toward them, unaware of Pitt's intention to run ashore. The searchlight illuminated the Grand Banks in its beam with unwavering steadiness, like a spotlight trained at a dancer on a stage. The two boats closed rapidly, running at an angle toward each other. Then the commander of the patrol boat sensed Pitt's intentions and steered to cut off the Grand Banks and block it from reaching the shore. With less than half the speed of his nemesis, Pitt was forced to accept the fact that he was engaged in a race he would surely lose. Yet he stood at the helm with unblinking eyes and a callous determination. The fight was extremely one-sided, but he wasn't about to turn the other cheek. The thought of failure never entered his mind.

Seeing an unexpected opportunity, Pitt yanked the gear lever and threw the Grand Banks into reverse. The boat shuddered from the strain under full throttle and came to a stop, its props beating the water in a maelstrom of froth. Then it began moving backward, its square transom pushing aside the water like a bulldozer.

Giordino appeared with Pat and Megan. He stared bemused at seeing the patrol boat about to cross the Grand Banks' bow while their own boat was surging backward. "Don't tell me. I'm keen to guess. You've conjured up another cunning plan."

"Not cunning, just desperate."

"You're going to ram him."

"If we play our cards right," answered Pitt quickly, "I do believe we can bloody his nose. Now, everyone lie on the floor. Use whatever solid cover you can find to shield yourselves. Because it's surely going to rain."

There was no time to say more. The commander of the second patrol boat, not comprehending the reverse movement of his prey, altered his course so that he would cross within ten feet of the Grand Banks' bow, come to a stop, and blast the Grand Banks at point-blank range. It was a naval tactic called crossing the T. He stood at the helm and raised one hand as a signal for the gunners to open fire.

Then two events happened in the same instant. Pitt crammed the gear lever back to full forward and the machine guns on the patrol boat opened up. The Grand Banks' props dug in the water and sent the boat surging forward, as bullets sprayed the bridge. The glass from the windshield shattered into a thousand shards and burst all through the cabin. Pitt had already thrown himself down behind the console, one hand raised and gripping the bottom arc of the helm. He didn't notice that the back of his hand had been gashed by flying glass until the blood began dripping into his eyes. The upper cabin of the Grand Banks was being methodically shot to pieces. The gunners were shooting high to throw sheer terror into the minds of those lying prone on the deck. The interior of the bridge was a bedlam of flying wreckage, as nine-millimeter shells shredded everything they smashed against.

The commander of the patrol boat had cut his speed and was drifting to a stop, since his gunners seemed to be enjoying close-up target practice. His satisfaction was premature, while Pitt's timing couldn't have been more perfect. The commander missed Pitt's intent until it was too late. Before he could steer his patrol boat out of the way, the Grand Banks had suddenly jerked forward, her engines pounding at full rpms.

There came a grinding sound of twisted and tortured fiberglass and wood. The Grand Banks' bow sliced through the starboard hull of the patrol boat and punched through to the keel. The patrol boat canted over on her port side, the crew grabbing at any solid object to keep from being pitched overboard, and began to settle almost immediately.

Pitt hauled himself to his feet, threw the gear lever into reverse, and backed the Grand Banks out of the gash in the hull of the patrol boat, allowing a rush of water to flood and gurgle into the cavity. For a moment, the patrol boat struggled back to an even keel, but then the black waters flowed over her deck and she slipped away, her searchlight still glaring as it plunged to the floor of the fjord, leaving her crew struggling to stay afloat in the frigid waters.

"Al," Pitt said in a conversational tone. "Check the forward compartment."

Giordino disappeared through a hatch and returned in seconds. "We're sucking in water like a giant douche bag. Another five minutes and we'll join our friends in the water, even faster if you don't stop this tub."

"Who said anything about going forward?" Pitt's eyes locked on the direction computer. The distance to shore and the mouth of the ravine was only fifty yards, but it was an impossible span for a fast-sinking boat. Trying to move ahead would only escalate the flood of water pouring in through the shattered bow. His mind raced with a strange clarity, as it always did during crisis, considering any and every option. He sent the Grand Banks barreling through the water in reverse, which lowered the stern and raised the bow. The flooding problem temporarily solved, he warned the others. "Go out on deck and brace yourselves for the shock when we strike the rocks."

"On deck?" Pat asked numbly.

"In case the boat rolls over when we ground, you're better off out in the open where you can jump in the water."

None too soon, Giordino herded the two females outside and made them sit down on the deck, backs against the cabin while reaching out and clutching the railing. He sat in the middle with both strong arms encircling their waists. Pat was frozen in pure fright, but Megan, looking into Giordino's unperturbed face, took courage from it. He and the man at the helm had brought them this far. It was utterly incomprehensible to her that they wouldn't make good on their word and take her safely home.

The Grand Banks was settling lower from the water coming through the damaged hull below the waterline aft of the bow. The mouth of the ravine was very close now. Black heaps of rock that Pitt and Giordino had waded past, before commencing their underwater journey to the shipyard earlier that night, rose from the blackness, ominous and beckoning. Pitt did his best to dodge around the largest of the rocks, barely distinguishing their shapes, as they were outlined by the white foam of the fjord's two-foot waves that slapped against them.

And then one of the propellers struck with a loud metallic smack and sheared off, sending the engine racing out of control. More rocks swirled by. Then came a heavier blow and the boat shuddered but kept going several more feet, before the port side of the transom crunched into a rock that smashed the yielding wood to pieces. As though a dam had burst, a gush of water flooded across the rear open deck, pulling down the stern. The next shock came with bone-jarring impact, as the boat struck hard on and split down the keel, the wooden-planked hull tearing itself to pieces. But then the terrible crunching and grinding sounds ceased as the battered Grand Banks finally came to a stop, with only ten feet separating her ruptured stern from the edge of the rocky shoreline.

Pitt snatched up the little directional computer and rushed out the bridge door. "Everybody ashore who's going ashore," he shouted. He snatched up Megan under one arm and smiled at her. "Sorry about this, young lady, but we can't hang around to find a ladder." Then he slid over the railing and lowered himself and Megan into the frigid water, his feet touching bottom in four feet. He knew Pat and Giordino were right behind him, as he struggled over the rocky bottom and slime-covered rocks toward dry land.

As soon as his feet cleared the water, he released Megan and checked his directional computer to make absolutely certain they had the right ravine. They did. The Skycar was only minutes away.

"You're hurt," said Pat, seeing the dark stream of blood on Pitt's hand under the light of the stars and falling crescent moon. "You've got a nasty gash."

"A glass cut," he said simply.

She inserted a hand under her red coveralls, ripped off her bra, and began using it to wrap Pitt's hand to stem the flow of blood. "Now, there's a bandage I've never seen before," he murmured with a grin.

"Under the circumstances," she said, tying the ends tightly in a knot, "it's the best I can do."

"Who's complaining?" He gave her a hug and then turned to the shadow that was Giordino. "All present and accounted for?"

Giordino had Megan by the hand. "Adrenaline still pumping."

"Then come on," said Pitt. "Our private plane awaits."

To Sandecker and Agent Little, the wait for the next contact from Pitt and Giordino seemed interminable. The fire had died to a few smoldering embers, and the admiral seemed to have no interest in rekindling it. He puffed on one of his big cigars, covering the ceiling with a haze of blue smoke. Both he and Little passed the time sitting spellbound, listening to the tales told by Admiral Hozafel, tales he had never told anyone in more than fifty-six years.

"You were saying, Admiral," said Sandecker, "that the Nazis sent expeditions to explore Antarctica several years before the war."

"Yes, Adolf Hitler was far more creative than people thought. I can't say what inspired him, but he acquired a fascination for Antarctica, primarily to populate and to use as a giant military establishment. He believed that if such a dream came true, his naval and air forces could control all the seas south of the Tropic of Capricorn. Captain Alfred Ritscher was put in command of a large expedition to explore the subcontinent. The *Schwabenland,* an early German aircraft carrier used to refuel seaplanes flying the Atlantic in the early 1930s, was converted for Antarctic exploration, and left Hamburg in December of 1938 under the pretense of studying the feasibility of setting up a whaling colony. After reaching their destination in the middle of the southern summer, Ritscher sent out aircraft with the newest and best German cameras. His flyers covered over two hundred and fifty thousand square miles and took more than eleven thousand aerial photographs."

"I've heard rumors of such an expedition," said Sandecker, "but until now I never learned the true facts."

"Ritscher returned with a larger expedition a year later, this time with improved aircraft with skis, so they could land on the ice. They also brought along a small zeppelin. This time they covered three hundred and fifty thousand square miles, landing at the South Pole and dropping flags with the swastika emblem every thirty miles as markers for their claim of Nazi territory."

"Did they discover anything of unusual interest?" asked Little.

"Indeed they did," replied Hozafel. "The aerial surveys recorded a number of ice-free areas, frozen lakes whose ice surface was less than four feet thick, and steam vents with signs of vegetation growing nearby. Their photographs also detected what looked like bits and pieces of roads under the ice."

Sandecker sat up straight and gazed at the old German U-boat commander. "The Germans found evidence of a civilization on Antarctica?"

Hozafel nodded. "Teams using motorized snow vehicles found natural ice caves. While exploring them, they stumbled onto the remains of an ancient civilization. This discovery inspired the Nazis to use their engineering and technical ingenuity to build a vast underground base in Antarctica. It was the best-kept secret of the war."

"To my knowledge," said Little, "Allied intelligence sources ignored rumors of a Nazi base in Antarctica. They considered them far-fetched propaganda."

Hozafel gave a crooked smile. "They were meant to. But once, Admiral Donitz nearly gave it away. During a speech to his U-boat commanders, he announced, 'The German submarine fleet is proud of having built for the Führer, in another part of the world, a Shangri-la on land, an impregnable fortress.' Fortunately for us, nobody paid attention. The U-boats I commanded earlier in the war were never sent to the Antarctic, so it wasn't until near the end, when I became commander of the U-699, that I learned of the secret base, whose code name was New Berlin."

"How was it built?" inquired Sandecker.

"After the war began, the first step the Nazis took was to send a pair of raiders into the southern waters to sink all hostile shipping and keep the Allies from obtaining any information concerning the project. Until they were eventually sunk by ships of the British navy, the raiders captured or destroyed entire fleets of Allied shipping and all fishing and whaling ships that strayed into the area. Next, an armada of cargo ships, disguised as Allied merchant vessels, and a fleet of huge U-boats, built not for warfare but to transport large cargoes, began moving men, equipment, and supplies to the area of the ancient civilization they thought might be Atlantis."

"Why build a base on ancient ruins?" said Little. "What military purpose did it serve?"

"The dead and lost city itself was not important. It was the vast ice cave they found under a field of ice that led from the city. The cave traveled twenty-five miles, before ending at a geothermal lake that covered a hundred and ten square miles. Scientists, engineers, construction teams, and every arm of the military—army, air force, navy—and, of course, a large contingent of SS to maintain security and oversee the operation, landed and began an immense excavation project. They also imported a large army of slave labor, mostly captured Russians from Siberia, who had built up a resistance to cold climates."

"What happened to the Russian prisoners after the base was completed?" asked Little, suspecting the answer.

Hozafel's face turned grim. "The Nazis could never allow them to be released and reveal Germany's best-kept secret. They were either worked to death or executed."

Sandecker studied the smoke spiraling from his cigar soberly. "So thousands of Russians lie under the ice, unknown and forgotten."

"Life was cheap to the Nazis," said Hozafel. "The sacrifice to build a fortress to launch the Fourth Reich was well worth the price to them."

"The Fourth Empire," Sandecker said darkly. "The last Nazi bastion and their final attempt at world domination."

"The Germans are a very obstinate race."

"Did you see this base?" asked Little.

Again, Hozafel nodded. "After leaving Bergen, Captain Harger and the U-2015, followed by my crew in the U-699, sailed across the Atlantic without surfacing, to a deserted port in Patagonia."

"Where you off-loaded your passengers and treasures," added Sandecker.

"You're familiar with the operation?"

"Only the basics, not the details."

"Then you couldn't know that only the passengers and medical specimens went ashore. The art treasures, hoards of gold and other valuables, as well as the sacred Nazi relics, remained on board the U-2015 and U-699. Captain Harger and I then cast off for the base in Antarctica. After rendezvousing with a supply ship and refueling, we continued the voyage, arriving at our destination in early June of 1945. The product of German engineering was a marvel to behold. A pilot came out and took the helm of the U-2015. We followed in her wake and were led into a large cavern that was invisible from a quarter of a mile at sea. A large dock facility carved out of ice, capable of handling several submarines and large cargo vessels, greeted our amazed eyes. Captain Harger and I were ordered to moor behind a military transport that was unloading disassembled aircraft—"

"They flew aircraft from the base?" Little interrupted.

"The very latest in German aviation technology. Junkers 287 jet bombers converted to transports, fitted with skis, and specially modified for subarctic conditions. The slave labor had cut a large hangar in the ice, while heavy construction equipment had smoothed a mile-long runway. Over five years, an entire mountain of ice was hollowed out to form a small city supporting five thousand construction workers and slaves."

"Wouldn't the ice inside the caverns and tunnels begin to melt from the heat generated by that many men and their equipment?" asked Little.

"German scientists had developed a chemical coating that could be sprayed on the ice walls that insulated and prevented them from melting. The heat inside the complex was maintained at a constant sixty degrees Fahrenheit."

"If the war was over," Sandecker put to Hozafel, "what useful purpose could the base serve?"

"The plan, as I understood it, was for the remaining elite Nazis of the old regime to operate secretly from the base, infiltrate into South America, and buy great tracts of land and many technical and manufacturing corporations. They also invested heavily in the new Germany and in the Asian countries, using the gold from their old national treasury, some of the looted treasures that were sold in America, and counterfeit American currency printed with genuine U.S. Treasury printing plates that were obtained by the Russians and captured by the Germans. Finances were not a problem to launch the Fourth Reich."

"How long did you remain at the base?" asked Little.

"Two months. Then I took my U-boat and crew and sailed to the Río de Plata River and surrendered to the local authorities. An officer of the Argentine Navy came on board and directed me to continue toward the Mar de Plata naval base. I gave the order, my last one as an officer in the Kriegsmarine before turning over a completely empty U-boat."

"How long after the war ended did this take place?"

"A week short of four months."

"Then what happened?"

"My crew and I were detained until British and American intelligence agents arrived and interrogated us. We were questioned for six solid weeks before we were finally released and allowed to return home."

"You and the crew, I assume, told Allied intelligence nothing."

Hozafel smiled. "We had three weeks during the voyage from Antarctica to Argentina to rehearse our stories. They were a bit melodramatic perhaps, but none of us broke and the interrogation teams learned nothing. They were highly skeptical. But who could blame them? A German naval vessel vanishes for four months and then turns up, its commander claiming that he believed that any radio contact stating that Germany had surrendered was an Allied scheme to make him reveal his position? Not a plausible story, but one they could not break." He paused and stared at the dying fire. "The U-699 was then turned over to the United States Navy and towed to their base at Norfolk, Virginia, where it was dismantled down to the last bolt and then scrapped."

"And the U-2015?" Sandecker probed.

"I don't know. I never heard what happened to her and never saw Harger again."

"You might be interested in knowing," said Sandecker, pleased, "that the U-2015 was sunk only a few days ago by a U.S. nuclear sub in the Antarctic."

Hozafel's eyes narrowed. "I've heard stories of German U-boat activity in the southern polar seas long after the war, but found no substance to them."

"Because many of the highly advanced XXI and XXII class of U-boats are still listed as missing," said Little. "We strongly suspect that a fleet of them was preserved by Nazi leadership for smuggling purposes during the years since the war."

"I would have to admit you're probably correct."

Sandecker was about to speak when the phone rang again. He engaged the speaker, almost afraid of what he might hear. "Yes?"

"Just to confirm," came Pitt's voice. "The pizza is on your doorstep and the delivery boy is on his way back to the store through heavy rush-hour traffic."

"Thank you for calling," said Sandecker. There was no sense of relief in his voice.

"I hope you call again when you get the urge for pizza."

"I prefer calzone." Sandecker closed the connection. "Well," he said wearily, "they reached the aircraft and are in the air."

"Then they're home free," said Little, suddenly buoyant.

Sandecker shook his head dejectedly. "When Dirk mentioned rush-hour traffic, he meant they were under attack by security force aircraft. I fear they have escaped the sharks only to encounter the barracuda."

UNDER its automatic guidance system, the Moller Skycar ascended into the night and skimmed across the black waters of the fjord, slowly increasing its altitude as it swept over the glacier flowing down from the mountains. If anyone on board thought that once they reached the Skycar, they had lifted off for a peaceful flight back to the NUMA ship waiting off Punta Entrada, they were sadly mistaken.

Not one but four helicopter gunships rose from the deck of the *Ulrich Wolf* and set a course to intercept the Skycar. One should have been enough, but the Wolfs sent out their entire fleet of security aircraft to stop the fleeing fugitives. There were no fancy formations, no tentative skirmishing; they came on abreast in a well-calculated deployment to cut off the Skycar before it could reach the sanctuary of the mountains.

Purchased by Destiny Enterprises from the Messerschmitt-Bolkow Corporation, the Bo 105LS-7 helicopter was designed and built for the Federal German Army primarily for ground support and paramilitary use. The aircraft chasing the Skycar carried a crew of two, and mounted twin engines that gave it a maximum speed of two hundred and eighty miles an hour. For firepower, it relied on a ventral-mounted, swiveling twenty-millimeter cannon.

Giordino sat in the pilot's seat this trip, with Pitt monitoring the instruments, while the women huddled in the cramped rear passenger seat. In a repeat performance of the incoming flight, there was little for Giordino to do but alter the throttle settings to maximum speed. Every other manipulation was computer-controlled and operated. Next to him, Pitt was studying the pursuing helicopters on the radar screen.

"Why, oh why, can't those big bullies leave us alone?" Giordino moaned.

"Looks like they sent the entire gang," said Pitt, eyeing the blips on the outer edge of the screen, which were closing in on the outline of the Skycar in the center as if it were a magnetic bull's-eye.

"If they have heat-seeking missiles that fly in and through canyons," said Giordino, "they may prove a nuisance."

"I don't think so. Civilian aircraft are rarely capable of carrying military missiles."

"Can we lose them in the mountains?"

"It will be a near thing," Pitt answered. "Their only hope is to take their best shot from half a mile before we're out of range. After that, we can outrun them. Their speed looks to be about thirty miles slower than ours."

Giordino peered through the canopy. "We're coming off the glacier and entering the mountains. Twisting through the canyons should make it awkward for them to get off a clean shot."

"Shouldn't you be concentrating on flying this thing?" said Pat, staring uneasily at the mountains silhouetted in the faint moonlight that were beginning to rise up on both sides of the Skycar. "Rather than chatting among yourselves?"

"How are you two getting on back there?" Pitt asked solicitously.

"This is like riding a roller coaster," said Megan excitedly.

Pat was more aware of the danger and not as enthusiastic as her daughter. "I think I'll keep my eyes closed, thank you."

"We'll be thrown around by turbulence, and the sudden shifts of direction through the mountains, because we'll be running at maximum speed," explained Pitt. "But not to worry. The computer is flying the aircraft."

"How comforting," Pat muttered uneasily.

"The bad guys are coming over the summit at nine o'clock," announced Giordino, warily staring at the glaring lights beamed by the helicopters that lit up the jagged mountain slopes.

The pilots of the assault helicopters played a smart game. They made no attempt to chase the faster Skycar through the hooks and crooks among the ravines that split the mountains. They realized they had one opportunity, and only one, to shoot down the strange-looking aircraft. They gained altitude as one and fired down into the ravine, their twenty-millimeter shells blasting through the dark in trajectories ahead of the Skycar.

Pitt instantly realized the tactic and elbowed Giordino's arm. "Take manual control!" he snapped. "Stop us in midair and back up!"

Giordino obeyed and completed the maneuver almost before the words were out of Pitt's mouth. He switched off the computer control and took command, bringing the Skycar to a gut-wrenching halt that threw them against their safety harnesses, then sending the aircraft back down the ravine in reverse.

"If we attempt to fly through that barrage," said Pitt, "we'll be shot to shreds."

"It's only a matter of seconds before they reposition and aim this way."

"That's the idea. I'm banking on them turning and deflecting their fire behind our path, expecting us to fly into it. But we shoot forward again, forcing them to realign—the same trick we pulled on the patrol boat. If things fall our way, we'll gain enough time to put a mountain between us before they can reconcentrate their fire again."

As they spoke, the gunships broke out of formation to converge their fire. In a few seconds, they had realigned and zeroed in, firing directly at the Skycar. It was the signal for Giordino to send the craft charging up the ravine again. The plan came within a hair of out-and-out success, but the seconds spent in reverse allowed the helicopters to move in closer. There was no concentrated barrage this time. The pilots reacted swiftly and began firing wildly at the rapidly fleeing Skycar.

Shells ripped into the vertical fins of the tail assembly. The landing wheels were shot off and the upper part of the canopy suddenly shattered and flew off into the darkness, allowing a rush of cold air to flood into the cockpit. The murderous but inaccurate fire sprayed all around the craft, but mercifully the engines remained unscathed. Unable to evade the salvo by twisting the Skycar obliquely—since the sides of the ravine were no more than fifty feet from the widest part of the aircraft—Giordino jerked it up and down instead.

The twenty-millimeter shells that missed chewed into the steep cliffs and threw up geysers of rocky fragments. Like a cat chased by a pack of dogs, Giordino hurled the Skycar up the canyon in a frenzied series of undulating maneuvers. Another two hundred yards, then a hundred, and suddenly, Giordino threw the aircraft into a sharp ninety-degree bank, skirting around a protruding rock-bound slope that blocked off the storm of shell fire.

By the time the Destiny Enterprises' gunships had reached the promontory and rounded it, the Skycar had vanished deep into the blackness of the mountains.

PART FOUR

CITY UNDER THE ICE

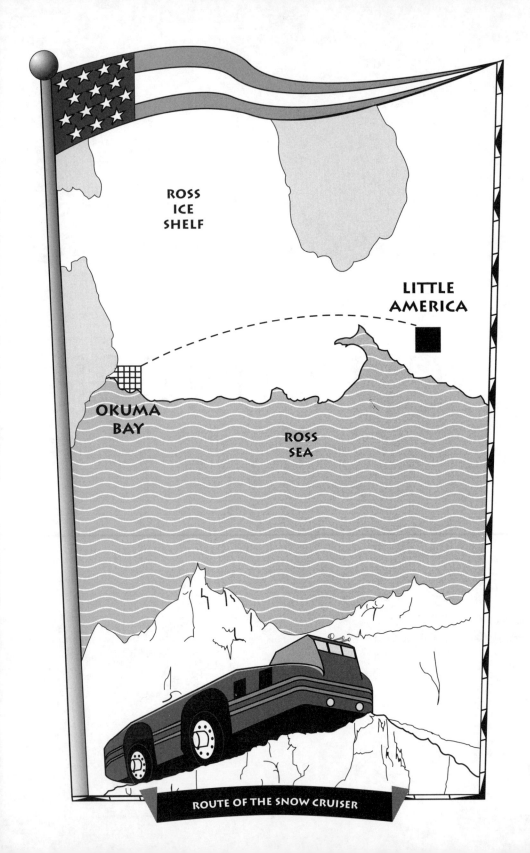

ROSS
ICE
SHELF

LITTLE
AMERICA

OKUMA
BAY

ROSS
SEA

ROUTE OF THE SNOW CRUISER

32

LIMOUSINES FORMED A LONG arc on the circular drive of the British Embassy in Buenos Aires. Ladies in ballgowns and men in tuxedos exited the long black cars and entered through high bronze doors into the foyer, where they were met by the British ambassador to Argentina, Charles Lexington, and his wife, Martha, a tall, serene woman with white hair cut in a pageboy. The social event of the year was a celebration in honor of Prince Charles's elevation to the throne, finally abdicated by his mother, Queen Elizabeth.

The elite of Argentina had been invited, and all attended. The President, the National Congress leaders, the mayor of the city, financiers and industrialists, and the nation's most admired celebrities. Those who entered the ballroom to the music of an orchestra in eighteenth-century costume were enthralled with the sumptuous buffet prepared by the finest chefs imported from England especially for the event.

When Karl Wolf and his usual entourage of sisters made their grand entrance into the vast room, they inevitably received the stares of everyone present. His personal bodyguard stayed close beside them at all times. In keeping with their family tradition, the gorgeous women were all wearing gowns of the same design but in different colors. After being greeted by the British ambassador, they swept into the ballroom, their radiance envied by almost all the women present.

Karl was accompanied by Geli, Maria, and Luci, who'd brought along their husbands, and Elsie, who had just returned from America. As his sisters and their spouses began dancing to a medley of Cole Porter tunes, Karl led Elsie to the buffet, stopping along the way to accept a glass of champagne from the liveried waiters. They selected a sampling of exotic dishes and moved into the library, where they found an empty table with two chairs next to a floor-to-ceiling bookcase.

Elsie was about to lift a fork with a delicate cheese to her mouth when her hand froze in midair and her face took on a look of disbelief. Karl studied her dazed expression but did not turn around, instead waiting quietly for an explanation. It came with the presence of a tall, rugged-looking man with a lovely woman at his side, flaming red hair cascading to her waist. The man wore a tuxedo with a maroon brocade vest, and a gold watch chain hung across the front. The woman was dressed in a black silk velvet jacket over a slim-fitting, black silk ankle-length gown, slit on the sides. A crystal-beaded choker adorned her slender neck.

They approached the Wolfs and stopped. "How nice to see you again, Elsie," said Pitt cordially. Before she could answer, he turned to Wolf. "You must be the infamous Karl Wolf I've heard so much about." He paused and turned to Pat. "May I introduce Dr. Patricia O'Connell?"

Wolf gazed at Pitt as a cutter might study a diamond before lifting his mallet to strike his wedge and cleave a stone. Though he didn't seem to recognize Pitt, Pat felt a chill ripple up her spine. The billionaire was extremely handsome, but he stared from eyes that were cold and threatening. There was a hardness about him that suggested an underlying savagery. If he knew who she was, he showed no sign of recognition at hearing her name, nor did he display gentlemanly grace by rising from his chair.

"Though we have never met," Pitt continued in a friendly fashion, "I feel as if I know you."

"I have no idea who you are," said Wolf in perfect English, with just a trace of a Teutonic accent.

"My name is Dirk Pitt."

For a brief moment, there was incomprehension in Wolf's eyes, then his face slowly took on a look of pure animosity. "You are Dirk Pitt?" he asked coldly.

"None other." He smiled at Elsie. "You look surprised to see me. You left Washington quite suddenly before we had a chance to chat again."

"Where did you come from?" she snarled.

"From the *Ulrich Wolf*," Pitt answered politely. "After taking a tour of the ship, Pat and I found ourselves in Buenos Aires and thought we'd drop by and say hello."

If her eyes were lasers, Pitt would have been fried and grilled. "We can have you killed."

"You've tried, and it didn't work out," Pitt replied casually. "I don't advise you to try again, certainly not inside the British Embassy in front of all these people."

"When you reach the street, Mr. Pitt, you will be in my country, not yours. You will be helpless to protect yourselves."

"Not a good idea, Karl. You'd only upset the United States Marines who escorted us here tonight under the protection of the American ambassador, John Horn."

One of Wolf's hefty bodyguards moved forward then as if to assault Pitt, but suddenly Giordino stepped from behind and stood toe-to-toe with the guard, blocking any movement. The guard, who outweighed Giordino by a good fifty pounds and stood ten inches taller, looked down contemptuously and said, "What makes you think you're so tough, little man?"

Giordino grinned condescendingly. "Would you be impressed if I told you that I'd just exterminated half a dozen of your fellow vermin?"

"He's not kidding," said Pitt.

The guard's reaction was amusing. He didn't know whether to be mad or wary. Wolf raised a hand and idly waved off his bodyguard. "I congratulate all of you on your escape from the *Ulrich Wolf*. My security forces proved most incompetent."

"Not at all," Pitt replied amicably. "They were really quite good. We were very lucky."

"From the report I received, luck had very little to do with it."

It was as close to a compliment as Karl Wolf could ever give. He came slowly out of his chair and stood facing Pitt. He was two inches taller and relished looking down at this thorn in Destiny Enterprises' side. His blue-gray eyes glinted, but their fixed stare was easily matched and returned by Pitt, who was more interested in studying his enemy than engaging in a childish game of stare-down.

"You are making a regrettable mistake in opposing me, Mr. Pitt. Surely you must be aware by now that I am dedicated to using every tool at my command to make the world as pure and as uncontaminated as it was nine thousand years ago."

"You have a strange way of going about it."

"Why did you come here tonight?"

Pitt did not back off. "I have suffered a great deal of inconvenience because of your family, and I was determined to meet the man who's been scheming to play master of the universe."

"And now that you've met me?"

"It seems to me you've bet the farm on a phenomenon that may not take place. How can you be so dead certain the twin of the comet that wiped out the Amenes will return next month and strike the earth? How do you know it won't miss, as it did then?"

Wolf looked at Pitt speculatively and smiled maliciously. It was obvious that a man of his wealth and power was not used to people who did not fear him, who did not grovel in his divine presence.

"The coming cataclysm is an established conclusion. The world, as it is known by every living creature, will no longer exist. With the exception of my family, everyone in this room, including yourself, will surely perish." He leaned forward with a wicked grin. "But I'm afraid, Mr. Pitt, that it will happen rather sooner than you think. The timetable's been advanced, you see. The end of the world . . . will begin precisely four days and ten hours from now."

Pitt tried to hide his shock. Less than five days! How was it possible?

Pat didn't bother to hide her dismay. "How could you do this? Why have you gone to so much trouble to keep it a secret?" she demanded impassionedly. "Why haven't you warned every living soul on Earth so they can prepare for whatever happens? Have you and your precious sisters no conscience? Have you no compassion? Don't the deaths of billions of children torment you, like any sane person? You're just as bad as your ancestors who slaughtered millions—"

Elsie shot to her feet. "How dare you insult my brother!" she hissed.

Pitt slid his arm around Pat's waist. "Don't waste your breath on these purveyors of slime," he said, his face taut with anger. The confrontation was getting too tense. But he couldn't resist getting in one more remark. He looked at Elsie and said pleasantly, with a chilling grin, "You know, Elsie, I'll bet that making love to you and your sisters is like making love to ice sculptures."

Elsie hauled back to slap Pitt, but Pat lunged forward and grabbed her arm. Elsie snatched it away, shocked that someone other than a family member would treat her roughly. For a moment, both Pitt and Wolf thought the two women were going to go at it, but Pat smiled brazenly and turned to Pitt and Giordino. "I'm bored. Why don't one of you gentlemen ask me to dance?"

Pitt decided it was wiser to hang around and attempt to milk the Wolfs for more information while he had their attention. He made a slight bow to Giordino. "You first."

"My pleasure." Giordino took Pat's hand and led her to the dance floor, where the orchestra was playing "Night and Day."

Pitt said to Karl Wolf, "Very clever of you, accelerating the schedule. How did you do it?"

"Ah, Mr. Pitt," Wolf said. "I must have some secrets to myself."

Pitt tried a different tack. "I compliment you on your ships. They are masterworks of marine architecture and engineering. Only the *Freedom,* the sea city built by Norman Nixon of Engineering Solutions, comes close to matching their magnificent scale."

"That is true." Wolf was intrigued, despite himself. "I freely admit that many of the qualities we built into the *Ulrich Wolf* came from those designs."

"Do you really think those immense vessels will float out to sea in the wash from the giant tidal wave?"

"My engineers have assured me their calculations are precise."

"What happens if they're wrong?"

The expression on Wolf's face suggested that he never considered the thought. "The cataclysm *will* come to pass, exactly when I said it would, and our ships *will* be safe."

"I'm not sure I'd want to be around after the earth was devastated and most of the humans and animals became extinct."

"That's the difference between you and me, Mr. Pitt. You see it as the end. I see it as a bold new beginning. Now, good night. We have much to do." And he gathered up his sister and walked away.

Pitt desperately wanted to believe that Wolf was simply another lunatic, but this man's passion and that of his entire family went far beyond mere fanaticism. Pitt stood there, uneasy. No man this intelligent would build an empire worth many billions of dollars to throw it away on a crackpot scheme. There had to be an underlying rationality, one that was too horrifying to envision. But what? According to Wolf's own timetable, Pitt now had only four days and ten hours to find the answer. And why was Wolf so forthcoming about the deadline? It was almost as if he didn't care that Pitt knew. Did he simply think that it didn't matter anymore, that there was nothing anyone could do about it? Or was there some other reason in that devious mind?

Pitt turned and walked away. He stepped up to the bar and ordered an *anejo*, 100 percent blue agave tequila on the rocks. Ambassador Horn came and stood beside him. Horn, a light-haired small man, had the look of a hawk gliding in a spiral over a forest, more interested in his sovereignty than scanning for a meal.

"How did you and Karl Wolf get along?" he inquired.

"Not too well," answered Pitt. "He has his mind set on playing God, and I never learned to genuflect."

"He's a strange man. No one I know has ever gotten close to him. Certainly, there's been no indication why he would believe in this fantastic story of the end of the world. I've told my colleagues here and in Washington, and they say there's no evidence at all of such an event coming—at least so far."

"Do you know much about him?"

"Not a great deal. Only what I've read in intelligence reports. His grandfather was a big Nazi who escaped Germany at the end of the war. He came here with his family and a group of Nazi cronies, along with their top scientists and engineers. Soon after arriving in Argentina, they established a huge financial conglomerate within less than two years, buying and operating the largest farms and ranches, banks and corporations in the country. Once their power base was solidified, they branched out internationally into everything from chemicals to electronics. One can only guess where the original capital came from. Rumors say it was gold from the German treasury and assets stolen from the Jews who died in the camps. Whatever the source, it must have been a tremendous hoard to have accomplished so much in so little time."

"What can you tell me about the family?"

Horn paused to order a martini from the bartender. "Mostly rumors. My Argentinian friends speak in hushed tones whenever the Wolfs come up in conversation. It's been reported that Dr. Josef Mengele, the 'Angel of Death' at Auschwitz, was involved with the Wolfs until he drowned several years ago. The stories, I admit, sound pretty outlandish. But they claim that Mengele, continuing his genetic experiments, worked with the first generations of Wolfs in producing offspring with high intelligence and exceptional athletic ability. These children then produced an even more controlled strain, which you see in the extraordinary likenesses in all the third generation of Wolfs, such as Karl and his sisters, who, by the way, all look identical to their brothers and cousins. One outlandish bit of gossip is that Adolf Hitler's sperm was smuggled out of Berlin in the closing hours of the war and used by Mengele in impregnating the Wolf women."

"Do you believe all this?" Pitt asked.

"I certainly don't want to," said Horn, sipping at his martini. "British intelligence is mum on the subject. But my embassy intelligence officer, Major Steve Miller, using a computer, has compared photos of Hitler with those of the Wolfs. As abhorrent as it sounds, except for hair and eye color, there *is* a marked resemblance in facial structure."

Pitt straightened and extended his hand. "Ambassador, I can't tell you how grateful I am for your invitation and protection. Coming to Buenos Aires was a wild scheme, and you were very generous with your time in helping me to meet Karl Wolf."

Horn gripped Pitt's hand. "We were lucky the Wolfs showed up for the party. But I have to tell you that it was a real pleasure to see someone tell that arrogant devil where to get off. Because I'm a diplomat, I couldn't afford the luxury of doing it myself."

"He claims the timetable's moved up, that now there's only four days until Armageddon. I should think the family will soon be boarding their superships."

"Really? That's odd," said Horn. "I have it on good authority that Karl is scheduled to make an inspection tour of his mineral retraction facility in Antarctica the day after tomorrow."

Pitt's eyes narrowed. "He's cutting it pretty thin."

"That project has always been a bit of a mystery. As far as I know, the CIA has never been able to get an agent inside."

Pitt smiled at Horn. "You're certainly abreast of intelligence matters, Ambassador."

Horn shrugged. "It pays to keep one's fingers in the pie."

Pitt swirled the tequila in his glass and stared thoughtfully at the liquid curling around the ice cubes. What is so important in Antarctica that Wolf has to squeeze in a visit, Pitt wondered. It seemed to him that the new leader of the Fourth Empire would be flying toward his fleet in preparation for the big event instead of to the polar continent. Getting there and back would take two days. It didn't figure.

33

THE FOLLOWING DAY, TWENTY-SEVEN of the two-hundred-member Wolf dynasty, the dominant principals of Destiny Enterprises and the chief architects of the Fourth Empire, met at Destiny's corporate offices. They assembled in the spacious boardroom with its teak-paneled walls and handsomely carved forty-foot-long conference table, also carved from teak. A large oil painting of Ulrich Wolf hung above the mantel of a fireplace at one end of the room. The family patriarch stood ramrod-straight in a black SS uniform, jaw thrust out, black eyes staring at some distant horizon beyond the painting.

The twelve women and fifteen men waited patiently while being served fifty-year-old port from crystal glasses. At precisely ten o'clock, Karl Wolf stepped from the chairman's suite and took his seat at the end of the table. For a few moments, his gaze swept the faces of his brothers, sisters, and cousins seated expectantly around the table. His father, Max Wolf, sat at his left. Bruno Wolf was to his right. Karl Wolf's lips were parted in a slight smile, and he looked to be in a cheerful mood.

"Before we begin our final meeting in the office of Destiny Enterprises and our beloved city of Buenos Aires, I should like to express my admiration for the way you and your loved ones have accomplished so much in so little time. Every member of the Wolf family has performed far beyond expectations, and we should all be proud that none has proved a disappointment."

"Hear, hear," exclaimed Bruno. The chant was taken up around the table, accompanied by a round of applause.

"Without my son's leadership," announced Max Wolf, "the great crusade, conceived by your grandfathers, could never have achieved fulfillment. I am proud of your eminent contribution to the coming new world order and elated that our family, with the blood of the Führer flowing through your veins, is now on the verge of making the Fourth Reich a reality."

More applause erupted around the table. To a stranger, everyone in the room, with the exception of Max Wolf, looked as if he or she had been cloned. The same facial features, body build, eyes and hair—it was as if the boardroom had become a hall of mirrors.

Karl shifted his eyes to Bruno. "Are those who are not present here today on board the *Ulrich Wolf?*"

Bruno nodded. "All family members are comfortably settled in their residence quarters."

"And the supplies and equipment?"

Wilhelm Wolf raised a hand and reported. "Food stocks have been loaded and stored aboard all four vessels. All ship's personnel are on board and accounted for. Every piece of equipment and all electronic systems have been tested and retested. They all function perfectly. Nothing has been left to chance or overlooked. Every contingency has been considered and alternatives prepared. The ships are in total readiness for the onslaught of even the strongest tidal waves anticipated by our computer projections. All that is left is for the rest of us to fly to the *Ulrich Wolf* and wait for the resurrection."

Karl smiled. "You will have to go without me. I will follow later. It is critical that I oversee the final preparations at our mining operation at Okuma Bay."

"Do not be late," said Elsie, smiling. "We might have to sail without you."

Karl laughed. "Never fear, dear sister. I have no intention of missing the boat."

Rosa raised her hand. "Did the American scientist decipher the Amenes inscriptions before she escaped the ship?"

Karl shook his head. "Unfortunately, whatever information she discovered, she took with her."

"Can't our agents retrieve it?" asked Bruno.

"I fear not. She is too well protected at the American Embassy. By the time we devised a plan and mounted an operation to seize her again, it would be too late. The deadline would be upon us."

Albert Wolf, the paleoecologist of the family, who was an expert in ancient environments and their effects on primeval plant and animal life, motioned to speak. "It would have been most beneficial to have studied a narrative by those who lived through the last cataclysm, but I believe our computer projections have given us a fairly accurate picture of what to expect."

"Once the ships are swept into open water," said Elsie, "our first priority is to ensure that they are rigidly sealed against all contamination from ash, volcanic gases, and smoke."

"You may rest easy on that problem, cousin," said Berndt Wolf, the family's engineering genius. "The ship's interiors are designed to become completely airtight in a matter of seconds. Then specially constructed filtering equipment takes over. All systems have been exactingly tested and have proven one hundred percent efficient. A pure, breathable atmosphere for an extended period of time is a confirmed reality."

"Have we decided on what part of the world we will come ashore after it's safe to do so?" asked Maria Wolf.

"We're still in the process of accumulating data and calculating projections," answered Albert. "We must determine exactly how the cataclysm and tidal waves will alter the world's coasts. It will be mostly a matter of analyzing the situation after the havoc has abated."

Karl glanced down the table at his kinsmen. "Much will depend on how the landmasses have changed. Europe may become inundated as far as the Urals in Russia. Water may fill the Sahara Desert. Ice will cover Canada and the United States. Our first priority is to survive the onslaught and wait patiently before deciding on where to establish a headquarters city for our new world order."

"We have several sites under consideration," said Wilhelm. "The prime considerations are a port, such as San Francisco, where we can moor the ships, preferably a location with nearby land suitable for growing crops and orchards, and a centralized area that facilitates transportation and the spread of our authority around the new world. Much will depend upon the extent of the cataclysm."

"Do we have any idea how long we must remain on board the ships before we can venture ashore?" asked Gerda Wolf, whose expertise was education and who had been chosen to supervise the fleet's school systems.

Albert looked at her and smiled. "Certainly no longer than we have to, my sister. Years will pass, but we have no way of predicting exactly how long it will take before we can safely begin our conquest of the land."

"The people who survive on high ground?" queried Maria. "How will we treat them?"

"There will be pitifully few," replied Bruno. "Those who we can find and round up will be placed in secure areas to cope as best they can."

"We're not going to assist them?"

Bruno shook his head. "We cannot weaken our own food supplies before our people have the opportunity to subsist off the land."

"In time, except for those of us of the Fourth Reich," said Max Wolf, "the rest of mankind will become extinct. Survival of the fittest. That is the way of evolution. It was ordained by the Führer that a master race would someday govern the world. We are that master race."

"Let us be honest, Uncle," said Felix Wolf. "We are not fanatical Nazis. The Nazi party died with our grandparents. Our generation pays homage to Adolf Hitler only for his foresight. We do not worship the swastika or shout 'Heil' in front of his picture. We are our own race, created to rid the present world of crime, corruption, and disease by establishing a higher level of mankind: one that will build a new society free from the sins of the old one. Through our genes, a new race will emerge, pure and untouched by the evils of the past."

"Well said." Otto Wolf spoke, after sitting quietly through the conference. "Felix has eloquently summed up our purpose and commit-ment. Now all that is left is for us to carry our great quest through to a triumphant conclusion."

There came a few moments of silence. Then Karl folded his hands and spoke slowly. "It will be most interesting to see the conditions around us this time next year. It will indeed be a world inconceivable to those who will have gone."

34

A SMALL ENCLOSED TRUCK, painted white with no logo or advertising on its sides, rumbled past the terminal of the Jorge Newbery city airport, located within the federal district of Buenos Aires, and came to a stop under the shade of a maintenance hangar. The airport normally served Argentina's domestic airlines, including those that operated out of Paraguay, Chile, and Uruguay. None of the flight line workers seemed to take notice of a turquoise executive jet with "NUMA" boldly outlined on its fuselage, as it landed and taxied to the hangar where the truck was waiting.

Three men and a woman came through the passenger door and stepped down to the concrete, which was heated by the noonday sun. Just as they were about to reach the maintenance office door of the hangar, they veered around the corner and approached the truck. When they were thirty feet away, the rear door opened and four United States Marines in battle gear jumped to the ground and formed a perimeter around the vehicle. The sergeant in command then helped Congresswoman Smith, Admiral Sandecker, Hiram Yaeger, and a third man enter the truck before reclosing the door.

The interior of the truck was a comfortably furnished office and command post. One of fifty constructed specifically for American embassies around the world, it was designed to protect and aid embassy personnel to escape their compound in the event of attack, such as the abduction and hostage situation in Iran during November of 1979.

Pitt stepped forward and embraced Loren Smith, who was shown aboard first. "You gorgeous creature. I wasn't expecting you."

Pat O'Connell felt a stab of jealousy at seeing Pitt with his arms around Loren. The congresswoman from Colorado was far more attractive than she had imagined.

"The admiral asked me to come, and there were no pressing votes on the floor, so here I am, even if it is for only a few hours."

"A pity," he said sincerely. "We could have done Buenos Aires."

"I would have liked that," she replied in a husky tone. Then she saw Giordino. "Al, it's good to see you."

He gave her a peck on the cheek. "Always a pleasure to see my government at work."

Sandecker climbed in, followed by Yaeger and the stranger. He merely nodded at Pitt and Giordino. He walked directly to Pat O'Connell. "You don't know how happy I am to shake your hand again, Doctor."

"You don't know how happy I am to be here," she said, kissing him on the forehead, to his obvious embarrassment. "My daughter and I are in your debt for sending Dirk and Al to rescue us."

"I didn't have to send them," he said wryly. "They would have gone on their own."

Yaeger greeted his old friends and Pat, who was introduced to Loren for the first time. Then Sandecker introduced Dr. Timothy Friend. "Tim is an old school pal. He helped me pass algebra in high school. When I went to the Naval Academy, he went to the Colorado School of Mines for a degree in geophysics. Not content with that, he obtained his Ph.D. in astronomy at Stanford, and became one of the country's most respected astronomers and director of the government's Strategic Computing and Simulation Laboratory. Tim is a wizard of innovative visualization techniques."

Friend's bald head was encircled by wisps of gray hair, like a school of silverfish swimming around a coral dome. A short man, he had to tilt his head back slightly to gaze up at the two women, who were considerably taller. Giordino, who stood five feet four, was the only one he could look straight in the eye. A quiet man among friends, he became outgoing and lively when lecturing before students, directors of corporations, or high government officials. It was easy to tell that he was in his element.

"Would you all care to sit down?" said Pitt, motioning to comfortable leather chairs and sofas spaced in a square in the center of the truck's cargo area. Once they were seated, an embassy staff member served coffee and sandwiches from a small galley behind the cab.

"Loren asked to come along," said Sandecker, without preamble. "She and her congressional aides investigated Destiny Enterprises and came up with some intriguing information."

"What I found in the past two days is quite worrisome," Loren began. "Very quietly, under astounding secrecy, the Wolf family and Destiny Enterprises have sold every business, every one of their shares in national and international corporations, every financial holding, all bonds, all stocks, all real estate, including every stick of furniture in their homes. All bank accounts have been cleaned out. Every asset large and small has been liquidated. Billions of dollars were converted into gold bullion that was transported to a secret location—"

"Where it is now stored in the cargo compartments of their fleet of ships," Pitt finished.

"It's as though the entire family of two hundred members has never existed."

"These are not stupid people," Pitt said convincingly. "I find it inconceivable that they are capable of irrational judgment. So is there a comet coming, or isn't there?"

"The very reason I've asked Tim to come along," explained Sandecker.

Friend laid out several small piles of papers on a table between the chairs and sofas. He picked up the first one and leafed through it before consulting his notes. "Before I answer that, let me go back a bit, so you can understand what the Wolfs have been preparing for. I think it best to begin with the comet's impact on earth sometime around seven thousand B.C. Fortunately, this is not an event that occurs on a regular basis. Although Earth is struck daily, it's by small asteroid fragments no larger than a fist that burn up upon entry into the atmosphere. About every century, one approximately a hundred and fifty feet in diameter strikes Earth, such as the one that produced the crater in Winslow, Arizona, and the other that exploded before impact in Siberia in 1908 that plastered eight hundred square miles. Once every million years, an asteroid half a mile wide strikes with a force equal to detonating every nuclear device on Earth simultaneously. Over two thousand of these big celestial missiles cross our orbit on a regular schedule."

"Not a pretty picture," said Pat.

"Don't lose any sleep over it," Friend said, smiling. "Your odds of dying from an asteroid are twenty thousand to one during your lifetime. We can't, however, discount the logical possibility that it's only a question of time before our luck runs out."

Pitt poured a cup of coffee. "I assume you're talking about a really stupendous bang."

"Indeed," said Friend, nodding vigorously. "Once every one hundred million years, a mammoth asteroid or comet strikes Earth, like the one that smacked into the sea off Yucatán sixty-five million years ago and caused the extinction of the dinosaurs. This impact came from an object six miles in diameter that left a crater one hundred and twenty miles wide."

Friend paused to scan his paperwork before continuing. "That was smaller than the one that struck nine thousand years ago. Our computer model indicates that it measured nearly ten miles in diameter and plunged into Hudson Bay, Canada. The resulting chain reaction annihilated nearly ninety-nine percent of all plant and animal life on the planet, which is twenty percent more than the asteroid that caused the extinction of the dinosaurs sixty-five million years earlier."

Loren stared at Friend with rapt interest. "A chain reaction comprising what type of disasters?"

"You take an object ten miles in diameter, weighing several billion tons, and then hurl it through a vacuum into a big soft ball at a speed of one hundred and thirty thousand miles an hour, and you're going to have a blast that is gargantuan beyond comprehension. The earth probably rang like a bell, as the shock of impact was transmitted into every corner. Using computer simulation and visualization techniques, which were very complicated and would take me two hours to explain, we determined that the comet came on an angle, punching into the southeastern section of Hudson Bay and blasting out a crater two hundred and thirty miles in diameter, or more than twice the size of the island of Hawaii. The entire mass of water in the bay was vaporized, as the bulk of the now-disintegrating comet plowed into the Earth to a depth of two miles. Astronauts have taken photos that show a perfect sphere where the shoreline circles the remains of the crater."

"How do you know it was a comet and not an asteroid or meteor?" asked Yaeger.

"An asteroid is a small body or minor planet that wanders the inner solar system and revolves around the sun. Some are rich in carbon; others contain minerals rich in iron, silicon, and other minerals. Meteorites for the most part, are smaller fragments from asteroids that have collided with one another and broken up. The largest ever found weighed seventy tons. A comet is quite different. It's often called a dirty snowball made up of ice, gas, and rocky dust particles. They usually travel in very long oval orbits on the outer edge of the solar system, and often beyond. Because of gravitational interaction from the sun and planets, a few are diverted and orbit around the sun. When they come close to the sun, the comet's surface ice vaporizes and forms a spectacular elongated cone or tail. It's generally thought that they are leftovers from the formation of the planets. By drilling and then analyzing the composition of the microscopic debris found in and around the Hudson Bay crater, geophysicists discovered tiny particles that they identified as part of the comet that slammed into the earth in seven thousand B.C. Tests revealed no traces of the usual minerals and metals associated with asteroids."

"So we have impact," said Sandecker. "Then what happened?"

"A measureless inverted cone of red-hot rock, steam, dust, and debris was hurled up and above the atmosphere, only to plunge in a fiery rain back down on Earth, igniting uncontrollable forest fires around the world. Huge amounts of sulfur, shock-heated nitrogen, and great doses of fluorides were injected into the atmosphere. The ozone layer would have been destroyed, skies blotted out, as winds of hurricane strength whipped across the land and seas. Our simulation suggests this cloud of debris and smoke lasted no less than fourteen months. This alone would have killed off most of Earth's life and collapsed the food chain."

"It sounds too horrible for me to imagine," said Loren quietly.

Friend made a taut smile. "Lamentably, that's only the opening act. Because Hudson Bay opened into the Atlantic Ocean, waves as high as seven or eight miles were formed that burst across the lowlands. Florida would have been totally inundated, along with most of the islands of the world. Much of Europe and Africa saw waves surging hundreds of miles inland from their shorelines. Because most of Australia's ancient inhabitants lived on or near the coasts, the continent would have suffered a ninety-nine-percent death rate within minutes. Southeast Asia would have been buried under water. Vast multitudes of sea life would have been carried far inland and left to die when the giant waves finally receded. The chemical balance of the oceans was altered. What the upheaval didn't kill in the oceans, the silt, mud, and debris would.

"Shuddering from the comet's impact, massive earthquakes far beyond the top end of the Richter scale forever changed the dimensions of the mountains, plains, and deserts. Then volcanoes around the globe, dormant or active, erupted; molten lava in great sheets as high as a mile stormed over whatever land wasn't submerged. If an astronaut had flown to Mars before the cataclysm and returned two years later, he would not have been able to recognize the world, nor would anyone he knew or loved still be alive. He could very well find himself the only man on Earth."

Pitt looked at the astronomer. "You don't paint a very pretty picture."

"The aftermath was ghastly to behold. Once the deluge waters retreated, boulders of every size and shape were dispersed throughout the landscape, where they still rest today and are a great puzzle to geologists, who otherwise can't explain how they came to be there. Vast deposits of mangled trees, along with the bodies of animals and sea life carried far inland, were heaped in huge deposits. These deposits can still be found in the frozen regions of the world, proving that they were hurled there by a giant cataclysm. Huge bodies of water were trapped, and formed lakes. In one known instance, the land strait that separated the Atlantic Ocean from the valley and rivers of the Mediterranean was swept away and the sea was formed. Old glaciers melted, new ones were formed. Tropical forests began to grow in mild climates that were once lashed by frigid winds and freezing temperatures. The Gobi, Sahara, and Mojave regions, then tropical forests, became dry and arid. The continental shelves that once stood above the water were now drowned. The magnetic poles reversed their polarity. Civilizations that existed were buried as deep as five hundred feet beneath the surface. It might have taken as long as twenty years before the world became completely stable again. The few humans who somehow survived were faced with a very grim existence, and it was a miracle any of them endured to become our ancestors."

Pat set down her cup. "The primitive people of the Earth were so badly decimated and fragmented, they kept no record of their activities for thousands of years. Except for the inscriptions by the Amenes, most of which were lost or buried, the only memories of the cataclysm that were passed down came by word of mouth. Only after the early Egyptians, the Sumerians, and the Indus civilization of India reinvented the written language did records and stories of the deluge begin to spread."

"Who knows what cities," said Pitt, "what palaces with their archaeological treasures lie scattered on the deep seafloor or buried under hundreds of feet of silt and rock? Except for the inscriptions left by the Amenes, we have no way of assessing the splendor of the distant past before civilizations began rebuilding themselves."

Friend had remained silent while each member of the group envisioned the nightmare. He let his eyes rove around the sitting area inside the command truck, curiously observing the expressions of abhorrence in their eyes. Only Pitt's eyes seemed to be composed. It was as if he was contemplating something much different, something far off in the distance.

"And thus ends the cataclysm," said Sandecker morosely.

Friend slowly shook his head. "I haven't yet come to the worst part," he said, his earlier smile gone. "Only in the past few years have scientists come to realize the major upheavals Earth has experienced in the past, with and without influence by objects from outer space. We know now that a significant impact by a large comet or asteroid has the capability to cause the earth's crust to shift. Charles Hapgood put forth the theory that because it literally floats on an inner molten core, the crust or shell, which is only twenty to forty miles thick, can and has rotated around the core's axis, causing great extremes in climate and the movement of the continents. It's called earth crust displacement, and its consequences can be catastrophic. At first, Hapgood's theory was laughed at by other Earth scientists. Then Albert Einstein focused his intellect on it and ended up agreeing with Hapgood."

"Sort of like the coating of Teflon around a soccer ball," suggested Yaeger.

"The same principle," Friend acknowledged. "Our computer simulation suggested that the impact exerted enough pressure to move the crust. The result was that some continents, islands, and other landmasses shifted closer to the equator, while others shifted farther away. The movement also caused the North and South Poles to shift from their former positions into warmer climates, unleashing trillions of tons of water that raised the surface of the oceans over almost four hundred feet. To give you an example, before the deluge, a man or woman could have walked from London across the English Channel to France without getting their feet wet.

"In the end, the whole world was rearranged. The North Pole that was in the center of Canada was now far to the north in what is now known as the Arctic Sea. Siberia also shifted north in an incredibly short time span, as evidenced by fruit trees with leaves and woolly mammoths that were found quick-frozen, with vegetation undigested in their stomachs that no longer grew within a thousand miles of that location. Because North America and most of Europe revolved south, the great ice age abruptly ended. Antarctica also shifted south, nearly two thousand miles from the region it had once occupied in the southern sea between the lower portions of South America and Africa."

"Was Earth's orbit affected?" Yaeger asked.

"No, the orbit remained on its present track around the sun. Nor was the Earth's axis altered. The equator remained where it had been since the beginning. The four seasons came and went as always. Only the face of the globe had changed."

"That explains a great deal," said Pitt, "such as how the Amenes could draw a map of Antarctica without its ice mass."

"And their city under the ice that the Germans discovered," said Pat. "Its climate was habitable before the shift."

"What about the Earth's axis of rotation?" queried Giordino. "Would that change?"

Friend shook his head. "Earth's tilt of twenty-three point four degrees would remain constant. The equator would also remain constant. Only the crust above the fluid core would move."

Sandecker said, "If we could get back to the comet for a moment, it's time for you to answer Dirk's question. Were the Amenes and the Wolf family right in predicting a cataclysmic collision with the twin of the comet that struck earth in seven thousand B.C.?"

"May I have another cup of coffee?" Friend asked.

"Certainly," said Loren, pouring from the pot on the center table.

Friend took a few sips and set the cup down. "Now, then, before I answer your question, Admiral, I'd like to describe briefly the new Asteroid and Comet Attack Alert System, which came online just last year. A number of telescope facilities and specially designed instruments have been set up in different areas of the world for the express purpose of discovering asteroids and comets whose orbits approach Earth. Already, astronomers manning the facilities have discovered over forty asteroids that will come unpleasantly close to Earth at some point within its orbit. But detailed calculations reveal that they will all miss by a comfortable margin in the years ahead."

"Have they known about the approach of the second comet," said Loren in dismay, "and suppressed any warning of the threat?"

"No," said Friend. "Though the astronomers agreed to keep news of such possible encounters secret for forty-eight hours, until computer projections could definitely say a collision was imminent. Only when they are certain a collision is imminent would news of the discovery be made public."

"So what you are saying—" said Yaeger.

"Is that there is no emergency."

Pitt looked at Friend. "Come again."

"The event in seven thousand B.C.," explained Friend, "was a million-to-one chance occurrence. The comet that struck Earth, and the comet that arrived a few days later and missed, were not twins. They were separate objects in different orbits that happened to cross paths with Earth at almost the same time. An incredible coincidence, nothing more."

"How soon is the second comet due to return?" Pitt inquired warily.

Friend thought a moment, then said, "Our best guess is that it will fly by no closer than eight hundred thousand miles from us—in another ten thousand years."

35

THERE CAME SEVERAL MOMENTS of stunned silence, as perplexity flooded the minds of the people seated around Dr. Friend. Pitt swore softly under his breath. He stared steadily at Friend, as if attempting to read something in the astronomer's eyes, an uncertainty maybe, but there was none.

"The comet—" he began.

"Its name is Baldwin, after the amateur astronomer who rediscovered it," Friend interrupted.

"You say the Murphy comet and the second comet that the Amenes recorded are one and the same?"

Friend nodded vigorously. "No doubt about it. Calculations confirm that its orbit coincided with the comet that caused the cataclysm of seven thousand B.C."

Pitt glanced at Sandecker and Pat, then back to Friend. "There can be no mistake?"

Friend shrugged. "A margin of error of perhaps two hundred years, but certainly no more. The only other large object to enter Earth's atmosphere in recorded history was the one that flattened those eight hundred square miles in Siberia. Only now are astronomers beginning to believe that, instead of a colossal impact, it was actually a near miss."

"Surely the Wolfs must have had access to the same data," said Loren, looking bewildered. "It doesn't make sense for them to liquidate every asset of the family after having spent billions of dollars building a fleet of ships to survive a cataclysm they know is not about to happen."

"We all agree with you," said Sandecker. "It may simply be that the Wolf family is nothing more than a bunch of fruitcakes."

"Not only the family," said Giordino, "but two hundred and seventy-five thousand other people who work for them and look forward to the voyage to nowhere."

"That doesn't sound like an insignificant cult of crazies to me," said Loren.

"Very true," Pitt agreed. "When Al and I infiltrated the supership, we found a dedicated fanaticism with surviving the deluge."

"I reached the same conclusion," added Pat. "The conversations I overheard regarding the coming cataclysm were resolute. There was not the slightest doubt in their minds that disaster would overtake the world and that they had been given the gift of rebuilding a new civilization without the handicaps of the old."

Giordino looked at Pat. "An echo of Noah and his ark."

"But on a far grander scale," Pitt reminded him.

Sandecker shook his head slowly. "I have to admit that this whole dilemma is a mystery to me."

"The Wolf family must have a solid motive." Pitt paused, as everyone stared at him in silence. "There can be no other answer. If they are convinced the civilized world is going to be swept away and buried for all time, they must know something no one else on Earth knows."

"I can assure you, Admiral," said Friend, "that disaster is not soaring in from the solar system. Certainly not in the next few days. Our tracking network sees no large asteroids or comets coming anywhere close to Earth's orbit in the foreseeable future, certainly not before the end of the next century."

"So what else could produce such a disaster? Is there any way of predicting a crust displacement or a polar shift?" Yaeger asked Friend.

"Not without the opportunity to study such a phenomenon at first hand. Earthquakes, volcanic eruptions, and tsunami waves have been witnessed and recorded. But no crust movements or polar shifts have occurred since earth science emerged from the Greeks. So we have no solid data upon which to draw enough conclusions to even attempt predictions."

"Are there conditions on Earth that could cause the crust and poles to shift?" asked Pitt.

"Yes," Friend answered slowly. "There are natural forces that could upset Earth's balance."

"Such as?"

"The most likely scenario would be an ice shift at one of the poles."

"Is that possible?"

"Earth is like a giant child's top or gyroscope rotating on its axis, as it spins every year around the sun. And, like a top, it is not in perfect balance, because the landmasses and poles are not ideally placed for perfect stabilization. So Earth wobbles as it rotates. Now, if one of Earth's poles grows until it becomes oversize, it affects the wobble, like an unbalanced wheel on your car. Then it could cause a crust displacement or polar shift. I know respected scientists who believe this happens on a regular basis."

"How often?"

"Approximately every six to eight thousand years."

"When was the last shift?"

"By analyzing cores pulled from deep beneath the seas, oceanographers have dated the last shift at nine thousand years ago, the approximate age your comet struck Earth."

"So you might say we're due," said Pitt.

"Actually, overdue." Friend made a helpless gesture with his hands. "We can't say with any confidence. All we know is that when the day comes, the shift will be very sudden. There will be no warning."

Loren stared at Friend uneasily. "What will be the cause?"

"The ice formation that accumulates on top of Antarctica is not distributed equally. One side of the continent receives much more than the other. Every year, over fifty billion tons of ice are added to the Ross Ice Shelf alone, a growing mass which increases Earth's wobble. In time, as the weight shifts, so will the poles, causing, as Einstein himself predicted, trillions of tons of water and ice thousands of feet high to race from both poles toward the equator. The North Pole will sweep south and the South Pole will sweep north. All the forces that were unleashed by a comet strike will be repeated. The major difference is that instead of a world population of about a million people nine thousand years ago, now we're looking at a world populated by seven billion people who will be swept to their deaths. New York, Tokyo, Sydney, Los Angeles will be completely inundated, while cities far inland will be leveled to the ground and disappear. Hardly a slab of concrete would be left where millions walked only a few days earlier."

"And if the Ross Ice Shelf were suddenly to detach itself from the rest of the continent and drift out to sea?" Pitt put to Friend, leaving the question hang.

Friend's face turned grim. "It's an event we've already considered. A simulation shows that a drastic movement by the Shelf would cause an imbalance broad enough to trigger a sudden shift of Earth's crust."

"What do you mean by drastic movement?"

"Our simulation demonstrated that should the entire ice shelf break away and drift sixty miles to sea, its relocated mass would increase Earth's wobble enough to trigger a pole shift."

"How long do you estimate it would take to drift sixty miles?"

Friend thought a moment, then said, "Taking into account the sweep of the currents in that part of the Antarctic, I should say no more than thirty-six hours."

"Is there no way to stop the drift?" asked Loren.

"I don't see how." Friend shook his head. "No, I doubt if a thousand nuclear bombs could melt enough of the ice shelf to make a difference. But, look, this is all theoretical. What else could possibly cause the Shelf to go drifting out to sea?"

Pitt looked at Sandecker, who returned the stare. Both men were envisioning the same nightmare, and both read each other's mind. Pitt's stare moved to Loren.

"The Wolfs' nanotech facility that processes minerals from seawater, how far is it from the Ross Ice Shelf?" he asked her.

Loren's eyes widened. "Surely, you don't think—"

"How far?" Pitt gently pressured.

Finally, she drew a deep breath. "The plant sits right on the edge."

Pitt turned his attention to Friend. "Do you have an estimate of the Ross Ice Shelf's size, Doctor?"

"It's immense," said Friend, stretching out his hands for effect. "I can't give you exact dimensions. All I know is that it's the world's largest body of floating ice."

"Give me a few minutes," said Yaeger, as he opened his laptop computer and began typing on the keyboard. They all sat quietly and watched while Yaeger linked up with his computer network at NUMA headquarters. Within a few minutes, he was reading off the data on his monitor. "Estimates of its mass range as high as two hundred and ten thousand square miles, making it approximately the size of Texas. The circumference, not counting the perimeter facing the sea, is nearly fourteen hundred miles. Thickness runs from eleven hundred to twenty-three hundred feet. Ice scientists liken it to a gigantic floating raft." Yaeger looked up at the faces absorbed in his report. "There is, of course, a mountain of additional information on the ice shelf, but those are the essentials."

"How is it possible," asked Pat, "for man to force two hundred and ten thousand square miles of ice to crack and move apart?"

"I haven't the foggiest clue," said Pitt. "But I'll bet the farm the Wolf family has planned and worked for three generations to do just that."

"Good Lord!" muttered Friend. "It's unthinkable."

"The pieces," said Giordino darkly, "are coming together."

"By whatever means, they intend to break the ice shelf away from land and move it out to sea, upsetting Earth's rotation and causing an increase in its wobble. Once the imbalance is in the critical stage, a polar shift and a crust displacement will occur. Then the Wolfs' mega-ships, after surviving the resulting tidal waves, will be swept out to sea, where they'll drift before cruising around the altered Earth for several years until the upheaval abates. When they are satisfied that Earth is livable again, they'll come ashore and establish a new order, the Fourth Empire, on the bodies of seven billion people, along with the mass destruction of animal and sea life."

Everyone seated in the truck looked stricken, faces locked in abhorrence and despair. No one could conceive of such a horror. No mind could grasp the total inhumanity of such an act.

"God help us all," Loren murmured softly.

Pitt looked at Sandecker. "You must inform the President."

"I've kept his science board and chief of staff, Joe Flynn, up to date on our investigation, but until now no one has taken the threat seriously."

"They'd better reconsider damned quick," said Giordino.

"We'd better rethink our options," said Pitt, "and come up with a plan of action. With only three days to go, we haven't got much time. Not if we want to stop the Wolfs from launching an apocalypse."

36

THE PILOT LINED UP the Destiny Enterprises company jet for his approach and settled down on the long ice runway without the slightest hint of a bump. The plane, the last one of the fleet that had been sold off, was a custom-built Japanese Dragonfire twin-engine jet with no markings or identification numbers on its fuselage, wings, or tail. It was painted white and blended in with the snowy landscape, as it taxied toward what looked like a steep cliff against a high mountain covered with ice.

When the aircraft was less than two hundred yards from smashing into the mountain, the ice cliff miraculously parted, revealing a vast grottolike interior. The pilot slowly pulled back on the throttles, bringing the jet to a stop in the middle of the hangar, which slave labor had carved out of the mountain nearly sixty years earlier. The jet engines whined briefly, before their turbines decreased their rotation and slowly came to a quiet rest. Behind, the ponderous ice doors closed on a series of solid rubber wheels.

There were two other aircraft parked in the hangar, both Airbus Industrie military versions of the A340-300. One was capable of carrying 295 passengers and twenty tons of freight. The other had been built purely as a cargo carrier. Both had maintenance men checking over the engines and filling the fuel tanks for the coming evacuation of Wolf personnel to the safety of the big superships waiting within the safety of the Chilean fjord.

The great hangar was a beehive of quiet activity. Workers in the various Wolf colored uniforms moved silently, conversing softly, as they packed the hundred or more wooden crates with the artifacts and wealth of Amenes, along with the looted art treasures from World War II and the sacred Nazi relics, all being readied for transportation to the *Ulrich Wolf.*

Fifty men in the standard Destiny Enterprises black security uniform stood at attention as Karl Wolf, along with his sister Elsie, exited the aircraft. He was wearing Alpine ski pants and a big suede jacket lined with alpaca wool. Elsie was dressed in a one-piece ski suit under a knee-length fur coat.

The man who directed the transportation project waited at the bottom of the boarding steps as they stepped to the ground.

"Cousin Karl, cousin Elsie, you do us an honor by coming."

"Cousin Horst," Karl greeted him. "I felt it my duty to observe the doomsday system in its final stages."

"An hour that is near at hand," Elsie added proudly.

"How goes the evacuation?" asked Karl.

"Cargo and passengers are scheduled to arrive on the *Ulrich Wolf* ten hours before the cataclysm," Horst assured him.

Then their brother, Hugo, and sister, Blondi, stepped forward to greet them. They took turns embracing.

"Welcome back to Valhalla," Blondi greeted Karl.

"Other business has kept me away too long," said Karl.

Hugo, who was the chief of the family security force, gestured toward a small electric automobile, one of a fleet of utility and heavy-equipment vehicles that ran on batteries, to prevent a buildup of carbon monoxide inside the caverns. "We'll take you to the control center, where you can see for yourself how we begin the end of the old world."

"After I inspect your guards," said Karl. Trailed by Elsie, he walked down the line of security guards in their black uniforms, who stood ramrod straight, with their P-10 automatics strapped to their hips and Bushmaster M17S rifles slung over their shoulders. He stopped occasionally and asked a guard his nationality and military history. When he reached the end of the line, he nodded in satisfaction.

"An intrepid company of men. You've done well, Hugo. They look like they can handle any intrusion."

"Their orders are to shoot to kill any unidentified intruder that enters our perimeter."

"I hope they perform with greater efficiency than Erich's men at the shipyard."

"There will be no failure at this end," Hugo said firmly. "I promise you, brother."

"Any sign of encroachment?"

"None," answered Blondi. "Our detection-control unit has seen no activity within a hundred and fifty miles of the facility."

Elsie looked at her. "One hundred and fifty miles does not seem far."

"It's the distance to Little America Number Six, the Yankee Antarctic research station. Since the station was built, they've shown no interest in our operations. Our aerial surveillance has yet to detect any attempt to trespass onto our mining facility."

"All is quiet with the Americans," added Hugo. "They'll give us no problems."

"I'm not so sure," said Karl. "Keep a tight eye on any activity. I fear their intelligence may be on the verge of discovering our secret."

"Any attempt to stop us," Hugo said confidently, "will come too late. The Fourth Empire is inevitable."

"I sincerely pray that will be the case," said Karl, as he entered the auto ahead of the women. Usually gallant around the ladies, Karl came from the old German school where men never yielded to women.

The driver of the electric car left the aircraft hangar area and entered a tunnel. After a quarter of a mile, they entered a vast ice cavern that enclosed a small harbor with long floating docks that rose and fell with the tide from the Ross Sea. The high-roofed channel that ran from the inner harbor to the sea curved gently, allowing large ships to navigate the passage while the ice cliffs blocked all view from the outside. Light throughout the complex came from overhead fixtures containing dozens of halogen bulbs. Four submarines and a small cargo ship were moored beside the docks. The entire harbor complex was deserted. The cargo cranes stood abandoned, along with a small fleet of trucks and equipment. There wasn't a soul to be seen on the docks or the vessels. It was as if their crews had walked off and never returned.

"A pity the U-boats that served our venture so efficiently all these years will be lost," said Elsie wistfully.

"Perhaps they will survive," Blondi consoled her.

Hugo smiled. "When the time comes, I will personally return to Valhalla to see how they fared. They deserve to be enshrined for their service to the Fourth Empire."

The old tunnel that ran nine miles through the ice between the hidden dock terminal, the aircraft hangar, and then to the sea-mining extraction facility had also been excavated by slaves from the old Soviet Union, their preserved bodies now frozen in a mass grave on the ice shelf. Since 1985, the tunnel had been expanded and constantly realigned because of the shifting ice.

In the beginning, the efforts to extract valuable minerals from the sea had proved a dismal failure, but with the nanotechnology revolution pioneered by Eric Drexler in California, along with his wife Chris Peterson, Destiny Enterprises had thrown its immense wealth and resources into a project to control the structure of matter. By rearranging atoms and creating incredibly tiny engines, they had totally reinvented manufacturing processes. Molecular machines could even produce a tree from scratch. The Wolfs, however, threw their efforts into extracting valuable minerals such as gold from seawater, a process they'd achieved and gone on to refine until they were producing a thousand troy ounces of gold a day from the Ross Sea, along with platinum, silver, and many other rare elements. Unlike ore pulled from the ground and then expensively processed by crushers and chemicals, the minerals extracted from the sea came in a nearly pure form.

The engineering center of the Destiny Enterprises sea-mining facility was a great domed structure whose interior looked similar to the vast control room at the NASA space center. Electronic consoles were manned by thirty scientists and engineers who monitored the computerized electronics of the nanotech mining operation. But this day, all operations for the extraction of rare metals from the sea had come to a halt, and all Wolf personnel were concentrating their efforts on the coming split of the ice shelf.

Karl Wolf entered the expansive room and stopped in front of a spacious electronic board that hung from the center of the domed ceiling. In the center, a large map of the Ross Ice Shelf was displayed. Around the edges, a series of neonlike tubing distinguished the ice from the surrounding land. The tubing, which stretched from the mining company around the ice shelf and ended three hundred miles from the opposite end, was green. The section from where the green ended was continued in red to the edge of the sea.

"The area in red is yet to be programmed?" Karl asked the chief engineer, Jurgen Holtz, who walked up to the Wolf party and gave a sharp nod of his head in greeting.

"Yes, that is correct." Holtz raised a hand and gestured at the board. "We are in the process of setting the molecular triggering devices. We have about another four hundred miles to program to the end of the tunnel at the sea."

Karl studied the constantly changing red letters and numbers on the digital displays spaced around the map. "When is the critical moment?"

"The final process for splitting off the ice shelf is timed for six hours . . ." Holtz paused to stare up at a series of numbers showing the time left until doomsday. "Twenty-two minutes and forty seconds from now."

"Any problems that might cause a delay?"

"None we're aware of. All computerized procedures and their backup systems have been inspected and scrutinized dozens of times. We have yet to find the slightest hint of a possible malfunction."

"An amazing feat of engineering," Karl said quietly, while gazing at the colored tubing surrounding the ice shelf. "A pity the world will never know of its existence."

"An amazing feat indeed," echoed Holtz, "boring a ten-foot-diameter tunnel fourteen hundred miles through the ice in two months."

"The credit goes to you and your engineers who designed and built the molecular tunneling machine," said Elsie, pointing at a large photo on one wall. The picture showed a hundred-foot-long circular boring machine with a thrust ram, a debris conveyor, and a strange-looking unit on the front that pulled apart selected molecular bonds within the ice, producing powder-snow-size chunks small enough to be transported to the rear of the conveyors to the open sea. A secondary unit rebonded the tiny chunks into near-perfect crystalline solid ice that was used to line the tunnel. When in full operation, the tunneler could bore through fifty miles of ice in twenty-four hours. Having accomplished its purpose, the great machine now sat under a growing sheet of ice outside the mining facility.

"Perhaps after the ice melts, we'll have an opportunity to use the tunneler again on subterranean rock," Karl said thoughtfully.

"You think the ice will melt away?" asked Elsie, puzzled.

"If our calculations are ninety-five percent correct, this section of the Antarctic will end up eighteen hundred miles north of here two months after the cataclysm."

"I've never quite understood how all this is going to break off the entire ice shelf and send it out to sea," said Elsie.

Karl smiled. "I'd forgotten that you were the family intelligence collector in Washington for the past three years and were not provided with details of the Valhalla Project."

Holtz held up one hand and pointed to the giant display board. "As simply as I can explain it, Miss Wolf, our nanocomputerized machine constructed a vast number of molecular replicating assemblers, which in turn constructed over many millions of tiny molecular ice-dissolving machines."

Elsie looked pensive. "In other words, the replicated assemblers, through molecular engineering, can create machines that can produce almost anything."

"That's the beauty of nanotechnology," replied Holtz. "The replicating assembler can copy itself in a few minutes. In less than twenty-four hours, tons of replicated machines, moving trillions of atoms around, drilled holes into the ice every six inches above and below the tunnel. Once the ice tubes were drilled to a predetermined depth, the nanocomputer closed down all further instructions to the machines. In sixteen hours, the moment our meteorologists have predicted a strong offshore wind in combination with a favorable current, a signal will be sent to reactivate the machines. They will then finish the job of dissolving the ice and separating the shelf from the continent, allowing it to drift out to sea."

"How long will that take?" asked Elsie.

"Less than two hours," answered Holtz.

"Then ten hours after the final break," Karl explained, "the displaced weight of the Ross Ice Shelf will have moved far enough away from the Antarctic continent to throw off Earth's delicately balanced rotation just enough to cause a polar shift in unison with a crust displacement, sending the world into a devastating upheaval."

"A world which we then can reshape into our image," said Elsie vaingloriously.

A man in the black uniform of a security guard came rushing out of an office and approached the group. "Sir," he said to Karl, handing him a sheet of paper.

Karl's face darkened for a brief instant, before turning reflective.

"What is it?" Elsie asked.

"A report from Hugo," Karl answered slowly. "It seems an unidentified aircraft is approaching from across the Amundsen Sea, and refuses to answer our signals."

"Probably the supply plane for the ice station at Little America," said Holtz. "Nothing to be concerned about. It flies in and out every ten days."

"Does it always pass over Valhalla?" asked Karl.

"Not directly, but it comes within a few miles as it makes its descent toward the ice station."

Karl turned to the security guard who had carried the message. "Please tell my brother to observe the approaching aircraft closely. If it deviates from its normal flight path to Little America, have him notify me immediately."

"Are you troubled, brother?" asked Elsie.

Karl looked at her, his face showing traces of concern. "Not troubled, my sister, merely cautious. I do not trust the Americans."

"The United States is a long way away," said Elsie. "It would take an

American assault force more than twenty-four hours to assemble and fly over ten thousand miles to Okuma Bay."

"Still," Karl said patiently, "it pays to be vigilant." He looked at Holtz. "Should a distraction arise, can the signal to split the ice be sent early?"

"Not if we want absolute success," Holtz replied firmly. "Timing is critical. We must wait until just before the peak of the flood tide to activate the molecular ice-dissolving machines. Then the ebb tide will carry the great mass of the ice shelf out to sea."

"Then it appears we have nothing to fear," said Elsie optimistically.

Karl dropped his voice, speaking slowly, softly. "I hope you're right, dear sister."

At that moment, another security guard approached and passed Karl a message from Hugo. He read it, looked up, and smiled faintly. "Hugo says that the American supply plane is on its normal course ten miles beyond our perimeter and is flying at an altitude of thirty-five thousand feet."

"Hardly the height to drop an assault team," said Holtz.

"No nation on Earth would dare fire missiles into our facility without their intelligence agencies penetrating our operation. And none have. Hugo's security force has diverted and blocked all outside probes into Valhalla."

"Diverted and blocked," Karl repeated. But his mind was not so sure. He recalled one man who had already defied too many of the Wolf family's aims, and Karl could not but wonder where he might be.

37

UNDER A SKY CONCEALED by a thick layer of clouds, a NUMA executive jet landed on a frozen airstrip, taxied toward a domed building, and rolled to a stop. Little America V was the fifth in the line of United States ice stations to bear the name since Admiral Byrd had established the first in 1928. Once situated several miles from the edge of the Ross Shelf near Kainan Bay, the sea was now only a short walk away, due to the calving of the ice pack over the years. The base served as a terminus for the 630-mile-long well-traveled ice road to the Byrd Surface Camp on the Rockefeller Plateau.

A man bundled up in a lime-green parka and fur-trimmed hood removed his sunglasses and grinned as Pitt opened the passengers door and stepped to the frozen ground.

"You Pitt or Giordino?" he asked in a rumbling voice.

"I'm Pitt. You must be Frank Cash, the ice station chief."

Cash merely nodded. "I didn't expect you for another two hours."

"We hurried."

Pitt turned as Giordino, who had closed the down the aircraft, joined them. Giordino introduced himself and said, "Thank you for working with us on such short notice, but it's a matter of extreme urgency."

"I have no reason to doubt you," said Cash astutely, "even though I received no instructions from a higher authority."

Unable to talk their way into joining the special force assault team that was being formed to raid the Wolf compound and halt the coming cataclysm, they had been told in no uncertain terms by Admiral Sandecker to remain in Buenos Aires out of harm's way. Pitt's reasoning had been that he and Giordino were essential to the raid, because it was they who had discovered the horrifying truth behind the man-induced cataclysm and knew more about the Wolfs and their security tactics than anyone else. And, since they were already in Buenos Aires and five thousand miles closer to the scene of conflict, they could get there before the assault team and scout the facility.

His plea had fallen on deaf ears. The argument by the high-ranking military had been that they were not professional fighting men who were trained and conditioned for such a strenuous and difficult operation. In Sandecker's case, he was not about to allow his best men to commit suicide in the frigid wastes of the southern polar continent. Pitt and Giordino, however, true to form, had taken a NUMA executive jet, and instead of flying it back to Washington as they had been ordered, they'd filled it to the brim with fuel and taken off for Antarctica, in hopes of entering the Wolf mining plant through the back door, without the slightest plan in their heads of how to cross sixty miles of frozen waste to the Wolf operation once they landed in Little America.

"We'll figure out something when we get there." Pitt was fond of saying this.

Followed by Giordino's "I'll tag along, since I don't have anything better to do."

"Come on inside," said Cash, "before we turn into ice sculptures."

"What's the temperature?" asked Giordino.

"Pretty nice today, with no wind. Last I looked, it was fifteen degrees below zero."

"At least I won't have to send for ice cubes for my tequila," said Pitt.

The domed building, which was 80 percent covered with ice, protruded only five feet above ground. The living and working quarters were a maze of rooms and corridors hacked under the ice. Cash led them into the dining area next to the kitchen and ordered them a hot lunch of lasagna from the station cook before producing a half-gallon bottle of Gallo burgundy. "Not fancy, but it hits the spot," he said, laughing.

"All the comforts of home," mused Giordino.

"Not really," Cash said, with a grim smile. "You have to be mentally deficient to want to live this life."

"Then why not take a job somewhere with a milder climate?" asked Pitt, noticing that all the men he'd seen at the station were bearded and the women had forsaken makeup and coiffures.

"Men and women volunteer to work in polar regions because of the excitement of pursuing a dangerous job exploring the unknown. A few come to escape problems at home, but the majority are scientists who pursue the studies of their chosen expertise regardless of where it takes them. After a year, they're more than ready to return home. By that time, they've either turned into zombies or they began to hallucinate."

Pitt looked at Cash. He didn't have a haunted look in his eyes, at least not yet. "It must take strength of character to subsist in such a bleak environment."

"It begins with age," Cash explained. "Men under twenty-five lack reliability, men over forty-five lack the stamina."

After waiting patiently for a few minutes, while Pitt and Giordino ate most of their lasagna, Cash finally asked, "When you contacted me from Argentina, did I hear right when you said you wanted to cross the ice shelf to Okuma Bay?"

Pitt nodded. "Our destination is the Destiny Enterprises mining operation."

Cash shook his head. "Those people are security fanatics. None of our scientific expeditions ever got within ten miles of the place before being chased off by their security goons."

"We're quite familiar with the goons," said Giordino, relaxing after filling his stomach.

"What did you have in mind for transportation? We have no helicopter here."

"All we'll need is a couple of snowmobiles," Pitt said, looking into Cash's face. The expression in the ice station chief's eyes was not encouraging.

Cash looked pained. "I fear you two have flown a long way for nothing. Two of our snowmobiles are in maintenance, waiting for parts to be flown in. And the other four were taken by scientists to study the ice around Roosevelt Island north of here."

"How soon before your scientists return?" asked Pitt.

"Not for another three days."

"You have no other transportation?" asked Giordino.

"A bulldozer and a ten-ton Sno-cat."

"What about the Sno-cat?"

Cash shrugged. "A section of one track shattered from the cold. We're waiting for a part to be flown in from Auckland."

Giordino looked across the table at his friend. "Then we have no choice but to fly in and hope we find a place to land."

Pitt shook his head. "We can't risk jeopardizing the special force mission by dropping in out of the blue. I had hoped that with snowmobiles we might have covered the distance, parked them a mile or two away from the mining compound, and then crept in unobserved."

"You fellas act like it's a matter of life or death," said Cash.

Pitt and Giordino exchanged glances and then both looked at the station chief, their faces set in grave expressions. "Yes," Pitt said severely, "it's life and death to more people than you can possibly conceive."

"Can you tell me what this is all about?"

"Can't," Giordino answered simply. "Besides, you wouldn't want to know. It might ruin your entire day."

Cash poured a cup of coffee and contemplated the dark liquid for a few moments. Then he said, "There is one other possibility, but it's highly improbable."

Pitt stared at him. "We're listening."

"Admiral Byrd's Snow Cruiser," Cash announced, as if he was launching a lecture, which indeed he was. "A jumbo four-wheel-drive, larger than any vehicle built in her day."

"When was that?" Giordino queried.

"Nineteen thirty-nine." There was a pause. "It was the inspiration of

Thomas Poulter, a polar explorer, who designed and built a monstrous machine he hoped could carry five men and his pet dog to the South Pole and back. I guess you might call it the world's first really big recreational vehicle. The tires alone were over three feet wide and more than ten feet in diameter. From front to back, it measured fifty-six feet long by twenty feet wide and weighed thirty-seven tons fully loaded. Believe you me, she's some vehicle."

"She sounds overly elaborate," said Pitt, "for a vehicle designed to travel to the South Pole."

"She *was* that. Besides a grand control cabin raised on the front, it had its own machine shop, living quarters for the crew, and a galley that also performed double duty as a photographer's darkroom. The rear end housed storage space for a year's supply of food, spare tires, and enough fuel for five thousand miles of travel. Not only that, she was supposed to have carried a Beechcraft airplane with skis on her roof."

"What did such a monster use for power?"

"Two one-hundred-and-fifty-horsepower diesel engines linked to four seventy-five-horsepower electric traction motors, which could feed power to all or any one of the wheels individually. The wheels could all be turned for a crabbing movement and sharp turns, and even retract when crossing a crevasse. Each wheel alone weighed six thousand pounds. The tires were twelve-ply and made by Goodyear."

"Are you saying this gargantuan machine not only still exists, but is available?" asked Pitt incredulously.

"Oh, she exists, but I can't say she's available or that she could travel across sixty miles of the ice shelf. Sixty miles may not seem like much distance, but after the Snow Cruiser was completed, shipped to the Antarctic, and unloaded at Little America Three, not far from this station, her designer's best-laid plans went down the sewer. The engines had the power, but Poulter had miscalculated the gear ratios. The behemoth would do thirty miles an hour on a level road, but couldn't pull her mass through ice and snow, especially up a grade. Given up as a white elephant, she was abandoned. In later years, she was covered over by the ice, lost, and forgotten. It was always thought that as the ice shelf moved toward the sea, the Snow Cruiser would eventually be carried away and dropped in the deep when the ice floe melted."

"Where is she now, still buried under the ice?" Pitt inquired.

Cash shook his head and smiled. "The Snow Cruiser is about two miles from here, dangerously close to the edge of the ice shelf. A rich old mining engineer got it into his head to find and rescue the vehicle, then transport it back to the States for display in a museum. He and his crew discovered it thirty feet deep in the ice and spent three weeks digging it out. They built an ice tent around it, and the last I heard actually got it running."

"I wonder if they'd let us borrow it?"

"Never hurts to ask," said Cash. "But I think you'd do better selling a basset hound on eating broccoli."

"We've got to try," Pitt said firmly.

"You got Arctic clothing?"

"In the plane."

"Better get it on. We'll have to hike to where the Snow Cruiser sits." Then Cash looked as though he'd suddenly thought of something. "Before I forget, I'll have a couple of our maintenance men throw a cover over your plane and set up an auxiliary heater to keep your engines, fuel, and hydraulic systems warm and the ice off the fuselage and wings. Leave a plane set for a week and she'll start to disappear under a buildup of ice."

"Good idea," Giordino acknowledged. "We may have to use it in a hurry if all else fails."

"I'll meet you back here in half an hour and I'll lead you to the vehicle."

"Who is the old guy who's heading up the salvage operation?" asked Pitt.

Cash looked lost for a moment. "I don't really know. He's an eccentric cuss. His crew usually calls him 'Dad.'"

WITH Cash in the lead, they walked a trail marked with orange flags across the ice for nearly an hour. After a while, Pitt could see figures moving about a large blue tent surrounded by a series of smaller orange polar tents. A light snow was falling and forming a thin white blanket over the tents. Strange as it seems, the Antarctic rarely experiences a heavy snow. It is one of the driest continents on Earth, and a few inches below the surface, the snow is ancient.

There was almost no wind, but not having yet built an immunity against the icy temperatures, Pitt and Giordino felt cold beneath their heavy Arctic clothing. The sun blazed through the remnants of the ozone layer, and the glare would have dazzled their eyes but for the darkly coated lenses of their glasses.

"It looks nice and peaceful," said Pitt, taking in the majestic view of the landscape. "No traffic, no smog, no noise."

"Don't let it fool you," Cash came back. "The weather can change into cyclonic hell in less time than you can spit. I can't count all the fingers and toes that have been lost to frostbite. Frozen bodies are found on a regular basis. That's why anyone who works in the Antarctic is required to provide a full set of dental X rays and wear dog tags. You never know when your remains will have to be identified."

"Bad as that."

"The windchill is the big killer. People have taken a short hike only to be overtaken by high winds that block out all vision, and they freeze to death before finding their way back to the station."

They trudged the final quarter of a mile in silence, stepping over the crusted, wind-carved ice that thickened and compressed as it went deeper. Pitt was beginning to feel the tentacles of exhaustion, too little sleep, and the pressures of the past few days, but the thought of falling into a bed never occurred to him. The stakes were too high, fantastically so. Yet his step was not as energetic as it should have been. He noticed that Giordino was not walking lively, either.

They reached the camp and immediately entered the main tent. The initial sight of the Snow Cruiser stunned them almost as much as when they'd viewed the Wolfs' gigantic ships for the first time. The great wheels and tires dwarfed the men working around them. The control cab that sat flush with the smooth front end rose sixteen feet into the air and brushed the top of the tent. The top of the body behind the cab was flattened to hold the Beechcraft airplane that had not been sent to

Antarctica with the big vehicle back in 1940. It was painted a bright fire-engine red, with a horizontal orange stripe running around the sides.

The loud sound they had heard when approaching across the ice came from a pair of chain saws held by two men who were cutting grooves in the massive tires. An old fellow with gray hair and a gray beard was supervising the crude method of cutting tread into rubber. Cash stepped up to him and patted one shoulder to get his attention. The old man turned, recognized Cash, and gestured for everyone to follow him. He led the way outside and then into a smaller tent next door that contained the galley, with a small cookstove. He offered them chairs around a long folding metal table.

"There, that's quieter," he said, with a warm smile, as he stared through blue-green eyes.

"This is Dirk Pitt and Al Giordino with the National Underwater and Marine Agency," said Cash. "They have an urgent mission for the government, and hope you can help them carry it out."

"My name is a bit strange, so my crew, who are all forty years younger than I am, just call me Dad," he said, shaking hands. "What can I do for you?"

"Haven't we met before?" asked Pitt, studying the old man.

"It's possible. I get around quite a bit."

"The Snow Cruiser," said Pitt, cutting to the heart of his request, "is it in any condition to drive to the South Pole?"

"That's what she was built to do, but if you'd have asked that question sixty years ago, or even a week ago, I'd have said no. On dry land it proved a remarkable machine, but on the ice it was a dismal failure. For one thing, the tires were smooth and spun ineffectively without friction. And the gearing in the reduction unit was all wrong. Driving her up a slight hill was like an eighteen-wheeler semi–truck and trailer attempting to pull a load up the Rocky Mountains in sixteenth gear. The engine would lug itself to death. By changing the gears and cutting treads in the tires, we think we can demonstrate that she might have lived up to expectations and actually reached the Pole."

"What if she came up against a crevasse too wide for her to drive over?" inquired Giordino.

"Thomas Poulter, the cruiser's designer and builder, came up with an ingenious innovation. The big wheels and tires were positioned close to the center of the body, which left an overhang front and rear of eighteen feet. The wheels were capable of retracting upward until they were level with the underside of the body. When the driver came to a crevasse, he lifted the front wheels. Then the rear-wheel traction pushed the forward section over the crevasse. Once the front wheels were safe on the opposite side, they were lowered. Finally, the rear wheels were retracted and the front then pulled the cruiser to the other side. A very ingenious system that actually works."

"Where did you find sixty-year-old gears that would fit the reduction unit?"

"The unit, or transmission, was not the only one built. We analyzed the problem and how to fix it before we came down here. The original manufacturer is still in business and had a bin of old parts buried deep in their warehouse. Fortunately, they had the gears we needed to make the necessary changes."

"Have you tested her yet?" asked Giordino.

"You've arrived at an opportune moment," replied Dad. "In the next hour, we hope to run her out onto the ice for the first time since she came to rest in 1940, and see what she can do. And just in time, too. Another couple of weeks and the ice floe would have broken and carried her out to sea, where she would have eventually sunk."

"How do you intend to transport her back to the States?" asked Giordino.

"I've chartered a small cargo ship that is moored off the ice shelf. We'll drive her across the ice, up a ramp, and onto the ship."

"If she performs according to expectations," said Pitt, "can we borrow her for a couple of days?"

Dad looked blank. Then he turned and stared at Cash. "He's joking."

Cash shook his head. "He's not joking. These men desperately need transportation to the Wolf mining facility."

Dad squinted at Pitt as he refilled his wineglass. "I should say not. By the time I'm finished, I will have spent over three hundred thousand dollars to pull her out of the ice, restore her to running condition, and transport her back to the Smithsonian in Washington. When I first discussed my dream of saving the vehicle, everyone laughed at me. My crew and I dug under the worst weather conditions imaginable. It was a major feat to lift her back to the surface again, and we're all damned proud. I'm not about to hand her over to a couple of strangers who want to go joyriding around the ice pack."

"Trust me," said Pitt earnestly. "We're not going for a joyride. As bizarre as it sounds, we are trying to avert a worldwide catastrophe."

"The answer is no!"

Pitt and Giordino exchanged cold looks. Then Pitt removed a small folder from the breast pocket of his arctic survival coat and pushed it across the table at Dad. "Inside, you will find several phone numbers. They list, in order, the Oval Office of the White House, the Joint Chiefs of Staff at the Pentagon, the chief director of NUMA, and the Congressional Security Committee. There are also names of other important people who will back up our story."

"And what, may I ask, is your story?" Dad asked skeptically.

So Pitt told him.

AN hour and thirty minutes later, Dad and his crew, along with Frank Cash, stood and watched silently as the big red vehicle, belching a black cloud of exhaust into the crystal blue sky, lumbered across the frozen landscape toward the horizon.

"I never got Dad's name," said Pitt, as he sat hunched over the steering wheel, gazing through the windshield and studying the ice field ahead for cracks and obstacles.

Giordino stood behind Pitt in the Snow Cruiser's confined chart and control room, studying a topographical map of the ice pack. "The name on an envelope that was sticking out of his pocket read 'Clive Cussler.' "

"That *is* an odd name. Yet it sounds vaguely familiar."

"Whoever," said Giordino indifferently.

"I hope I didn't step into a minefield when I promised to bring back his off-road vehicle in the same condition he loaned it to us."

"If we put a scratch on it, have him send the bill to Admiral Sandecker."

"Got a heading for me?" Pitt asked.

"Where's your GPS unit?"

"I forgot it in the rush. Besides, they didn't have a Global Positioning System in 1940."

"Just head that way," Giordino said, pointing vaguely into the distance.

Pitt's eyebrows rose. "That's the best you can do?"

"No directional instrument ever created can beat an eyeball."

"Your logic defies sanity."

"How long do you think it will take to get there?" Giordino asked.

"Sixty miles, at only twenty miles an hour," Pitt murmured. "Three hours, if we don't run into any barriers in the ice and have to detour around them. I only hope we can get there before the assault team. A full-scale attack might force Karl Wolf to slice off the ice shelf ahead of schedule."

"I have a sour feeling in my stomach that we won't be as lucky sneaking in here as we were at the shipyard."

"I hope you're wrong, my friend, because a lot of people are going to be very unhappy if we fail."

38

THE SUN BLAZED FROM an azure blue sky, its intensity tripled by the reflection off the crystallized surface as the big red Snow Cruiser crawled over the freeze-dried landscape like a bug over a wrinkled white sheet. Veiled by a gossamer of snow, she trailed a light haze of blue from her twin diesels' exhaust drifting in the air. The huge wheels crunched loudly as they rolled over the snow and ice, their crude cross-cut tread gripping without slippage. She moved effortlessly, almost majestically, as she was meant to do, created by men who had not lived to see her fulfill their expectations.

Pitt sat comfortably straight in the driver's seat, and gripping the buslike steering wheel, drove the Cruiser in a straight line toward a range of mountains looming far off to the horizon. He peered through heavily polarized sunglasses. Snow blindness was an ominous threat in cold climates. It was caused by conjunctiva inflammation of the eye by the sun, whose glare reflected a low-spectrum ultraviolet ray. Anyone unlucky enough to suffer the malady felt like sand was being rubbed in their eyes, followed by blindness that lasted anywhere from two to four days.

Frostbite, though, wasn't a hazard. The heaters in the Snow Cruiser kept the cabins at a respectable sixty-five degrees. Pitt's only small but irritating problem was the constant buildup of frost on the three windshields. The window vents did not put out enough air to keep them clear. Though he drove wearing only an Irish-knit wool sweater, he kept his cold-weather clothing nearby, in case he had to leave the cruiser for whatever emergency might rear its unwelcome head. As beautiful as the weather looked, anyone familiar with either pole knew it could turn deadly in less time than it took to tell about it.

When added up, more than a hundred and fifty deaths had been recorded in Antarctica since exploration had begun, when a Norwegian sailor on a whaling ship, Carstens Borchgrevink, had become the first man to step ashore on the continent in 1895. Most were men who had succumbed to the cold, like Captain Robert Falcon Scott and his party, who'd frozen to death on their return trip after trekking to the South Pole. Others had become lost and wandered aimlessly before they died. Many were killed in aircraft crashes and other unfortunate accidents.

Pitt wasn't in the mood to expire, certainly not yet; not if he and Giordino were to stop the Wolfs from launching a frightful horror on mankind. Besides manhandling the Snow Cruiser over the ice shelf, his first order of business was to get to the mining facility as quickly as possible. His handheld GPS was of no use. The geographic display on Pitt's unit was incapable of showing his exact position within a thousand miles of the pole. Because the satellites that relayed the position belonged to the military, who had not planned on conducting a war in Antarctica, they were not in orbit over that part of the globe.

He called down to Giordino, who was standing below and behind him, hunched over a chart table studying a map of the Ross Ice Shelf. "How about giving me a heading?"

"Just keep the front end of this geriatric antique aimed toward the highest peak of those mountains dead ahead. And, oh yes, be sure to keep the sea on your left."

"Keep the sea on my left," Pitt repeated in exasperation.

"Well, we certainly don't want to run off the edge and drown, do we?"

"What if the weather closes in and we can't see?"

"You want a heading," Giordino said cynically. "Pick any compass direction you want. You've got three hundred and sixty choices."

"I stand chastised," Pitt said wearily. "My mind was elsewhere. I'd forgotten that all compass readings down here point north."

"You'll never get on *Jeopardy*."

"Most of the category questions are beyond my meager mental capacity anyway." He turned to Giordino and made a shifty grin. "I'll bet you tell bloody horror bedtime stories to little children."

Giordino looked at Pitt, trying to decipher his meaning. "I what?"

"The cliffs at the edge of the Ross Ice Shelf reach two hundred feet above and nine hundred feet below the surface of the sea. From the top edge to the sea is a sheer drop. We drive off the ledge, there won't be enough left of us to sail anywhere."

"You have a point," Giordino grudgingly conceded.

"Besides falling into a bottomless crevasse or becoming lost and freezing to death in a blizzard, our only other dilemma is if the ice we're driving on breaks loose or calves and carries us out to sea. Then all we'll be able to do is sit and wait for a cataclysmic tidal wave launched by the polar shift to sweep us away."

"You should talk," Giordino said, his voice heavy with sarcasm. "Your bedtime stories make mine sound like Mother Goose science fiction tales."

"The skies are darkening," Pitt said, staring upward through the windshield.

"Do you still think we can make it in time?" asked Giordino.

Pitt glanced down at the odometer. "We've come twenty-one miles in the last hour. Barring unforeseen delays, we should be there in just less than two hours."

They had to make it in time. If the special assault team failed, then he and Giordino were the only hope, as inadequate for the job as any two men seemed. Pitt did not bask in an aura of optimism. He well knew the terrain ahead was fraught with obstacles. His biggest fears were rotting ice and crevasses seen too late. If he wasn't constantly alert, he could drive the Snow Cruiser into a deep crevasse and send it plunging hundreds of feet into the Antarctic Sea below. So far, the frozen wasteland lay fairly flat. Except for thousands of ripples and ruts like those found in a farmer's plowed field, the ride was reasonably smooth. Occasionally, he'd spot a crevasse hiding in the ice ahead. After a quick stop to appraise the situation, he'd find a way to detour around it.

The thought that he was driving a thirty-five-ton lethargic monster of steel across an icy plain with deep fissures looming unseen in every direction was not comforting. Few words in a dictionary could describe the feeling. Suddenly, a crack in the ice became visible, but only after he was almost on top of it. With a hard twist of the wheel, he slewed the Snow Cruiser around sideways, stopping it within five feet of the edge. After driving parallel to the chasm for half a mile, he finally found a firm surface five hundred yards from where it vanished in the ice.

He glanced at the speedometer and noted that the speed had slowly crept up to twenty-four miles an hour. Giordino, down in the engine room, was fussing with the two big diesel engines, delicately adjusting the valves on the fuel intake pumps and increasing the flow. Because Earth's air is thinner at the poles due to a faster rate of spin, and because it is extremely dry and cold, the fuel ratio needed to be reset, a chore Dad and his crew had not yet performed. Fuel injection was constant on newer diesel engines, but on the sixty-year-old Cummins, the fuel flow to the injectors could be altered.

The frozen desert ahead was bleak, desolate and menacing, while at the same time a landscape of beauty and magnificence. It could be tranquil one moment and frightening the next. In Pitt's mind, it suddenly became frightening. His feet stomped the brake and clutch of the Snow Cruiser, and he watched stunned as a crevasse no more than a hundred feet away opened and spread apart, the crack stretching as far as he could see in both directions across the ice pack.

Dropping down the ladder from the control cabin, he threw open the entry door, stepped outside, and walked to the edge of the crevasse. It was a terrifying sight. The color of the ice on the sides that fell out of sight turned from white at the edge of a beautiful silver-green. Its gap spanned almost twenty feet. He turned as he heard the crunch of Giordino's feet behind him.

"What now?" questioned Giordino. "This thing must run forever."

"Frank Cash mentioned that the wheels could retract to cross a crevasse. Let's check out the operation manual that Dad gave us."

As Dad had told them, the Snow Cruiser's designer, Thomas Poulter, had come up with an ingenious solution for the crevasse problem. The underside of the cruiser's belly was flat like a ski, with a front and rear overhang of eighteen feet on both ends from the wheels. Following the instructions in the manual, Pitt pressed the levers that retracted the front wheels vertically until they were level with the body. Then, using the rear wheels for traction, he drove the Cruiser slowly forward until the front section slid across the crevasse and rolled past the opposite edge a safe distance for stability. Next Pitt extended the front wheels and retracted the wheels in the rear. Now using the front-wheel drive, the rear half of the cruiser was pulled the rest of the way over the chasm. After, extending the rear wheels, they were on their way again.

"I do believe I'd call that a brilliant innovation," Giordino said admiringly.

Pitt shifted gears and turned the bow of the Snow Cruiser back toward the peak that had expanded into a range of mountains. "Amazing how he could be farsighted on one mechanism and yet badly underestimate the gearing and tire tread."

"No one is flawless. Except me, of course."

Pitt accepted the bluster with practiced patience. "Of course."

Giordino took the manual with him into the engine compartment, but not before pointing to the twin temperature gauges on the instrument panel. "The engines are running hotter than normal. Better keep an eye on them."

"How can they run hot when it's twenty degrees below zero outside?" Pitt queried.

"Because their radiators are not exposed. They're mounted directly in front of the engines inside the compartment. It's almost as if they overheat themselves."

Pitt had hoped darkness would cloak their arrival at the mining compound, but at this time of year in the Antarctic, the sunset had barely occurred before it was dawn again. He didn't fool himself into thinking they could infiltrate the facility without being detected, certainly not in a gargantuan fire-engine-red snow vehicle. He knew he'd have to think of something in the next hour and a half. Soon, very soon, the buildings of the extraction plant would appear on the horizon along the base of the mountains.

He began to feel a tinge of hope, but then, as if an unseen force was working against him, the atmosphere grew heavy and congealed like a lace curtain. The wind suddenly swept in from the interior of the continent with the force of a tidal wave. One minute, Pitt could see for sixty miles; the next it was as though he was gazing through a film of water, fluid in motion, iridescent and ephemeral. The sky was gone in the blink of an eye and the sun totally blotted out, as the wind charged over the ice shelf like a raging monster. The world became a swirling pall of pure white.

He kept the accelerator pressed to the metal floor and clenched the steering wheel, not turning it, keeping the big vehicle moving in a straight line. They were in a hurry, and no tempestuous behavior from Mother Nature was going to slow them down.

A man wanders in circles during a whiteout, not because he's right-handed and tends to go in that direction, but because almost all humans unknowingly have one leg that is a millimeter shorter than the other. The same factor held true with the Snow Cruiser. None of the tires had come out of the mold symmetrically perfect with each other. If the steering wheel was locked in place while the vehicle was moving straight, it would gradually begin turning in an arc.

Nothing held substance. It was as if the world no longer existed. The gale-force windstorm seemed to drain the color out of everything. The ice storm swirled and gusted with such force that the driving hail of ice particles bombarded the windshield like tiny nails. Their impact against the glass came like a crescendo of clicking sounds. Pitt felt himself idly wondering if the onslaught would mar the old prewar safety glass. He lurched forward as the Snow Cruiser bounced over a frozen ice ridge unseen under the white maelstrom. He braced for a second bump, but it never came. The ice ran smooth.

The old line "It never rains but it pours" flashed through Pitt's mind when Giordino shouted through the hatch from the engine compartment, "Check your gauges. The engines are still running hot. With no air circulation down here, I have steam coming out of the radiator overflow tubes."

Pitt stared at the temperature gauges on the instrument panel. He'd spent so much effort concentrating on keeping the great vehicle moving on an undeviating course, he'd neglected to check the gauges. Oil pressure was slightly low, but the water temperatures were already crossing into the red zone. In less time than it takes to boil an egg, the radiators would boil over and blow a water hose from the engine. After that, there was no way of telling how long the engines would turn until their pistons burned and froze inside the cylinders. Already, he could hear the engines beginning to misfire as combustion occurred early from the acute heat.

"Throw on your cold-weather gear," Pitt shouted. "When you're ready, open the outside door. The flood of cold air should cool down the engines."

"And freeze us into Popsicles at the same time," Giordino came back.

"We'll have to suffer until they're running at normal temperatures again."

Both men donned their heavy-weather coveralls and hooded parkas again, Pitt struggling with the heavy clothing while he kept the Cruiser on a steady course through the storm. When they were fully dressed and fortified for the cold, Giordino opened the door. A howling chaos surged into the control cabin, the wind moaning and screaming as it whipped through the doorway. Pitt huddled over the steering wheel and stared through half-screwed-shut eyes as the blast of cold flung itself into the control cabin with a banshee shriek that drowned out all sounds from the diesel engines.

He could not have envisioned the profound shock that came from having the temperature inside the cabin drop eighty degrees within thirty seconds. When a human is appropriately clothed for extreme cold, he can endure temperatures of 120 degrees below freezing for twenty to thirty minutes at a time without suffering injury. But when the windchill factor adds another fifty degrees to the temperature, the drastic frigidness can kill within a few short minutes. Pitt's cold-weather clothing could protect him from mere cold, but the chill from the gale sucked the body heat right out of him.

Down in the engine compartment, Giordino sat between the two engines and savored what little heat he could soak up from the exhaust heaters and the radiator fans. He was deeply concerned about how Pitt could survive until the engine temperatures dropped. There was no more communication. The screaming wind made voice contact impossible.

The next few minutes were the longest Pitt had ever spent. He had never known such cold. It felt as if the wind went right through him, cutting his insides as it traveled. He stared at the needles on the engine temperature gauges and saw them drop with agonizing slowness. The ice crystals smashed into the windshields like a never-ending swarm. They hurtled through the door and into the control cabin, quickly covering Pitt and the instrument panel in a white glaze. The heater could no longer cope with the frozen air, and the inside of the windshield quickly frosted over, while the wipers on the outside were overwhelmed and soon became locked in a thickening blanket of ice. Unable to see past the steering wheel, Pitt sat like a rock as the torrent of white curled around him. He felt as though he were being swallowed by a ghost with thousands of tiny teeth.

He clenched his own teeth to keep them from chattering. Fighting forces far beyond his control, and realizing that he might be responsible for saving billions of lives, was not pleasant, but it drove him to stay the course against the screaming wind and stinging ice. What frightened him most was the prospect of driving into a crevasse that was impossible to see before it was too late. The sane thing to do was to slow the Snow Cruiser to a snail's crawl and send Giordino ahead to test the ice, but besides risking his friend's life, it would have cost them precious time, and time was an extravagance they did not have. His numbed right foot could no longer move up and down on the accelerator pedal, so he kept it fully pressed down, frozen in place to the floorboard.

Their drive across that deceptive and treacherous ice field had turned into a freezing nightmare.

There was no point of no return. It was finish the mission or die.

The shrieking fury of the ice storm showed no signs of diminishing. Pitt wiped the thickening veneer of ice from the instrument panel at last. The temperature gauge needles were slowly dropping out of the red now. But if he and Giordino wanted to reach their destination without further interruption, the needles would have to fall another twenty degrees.

He was a blind man in a world of the blind. He was even denied a sense of touch. His hands and legs soon went numb, with all feeling lost. His body no longer felt a part of him and refused to respond to his commands. He found it next to impossible to breathe. The bitter cold seared his lungs. The thickening of the blood, the chill seeping through his skin, the stinging pain that was torturing his flesh, despite the insulation of his clothing, drained his strength. He never knew a man could freeze to death so fast. It required a concentrated effort of willpower not to give in and order Giordino to close the door. His bitterness against failing was as strong as the terrible wind.

Pitt had stared the grim reaper in the face before, and he had spat on him. As long as he was still breathing and able to think straight, he still had a chance. If only the wind would die. He knew that storms could vanish as quickly as they were born. Why can't this one die? he implored no one but himself. A horrible emptiness settled over him. His vision was darkening around the edges of his eyes, and still those vexing needles hadn't wavered into the normal temperature range.

He did not exist by any preposterous illusion of hope. He believed in himself and in Giordino and in luck. The Almighty could come along, too, if He was agreeable. Pitt had no wish to welcome the great beyond with open arms. He'd always believed he'd have to be dragged away by either angels or demons, fighting to the end. The jury was still out on whether his good virtues outweighed the bad. The only undeniable, uncontested reality was that he had little to say in the matter and was within minutes of freezing into a block of ice.

If there was a purpose for adversity, Pitt was damned if he knew what it was. Somewhere beyond it all, he stepped from being a mere mortal to a man outside himself. His mind was still clear, still capable of weighing the odds and the consequences. He pushed back the dark nightmare that was closing in on him. Suffering and foreboding no longer had meaning for him. He refused to accept an inevitable end. Any thought of dying became abhorrent and stillborn.

He almost gave way to an overpowering instinct to throw in the towel and surrender, but steeled himself to hold out another ten minutes. There was never a doubt in his mind that he and Giordino would see it through together, nor was there a moment of panic. Save the engines, save himself, and then save the world. That was the line of priority. He rubbed the frost from his glasses and saw that the needles on the gauge were falling faster and rapidly approaching their normal operating temperature.

Twenty more seconds, he told himself, then another twenty. What was the old ditty, "Ninety-nine bottles of beer on the wall"? Then came relief and exultation, as the temperature gauges registered nearly normal again.

There was no need to shout through the hatch down to Giordino in the engine compartment. The little Italian sensed when the time was ripe by placing a hand momentarily on the top of a radiator. He slammed shut the door, sealing off the frightful force of wind and ice, but not before throwing the interior heater switches as high as they could go. Then he rushed up to the control cabin and roughly pulled Pitt from behind the steering wheel.

"You've done enough for the cause," he said, troubled at seeing Pitt so close to death from hypothermia. "I'll help you down to the engine compartment where you can warm up."

"The Snow Cruiser . . ." Pitt barely murmured through frozen lips. "Don't let it wander."

"Don't burden yourself. I can drive this mechanical mastodon as well as you."

After setting Pitt on the floor between the big diesels where he could get warm again, Giordino climbed back into the icy control cabin, sat behind the steering wheel, and engaged first gear. Within sixty seconds, he had the grand vehicle boring through the storm once again at twenty-four miles an hour.

The consistent knock of the diesels, running smoothly once again, was more than music to Pitt's ears, it was a symbol of renewed hope.

Never in his entire life had anything ever felt so good as the warmth that emanated from the engines and was absorbed by his half-frozen body. His blood soon thinned and circulated again, and he allowed himself the luxury of simply relaxing for half an hour while Giordino held the wheel.

Almost morbidly, he began to wonder: had the special military force landed? Were they lost and dying in the same treacherous blizzard?

39

PAINTED IN A CHARCOAL gray with no markings but a small American flag on the vertical stabilizer, the McDonnell Douglas C-17 soared above an ocean of pearl-white clouds blanketing the glaring ice of Antarctica like a giant, featherless pterodactyl over a Mesozoic landscape.

Air Force Captain Lyle Stafford was quite at home in his cockpit office flying over the frozen continent. Normally, he flew back and forth between Christchurch, New Zealand, and the American ice stations scattered around Antarctica, transporting scientists, equipment, and supplies. This trip they had been abruptly pressed into service to fly the hurriedly assembled assault teams to the Ross Ice Shelf and drop them over the Destiny Enterprises mining facility.

Stafford looked more like a public relations director than a pilot. Graying hair neatly trimmed, always ready with a smile, he was always volunteering to help out Air Force service and charity organizations. On most flights, he read a book, while his copilot, Lieutenant Robert Brannon, a long-boned Californian whose knees came halfway to his chin when he was seated, tended the controls and instruments. Almost reluctantly, he glanced from his book, *The Einstein Papers* by Craig Dirgo, out his side window and then at the Global Positioning System display.

"Time to go back to work," he announced, putting aside the book. He turned and smiled at Major Tom Cleary, who sat perched on a stool behind the pilots. "It's almost time to begin prebreathing, Major, and acclimate yourselves to the oxygen."

Cleary stared through the windshield over the pilot's heads, but all he saw was cloud cover. He assumed that a corner of the Ross Ice Shelf was looming unseen ahead and below the aircraft. "How's my time?"

Stafford nodded at the instrument panel. "We'll be over your release point in one hour. Are your men ready and eager?"

"Ready, maybe, but I'd hardly describe them as eager. They've all jumped from a jet aircraft at thirty-five thousand feet at one time or another, but not while it was traveling at four hundred miles an hour. We're used to feeling the aircraft slow down before the ramp lowers."

"Sorry I can't bring you in closer, slower, and lower," said Stafford sympathetically. "The trick is for you and your men to land on the ice without your chutes being discovered in the air. My orders state in no uncertain terms for me to make my routine supply run to McMurdo Sound in my normal flight pattern. I've shaved it as close as I dare without raising suspicion. As it is, you'll have to glide nearly ten miles to your target zone just outside the security fences."

"The wind is blowing from the sea, so that's in your favor," offered Brannon.

"The cloud cover helps, too," Cleary said slowly. "And if they have a functioning radar system, the operator will have to have four eyes to detect us from the exact moment we exit until we deploy our canopies."

Stafford made a slight course change and then said, "I don't envy you, Major, jumping from a nice warm airplane into an icy blast one hundred degrees below zero."

Cleary smiled. "At least you didn't hand me the tired old pilot's line about 'jumping from a perfectly good airplane.' I appreciate that."

They all laughed for a few moments at the inside joke among professionals. For decades, parachutists had been posed the question, "Why do you jump from a perfectly good airplane?" usually by pilots. The stock answer Cleary usually gave was "When a perfectly good airplane exists, then I'll quit jumping."

"As for the cold," Cleary continued, "our electrically heated thermal suits will keep us from turning into icicles while we descend to a warmer altitude."

"The clouds extend, too, within a thousand feet of the ground, so you'll be falling blind most of the way, since your compasses and GPS instruments are ineffective," said Brannon.

"The men are well trained for that. The key to a successful high-altitude, low-opening infiltration jump is to exit at the correct grid coordinate upwind, and have everyone under canopy at relatively the same altitude."

"We'll put you out on a silver quarter. But it won't be no picnic."

"No," said Cleary solemnly. "I'm sure that in the first minute after we drop from the plane, we'll wish we were falling into a fiery hell instead."

Stafford checked the instrument panel again. "After you and your men finish prebreathing, I'll decompress the cabin. Immediately afterward, I'll pass on the twenty- and ten-minute warnings to you and my crew. Then I'll notify you over the intercom when we're six minutes from the release point. At two minutes out, I'll lower the ramp."

"Understood."

"At one minute out," Stafford went on, "I'm going to ring the alarm bell once. Then, when we're directly over the release point, I'll turn on the green light. At the airspeed we'll be flying, you'll have to get out quickly as a group."

"Our intentions exactly."

"Good luck to you," said Stafford, twisting in his pilot's seat and shaking hands with the major.

Cleary smiled faintly. "Thanks for the ride."

"Our pleasure," Stafford said genuinely. "But I hope we don't have to do it again anytime soon."

"Nor do I."

Cleary stood and straightened, left the cockpit, and walked aft into the aircraft's cavernous cargo bay. The sixty-five men seated inside were a serious-faced group, dogged and dead calm, considering the uncertain peril they were about to encounter. They were young. Their ages ranged from twenty to twenty-four. There was no laughter or unproductive conversation, no grousing or complaining. To a man they were absorbed in checking and rechecking their equipment. They were a composite of America's finest fighting men, hastily thrown together on the spur of the moment from special units nearest to Antarctica that were on counter-drug operations throughout South America. A team of Navy SEALs, members of the Army's elite Delta Force and a Marine Force Recon team . . . a combined band of secret warriors on a mission unlike any ever conceived.

Once the alert had been given the Pentagon by the White House, the one thing they had in short supply was time. A larger Special Forces unit was on the way from the United States but was not expected to reach Okuma Bay for another three hours, a time span that might prove too late and disastrous. Admiral Sandecker's warning was not received with enthusiasm by the President's top aides, nor the Armed Forces chief of staff. At first, none dared believe the incredible story. Only when Loren Smith and various scientists added their weight to the plea for action was the President persuaded to order the Pentagon to send a special force to stop the rapidly approaching cataclysm.

An air assault with missiles was quickly ruled out because of an utter lack of intelligence data. Nor could the White House and Pentagon be absolutely sure that they might not find themselves in hot water with the world for destroying an innocent plant and hundreds of employees. Nor could they be certain of the specific location for the command center for Earth's destruction. For all they knew, it could be hidden in an underground ice chamber miles from the facility. The Joint Chiefs decided that a manned assault offered the best chance of success, without an international outcry if they were wrong.

The men were seated on their heavy rucksacks, wearing parachutes, and were engaged in completing jumpmaster inspections. The rucksacks were full of survival gear and ammunition for the new Spartan Q-99 Eradicator, a ten-pound deadly killer weapon that integrated an automatic twelve-gauge shotgun, a 5.56-millimeter automatic rifle with sniper scope, and a large-bore barrel in the center that fired small shrapnel-inflicting missiles that exploded with deadly results at the slightest impact. The spare magazines, shotgun shells, and shrapnel missiles weighed nearly twenty pounds and were carried in belly packs slung around their waists. The top flap of the belly pack held a navigation board, complete with a Silva marine compass and digital altimeter, both clearly visible to the jumper while gliding under his canopy.

Captain Dan Sharpsburg led the Army's Delta Force, while Lieutenant Warren Garnet was in command of the Marine Recon Team. Lieutenant Miles Jacobs and his SEAL team, which had aided NUMA on St. Paul Island, was also part of the assault force. The combined group was under the command of Cleary, a Special Forces veteran who had been on leave with his wife enjoying the Kruger Game Park in South Africa, when he was whisked away on a minute's notice to take command of the elite makeshift assault unit. It had to be the first time in American military history that separate special units were merged to fight as one.

For this mission, every man would be utilizing a new ram-air parachute system for the first time, called the MT-1Z or Zulu. With a four-to-one lift-to-drag ratio, the canopy could travel four meters horizontally for every meter descended, an advantage that did not go unappreciated among the three teams.

Cleary scanned the two rows of men. The nearest officer, Dan Sharpsburg, tilted his head and grinned. A red-haired wit with a gross sense of humor, and an old friend, he was one of the few who actually looked forward to the suicidal plunge. Dan had been "chasing airplanes" for years, achieving the status of Military Free Fall Instructor at the U.S. Army's prestigious Special Forces Military Free Fall School in Yuma, Arizona. When not off on a mission or training, Dan could be found skydiving with civilians for the fun of it.

Cleary had barely had time to glance at the service records of Jacobs and Garnet, but he knew they were the best of the best turned out by the Navy and Marines for special force missions. Though he was an old Army man, he well knew the SEALs and Marine Recon teams were among the finest fighting men in the world.

As he looked from face to face, he thought that if they survived the jump and glide to the target site, they then had the Wolfs' security force to contend with. A well-armed and trained small army of mercenaries, he was told, many of whom had served the very same forces as the men on the plane. No, Cleary concluded. This would be no picnic.

"How soon?" Sharpsburg asked tersely.

"Less than an hour," Cleary answered, moving down the line of men and alerting Jacobs and Garnet. Then he stood in the middle of the united fighting men and gave them final instructions. Satellite aerial photos were carried by everyone in a pocket of their thermal suits, to be studied once they had fallen into the clear and opened their canopies. Their target landing site was a large ice field just outside the mining facility, whose broken, uneven landscape offered them a small degree of protection when regrouping after the jump. The next part of the plan was the assault on the main engineering center of the facility, where it was hoped the doomsday controls were housed. Expert military minds judged that fewer casualties would occur if they landed and attacked from the outside rather than landing in the maze of buildings, antennas, machinery, and electrical equipment.

Coordination was to take place once each unit was on the ground and assembled for the assault. Any who were injured upon landing would have to suffer the cold and be dealt with later, after the facility had been secured and any systems or equipment that were designed to separate the ice shelf destroyed.

Satisfied that each man knew what was expected of him, Cleary moved to the rear of the cargo bay and donned his parachute and rucksack. Then he had one of Sharpsburg's men give him a complete jumpmaster inspection, with emphasis on his oxygen-breathing equipment for the long fall.

Finally, he silhouetted himself with his back to the closed cargo ramp in the floor and waved his hands to get the men's attention. From this point on, communication with the entire assault team would be conducted by hand and arm signals, which was standard operating procedure. The only voice communications until the jump would be between Cleary, Sharpsburg, Jacobs, Garnet, and Stafford in the cockpit. Once they exited the aircraft and were under canopy, each man could communicate with individual Motorola radios over secure frequencies.

"Pilot, this is the jumpmaster."

"I read you, Major," came back Stafford's voice. "Ready on the mark?"

"Jumpmaster checks complete. Oxygen prebreathing is under way."

Cleary took an empty seat and studied the men. So far, it was going well, almost too well, he thought. This is the time when Murphy's Law came sneaking around, and Cleary wasn't about to allow Mr. Murphy any opportunities. He was pleased to see the men were fully alert and primed.

They wore hoods under gray Gentex flight helmets to gain additional protection from the harsh subzero temperatures. Adidas Galeforce yellow-lens goggles for fog and overcast were attached to the helmets, resting up and leaving the men's eyes clearly visible to Cleary and the oxygen technician so they could check for any signs of hypoxia. The heating units in their thermal suits were activated, and each man checked his buddy to make certain that all equipment was properly organized and in place. Bungee cords and web straps were strategically laced around each man's clothing and equipment to prevent them from being torn away by the great burst of air expected upon their exit from the ramp.

After they checked their radios to confirm that each was transmitting and receiving, Cleary stood up and moved near the closed ramp. Facing his assault force again, he saw that all the men were giving him their undivided attention. Once again, he motioned to the man nearest his left with a thumbs-up signal.

IN the cockpit, carefully studying his computerized course and the programmed target, Captain Stafford was concentrating his mind and soul on dropping the men waiting aft over the precise spot that would give them every chance of surviving. His primary concern was not to send them out ten seconds too early or five seconds too late and scatter them all over the frozen landscape. He disengaged the automatic pilot and turned the controls over to Brannon so his perspective and timing would not be diverted. Stafford switched to the cockpit intercom and spoke through his oxygen mask to Brannon. "Deviate one degree and it will cost them."

"I'll put them over the target," Brannon said self-assuredly. "But you have to put them *on* it."

"No confidence in your aircraft commander's navigational abilities? Shame on you."

"A thousand pardons, my captain."

"That's better," Stafford said expansively. He switched to the cargo bay intercom. "Major Cleary, are you ready?"

"Roger," Cleary answered briefly.

"Crew, are you ready?"

The crewmen, wearing harnesses attached to cargo tie-down rings and portable oxygen systems, were standing a few feet forward of the ramp on opposite sides.

"Sergeant Hendricks ready, Captain."

"Corporal Joquin ready, sir."

"Twenty-minute warning, Major," Stafford announced. "Depressurizing cabin at this time."

Hendricks and Joquin moved cautiously close to the ramp, carefully guiding their harness anchor lines, following checklists and preparing for what was about to become one of the most unusual duties of their military careers.

As the cabin decompressed, the men could feel the temperature drop, even within the protective confines of their electrically heated thermal jumpsuits. The air hissed from the cargo bay as it slowly equalized with the outside atmosphere.

Time passed quickly. And then Stafford's voice came over the intercom.

"Major, ten-minute warning."

"Roger." There was a pause, then Cleary asked sarcastically, "Can you give us any more heat back here?"

"Didn't I tell you?" Stafford replied. "We need ice for cocktails after you leave."

For the next two minutes, Cleary went over the infiltration plan of the mining facility in his mind. They were combining the elements of a high-altitude, low-canopy opening jump with a high-altitude, high-canopy opening jump to keep detection to a minimum. The plan was for the team to free-fall to 25,000 feet, open their canopies, assemble in the air, and fly to the target landing zone.

Sharpsburg's Delta Force would exit first, closely followed by Jacobs and his SEALs, and then by Garnet and his Marine Recon Team. Cleary would be the last man to jump, in order to have an overview of his men and be in the most advantageous position to give course corrections. Sharpsburg would be the Mother Hen, the term tagged to the lead jumper. All of the Ducks in Line would then follow. Where Sharpsburg went, so would they.

"Six minutes to jump," came Stafford's voice, interrupting Cleary's thoughts.

STAFFORD'S eyes were on the computer monitor, linked to a newly installed photo system that revealed the ground in astonishing detail through the clouds. Brannon handled the big aircraft as tenderly as if it were a child, his course rock-steady on the line that traveled across the monitor, with a small circle depicting the jump target.

"Damn the orders!" Stafford suddenly snorted. "Brannon!"

"Sir?"

"At the one-minute warning, cut our airspeed to 135 knots indicated. I'm going to give those guys every chance at surviving I can. When Sergeant Hendricks reports that the last man has jumped, ease the throttles to two hundred knots."

"Won't the Wolfs' ground radar pick up our reduction in speed?"

"Radio McMurdo Station on an open frequency. Then say we're experiencing engine trouble, will have to reduce speed and arrive late."

"Not a bad cover," Brannon conceded. "If they're monitoring us on the ground, they'd have no reason not to buy the story."

Brannon went on his radio and announced the deception to anyone who was listening. Then he gestured at the numerals flashing on the computer monitor indicating the approaching jump mark. "Two minutes coming up."

Stafford nodded. "Begin reducing speed, *very gradually.* At one minute to drop, just after I ring the bell, cut the airspeed to 135."

Brannon flexed his fingers like a piano player and smiled. "I shall orchestrate the throttles like a concerto."

Stafford switched to the cargo bay intercom. "Two minutes, Major. Sergeant Hendricks, begin opening the ramp."

"Ramp opening," came back Hendricks's steady voice.

Stafford turned to Brannon. "I'll take the controls. You handle the throttles so I can concentrate on timing the drop."

After monitoring the transmission, Cleary stood up and moved to the port side of the ramp, keeping his back turned to one side of the fuselage so he had a clear view of his men, the jump/caution lights, and the ramp. He raised and extended his right arm in an arc, palm facing from his side to a perpendicular position. This was the command to stand up.

The men rose from their seats and stood, checking their rip cords and equipment again, adjusting the heavy rucksacks they wore to the rear below their main parachute container. The huge ramp began to creep open, allowing a great rush of frigid air to sweep through the cargo bay.

The next seconds passed with cruel sluggishness.

In grim determination, they gripped the steel anchor line cables with gloved hands for support against the immense whirlwind they expected when the ramp fully opened, and as guides as they moved to the edge of the ramp to execute their exit. Although they exchanged self-assured glances, it was as if they didn't see their buddies around them. No words were needed to describe what they would experience once the ramp opened, and they dove into air so cold it was unimaginable.

IN the cockpit, Stafford turned to Brannon. "I'll take the controls now, so I can concentrate on timing. The throttles are yours."

Brannon raised both his hands. "She's all yours, Cap."

"Cap? Cap?" Stafford repeated as if in pain. "Can't you show me at least a smidgen of respect?" Then he switched the intercom aft. "One-minute warning, Major."

———

CLEARY did not acknowledge. He didn't have to. The alarm bell rang once. He gave the next signal, right arm straight out to his side at shoulder level, palm up, then bent it at the elbow until his hand touched his Gentex helmet, giving the command to move to the rear, the men in front coming to a stop three feet from the ramp hinges. He lowered his goggles into place and silently began counting off the seconds until exit. Suddenly, he sensed something out of place. The aircraft was noticeably slowing.

"Ramp opened and locked, Captain," Hendricks informed Stafford.

The sergeant's voice took Cleary by surprise. He immediately realized that he had forgotten to disconnect his communications cord from the intercom jack.

Cleary gave the men the hand and arm signal indicating fifteen seconds from exit. His eyes were fixed on the red caution light. The sixty-five-man team was massed into a tightly compressed group, with Sharpsburg now perched inches from the edge of the ramp.

Simultaneously, as the crimson caution light blinked off and the jump light flashed a vivid green, Cleary pointed to the open ramp.

As if jolted by a shock of electricity, Lieutenant Sharpsburg dove from the aircraft, soaring off into cloud-shrouded nothingness. With his arms and legs spread, he was swept out of sight as swiftly as if he'd been jerked by a giant spring. His team was no more than a few feet behind as they were also swallowed up in the clouds, followed swiftly by Jacobs and his SEAL team. Then came Garnet and his Marines. As the last Marine stepped off the ramp edge, Cleary leaped and was gone.

For a long moment, Hendricks and Joquin stood and stared into the white oblivion, unable to believe what they had just witnessed. Almost as if mesmerized, Hendricks spoke into the intercom on his oxygen mask. "Captain, they're gone."

BRANNON lost no time in easing the throttles forward until the airspeed instruments read two hundred knots, half the C-17's cruising speed. The cargo door was closed and the oxygen system in the cargo bay replenished. Stafford's next act of business was to switch to a secure frequency and radio the U.S. South Atlantic Command Headquarters to report that the jump went as scheduled. Then he turned to Brannon.

"I hope they make it," he said quietly.

"If they do, it will be because you sent them out into a blast of air a good two hundred and fifty miles an hour less in strength than our normal cruising speed."

"I hope to God I didn't give them away," said Stafford, without remorse. "But it seemed certain death to subject them to such an explosive gust."

"You won't get an argument from me," Brannon said somberly.

Stafford sighed heavily as he reengaged the automatic pilot. "Not our responsibility any longer. We dropped them right on a dime." Then he paused, staring into the ominous white clouds that whipped past the windshield and obscured all view. "I pray they all get down safely."

Brannon looked at him askance. "I didn't know you were a praying man."

"Only during traumatic times."

"They'll make it down," said Brannon, with a sense of optimism. "It's after they hit the ground that hell could break loose."

Stafford shook his head. "I wouldn't want to go up against those guys that just jumped. I'll bet their attack will be a walk in the park."

Stafford had no idea how dead wrong he was.

THE radar operator in the security building headquarters next to the control center picked up a phone as he studied the line sweep around his radar screen. "Mr. Wolf. Do you have a moment?"

A few minutes later, Hugo Wolf walked briskly into the small darkened room filled with electronic units. "Yes, what is it?"

"Sir, the American supply aircraft suddenly reduced its speed."

"Yes, I'm aware of that. Our radio intercepted a message from them saying they were having engine trouble."

"Do you think it might be a ruse?"

"Has it strayed from its normal flight path?" asked Hugo.

The radar operator shook his head. "No, sir. The plane is ten miles out."

"You see nothing else on the screen?"

"Only the usual interference during and immediately after an ice storm."

Hugo put a hand on the operator's shoulder. "Follow her course to make sure she doesn't double back, and keep a sharp eye for a hostile intrusion from the sea or air."

"And behind us, sir?"

"Now, who do you think would have the powers to cross the mountains or trek over the ice shelf in the middle of an ice storm?"

The operator shrugged. "No one. Certainly no one who is human."

Hugo grinned. "Exactly."

AIR Force General Jeffry Coburn laid the phone back in its receiver and looked across the long table in the war room deep beneath the Pentagon. "Mr. President, Major Cleary and his unified command have exited the aircraft."

The Joint Chiefs and their aides were seated in a theaterlike section of a long room whose massive walls were covered with huge monitors and screens showing scenes of Army bases, Navy ships, and Air Force fields around the globe. The current status of ships at sea and military aircraft in the air were constantly monitored, especially the big transports carrying the hastily assembled Special Forces from the United States.

One huge screen that lay against the far wall held a montage of telephoto images taken of the Destiny Enterprises mining facility at Okuma Bay. The photos in the montage were not from an overhead view, but appeared to be pieced together and conceptualized after being shot from an aircraft several miles off to one side of the facility. There were no overhead images because the military had no spy reconnaissance satellites orbiting over the South Pole. The only direct radio contact with Cleary's assault force came from a civilian communications satellite used by United States ice research stations on the Ross Ice Shelf that was linked to the Pentagon.

Another screen revealed President Dean Cooper Wallace, six members of his cabinet, and a team of his close advisers, who were seated around a table in the secure room deep beneath the White House. The directors of the CIA and FBI, and Ron Little and Ken Helm, were also present on a direct link with the war room, along with Congresswoman Loren Smith, who had been invited because of her intimate knowledge of Destiny Enterprises. While they acted as advisers to the President on what had been given the code name Apocalypse Project, Admiral Sandecker sat with the Joint Chiefs at the Pentagon and acted as consultant on their end.

"What is the countdown, General?" asked the President.

"One hour and forty-two minutes, sir," General Amos South, head of the Joint Chiefs, answered. "That is the time our scientists tell us when tidal currents are at their height to separate the ice shelf and carry it out to sea."

"Just how accurate is this intelligence?"

"You might say it comes from the horse's mouth," Loren replied. "The timetable was revealed by Karl Wolf himself and was confirmed by the nation's top glaciologists and experts on nanotechnology."

"Since Admiral Sandecker's people penetrated Wolf's organization," explained Ron Little, "we have accumulated considerably more intelligence on what the Wolfs call the Valhalla Project. It all adds up to them doing exactly what they threaten, cutting off the Ross Ice Shelf and upsetting Earth's rotational balance in order to cause a polar shift."

"Triggering a cataclysm of unimaginable destruction," added Loren.

"We've come to the same conclusion at the FBI," said Helm, backing up Little. "We've asked experts in the field of nanotechnology to study the facts, and all agree. The Wolfs have the scientific and engineering capability to execute such an unthinkable act."

The President stared into the monitor at General South. "I still say, send in a missile and stop this insanity before it can get off the ground."

"Only as a last resort, Mr. President. The Joint Chiefs and I strongly agree that it is too risky."

Admiral Morton Eldridge, Chief of the Navy, entered the discussion. "One of our aircraft equipped with radar intercept systems has arrived on site. They've already reported that the Wolf mining facility has superior radar equipment that could detect an incoming missile from an aircraft or nearby submarine with a warning time of three minutes. That's more than enough time to alert and panic them into throwing the doomsday switch early, a situation that may or may not break off the ice shelf. Again, a risk that is a poor gamble at best."

"If, as you say," said Wallace, "their radar equipment is rated as superior, haven't they already been alerted by your aircraft and the signals it sends out?"

Admiral Eldridge and General Coburn exchanged bemused glances before Eldridge replied. "Because it is highly classified, it is known only by a select few that our new radar warning systems are virtually undetectable. Our radar interception aircraft is below the horizon. We can bend our signals to read theirs, but they cannot find or read ours."

"Should our ground force be unable to penetrate the Wolf security defenses," said South, "then, of course, as a last resort, we'll send in a missile from our nuclear attack sub *Tucson.*"

"She's already on station in the Antarctic?" asked Wallace incredulously.

"Yes, sir," answered Eldridge. "A fortunate coincidence. She was on an ice data-gathering patrol when she successfully destroyed the Wolfs' U-boat that was firing on the NUMA research ship *Polar Storm*. Admiral Sandecker alerted me in time to send her to Okuma Bay before the final countdown."

"What about aircraft?"

"Two Stealth bombers are in the air and will begin a holding pattern ninety miles from the facility in another hour and ten minutes," answered Coburn.

"So we're covered from air and sea," said Wallace.

"That is correct," General South acknowledged.

"How soon before Major Cleary and his force begin their assault?"

South glanced up at a huge digital clock on one wall. "Depending on wind and overcast conditions, they should be gliding toward their target and landing in a few minutes."

"Will we receive a blow-by-blow account of the assault?"

"We have a direct link to Major Cleary's ground communications through the satellite that's servicing our ice stations at the Pole and Mc-

Murdo Sound. But since he and his men will be extremely busy for the next hour, and possibly coming under hostile fire, we do not think it wise to interfere or interrupt their field communications."

"Then we have nothing to do but wait and listen." Wallace spoke mechanically.

Silence greeted his words. No one in either war room offered him a reply.

After a long moment, he murmured, "God, how did we ever get in this mess?"

40

HURTLING MORE THAN 120 miles an hour through the thickly layered cloud mist from 35,000 feet, Cleary spread his arms apart and faced what he could only assume was the ground, since the cloud cover hid all evidence of a horizon. His mind boycotted the frigid blast of air that engulfed him, and he concentrated on maintaining a stable body position. He mentally reminded himself to personally thank Stafford someday for slowing the aircraft. It was a gesture that had provided the assault team with near-perfect conditions for exiting in a tightly knit group and enabled them to achieve a stable attitude without tumbling uncontrollably for several thousand feet. That situation would have scattered the teams over several miles, making the infiltration of a cohesive, intact fighting element nearly impossible.

He moved his left wrist within a few inches of his goggles, bringing the face of the MA2-30 altimeter within easy view. He was rapidly descending past 33,000 feet. Given the low air density at this altitude, he expected to speed up considerably.

Cleary concentrated on preserving his heading, 180 degrees from the

C-17's course at exit time, and he scanned the air immediately around him for signs of the other men in free fall. He passed through a heavy layer of moisture and felt the stinging pellets of hail stab the front of his body, mask, and goggles. Off to his right, about forty feet, he could barely see the flashing of several high-intensity firefly lights in the gray emptiness.

The lights were attached to the top of each man's Gentex helmet with the beam facing backward. They were set in that direction as a preventive measure to warn a man falling directly on top of another at the moment of canopy pull.

He briefly wondered if they might have exited over the incorrect grid. It hardly made any difference now. They were committed. They were either upwind of the target landing zone or not. It was a fifty-fifty chance. Only his faith in Stafford's flying ability gave him a healthy measure of optimism.

In the seconds between the time that Captain Sharpsburg had dived from the ramp and Cleary followed, the point of no return had passed into oblivion. He looked down at the airspace directly beneath him and saw no one. Next he checked his altitude. He was approaching 28,000 feet.

The plans called for the men to free-fall to 25,000 feet, open their canopies, assemble in the air, and glide to the target landing zone. Slightly before reaching that altitude, each man would have to initiate his pull sequence. That meant clearing his airspace and arching his body as perfectly as possible, then locating and maintaining eye contact with his main rip cord on the right, outboard side of his parachute harness. The next step was to grasp and pull the rip cord and check over his right shoulder to be sure that his canopy was deploying properly. He would need a thousand feet of working altitude in order for his main canopy to open at 25,000 feet on the mark.

Off in the distance, he could now see more firefly lights, ten, perhaps twelve. The cloud layer was thinning and visibility was increasing as they penetrated the lower altitudes. Cleary's altimeter read 26,000 feet. Rational thoughts ceased and years of training took over. With no hesitation, Cleary reacted decisively, silently repeating the commands as he executed the action sequence. Arch, look, reach, pull, check, check, and check.

Cleary's MT-1Z main canopy deployed in a near-perfect attitude and heading, softly, smoothly, and without the slightest indication that it had slowed him from an airspeed of 150 miles an hour straight down to nearly zero. He was now suspended underneath the fully inflated wing, drifting with the wind like a lethargic marionette.

As if booming stereophonic loudspeakers had been switched off, the sound of wind howling past him had ceased. The earpiece speakers inside his Gentex helmet crackled with static, and for the first time since he'd stepped from the ramp, Cleary distinctly heard the sounds of his breathing through the oxygen mask. He looked up immediately and meticulously inspected every square inch of his canopy for any signs of damage, including the suspension lines from their attaching points to the risers.

"Wizard, this is Tin Man, requesting a common check, over," Lieutenant Garnet's voice came over the earpiece receivers. Every man was capable of communicating via throat microphones attached to Motorola radios in a secure mode.

Cleary answered, initiating a communications check that used the team sub-element call signs. "All teams, this is Wizard, report your status in sequence, over." Because of the lack of visibility, Cleary could not see the entire group. He had to rely on his sub-element leaders for details.

Captain Sharpsburg responded first. "Wizard, this is Lion. I have the point at twenty-three thousand feet. Also, visual contact with all but two of my men. Standing by to lead the stick to target." Stick was the term for a team of men descending in a line.

"Roger that, Lion," acknowledged Cleary.

"Wizard, Scarecrow here," announced Jacobs. "At twenty-four thousand feet and in visual contact with all my men. Over."

Garnet of the Marines was next. "Wizard, this is Tin Man. I have visual contact with all but one of my men."

"I copy, Tin Man," said Cleary.

Reaching up, Cleary grasped the control toggles of the left and right risers, giving them a simultaneous tug and unstowing the breaks, placing the canopy in full flight mode. He felt a surge of acceleration as the canopy picked up airspeed. Cleary's earpiece speakers were humming with the sounds of team members checking in with their respective leaders. He mentally reviewed the events that lay ahead. If the assault team had been released at the correct coordinates, they should land in the middle of a large open space on the ice near the security fence of the mining facility. The terrain afforded them safe cover and concealment from which they could assemble and conduct a final equipment check prior to moving into the assault position.

He could lightly feel the wind rushing by as his canopy gained airspeed, an indication that he was traveling with predominant winds and not against them. At 19,000 feet, the cloud layers opened up, revealing the stark white expanse of the frozen Antarctic landscape. Canopies were strung out in a jagged, stairstep line to his front, with the firefly beams looking like a string of Christmas lights hung above an empty horizon.

Suddenly, he was called by Garnet. "Wizard, this is Tin Man. I am one man short, repeat, one man short, over."

Damn! Cleary thought. It was going too smoothly, and now Murphy stepped in to remove any false sense of security.

Cleary didn't ask the name of the missing man. It wasn't necessary. If he had a malfunction and jettisoned his main canopy, he should be somewhere below the stick of canopies heading toward the assembly area, suspended beneath his reserve canopy. There was no thought of the man falling to his death. It rarely ever happened. Once on the ground, the missing man would have to rely on his skills to survive until a search team could be sent out after the facility was secured.

Cleary's only concern was the man's equipment. "Tin Man. This is Wizard. What arsenal was the man carrying?"

"Wizard, we are missing one complete demolition kit and two LAWs, over."

Not good. The LAW was a Light Antitank Weapon, a powerful, one-shot, throwaway unit that could take out an armored vehicle. Two men had cross-loaded a LAW each, so there were still two in reserve. The demolition kit was critical. It contained thirty pounds of C-4 plastic explosive, detonation cord, and time fuses. They badly needed the kit if they encountered barricades or fortifications. Of all the men to lose, Cleary cursed, it had to be the one carrying the only demo kit and two LAWs.

So be it. "Wizard to all elements. Target is eight miles out. Extinguish all firefly lights and maintain maximum radio silence. Close up the stick as tight as possible. Wizard, out."

They were down to a fifteen-minute canopy flight to the target landing zone. Cleary checked his watch. They were still racing the clock, with little time in reserve. He hoped the missing man was not an omen. Myriad things could go wrong in the next half hour. They couldn't afford to lose another man and vital equipment. The tailwind was pushing them along nicely. Cleary looked ahead and down, satisfied that the stair-step formation was tight and the new-model canopies were exceeding all expectations for glide and stability. The plan was to be over the target landing site at 500 feet.

The mining facility was getting closer. Details of the buildings could be recognized through occasional breaks in the clouds. Now they were at 8,000 feet altitude and moving into a phase of the operation where they were most vulnerable before they were safely on the ground.

At 7,000 feet, Cleary felt something out of place. He was losing airspeed. His canopy began to buck and flutter from a crosswind that had swept in from nowhere. He intuitively reached up for the toggles nestled on the rear side of the front risers. These were canopy "trim tabs," which increased the canopy's angle of attack to counter the crosswind.

"Wizard, this is Lion. We've got one hell of a crosswind."

"Roger, Lion. I have it at my altitude as well. All elements, use trim tabs and maintain heading."

Cleary looked down and saw the icy landscape moving by, considerably slower than before. At 2,000 feet, the tailwind thankfully picked up again and the crosswind died off. He scanned the mining facility for movement or activity. Everything on the ground appeared normal. Puffs of white vapor revealed where warm air and exhaust escaped from within the facility's buildings. It looked deceivingly unthreatening.

At last, Cleary heard the message he was hoping for.

"Wizard, this is Lion. I have cleared the security fence and have visual of the target landing zone. We're almost home."

"Roger that, Lion," Cleary answered with relief.

He watched as the front element of the stick moved slightly to the right. They were preparing to fly a downwind and base leg of their flight in preparation for turning into the wind and landing. Sharpsburg, the lead man, turned perpendicular to the direction of flight. The stick of canopies immediately behind him followed suit, turning on the same imaginary point in the sky as Sharpsburg.

"Wizard," Lion reported, without bothering to identify himself, "five hundred feet and preparing to land."

Cleary did not reply. There was no need. He watched as the first canopy landed on target and deflated, followed by the second, then the third. As the men touched down, they jettisoned as much gear as possible and took up a hasty defensive perimeter.

Now at 500 feet, Cleary observed Jacobs's SEAL team mirror the landing of the Delta team. Next came Garnet and his Marines. Now directly over the imaginary turning point, he tugged at the left toggle and slid around ninety degrees for one hundred meters, repeating the maneuver until he was facing the wind. He felt it push into his body, slowing the canopy's forward movement. Then Cleary brought both toggles to the halfway point and studied the frozen ground and his altimeter collectively.

Two hundred feet came quickly. The ground was rushing up to meet him. Past the one-hundred-foot mark, he let up on his toggles, completely entering free flight. Then, relying on his expertise and experience, Cleary pulled the toggles all the way down until they reached full extension, and he touched the Antarctic's icebound surface as lightly as if he'd stepped off a curb.

He quickly unbuckled his harness and dropped the parachute system that had carried him safely to his destination. Then he knelt down and prepared his Spartan Q-99 Eradicator, locking and loading it for immediate use.

Garnet, Sharpsburg, and Jacobs were at his side within thirty seconds. They coordinated briefly, checking their position and making final preparations for their movement toward the control center of the facility. After issuing final instructions to Sharpsburg, who would be in charge of the assault team if Cleary was killed or badly wounded, he peered at the facility through his field glasses. Not seeing any signs of defensive activity, Cleary ordered the teams to move out tactically, with himself in the middle of the patrol.

41

LOATH TO DIE, THE wind struggled to stay alive until there was no more strength left in it. Then it was gone, leaving the sun to transform the last of the windblown ice crystals into sparkling diamond dust. The dismal gray light gave way to a blue sky that returned as the Snow Cruiser forged relentlessly across the ice shelf. The mighty machine had proven herself a tough customer. Engines running faultlessly, wheels churning through the snow and ice, she never stalled or floundered during the malicious blizzard. But for the muffled tone of her exhaust, the stillness that settled over the desolate ice shelf made it seem like oblivion.

Warmed finally by the engines, Pitt felt ready to face reality again. He took over the wheel from Giordino, who found a broom in the bunk compartment and used it to brush the ice buildup off the windshields. Released from their frozen bondage, the windshield wipers finished sweeping the glass clean. The Rockefeller Mountains materialized in the distance and rose above the bow of the vehicle. They were that close.

Pitt pointed to a series of black smudges on the sun-splashed white horizon slightly off to his left. "There lies the Wolf mining works."

"We did good," said Giordino. "We couldn't have wandered more than a mile off our original track during the storm."

"Another three or four miles to go. We should be there in twenty minutes."

"Are you going to crash the party unannounced?"

"Not a wise move against an army of security guards," answered Pitt. "That low rock ridge protruding from the ice that angles toward the base of the mountains?"

"I see it."

"We can run along out of sight of the compound, using it for cover while we close the final two miles."

"We just might make it," said Giordino, "if they don't spot our exhaust."

"Keep your fingers crossed," Pitt said with a tight grin.

They left the great ice plain of the Ross Ice Shelf and crossed onto ice-mantled land and skirted the ridge that trailed down from the mountain like a giant tongue, keeping below the summit out of sight of the mining compound as they crept ever closer. Soon they were driving beneath towering gray rock cliffs, with streams of ice hanging from their crests like frozen waterfalls, gleaming blue-green under the radiant sun. The path they took along the base of the mountains was not flat or smooth but strewn with wavelike undulations.

Pitt downshifted the Snow Cruiser into second gear to climb the series of low mounds and valleys. The burly machine took the uneven terrain in stride, her wide wheels moving the great mass up and down the grades without effort. His eyes swept the instrument panel for the tenth time in as many minutes. The temperature gauges indicated that the slow speeds at high rpms were causing the diesels to overheat again, but this time they could keep the door open without suffering the agonies of a blizzard.

They were passing the mouth of a narrow box canyon when Pitt suddenly stopped the Snow Cruiser.

"What's up?" Giordino asked, staring at Pitt. "You see something?"

Pitt pointed downward through the windshield. "Tracks in the snow leading into the canyon. They could have only been made by the treads from a big Sno-cat."

Giordino's eyes followed Pitt's outstretched finger. "You've got good eyes. The tracks are barely visible."

"The blizzard should have covered them," said Pitt. "But they still show because the vehicle that made them must have passed through just as the storm was ending."

"Why would a Sno-cat travel up a dead-end ravine?"

"Another entrance to the mining compound?"

"Could very well be."

"Shall we find out?"

Giordino grinned. "I'm dying of curiosity."

Pitt cranked the steering wheel to its stop and sharply turned the Snow Cruiser into the canyon. The cliffs rose ominously above the ravine, their height escalating until the sun's light paled the deeper they drove into the mountain. Fortunately, the twists and turns were not severe, and the Snow Cruiser was able to deftly navigate her bulk around and through them. Pitt's only worry was that they'd find nothing but a rock wall, and then have to back the vehicle through the canyon, since there was no room to turn her around. A quarter of a mile from the canyon's mouth, Pitt braked the vehicle to a stop before a solid wall of ice.

It was a dead end. Disillusionment circled their minds.

They both stepped down from the Snow Cruiser and stared at the vertical sheet of ice. Pitt peered down at the tracks that traveled up the canyon and stopped at the wall. "The plot thickens. The Sno-cat could not have backed out of here."

"Certainly not without making a second set of tracks," observed Giordino.

Pitt moved until his face was inches from the ice, cupped his hands around his eyes to block out the light, and stared. He could make out vague shadows beyond the ice barrier. "Something is in there," he said.

Giordino gazed into the ice and nodded. "Is this where somebody says, 'Open Sesame'?"

"No doubt the wrong code," Pitt said pensively.

"It has to be a good three feet thick."

"Are you thinking what I'm thinking?"

Giordino nodded. "I'll stay on the ground outside and cover you with my Bushmaster."

Pitt climbed back into the Snow Cruiser, shifted the gear lever into reverse, and sent the vehicle back about fifty feet, keeping the tires in the packed depressions made by the Sno-cat for better traction. He paused, grasped the wheel tightly in both hands, and burrowed down in the seat, in case the ice should crash through the windshield. Then he shifted into first and jammed the accelerator pedal flat against the floorboards. With a roar from its exhaust, the big mechanical goliath leaped forward, gathered speed, and then smashed into the frozen wall, rumbling the ground beneath Giordino's feet.

The ice exploded and shattered into a great splash of glittering fragments that showered over the red Snow Cruiser like so many glass shards from a fallen crystal chandelier. The sound of the impact came like a giant gnashing his teeth. At first, Giordino thought the vehicle might have to ram the thick, solidified ice wall several times before breaking through, but he was almost left behind as it bulldozed its way through on the first try and disappeared on the other side. He chased after it, gun cradled in his arms, like an infantryman following a tank for cover.

Once through, Pitt brought the Snow Cruiser to a halt and brushed the glass from his face and chest. A large block of ice had burst through the center windshield, narrowly missing him before it fell to the floor and shattered. His face was cut on one cheek and across the forehead. Neither gash was deep enough to require stitches, but the blood that flowed made him look as though he were badly injured. He wiped the crimson from his eyes onto his sleeve and looked to see where the Snow Cruiser had come to rest.

They were sitting inside a large-diameter ice tunnel, with the vehicle's front end firmly embedded in a frozen wall opposite the shattered entry. In both directions the tunnel looked deserted. Seeing no sign of hostility, Giordino rushed into the Snow Cruiser and climbed the ladder to the control cabin. He found Pitt smiling hideously through a mask of blood.

"You look bad," he said, attempting to help Pitt from the driver's seat.

Pitt gently pushed him away. "It's not nearly as bad as it looks. We can't afford time for a clinical repair. You can patch me up with that old first-aid kit in the crew cabin. In the meantime, I vote we follow the tunnel toward the left. Unless I miss my guess, that will lead us to the mining compound."

Giordino knew it was senseless to contest the issue. He dropped down to the crew cabin and returned with a first-aid kit that hadn't been opened since 1940. He cleaned away the congealing blood on Pitt's face, then smeared the cuts with the antiseptic of the era, iodine, whose sharp sting had Pitt cursing in no quiet tones. Then he dressed the skin cuts. "Another life saved by the capable hands of Dr. Giordino, surgeon of the Antarctic."

Pitt looked into the face that was reflected in a side-view mirror. There was enough gauze and tape to cover a brain transplant. "What did you do?" he asked sourly. "I look like a mummy."

Giordino feigned a hurt look. "Aesthetics is not one of my strong points."

"Neither is medicine."

Pitt gunned the engines and maneuvered the hulking vehicle back and forth until he was able to straighten it around for a journey through the tunnel. For the first time, he wound down his window and studied the width of the tunnel. He figured the clearance between the ice and the vehicle's wheel hubs and its roof was no more than eighteen inches. He turned his attention to a large round pipe that ran along the outer arc of the tunnel, with small tubes running vertically from its core into the ice.

"What do you make of that?" he said, pointing to the pipe.

Giordino stepped from the Snow Cruiser, squeezed himself between the front tire and the pipe, and laid his hands on it. "Not an electrical conduit," he announced. "It must serve another purpose."

"If it's what I think it is . . ." Pitt's voice dropped portentously.

"Part of the mechanism to break loose the ice shelf," said Giordino, finishing his friend's train of thought.

Pitt stuck his head out his window and stared back into the long tunnel that stretched away to a vanishing point. "It must extend from the mining compound fourteen hundred miles to the opposite end of the ice shelf."

"An inconceivable feat of engineering to bore a tunnel that was equal to the distance between San Francisco and Phoenix."

"Inconceivable or not," said Pitt, "the Wolfs did it. You must remember, it's much easier to bore a tunnel through ice than hard rock."

"What if we cut a gap in the line and stop whatever activation system they've created to split off the ice shelf?" asked Giordino.

"A break might trigger it prematurely," answered Pitt. "We can't take the chance unless we find ourselves left with no other alternative. Only then can we risk dividing the line."

The tunnel looked like a great gaping black mouth. Except for the dim glow of the sun through the thick ice, there was no illumination. An electrical conduit with halogen bulbs spaced every twenty feet ran along the ceiling, but the power must have been shut down at the main junction box, because the lights were dark. Pitt turned on the two small headlights mounted on the lower front end of the Snow Cruiser, engaged gears, and drove off, increasing his speed through the tunnel until they were moving at twenty-five miles an hour. Though it was a pace easily sustained by a bicycle rider, it seemed a breakneck speed through the narrow confines of the tunnel.

While Pitt focused on keeping the Snow Cruiser from brushing against the unsympathetic ice, Giordino sat in the passenger seat, his rifle propped on one knee, eyes fastened as far as the headlights could throw their beams, watching for a sign of movement or any object other than the seemingly unending pipe with its intersecting tubes that ran down into the floor and through the roof of the tunnel.

The ominous fact that the tunnel was deserted suggested to Pitt that the Wolfs and their workers were abandoning the mining facility and preparing to escape to their giant ships. He pushed the Snow Cruiser as fast as it would go, occasionally spinning the wheel hubs into the ice walls and carving a trench before steering the vehicle straight again. Dread began clouding his mind. They had lost too much time crossing the ice shelf. The timetable that Karl Wolf had boasted of in Buenos Aires at the ambassador's party had been four days and ten hours.

The four days had passed, as had eight hours and forty minutes, leaving only an hour and twenty minutes until Karl Wolf threw the doomsday switch.

Pitt estimated that one mile, maybe one and half, separated them from the heart of the facility. He and Giordino were not given satellite maps of the layout, so finding the control center once they were inside would be pure guesswork. The questions nagging his mind were whether the Special Forces team had arrived and had been successful in eliminating the army of mercenaries. The latter would put up a bitter fight—the Wolfs had surely promised to save them and their families from the cataclysm. Any way he looked at it, the thought did not present a rosy picture.

AFTER another eighteen minutes of negotiating the tunnel in silence, Giordino hunched forward and gestured ahead. "We're coming to a crossroads."

Pitt slowed the Snow Cruiser, as they came to an intersection where five tunnels spread off into the ice. The dilemma was maddening. Time did not allow them to make the wrong choice. He leaned out the side window again and studied the frozen floor of the tunnel. Wheeled tracks branched into them all, but the deepest ruts appeared to travel into the one on the right. "The tube on the right looks like it's had the heaviest traffic."

Giordino jumped down out of the Snow Cruiser and disappeared up the tunnel. In a few minutes, he returned. "About two hundred yards farther on, it looks like the tunnel opens into a large chamber."

Pitt gave a brief nod and turned the vehicle and followed the tracks into the tunnel on his right. Strange structures began appearing locked in the ice, vague and indistinguishable but with the straight lines of objects that were man-made rather than a creation of nature. As Giordino had reported, the tunnel soon widened into a vast chamber whose curved roof was covered by ice crystals that hung down like stalactites.

Light filtered down from several openings in the roof that illuminated the interior with an eerie glow. The effect seemed extraterrestrial, magical, timeless, and miraculous. Awed by the sight, Pitt slowly brought the Snow Cruiser to a halt.

The two men went silent in astonishment.

They found themselves parked in what was once the main square, surrounded by the icebound buildings of an ancient city.

42

No longer covered by the security blanket of the ice storm, the wind having dropped to only five miles an hour, Cleary felt naked, as his white-clad force fanned out and began advancing toward the mining facility. They took advantage of a series of hummocks that rose like camel humps for cover, until they reached the high fence that ran from the base of the mountain to the cliff above the sea and encircled the main compound.

Cleary had no prior intelligence on the force his men were up against. None had been gathered on the facility, simply because the CIA had never considered it a threat to the nation's security. Discovering the true horror of the menace at the last minute had left no time for covert penetration, nor had this simple hit-and-run strategy. It was a surgical operation, uncomplicated, requiring a quick conclusion. The orders were to neutralize the facility and deactivate the ice shelf breakaway systems before being relieved by a two-hundred-man Special Force team that was only an hour away.

All Cleary had been told was that the Wolf security guards were hardened professionals who came from elite fighting units around the

world. This was information provided by the National Underwater &
Marine Agency—hardly an organization practiced in intelligence gathering, Cleary mistakenly concluded. He was confident his elite force
could handle any hostiles they encountered.

Little did he know that his small force was outnumbered three to
one.

Moving in two columns, they reached what at first looked like a single fence but became two that were divided by a ditch. It looked to
Cleary as if it had been built decades before. There was an old sign
whose paint was badly faded but could still be translated as 'No Trespassing' in German. Made up of a common chain link, it was topped
by several strings of wire whose barbs had become impotent long before from a thick coating of ice. Once many feet higher than now, ice
drifts had built up against it until one could easily hoist one leg and step
over it. The ditch had also filled in and was little more than a low,
rounded furrow. The second fence was higher and still protruded seven
feet above the snow, but posed no serious hazard. They lost precious
minutes cutting through the strands until they could enter the grounds
of the compound. Cleary took it as a good omen that they had penetrated the outer perimeter without discovery.

Once inside, their movements were shielded by a row of buildings
with no windows. Cleary called a halt. He paused to examine a fifteen-
by-eighteen-inch aerial photo of the compound. Though he had etched
every street, every structure, in his mind during the flight from Cape
Town, as had Sharpsburg, Garnet, and Jacobs, he wanted to compare
a mark on the map to where they had passed through the outer fences.
He was pleased to see they were only fifty feet from their intended infiltration point. For the first time since they had landed, regrouped,
and advanced across the ice, he spoke into the Motorola radio.

"Tin Man?"

"I copy you, Wizard," replied the gravel voice of Lieutenant Warren
Garnet.

"We split up here," said Cleary. "You know what is expected of you
and your Marines. Good luck."

"On our way, Wizard," acknowledged Garnet, whose mission, as assigned to his Marine Recon Team, was to secure the generating plant and cut off all power to the facility.

"Scarecrow?"

Lieutenant Miles Jacobs of the Navy SEALs answered quickly. "I hear you, Wizard." Jacobs and his team were to circle around and assault the control center from the side facing the sea.

"You have the farthest to go, Scarecrow. You'd better get a move on."

"We're halfway there," Jacobs replied confidently, as he and his SEALs began moving out down a side road that led in the direction of the control center.

"Lion?"

"Ready to sweep," answered Captain Sharpsburg of the Army Delta Force cheerfully.

"I will accompany you."

"Happy to have an old hand along."

"Let's move out."

There was no synchronizing of watches, no further voice contact, as the teams divided and made their way to their assigned targets. There was no need. They all knew what they had to do, having been fully briefed on the horrendous consequences should they fail. Cleary had no doubts that his men would fight like demons or die without hesitation to stop the Wolfs from launching the apocalypse.

They moved lightly, almost fluidly, in offensive formation, two men ten yards ahead on either flank, and two men covering their rear. Every fifty yards, they stopped, dropped to the ground, or took whatever available cover presented itself, while Cleary studied the terrain and checked with the Marines and the SEAL teams.

"Tin Man, report."

"Sweep is clear. Approaching within three hundred yards of target."

"Scarecrow? Have you encountered anything?"

"If I wasn't sure, I'd say the place is abandoned," answered Jacobs.

Cleary did not reply. He rose from his crouched position as Sharpsburg moved his Lion team forward.

On the face of it, the facility seemed like a bleak and austere layout. Cleary saw nothing special about it, but then trepidation began to mount. The compound appeared totally deserted. No workers showed themselves. No vehicles moved. It was too quiet. The entire inner compound was cloaked in a cold, eerie silence.

KARL Wolf stared at an array of monitors in the headquarters of his security guards on a floor below the main control center. He watched with bemused interest as Cleary and his assault teams made their way through the roads of the complex.

"You'll have no problem preventing them from interrupting our launch time?" he asked Hugo, who was standing next to him.

"None," Hugo assured him. "We have contemplated and drilled for such an intrusion many times. Our fortifications are in place, the barricades raised, and our armored Sno-cats awaiting my orders to move into battle."

Karl nodded in satisfaction. "You have done well. Still, these are the elite of the American fighting forces."

"Not to worry, brother. My men are just as well trained as the Americans. We heavily outnumber them and have the advantage of fighting on our ground. The element of surprise is in our favor, not theirs. They do not suspect that they are walking into a trap. And we can travel through the facility's underground utility tunnels, emerge inside buildings, and attack their flanks and rear before they realize what is happening."

"Your overall strategy?" Karl asked.

"To gradually siphon them into a pocket in front of the control center, where we can destroy them at our leisure."

"Our ancestors who fought so many heroic battles against the Allies during the war would be proud of you."

Obviously pleased by his brother's compliment, Hugo clicked his heels and made a stiff bow. "I am honored to serve the Fourth Empire." Then he looked up and gazed at the monitors, studying the progress of the American fighting teams. "I must go now, brother, and direct our defenses."

"How long do you estimate it will take your men to crush the attackers?"

"Thirty minutes, certainly no more."

"That doesn't leave you and your men much time to reach and board the aircraft. Do not delay, Hugo. I have no wish to leave you and your brave men behind."

"And lose our dream of becoming the founding fathers of a brave new world?" Hugo said spiritedly. "I don't think so."

Karl motioned toward the digital clock mounted between the monitors. "Twenty-five minutes from now, we shall set the ice shelf detaching systems on automatic. Then everyone in the control center will leave through the underground tunnel that leads to the worker's main dormitory safely beyond the battlefield. From there, we'll take electric vehicles to the aircraft hangar."

"We shall not fail," said Hugo, with iron resolve.

"Then good luck to you," said Karl. He solemnly shook Hugo's hand, before turning and stepping into the elevator that would take him to the control room above.

CLEARY and the Lion team were only a hundred and fifty yards from the entrance of the control center when Garnet's voice came over his intercom. "Wizard, this is Tin Man. There's something wrong here. . . ."

In that instant, Cleary spotted the barricade blocking the road in front of the control center, saw the dark muzzles of guns propped on its crest. He opened his mouth to shout, but it was too late. A deafening volley laid down by the security guards exploded in front of the Delta Force from every direction. The blasts from two hundred guns swamped and reverberated off the walls of the buildings, cutting the icy air with a deafening roar.

Garnet and his Marines were caught in the open and exposed, but they laid down a covering fire and took whatever cover they could find along the buildings. Despite the ruthless fusillade, they continued advancing toward the power station, until Garnet recognized an ice barricade that was nearly impossible to distinguish against the white background until he was less than a hundred yards away. His men began a counterfire, firing their Eradicator rifles' fragmentation missiles at the security guards behind the barricades.

In front of the control center, at almost the same moment, Cleary found himself facing the same type of ice wall and blistering fire that Garnet was experiencing. Vulnerable to the heavy fire, the lead man on the left flank of the Delta Force caught bullets in a knee and thigh and he went down. Moving flat on his stomach, Sharpsburg grabbed the wounded man by his boots and pulled him around the corner of the building.

Cleary ducked below a stairway leading into a small storehouse. Shards of ice rained down on his shoulders as a stream of shells burst into the icicles hanging from the roof above him. Then a shot struck his body armor square-on above his heart, sending him staggering backward, alive but with a pain in his chest as if someone were pounding it with a sledgehammer. Sergeant Carlos Mendoza, who was the best shot of the team, lined up the crosshairs through the scope of his Eradicator on the Wolf security guard who'd shot Cleary and squeezed the trigger. A black figure jerked up from the crest of the barricade before falling back and disappearing. The sergeant then selected his next target and fired away.

More bullets slammed into the roof above Cleary, scattering ice slivers in a hundred different directions. He saw too late that Wolf's security force was prepared and waiting for them. The fortifications had been designed and constructed for just such an attack. He painfully discovered that the lack of proper intelligence was killing them. He also began to perceive that his attacking force was badly outnumbered by the defenders.

Cleary cursed himself for relying on untested information. He cursed the Pentagon and the Central Intelligence Agency, who'd estimated the Wolf security force at no more than twenty to twenty-five men. He cursed his lack of intuition, and in the heat of the moment he cursed himself for making the biggest mistake in his military life. He had badly underestimated his enemy.

"Tin Man!" he shouted into his microphone. "Report your situation!"

"I count sixty or more hostiles blocking the road in front of us," Garnet's voice replied in a monotone, as steady as if he were describing cows in a pasture. "We are under heavy fire."

"Can you force the issue and secure the power plant?"

"We are unable to advance due to extremely accurate fire. These are not your garden-variety security people we're facing. They know what they're doing. Can you send a team to relieve the pressure, Wizard? If we could band together in a flanking movement, I think we can take the barricade."

"Negative, Tin Man," replied Cleary. He well knew that the Recons were the elite of the Marine Corps. If they couldn't advance, nobody could. "We're also halted by heavy fire from at least eighty hostiles and cannot send support. I repeat, I cannot spare men to support you. Extricate as best you can and link up with Lion."

"Understood, Wizard. Withdrawing now."

With his Marines open and exposed, Garnet was frustrated to learn that he could expect no support, but had to retreat and find Cleary and Sharpsburg's Delta Force team through the maze of roads running through the facility. He wasted no time in considering going against orders and continuing the assault. Charging a barricade manned by three times his force across an open road was suicidal and would accomplish nothing but the massacre of his command. He was left with no choice but to begin an orderly withdrawal, carrying out their wounded as they withdrew from the murderous fire.

Having advanced halfway around the control center, Jacobs and his SEALs were jolted by the thunder of conflict and the shocking reports from Cleary and Garnet. He urged his men forward in hopes of securing the control center from the rear and removing the heat from teams Tin Man and Lion. The SEALs were only a hundred yards from the control center building when two armored Sno-cats turned the corner ahead and opened fire on them.

Jacobs watched helplessly as two of his men were cut down. Madder than hell, he held the trigger on his Eradicator rifle until the final round ejected from the clip, then his sergeant grabbed him by the collar of his parka and pushed him behind a trash bin before a barrage of counterfire could strike him. A volley of fragmentation missiles from the SEAL team temporarily halted the Sno-cats, but they began to come on again.

The SEALs fought tenaciously as they executed their withdrawal up the road, using whatever cover they could find. Then, unexpectedly, two more Sno-cats suddenly appeared at their rear and unleashed a torrent of fire. Jacobs felt a knot form in his stomach. He and his team had nowhere to go except into a narrow side alleyway. He prayed they were not being forced into an ambush, but the alley looked clear for at least seventy yards.

As he ran after his men, hoping they could reach cover before the Sno-cats turned the corner of the alley and achieved a field of unobstructed fire, he reported to Cleary. "Wizard, this is Scarecrow. We are under attack by four armored Sno-cats."

"Scarecrow, do they carry heavy weapons?"

"None that show. I make four hostiles with automatic weapons in each vehicle. Our fragmentation missiles have little effect on them."

Cleary crawled under a stairway, using it as a shield, and studied his map of the mining facility. "Give me your location, Scarecrow."

"We are moving down a narrow road toward the sea behind what looks like a row of maintenance shops about a hundred and fifty yards from the control center."

"Scarecrow, go another fifty yards, then bend a right turn and advance between a series of fuel storage tanks. That should bring you close to the front of the control center from a side road, where you can flank the hostiles pinning us down."

"Roger that, Wizard. On our way." Then, as an afterthought, Jacobs asked, "What have we got for defense against the armored Sno-cats?"

"Tin Man has two LAWs."

"We'll need four."

"The man carrying the other two went missing during the jump."

"Tin Man is at the power station," Jacobs said, frustrated. "He's not facing the armored cats, we are."

"I ordered him to withdraw from his objective because of overwhelming concentrated fire. He should be converging with Lion shortly."

"Tell him to load up, because four of those nasty vehicles will be right on our tail when we step into your front yard."

Jacobs and the SEALs soon circled the fuel storage tanks without encountering organized gunfire. Frequently glancing at his map of the facility, he led his men around a long wall that appeared to end near the front of the control center. It seemed like perfect cover, as they rushed to outflank the security guards behind the barrier who were blasting hell out of Sharpsburg and his Delta Force. Hardly had the SEALs come within fifty yards of the end of the wall when a blaze of concentrated fire struck them from the rear.

Unknown to them, a group of security guards had rushed through an underground tunnel and appeared from a building behind, a tactic that was happening with increasing frequency. Jacobs saw that it was virtually impossible to continue on his flanking maneuver, so he took his men along the path of least resistance and led them down a street strangely free of hostile gunfire.

Only eighty yards away, Cleary lay flat and peered through his binoculars, searching for a weak spot in the barricade blocking the entrance to the control center. He found none and realized that, like Garnet's, his position was rapidly becoming untenable, yet he was determined to make an assault on the control center as soon as he was reinforced by the Marine Recon Team, and the SEALs had begun their flanking attack on the barricade.

But down deep, doubts were starting to form as to whether he could still pull the coals of final victory out of the fire.

THE security guards were waging war with a vengeance. In their minds, they were fighting not only for their own lives but for the lives of their families who were waiting on board the *Ulrich Wolf*. Hugo himself was in the thick of the fighting in front of the control center, directing his forces and tightening the noose on the American assault team. His arrogance while issuing orders reflected his supreme confidence and optimism. His battle strategy was going exactly as he'd planned it. Hugo was in the enviable position of a commander who could dictate the terms of the fight.

He was flushing his enemy into one concentrated area for annihilation, as he had promised his brother Karl.

He spoke into an intercom mike inside his battle helmet. "Brother Karl?"

There was a moment or two of slight static before Karl responded. "Yes, Hugo."

"The intruders are contained. You and Elsie and the others can leave for the hangar as soon as the engineers set the nanotech systems on automatic."

"Thank you, brother. I'll soon meet you at the aircraft."

Two minutes later, as Hugo was ordering his two remaining armored Sno-cats to charge the American team, a security guard rushed to him behind the barricade and shouted, "Sir, I have an urgent message from the aircraft hangar!"

"What is it?" Hugo yelled above the gunfire.

But in that instant, Sergeant Mendoza squinted at the head behind the crosshairs inside his sniper scope and gently pulled the trigger of his Eradicator. The guard dropped dead at Hugo's feet, neither hearing nor feeling the bullet enter his right temple and exit the left. The message he had urgently wished to report, on the destruction in the aircraft hangar by a strange vehicle, died with him.

GARNET'S Marines linked up with Sharpsburg's Delta team and took cover, as the four Sno-cats withdrew from chasing Jacobs and attacked them in a double column from the rear. They came on oblivious to the two antitank weapons aimed at them by the Marines, who at less than a hundred yards couldn't miss. The lead Sno-cats went up in an explosion of fire and flying debris and bodies, forming an effective roadblock that prevented the remaining vehicles from striking the already beleaguered Americans.

Cleary realized quickly that the reprieve had only short-term benefits and was temporary. It would be only a question of time before the security guards wised up to the fact that no more antitank shells were being fired because the supply was exhausted. Then the armored Sno-cats would attack, and there would be no stopping them. When Jacobs and his team hit the barricade from the flank, hopefully the advantage would swing to their side.

IN Washington, the battlefield reports from the men under fire made it evident that the assault force was in deep trouble. It was becoming more obvious by the minute that Cleary and his men were being shot to pieces. The President and the Joint Chiefs could not believe what they heard. What had been launched as a daring mission had turned into a slaughter and a disaster. They were shocked by the growing realization that the mission had failed, and that the entire inhabited world was in jeopardy of vanishing, a nightmare they found impossible to accept.

"The aircraft carrying the main force," the President said, his thinking becoming disoriented, "when . . . ?"

"They won't be over the compound for another forty minutes," answered General South

"And the countdown?"

"Twenty-two minutes until the currents are right for the ice shelf to break off."

"Then we've got to send in the missiles."

"We will be killing our own men as well," cautioned General South.

"Do we have another option?" the President put to him.

South looked down at his open hands and slowly shook his head. "No, Mr. President, we don't."

Admiral Eldridge asked, "Shall I alert the commander of the *Tucson* to launch missiles?"

"If I may suggest," said the Air Force chief of staff, General Coburn, "I think it best that we send in the Stealth bombers. Their aircrews are more accurate in guiding their missiles to a target than an unmanned Tomahawk launched from a submarine."

The President quickly made his decision. "All right, alert the bomber pilots, but tell them not to fire until ordered. We never know when a miracle might happen and Major Cleary can force his way into the control center and halt the countdown."

As General Coburn issued the order, General South muttered under his breath, "A miracle is exactly what it will take."

43

STREETS RAN OFF THE square between buildings that protruded from the ice. They were not on the massive scale of much later civilizations, but their architectural characteristics were unlike any Pitt and Giordino had ever seen in their travels. There was no telling how many acres or square miles the city covered. What they saw was only a fraction of the magnificence that was the Amenes.

Rising up from one end of the square, an immense, richly ornate structure with triangular columns supported a pediment decorated with fleets of ancient ships in relief over a frieze carved with intricate sculptures of animals mingling with people wearing the same dress found on the mummies at St. Paul Island. The basic design of the colossal building was unlike any still standing from the ancient world. It would have been obvious to the eye of an architect that its basic structural form had been passed down through the millennia and copied by later builders of the great temples of Luxor, Athens, and Rome. The columns, however, were triangular, and looked foreign when compared to the much later round, fluted Doric, Ionic, and Corinthian columns.

A large entrance yawned beyond the columns. There were no stairs.

The upper levels were reached by gradually sloping ramps. Spellbound, Pitt and Giordino exited the Snow Cruiser and walked past the columns. Inside the main chamber, a vast corbeled triangular roof soared above the ice-covered, rock-hewn floor. In huge niches along the walls were stone statues of what must have been Amenes kings, powerful-looking creations with round eyes and narrow faces carved out of granite rich in quartz that shimmered as they walked past them. Sculptured heads of men and a few women were set in the floor, staring upward through their thin coating of ice, with Amenes inscriptions engraved above and below them.

In the center of the great chamber, a life-size sculpture of an ancient ship, complete with banks of oars, full sails, and crews, stood on a pedestal. The sight was nothing less than spectacular. The sheer artistry, craft, and technical mastery of stone gave it an eerie mystique that mocked modern sculpture.

"What do you make of it?" asked Giordino reverently, as if he were standing in a cathedral. "A temple to their gods?"

"More likely a mausoleum or a shrine," said Pitt, gesturing at the heads rising from the floor. "These look like memorials, perhaps to revered men and women who explored the ancient world and those who were lost at sea."

"It's amazing the roof didn't collapse after the comet's impact or the later accumulation of ice."

"Their builders must have worked under exceptionally high standards that were possible only under a structured culture."

They gazed in fascination down a network of windowless corridors whose interior walls were beautifully painted with scenes of spectacular seascapes that began with calm waters and progressed to waves whipped by hurricane furies beating against rocky shorelines. If modern men and women looked to the heavens for their God, the Amenes had looked to the seas. Their statuaries were of men and women, not stylized versions of gods.

"A long-lost race who discovered the world," Giordino said philosophically. "And yet there are no artifacts lying around, and no sign of the inhabitants' remains."

Pitt nodded at the network of narrow passages carved into the ice.

"No doubt recovered by the Nazis who discovered it, and later taken by the Wolfs to their museums on board the *Ulrich Wolf*."

"Doesn't look like they excavated more than ten percent of the city."

"They had more mundane things on their mind," said Pitt sardonically, "like hiding Nazi treasures and secret relics, extracting gold from seawater, and planning to destroy the world so they could make it over into *their* image."

"Too bad we haven't the time to explore the place."

"There's nothing I'd like better than to take the grand tour," said Pitt, shaking off his captivation, "but we have twenty-five minutes or less to find the control center."

Wishing they could linger, Pitt and Giordino reluctantly turned their backs on the great edifice and hurried back to the square and climbed into the Snow Cruiser. Still following the tracks left by a Sno-cat, Pitt steered the big cruiser through the heart of the haunting ghost city and rolled it into a tunnel beyond the mausoleum of the Amenes. Pitt drove less cautiously the closer they came to the mining compound, while Giordino crouched below the instrument panel with his Bushmaster sticking through the shattered middle windshield.

Almost a mile deeper into the tunnel, they rounded a bend and found themselves confronted with an electric auto coming in the opposite direction. The three startled security guards in the other vehicle, easily recognizable in their black uniforms, stared incredulously at the monster bearing down on them. The driver panicked and slammed on his brakes, skidding across the ice floor of the tunnel without reducing his speed in the slightest. The other two guards had a higher regard for self-preservation and leaped from the auto in a futile attempt at prolonging their lives.

There was a series of shrill screeches from shredding and grinding metal as the Snow Cruiser smashed into the electric auto and rolled over it as though it were a tricycle mashed by a garbage truck. The driver disappeared, along with his crumpled vehicle, under the Cruiser, while the other two guards were crushed against the ice walls of the tunnel by the great tires. As Pitt stared back in his side-view mirror, he saw only a pile of twisted junk sitting flattened on the floor of the tunnel.

Giordino twisted around in his seat and stared back through the slanted rear window of the control cab. "I hope you paid your insurance premiums."

"Only liability and property damage. I never take out collision."

"You should reconsider."

Another two hundred yards through the tunnel, groups of workers in red coveralls were moving wooden crates onto a train of flatbed cars that were connected to a large Sno-cat. Forklifts were transporting the crates past a thick silver steel door whose mounting bolts led deep into the ice. The massive door looked like the types that were used in banks to safeguard the contents of their vaults. A short entryway through the ice led into a spacious cavern.

Two security guards stood stunned at the sight of the gargantuan Snow Cruiser, plunging from what should have been an abandoned tunnel. They stood transfixed in the glare of the headlights. Only when Giordino fired a short burst from his Bushmaster through the broken windshield into the forklift did workers and security guards come alive and scramble back into the cavern to save themselves from being mashed by the mechanical avalanche bearing down on them.

"The door!" Pitt shouted, slamming on the brakes.

Giordino did not acknowledge or question. Almost as if he'd read Pitt's mind, he leaped from the Snow Cruiser and ran to the steel door, as Pitt squeezed off several rounds from his Colt .45 through the doorway to the cavern to cover him. Giordino was surprised by the light touch it took to push the door closed. He'd expected to exert every ounce of strength in his body, but the heavy steel door swung as easily as if it hung in air. Once it clicked against its stops, he turned the locking wheel until the bars slid into their sockets, sealing it closed. Then he found a chain on the forklift and wrapped it around the wheel, securing the end to a wheel of a flatbed car loaded with crates, until it was impossible to turn from the inside. Now the Wolf security guards and workers were effectively imprisoned without any prospect of a quick escape.

"I wonder what's inside the crates?" Giordino said, as he climbed back into the control cab.

"Artifacts from the city of the Amenes, I'd guess." Pitt ran the Snow Cruiser through the gears until he had regained top speed again. An angel perched on the roof of the cab might have helped them this far on their wild passage, but they still had a long way to go. True, surprise was theirs, but it seemed remarkable that they had come this far without a shot being fired at them, a situation that could quickly change, Pitt well knew. The powers of their angel had her limits, assuming that it was a she. Events had been met and overtaken. Once the Snow Cruiser burst out into the open, it would be a different story. Every gun in the compound would train on it.

At a wide bend in the tunnel, they suddenly burst out into the almost measureless hangar housing the Destiny Enterprises jet aircraft. Without lifting his foot from the gas pedal, Pitt quickly surveyed the two Airbus A340-300 passenger and cargo planes parked in the center of the hangar. A Sno-cat with a train of flatbed cars was stretched beneath the cargo door of the first aircraft, the familiar wooden crates riding up inside the fuselage on a conveyor belt. Wolf Enterprise engineers and workers were climbing boarding steps at the other plane for the trip to the giant superships. Sitting off to one side was a sleek executive jet that was in the process of being refueled.

Pitt relaxed slightly at seeing no security guards. "What have we here?"

"Ah-ha!" Giordino tensed, seeing Pitt's leg stiffen as if he were trying to push the accelerator pedal through the floorboard. He raised a prudent eye over the instrument panel and groaned softly. "Are you going to do what I think you're going to do?"

"Once you drive in a demolition derby," said Pitt, with a diabolical gleam in his eyes, "you never get it out of your blood."

The reaction from everyone in the hangar at seeing the Snow Cruiser appear out of nowhere was the same as that of the others who had confronted it in the tunnel earlier. They all froze in pure astonishment, the expressions on their faces quickly turning to incomprehension and cold fear at seeing a red mechanical demon incarnate burst out of nowhere.

Pitt took less than three seconds to assess his route of destruction. It took the same amount of time for all to realize that his intentions were unmistakable. With a mind-set two notches beyond tenacious, he set a course across the ice floor of the hangar, as straight as the crow flies, toward the first Airbus. The aircraft sat high off the ground, but not high enough for the side fenders of the Snow Cruiser. The right front panel immediately below the side windows of the control cabin caught the aircraft eight feet inside the aft section of the port wing, crushing the ailerons and shredding the wingtip.

The cargo loaders and aircraft maintenance crew were galvanized into action and flung themselves clear as the leviathan struck the aircraft, pivoting it around at a ninety-degree angle as the tires on the landing gear skidded over the ice. They sprawled, desperately slipping and scrambling to get as far away as possible from the thundering titan gone mad. The only sounds they identified were the engines racing through the gear changes. Nothing else about the giant machine looked remotely familiar. But they briefly glimpsed the face of a heavily bandaged Pitt twisting the steering wheel back and forth, and Giordino pointing his Bushmaster menacingly out the side window. They'd seen more than enough to call for security guards, but their frantic appeal came much too late to stop the destruction.

The Snow Cruiser ripped into the outer wing of the second Airbus. This time Pitt cut too far inside the wing. In a horrible screeching sound, the devastated wing jackknifed around the front end of the Snow Cruiser tire and hung there. Pitt crammed the gearshift into reverse and jammed down the gas pedal. The Cruiser backed up, pulling the aircraft with it. Pitt wrenched the steering wheel as far as it could go, desperately attempting to shake free from the aircraft, but the tangled wreckage held, and the Cruiser's mammoth tires began to lose their grip on the ice and spin uselessly.

Pitt threw the Snow Cruiser into forward and then reverse, as if he were trying to rock a car mired in mud. Finally, after a series of vicious metallic shrieks, the wing released its grip and dropped awkwardly, its wingtip touching the ice and looking like a piece of torn and tangled aluminum with a reservation at the scrap yard. Then, without flinching or betraying the slightest expression of emotion, Pitt pitched the Snow Cruiser in the direction of the executive jet.

"You don't screw around, do you?" Giordino said in resigned amusement.

"Listen!" Pitt snarled. "If this scum fixed it for an apocalypse to strike the world, they can damn well stay here and suffer along with everyone else."

The words were hardly out of his mouth when the battered Snow Cruiser pulverized the tail assembly of the Wolfs' private jet that sat much lower to the ground than the much larger aircraft. No contest this time, the Snow Cruiser ripped off the vertical and horizontal stabilizers as if they were a balsawood tail on a model airplane. Its fuselage effectively sliced into two parts, the executive jet collapsed disjointedly, the wings and bow pointing upward as if in a takeoff mode.

Giordino shook his head in wonder and said admiringly, "You'll never get invited back if you leave a mess everywhere you go."

Pitt turned to Giordino, a smile as wide as the horizon on his face. "Time sure flies when you're having fun."

Pitt looked up and saw a Sno-cat suddenly appear in the cracked and broken remains of the rearview mirror. He wasn't overly concerned, at least not yet. The Snow Cruiser, he estimated, was probably five miles an hour or more faster.

He threw the big Cruiser through the tunnel, striking and skidding off the ice walls in a daring attempt to inch ahead of the security guards in the Sno-cat. He careened through the bends, temporarily out of the line of fire, gaining time and widening the gap until the Sno-cat no longer came into view.

"You've lost them," said Giordino, brushing the shattered glass from the rear window off his shoulders as calmly as if it were dandruff.

"Not for long," said Pitt patiently. "Once we break into the open, we'll be fair game."

Four minutes later, they cleared the final bend in the tunnel, running past equipment that had been abandoned and doors leading into empty storerooms, and two minutes after that, the Snow Cruiser roared free under a blue sky, exiting less than half a mile from the center of the main compound.

At long last they reached their destination and had their view of the mining facility for the first time. They had exited the tunnel at one end of the compound. Unlike most ice stations, which were mostly buried under snow and ice, the Wolfs had kept the buildings and roads running between them swept clean and clear. The smaller buildings stood in circular fashion around the two main structures comprising the extraction plant and the control center.

The thunder of gunfire abruptly tore the chilling air, as flames clawed upward from several buildings, with black smoke rolling high into the sky before flattening under an inversion layer. Explosions sent debris flying into the air, accented with bursts from automatic weapons. Bodies could be seen sprawled in the streets, bloodied red and grotesque in the snow, two black uniforms for every one in white camouflage fatigues.

"It would appear," Pitt said grimly, "the party has started without us."

44

DESPITE THE LONG, HARD training, and the bravery and dedication of Team Apocalypse in attempting to stop the cataclysm, the mission was about to collapse. They were taking hits and falling wounded and dead for nothing. They had not achieved one fragment of advantage. Disaster was piling on disaster, when Cleary's worst fears were realized. Jacobs's SEALs, unable to strike the flank of the barricade, were inexorably driven into the same perimeter along with the other teams. The trap was complete. Every hole was plugged. The entire assault force was boxed in with no way out.

Grenade shrapnel slashed Cleary's chin and a bullet struck him in the hand. Of his officers, Sharpsburg was down with wounds in an arm and shoulder. Garnet was coughing blood from a hit in the throat. Only Jacobs was still unscathed, as he shouted encouragement to the men and directed their fire.

Then, unexpectedly, the security guards ceased firing. The Special Forces maintained a ragged counterfire until Cleary ordered them to stop all action, wondering what card the Wolfs were about to play next.

A voice, distinct and refined, came over loudspeakers on the buildings around the facility, echoing up and down the roads—a voice whose message was relayed to Washington through the microphones worn by the special force.

"Please give me your attention. This is Karl Wolf. I send greetings to the American assault teams who are attempting to infiltrate the Destiny Enterprises mining facility. You must know by now that you are heavily outnumbered, surrounded, and entrapped with no means of escape. Further bloodshed is pointless. I advise you to disengage and retire back to the ice shelf, where you can be evacuated by your own people. You will be allowed to carry your dead and wounded with you. If you do not comply in the next sixty seconds, you will all die. The choice is yours."

The message came as a jolt.

Cleary refused to accept inevitable defeat. He stared helplessly at the huddled and bullet-torn corpses of the dead and the bleeding bodies of the wounded. The eyes of those ready and able to fight on still reflected fearlessness and tenacity. They had fought savagely, bled, and died. They had given all that was humanly possible. But they could do no more than go down fighting, a last stand, unknown and unmourned.

The redoubtable Cleary by now had only twenty-six men in fighting condition left out of the original sixty-five who had parachuted from the C-17. They were assailed from the front and scourged from the rear by the remaining armored Sno-cats. He fought off a venomous pessimism and a bitterness he'd never known before. It seemed hopeless to mount another assault, but he was determined to make one more try. To push forward would amount to nothing more than a suicide charge. And yet there was no thought of disengaging. Every man knew that if they didn't die here and now, they would certainly die when the Earth went mad. With deep misgivings, Cleary regrouped what was left of his command for a final assault on the control center.

Then, in the silence of the temporary ceasefire, he heard what sounded like a car horn blaring in the distance. Soon it became louder, and every head on the battlefield turned and stared, mystified.

And then the thing was upon them.

"WHAT is happening?" Loren burst over the murmur of male voices at hearing the vocal burst of confusion over the speakers.

Everyone in the war rooms of the Pentagon and White House automatically glanced up at the monitors displaying static photos of the facility. For long, disbelieving moments, everyone sat in open amazement, listening spellbound to what they heard through the communications speakers.

"My God!" Admiral Eldridge uttered in a stunned croak.

"What in the devil is going on down there?" demanded the President.

"I have no idea, Mr. President," muttered General South, unable to comprehend the chaotic words of the Special Forces teams, who all seemed to be shouting at once. "I have no idea," he repeated vaguely.

SOMETHING totally macabre was happening on the battle site of the mining facility. The men of the Special Forces team, as well as the security guards, swung in shock. Cleary found himself staring through unblinking eyes with a stark, unfettered expression of bewilderment at a monstrous red juggernaut rolling on enormous donut tires that burst into view like a crazy man's nightmare. He watched in hypnotic fascination as the giant vehicle smashed into both armored Sno-cats, knocking them on their sides and squashing them, as the force of the impact hurled the startled guards into the air before they fell in broken heaps on the ice. Flames mushroomed in curling spires over a bursting canopy of screeching, tumbling doors, tractor treads, steel splinters, and armor plate. The monster never slowed, its driver never decelerating, as it relentlessly continued its spree of destruction.

Jacobs shouted for his men to leap aside, as Sharpsburg, in frantic disregard for his wounds, scrambled out of the way of the rapidly approaching monster. Garnet and his team gawked in blank disbelief, before they were abruptly galvanized into diving against the walls of the buildings to save themselves.

Then the thing was upon them, rushing past with an earsplitting roar from the exhaust headers whose mufflers had been torn off when crashing into the Sno-cats. It was a sound that none of the warriors, crouched dazed and stunned in the snow, could ever forget. And then it rampaged into the ice barricade as if it were made of cardboard.

The security guards froze in stunned astonishment along with every member of the Special Forces team, wounded or not, and watched in involuntary fascination as the colossus, not content with demolishing the barricade, rumbled on toward the high archway entrance of the control center like an out-of-control express train, callous of the devastation it was causing.

Bedlam! Security guards came alive and scattered frantically in every direction, trying to leap clear. For that one brief, fleeting moment, Cleary couldn't believe the rescuer of his command hadn't really been the work of aliens or demons from a hallucination. The curtain quickly parted in Cleary's mind and he realized that, thanks to the ponderous machine, victory had suddenly risen from the ashes.

Cleary always retained an image of that grand vehicle, its red paint transparent and glistening under the bright sun, its driver gripping the steering wheel with one hand, the other firing an old 1911-model Colt automatic out the window at the security guards as fast as he could pull the trigger, while another man sprayed any black uniform that moved with a Bushmaster rifle. It was a spectacle entirely unexpected, without precedent, a spectacle to make men doubt their sanity.

The thirty or fewer security guards who had not been laid dead and injured by the Special Force teams, and who'd survived the onslaught, soon recovered and began blasting at the murderous, freakish vehicle. Their gunfire slammed deafeningly in wave after wave. Bullets peppered the red body and great tires, tearing into metal and rubber, and still the monster refused to stop, horns atop the roof still trumpeting until they were shot away. Every shard of glass was shot out of the control cabin, and still the driver and his passenger blazed away at the security guards.

With brutal ferocity and with appalling savagery, the Snow Cruiser slammed into the control center, hurling her thirty-plus-ton mass, propelled at twenty miles an hour, through the metal walls and roof surrounding the entrance like a fist ramming into the front door of a dollhouse. The shattering impact tore off the roof of the Cruiser's control cabin as cleanly as if it had been chopped away by a giant ax. The front end of the raging monster crumpled as she bit deeply and plunged into the control room in a chaos of tearing, twisting metal and an explosion of electronic equipment, wiring, office furniture, and computer systems.

Her great body rent by a hurricane of small-arms fire, the control cabin nearly disintegrated, the massive tires torn to shreds and sitting flat under the wheels, the Snow Cruiser lost her momentum, rammed into the far wall, and finally came to a stop.

At such times, logic vanishes and men rise magnificently to the occasion. Stirred to action, shouting and cursing and without a spoken command, the surviving Marines, Delta Force, and SEALs leaped from their pitifully sheltered positions in the ice and rushed forward. Running through the breach left by the Snow Cruiser, they overran the barricade, concentrating their fire and eliminating most of the surprised security guards, who were caught unaware of the assault while they were still concentrating their attention and fire on the rampaging vehicle.

HUGO Wolf stood in pure horror. The gigantic red monstrosity from nowhere had, within the space of two short minutes, turned the tide of battle, wiping out two Sno-cats and their crews, and crushing nearly twenty of his men. Like a football quarterback who'd thrown a surefire touchdown pass in the closing minutes of the game, only to have the ball intercepted by the opposing team and run back for a touchdown, Hugo could not believe it was happening. Abruptly overtaken by panic, he leaped astride a nearby snowmobile, gunned the engine, and roared away from the turmoil toward the aircraft hangar.

Left abandoned and leaderless, the security guards saw faint hope of escape, and one by one, they surrendered their weapons and placed their hands on their heads. A few melted away and circled Cleary's assault teams in an attempt to reach the hangar before the aircraft took off. Suddenly, mercifully, the scene of carnage became strangely still and quiet. The bloody and nasty fight was over.

THE control room was in unspeakable shambles. Consoles had been catapulted from their bases and hurled against the walls. The contents of desks, shelves, and cabinets were spilled across the floor, carpeting it in files and paper. Tables and chairs were twisted and smashed. Monitors hung from their mountings in crazy angles. The Snow Cruiser sat astride the insane havoc like some great wounded dinosaur, showered by a thousand bullets. Astoundingly, she did not die. In defiance of all the laws of mechanical engineering, her diesels still turned over at idle, with a low rapping sound coming from her shattered exhaust pipes.

Pitt pushed aside the bullet-riddled door of the Snow Cruiser and carelessly watched it drop off its fractured hinges and fall away. Remarkably, he and Giordino had not been killed. Bullets had cut through their clothes, Pitt had taken a shot that had cut a small gouge in his left forearm, and Giordino was bleeding from a scalp wound, but they had survived without serious injury, far beyond their wildest expectations.

Pitt searched the mangled control room for bodies, but the Wolfs, their engineers, and their scientists had evacuated the building for the hangar. Giordino stared through those smiling yet brooding dark eyes of his at the scene of havoc.

"Is the clock still ticking?" he asked gravely.

"I don't think so." Pitt nodded at the remains of the digital clock lying amid the debris and pointed at the numerals. They were frozen at ten minutes and twenty seconds. "By destroying the computers and all electronic systems, we stopped the countdown sequence."

"No ice shelf breaking and drifting out to sea?"

Pitt simply shook his head.

"No end of the earth?"

"No end of the earth," Pitt echoed.

"Then it's over," Giordino muttered, finding it hard to believe that what had begun in a mine in Colorado had finally reached a conclusion in a demolished room in the Antarctic.

"Almost." Pitt leaned weakly against the wrecked Snow Cruiser, feeling relief dulled with anger against Karl Wolf. "There are still a few loose ends we have to tie up."

Giordino stared as if he were on another planet. "Ten minutes and twenty seconds," he said slowly. "Could the world have really come that close to oblivion?"

"If the Valhalla Project had truly gone operational? Probably. Could it have truly altered Earth for thousands of years? Hopefully, we'll never know."

"Do not move a finger or twitch an eye!" The command came as hard as cold marble.

Pitt looked up and found himself face-to-face with a figure in white fatigues pointing a mutant-looking firearm at him. The stranger was bleeding from the chin and a wound in one hand.

Pitt stared at the apparition, trying unsuccessfully to gauge the eyes behind the polarized goggles.

"Can I wiggle my ears?" he asked, perfectly composed.

From his point of view, Cleary couldn't be sure whether the nondescript characters standing in front of him represented enemy or friend. The shorter one looked like a pit bull. The taller of the two was disheveled and had slipshod bandages covering half his face. They looked like men dead on their feet, their gaunt, barely focused, sunken eyes set over cheeks and jaws showing the early stages of scraggly beards. "Who are you and where did you two characters come from, wise mouth?"

"My name is Dirk Pitt. My friend is Al Giordino. We're with the National Underwater and Marine Agency."

"NUMA," Cleary repeated, finding the answer little short of lunacy. "Is that a fact?"

"It's a fact," Pitt answered, perfectly composed. "Who are you?"

"Major Tom Cleary, United States Army Special Forces. I'm in command of the team that assaulted the facility."

"I'm sorry we couldn't have arrived sooner and saved more of your men," Pitt said sincerely.

Cleary's shoulders sagged and he lowered his gun. "No better men have died today."

Pitt and Giordino said nothing. There was nothing fitting they could say.

Finally, Cleary straightened. "I can't believe a couple of oceanographic people from NUMA, untrained to fight hostiles, could do so much damage," said Cleary, still trying to figure the men standing in front of him.

"Saving you and your men was a spur-of-the-moment action. Stopping the Wolfs from launching a cataclysm was our primary goal."

"And did you accomplish it?" asked Cleary, looking around at the wreckage of what had once been a high-tech operational control center, "or is the clock still ticking?"

"As you can see," Pitt replied, "all electronic functions are disabled. The electronic commands to activate the ice-cutting machines have been terminated."

"Thank God," Cleary said, the stress and strain suddenly falling from his shoulders. He wearily removed his helmet, pulled his goggles over his forehead, stepped forward, and extended his unwounded hand. "Gentlemen. Those of us still standing are in your debt. Lord only knows how many lives were spared by your timely intervention with this . . ." As he shook their hands, he paused to gaze at the twisted shambles of the once-magnificent Snow Cruiser, her Cummins diesel engines still slowly clacking over like a pair of faintly beating hearts. "Just what exactly is it?"

"A souvenir from Admiral Byrd," said Giordino.

"Who?"

Pitt smiled faintly. "It's a long story."

Cleary's mind shifted gears. "I see no bodies."

"They must have all evacuated the center during the battle and headed for the hangar to board the aircraft and make their escape," Giordino speculated.

"My map of the facility shows an airstrip, but we didn't see any sign of aircraft during our descent."

"Their hangar can't be seen from the air. It was carved into the ice."

Cleary's expression turned to fury. "Are you telling me the fiends responsible for this shameful debacle have vanished?"

"Relax, Major," Giordino said with a canny smile. "They haven't left the facility."

Cleary saw the pleased look in Pitt's eyes. "Did you arrange that, too?"

"As a matter of fact, yes," Pitt answered candidly. "On our way here, we happened to run into their aircraft. I'm happy to announce that all flights from the facility have been canceled."

SHOUTS and cheers erupted unabashedly in the Pentagon and White House war rooms at hearing Cleary's voice announce the termination of the ice shelf detachment systems, followed by Lieutenant Jacobs's report that the survivors of Wolf's security force were laying down their arms and surrendering. Elation washed over the two rooms at learning the worst of the deadly crisis was over. They heard Cleary's voice carrying on a one-sided conversation with the saviors of the mission, who carried no radios and whose words could not be heard intelligibly over Cleary's throat microphone.

Unable to contain his exhilaration, the President snatched up a phone and spoke sharply. "Major Cleary, this is the President. Do you read me?"

There was a flicker of static, and then Cleary's voice answered. "Yes, Mr. President, I hear you loud and clear."

"Until now, I was told not to interfere with your communications, but I believe everybody here would like a coherent report."

"I understand, sir," Cleary said, finding it next to impossible to believe he was actually talking to his commander in chief. "I'll have to make it quick, Mr. President. We still have to round up the Wolfs, their engineers, and the last of their security guards."

"I understand, but please brief us on this macabre vehicle that came on the scene. Who does it belong to and who was operating it?"

Cleary told him, but failed miserably at attempting to describe the snow monster that had burst forth from the ice at the last minute and snatched victory virtually from the mouth of defeat.

Everyone sat and listened, bewildered, but nobody was more bewildered than Admiral Sandecker when informed that two men from his government agency who were under his direct authority had driven sixty miles across the barren ice in a monstrous 1940 snow vehicle and helped crush a small army of mercenary security guards. He was doubly stunned when he heard the names Dirk Pitt and Al Giordino, who he thought were due to land in Washington within the hour.

"Pitt and Giordino," he said, shaking his head in wonderment. "I should have known. If anyone can make a grand entrance where they're not expected, it's them."

"I'm not surprised," said Loren, with a smile across her lovely face. "There was no way Dirk and Al were going to stand by passively and wait for the world to stop."

"Who are these people?" demanded General South, angrily. "Where does NUMA get off interfering in a military operation? Who authorized their presence?"

"I would be proud to say I did," Sandecker said, staring directly at South without giving an inch, "but it simply would not be true. These men, make that *my men,* acted on their own initiative, and it looks to me that it was a damned good thing they did."

The argument died before it had begun. It never left the minds of those present in the war rooms of the Pentagon and White House that without the intervention of Pitt and Giordino, there would have been no estimating the frightful aftermath.

Pitt's and Giordino's ears should have been burning, but without a link to Cleary's headgear radio, they could not hear what was said half a world away. Pitt sat on the step of the Snow Cruiser and pulled the bandages off his face, revealing several cuts that would require stitches.

Cleary looked down at him. "You're certain the Wolfs are still here?"

Pitt nodded. "Karl, the head of the family, and one sister, Elsie, must be in tears at seeing the aircraft they'd planned to use to flee the facility has been rendered nonflyable."

"Can you and Mr. Giordino lead me to the hangar?"

Pitt cracked a smile. "I'd consider it an honor and a privilege."

General South's voice cut into the brief conversation. "Major Cleary, I am directing you to regroup, do what you can for your wounded, and secure the rest of the facility. Then wait for the main Special Forces unit, which should be landing inside half an hour."

"Yes, sir," answered Cleary. "But first there is a little unfinished business to settle." He pulled out the connector between his mike and receiving unit, turned to Pitt, and fixed him with an enigmatic stare. "Where is this hangar?"

"About half a mile," said Pitt. "Are you thinking of rounding up a hundred people with the few men you have left?"

Cleary's lips spread in a shifty grin. "Don't you think it only fitting and proper that the men who have gone through hell should be in on the final kill?"

"You'll get no argument from me."

"Are you two up to acting as guides?"

"Did you get permission from Washington?"

"I neglected to ask."

Pitt's opaline green eyes took on a wicked look. Then he said, "Why not? Al and I never could pass up a diabolical scheme."

45

IT WOULD BE A classic understatement to say that Karl Wolf was horrified and enraged when he laid eyes on the broken wreckage of his aircraft. His grand scheme was in tatters, as he and his scientists and engineers milled around the hangar in fear and confusion. To his knowledge, the mechanism to break away the ice shelf was still set to come online in less than four minutes.

Misguided by Hugo, who told them his guards at the control center were still locked in a life-or-death struggle with the Special Forces teams, Karl had no perception that the Fourth Empire had died before it was born, or that Project Valhalla was aborted.

The Wolfs stood in a solemn group, unable to accept the full impact of the disaster, unable to believe the incredible story of a huge vehicle that had run amok and smashed their aircraft, before heading off toward the battle raging in front of the control center. They stood stunned with disbelief at the sudden reversal of their long-cherished plans. Hugo was the only one missing from his family members. Committed to the end, he had disregarded their predicament and was feverishly organizing the remaining members of his security force for the final resistance against the Americans he knew for certain were short minutes away from assaulting the hangar.

Then Karl said, "Well, that's it, then." He turned to Blondi. "Send a message to our brother Bruno on board the *Ulrich Wolf*. Explain the situation and tell him to send backup aircraft here immediately with all speed. We haven't another moment to lose."

Blondi didn't waste time with questions. She took off at a run toward the radio inside the control room at the edge of the airstrip.

"Will it be possible to land on the *Ulrich Wolf* during the early stages of the cataclysm?" Elsie Wolf asked her brother. Her face was pale with anguish.

Karl looked at his chief engineer, Jurgen Holtz. "Do you have an answer for my sister, Jurgen?"

A frightened Holtz looked down at the icy floor of the hangar and replied woodenly. "I have no way of calculating the exact arrival time of the expected hurricane winds and tidal waves. Nor can I predict their initial strength. But if they reach the *Ulrich Wolf* before our flight can land, I fear the result can only lead to tragedy."

"Are you saying we're all going to die?" demanded Elsie.

"I'm saying we won't know until the time comes," Holtz said soberly.

"We'll never have time to transfer the Amenes artifacts from the damaged planes after Bruno arrives," said Karl, staring distraught at the family's personal executive jet, sitting broken like a child's toy. "We'll take only relics of the Third Reich."

"I'm going to need every able-bodied male and female who can shoot a weapon." The voice came from behind Karl. It was Hugo, whose black uniform was splattered with blood from the dead guard who'd failed to tell him of the havoc in the hangar. "I realize we have many frightened and disoriented people on our hands, but if we are to survive until rescued by our brothers and sisters at the shipyard, we must hold out against the American fighting force."

"How many of your fighting men have survived?" asked Karl.

"I'm down to twelve. That's why I require all the reserves I can find."

"Do you have enough weapons for us all?"

Hugo nodded. "Guns and ammo can be found in the arsenal room at the entrance of the hangar."

"Then you have my permission to recruit any and everyone who wants to see their loved ones again."

Hugo looked his brother in the eyes. "It is not my place, brother, to ask them to fight and die. You are the leader of our new destiny. You are whom they respect and venerate. You ask, and they will follow."

Karl stared into the faces of his brother and two sisters, seeing his own expression of foreboding in their eyes. With a mind as cold as an iceberg and a heart of stone, he had no misgivings about ordering his people to lay down their lives so that he and his siblings might survive.

"Assemble them," he said to Elsie, "and I will tell them what they must do."

LEAVING four of his men who were not hurt seriously to tend the wounded and stand guard over the surviving security guards, Cleary and twenty-two able-bodied men of his remaining team, led by Pitt and Giordino, who knew the way to the hangar, entered the main tunnel in tactical formation, with two of Garnet's Delta Force acting as forward flanking scouts.

Lieutenant Jacobs was more than surprised to meet up with Pitt and Giordino again, and even more amazed to find that they were the mad-men who'd driven the Snow Cruiser into the battle zone only minutes before Cleary and his men would have ended up like Custer and the Seventh Cavalry at the Little Bighorn.

Moving cautiously, the column rounded the first bend in the tunnel and moved past the deserted construction equipment and the doorways leading into the empty storerooms. Walking through the ice tunnel seemed far different to Pitt and Giordino than when they had careened through it in the Snow Cruiser. Pitt smiled to himself at seeing the long gouges in the ice caused by his reckless driving when escaping the armored Sno-cat.

When they reached an abandoned tow vehicle, attached to a small train of four flatbed cars that had been used to haul supplies and cargo throughout the tunnel labyrinth, they halted their advance and used the equipment for cover, as Cleary questioned Pitt and Giordino.

"How far to the hangar from here?" he asked.

"About another five hundred yards before the tunnel opens into it," Pitt answered.

"Is there any place between here and there they could set up a barricade?"

"Every ten feet, if they had the time and blocks of ice. But I doubt they could have built anything substantial in the few short minutes since they lost their battle for the facility." He pointed down on the ice. Besides the rotund indentations from the tires of the Snow Cruiser, the only other tracks came from a single snowmobile and the footprints of several men that suggested that they had been running from the battle.

"Can't be more than a dozen security guards left. If they intend to mount a defense, it will have to be within a hundred yards of the hangar."

"Don't forget the Sno-cat," said Giordino quietly, "the one you didn't mash into scrap."

"There's another one of those devilish vehicles still lurking around?" growled Cleary.

Pitt nodded. "Very well could be. What's in your traveling arsenal that can disable it?"

"Nothing that will penetrate its armor," Cleary admitted.

"Hold up your men, Major. I think I see something that might be of use."

Pitt rummaged around in the toolbox of the tow vehicle until he came up with an empty fuel can. He found a steel pry bar and used it to perforate the top of the can. Then he took the bar and punched the bar through the bottom of the tow vehicle's fuel tank. When the can was full, he held it up. "Now all we need is an igniting device."

Lieutenant Jacobs, who was observing Pitt's actions, reached into his pack and retrieved a small flare gun used for signaling purposes at night or in foul weather. "Will this do?"

"Like a beautiful woman and a glass of fine Cabernet," said Pitt.

Cleary raised his arm and swung it forward. "Let's move out."

There were no haunting fears of the unknown now, no urgencies or trepidations. Flankers moving like cats, followed by men unshakable and committed, bent on avenging friends who'd died back at the control center, they advanced into the tunnel like wraiths under the obscure light refracting through the ice. Pitt felt a swell of pride, knowing that he and Giordino were accepted by such men as equals.

Suddenly, the flankers motioned a halt. Everyone froze, listening. An engine's exhaust faintly heard in the distance signaled the approach of a vehicle. Soon the sound grew louder and echoed through the tunnel. Then twin lights appeared, their beams dancing on the ice before rounding the bend.

"The Sno-cat," Pitt announced calmly. "Here it comes." He pointed at one of the nearby empty storerooms. "I suggest you and your men get inside quickly before we're all exposed by the headlights."

A terse, quiet command, and twenty seconds later, every man was inside the storeroom, with the door cracked open an inch. The lights grew brighter as the Sno-cat trod its way through the tunnel. Just behind the storeroom door, Pitt crouched with the fuel can clutched in both hands. Behind him, Jacobs stood poised and ready to fire the flare pistol, and behind him, the entire team primed and ready to pour from the storeroom and lay down a hail of lethal fire on the occupants of the Sno-cat or any guards who might be following on foot.

Timing was critical. If Pitt threw the can too soon or too late and the guards inside survived, the entire Special Force team was trapped inside the storeroom like ducks in a closet, and would be wiped out in less time than it would take to tell about it. Jacobs had to be on target, too. A miss and it was all over.

The Sno-cat came closer. Pitt judged its speed at about ten miles an hour. The driver was moving cautiously. Through the narrow slit between the door and frame, he saw no sign of guards following the vehicle on foot. "She's coming too fast for support to follow behind," Pitt reported softly to Cleary. "My guess is they're on a scouting mission."

"They carry four men," Cleary murmured. "I know that much."

Pitt shied his head and closed his eyes to keep from being temporarily blinded by the bright lights of the Sno-cat. It was so close now he could hear its treads crunch against the icy floor of the tunnel. With infinite caution, without using any sudden movement that might catch the eye of the vehicle's occupants, he inched the door open. The front end of the Sno-cat was now close enough to the storeroom that he could hear the muted beat of its engine. Nimbly, focused, and precise, he threw the door open, raised himself to his full height and hurled the gas can into the open compartment of the Sno-cat. Then, without the slightest suggestion of a pause, he ducked to his side and dropped to the ice.

Jacobs was not one to let the grass grow under his feet. He was aiming the flare pistol before Pitt cast aside the door. A millimeter's adjustment and he fired, the shell missing Pitt's head by the width of two fingers a heartbeat after the fuel can sailed into the open Sno-cat and splashed its contents inside.

The interior erupted in a holocaust of flame. The horrified guards, their uniforms ablaze, leaped from the Sno-cat and rolled frantically on the ice to smother the fire. Even if they had been successful, their lives would not have been spared. The men of Cleary's command who had suffered so appallingly from the guards earlier were not in a benevolent mood. They burst from the storeroom and put the guards out of their agony in a flurry of gunfire. The Sno-cat, now hardly identifiable as a mechanical transport, lurched driverless through the tunnel, grazing the slick walls of ice that did little to slow it down.

No time was spent inspecting the death scene. Cleary regrouped his men and got them moving again. Not one man turned and looked back or showed a sign of remorse. They pushed on through the tunnel, anxious to end the nightmare and punish those responsible. With a conscious effort of will, Pitt rose to his feet and leaned on Giordino's rock-strong shoulder for a few steps until his legs worked efficiently again, then set off after Cleary.

WHEN his radio calls to the Sno-cat went unanswered and the sounds of gunfire reverberated from the tunnel, Hugo Wolf assumed the worst. With no more armored vehicles, he had one more hand to play before the Americans reached the hangar and engaged in another free-for-all battle with his eight remaining security guards. He had little confidence in the small army of engineers, who hardly knew how to handle weapons or had the fortitude to shoot down another human, especially a trained professional who was shooting back. What he was about to attempt, Hugo thought morosely, was the last throw of the dice.

He walked over to where Karl, Elsie, and Blondi were conversing with Jurgen Holtz. Karl turned and looked at Hugo, seeing the dark expression. "Problems, brother?"

"I believe I have lost my last armored Sno-cat and four men who were not expendable."

"We've got to hold out," said Elsie. "Bruno is on his way with two aircraft and is scheduled to arrive five hours from now."

"Three and a half hours after the ice shelf breaks free," Holtz remarked. "The activation sequence for the ice machines has begun and there can be no stopping it."

Karl swore softly. "Can we hold out until then?"

Hugo stared at the tunnel leading to the mining facility as if he were expecting an army of phantoms. "They can't have but a handful of men left. If my guards can eliminate them in the tunnel or at least whittle them down to a pitiful few, then between the rest of us, we easily have enough firepower to stop them for good."

Karl faced Hugo and laid a hand on his shoulder. "Regardless of the outcome, brother, I know you will have conducted yourself bravely and with honor."

Hugo embraced Karl, then moved off to join the last of his guards and lead them into the tunnel. They were followed by a tow vehicle pulling a flatcar loaded with a fifty-five-gallon drum and a large six-foot-diameter fan.

THE Special Forces team stopped short of the last bend in the tunnel before it straightened and ran another fifty yards into the hangar. A light mist appeared ahead that seemed to grow thicker as it rolled through the tunnel and began to envelop the men.

"What do you make of it?" Cleary asked Pitt.

"Nothing good. We encountered nothing like it when we passed through here with the Snow Cruiser." Pitt raised a finger as if testing for wind. "It's not a natural phenomenon. Not only does it have a strange smell, but it's being sent by some sort of mechanism, probably a large fan."

"Not poisonous," said Cleary, sniffing the mist. "Part of our training is in recognizing toxic gas. My guess is they're laying a harmless chemical on us to screen their movements."

"Could be they're short on manpower and making a desperation play," suggested Jacobs, who came up alongside the major.

"Close up," Cleary ordered his men through his helmet radio. "We'll keep going. Be ready to take whatever cover you can find, should they advance and fire out of the mist."

"I don't recommend that course of action," Pitt warned him.

Cleary simply asked, "Why?"

Pitt grinned at Giordino. "I think we've been here before."

"And done that," Giordino added.

Pitt stared appraisingly at the mist, then put his hand on Giordino's arm. "Al, take one of the Major's men, run back to the tow vehicle, and bring back its spare tire."

Cleary eyes reflected curiosity. "What good is a tire?"

"A little subterfuge of our own."

MINUTES later, a tremendous detonation tore through the heart of the tunnel. No flame or swirling smoke, but a blinding flash followed by an enormous shock wave that crushed the confined air before it shot away like a missile through a pneumatic tube. The explosive sound came like a giant clap of thunder before it rumbled away and its echoes slowly faded.

Very slowly, stunned by the sheer density of the shock, his ears ringing like cathedral bells, Hugo Wolf and his eight remaining security guards staggered with numbed senses to their feet and began to advance through mounds of fallen ice, expecting to find nothing but the disintegrated bodies of the Americans. The sheer concussion was far beyond what they'd expected, but their hopes were buoyed into thoughts that their enemy had been eliminated.

Rounding the bend and using flashlights to penetrate the remnant of the mist and vapors from the explosion, they slowly moved forward until they could distinguish bodies lying gruesomely in and under the ice dislodged from the tunnel's roof. Hugo's eyes wandered from figure to figure, satisfaction and elation rising inside him at the sight of the dead Americans. Not one had survived. He looked down at two men who were dressed as civilians and wondered who they were and where they had come from. They were lying facedown, and he failed to recognize them as the two men who'd driven the abominable vehicle that had caused so much death and destruction at the control center.

"Congratulations on a great triumph, Mr. Wolf," one of his guards complimented him.

Hugo slowly nodded. "Yes, but it was a triumph that came with too high a cost." Then, mechanically, he and his men turned their backs on the seeming carnage and began walking back to the hangar.

"Freeze!" Cleary shouted.

Hugo and his men whirled around, aghast at seeing dead men suddenly leap to their feet with their guns leveled and trained. He might have surrendered then and there. Any sane man would have seen that resistance could only end in certain death. But Hugo, more on reflex than with a stable mind, threw up his gun to fire, the guards following his action.

The Special Forces weapons roared as one. The security guards managed to fire only a few frenzied rounds before they were cut down. Hugo stumbled backward, stood motionless in his tracks, his face contorted as he dropped his gun and stared through shocked and glazed eyes at the neatly spaced bullet holes that crossed the stomach of his black uniform from chest to waist. Finally, with sick certainty that he had failed, and knowing he had only a few seconds to live, he crumpled to the ground.

The gunfire had died away, and Jacobs, followed cautiously by his men, began inspecting the bodies and removing all weapons clutched in dead hands. Pitt, with his Colt hanging loosely in his right hand, came over and knelt at Hugo's side. The leader of the Wolf family's annihilated security force became aware of a presence and stared up expressionlessly.

"How did you know?" he murmured.

"Your people used the same booby-trap trick on me in the mine in Colorado."

"But the explosion . . . ?"

Pitt knew the man was going, and he had to get it in fast. "We rolled the spare tire and wheel from a tow vehicle down the tunnel, tripping the wire to your explosive charge. We then took cover in a storeroom. Immediately after the blast, we ran out and scattered ourselves in the ice debris caused by the concussion and played dead."

"Who are you?" he whispered.

"My name is Dirk Pitt."

The eyes widened briefly. "Not you," he whispered. Then the eyes froze open and his head slumped to the side.

46

THE EXPLOSION, FOLLOWED BY a storm of gunfire, resounded
through the tunnel and into the hangar like thunder rumbling from the
other end of a drainage pipe. Then the racket abruptly stopped and the
sounds ebbed, until an ominous silence spread and hung heavy inside
the hangar. Minutes passed, with everyone standing frozen, staring into
the yawning darkness, waiting with uneasy trepidation. Then the eerie
stillness was broken by the approaching sound of footsteps echoing
along the ice floor of the tunnel.

A figure slowly took form and walked into the refracted light falling
through the roof of the hangar. A tall man, holding a stick with a white
rag flowing from the top, advanced toward the semicircle of a hundred
men and women holding guns, every muzzle pointed at the stranger. A
scarf was wrapped around the lower half of his face. He walked directly
up to Karl Wolf and his sisters, stopped, and pulled away the scarf, revealing a craggy face darkened with bearded stubble and haggard with
fatigue.

"Hugo sends his regrets, but he is unable to join your little bon voyage party."

There was a moment of incredulous confusion throughout the hangar. Blondi stared in amazed fascination. Elsie's face took on an expression of shock and baffled rage. Predictably, Karl was the first to recover and come back on keel. "So it's you, Mr. Pitt," he said, observing Pitt through suspicious eyes. "You're like a curse."

"Forgive the casual dress," said Pitt cordially, "but my tux is at the cleaners."

Glaring at Pitt, her blue eyes furious, Elsie stepped forward and thrust an automatic pistol into Pitt's stomach. He grunted in pain, stepped back, and clutched his midriff, but the smile never left his face.

"You will notice," Pitt spoke tautly, "that I am unarmed and carrying a flag of truce."

Karl pushed Elsie's gun hand away. "Let me kill him," she hissed venomously.

"All in good time," he said conversationally. He looked Pitt in the eyes. "Hugo is dead?"

"As we say back home, Hugo bought the farm."

"And his men?

"In the same category."

"Were you responsible for the destruction of my aircraft?"

Pitt looked around at the smashed aircraft and shrugged. "I drove rather recklessly, I must admit."

"Where did you come from?" Wolf asked sharply.

Pitt smiled, ignored him completely, and said, "I suggest you order your people to lay down their weapons before they get hurt very badly. More than enough blood has been spilled here today. It would be the height of stupidity to add to the carnage."

"Your men, Mr. Pitt, how many of the American force are left?"

"See for yourself." Pitt turned and made a motion with his arm. Giordino, Cleary, and his remaining twenty men stepped from the tunnel into the hangar and spread out in an even line nearly ten paces apart, guns held at the ready.

"Twenty against a hundred." Karl Wolf smiled for the first time.

"We're expecting reinforcements momentarily."

"Too late," Karl said, firmly believing that Pitt was desperately attempting to save himself through deception. "The nanotech systems created to break away the ice shelf have been activated by now. The world is headed for a cataclysm as we talk. Nothing can stop it."

"I beg to differ," Pitt said, his tone purposefully neutral. "All systems were shut down ten minutes before they were to be set in motion. I'm sorry to disrupt your plans, Karl, but there will be no cataclysm. There will be no New Destiny, no Fourth Empire. The world will go on spinning around the sun as before, far from perfect, with all its man-made weaknesses and frailties. Summer and winter, blue skies and clouds, rain and snow, will continue uninterrupted until long after the human race has ceased to exist. If we become extinct, it will be from natural causes, not from some outlandish scheme by a megalomaniac bent on world domination."

"What are you saying?" Elsie snapped in growing alarm.

"No need to panic, dear sister," said Karl, his tone a shade less than congenial. "The man is lying."

Pitt shook his head wearily. "It's all over for the Wolf family. If anyone deserves to be indicted by a world tribunal for attempted crimes against humanity, it's you. When seven billion souls find out how you and your family of ghouls tried to exterminate every man, woman, and child on the planet, you're not going to be very popular. Your giant ships, wealth, and treasures will be seized. And if any of your family members *do* escape a lifetime in jail, their every move will be closely watched by international intelligence and police agencies to ensure that they won't have any ambitions for a Fifth Empire."

"If what you say is true," Karl said with a sneer, only slightly diminished by uncertainty, "what do you plan to do with my sisters and me?"

"Not my call." Pitt sighed. "Sometime, someplace, you'll be hanged for your crimes, for all the murders you've ordered of those who stood in your way. My satisfaction will be sitting in the front row and watching you drop."

"A most provocative illusion, Mr. Pitt, and most intriguing. A pity it's pure fantasy."

"You're a hard man to convince."

"Give the order to fire, brother," Elsie demanded. "Shoot the vermin. If you don't, I will."

Karl Wolf stared at the weary and battle-exhausted veterans of

Cleary's command. "My sister is right. Unless your men surrender within the next ten seconds, my people will cut them down."

"Never happen," said Pitt, his voice hard and abrupt.

"One hundred guns against twenty? The battle will not last long, and there can only be one conclusion. You see, Mr. Pitt, too much is at stake. My sisters and I will gladly sacrifice our lives in the name of the Fourth Empire."

"It's stupid to waste lives for a dream that's already dead and buried," Pitt said casually.

"The hollow statement of a desperate man. At least I will have the gratification of knowing you'll be the first to die."

Pitt stared at Wolf for a long moment, then glanced down at the automatic rifle in the madman's hands. Then he shrugged. "Have it your way. But before you get carried away with blood lust, I suggest you look behind you."

Wolf shook his head. "I'm not taking my eyes off you."

Pitt turned slightly to Elsie and Blondi. "Why don't you girls explain the facts of life to your brother?"

The Wolf sisters turned and looked.

Every neck in the hangar turned and every pair of eyes looked toward the rear wall and the entrance of the far tunnel. If there was one thing the hangar was lacking, it wasn't an arsenal of automatic weapons. Another two hundred had joined the drama being enacted around the wrecked aircraft. Two hundred nasty-looking Eradicator rifles all aimed at the backs of Destiny Enterprises engineers and scientists and held in the hands of men whose faces were hidden by helmets and goggles. They were ranged in an orderly semicircle, the front row kneeling, the back row standing, dressed in Arctic battle gear similar to that worn by Cleary and his team.

One of the figures stepped forward and spoke loudly with authority. "Lay down your weapons very slowly and back away! At the first sign of hostility, I will order my men to open fire! Please cooperate and no one will be hurt!"

There was no sign of hesitation or resistance. Far from it. The men and women who made up the scientific team for Destiny Enterprises were only too happy to rid themselves of weapons few of them knew how to operate properly. There was an almost universal sigh of relief as they backed away from the Bushmaster rifles and raised their hands in the air.

Elsie looked as if she had taken a knife in the heart. She stood with a stunned, uncomprehending look on her face. Blondi, her eyes stricken and bewildered, looked as if she was going to be sick. Karl Wolf's face went tense and hard as stone, more angry than fearful at the certainty of seeing his grand plan to launch a new world order suddenly evaporate.

"Which one of you is Dirk Pitt?" inquired the leader of the newly arrived Special Forces.

Pitt slowly raised his hand. "Here."

The officer strode up to Pitt and gave a slight nod of his head. "Colonel Robert Wittenberg, in charge of the Special Forces operation. What is the status of the Ross Ice Shelf operation?"

"Terminated," Pitt answered steadily. "The Valhalla Project was shut down ten minutes short of the ice-cutting system's activation."

Wittenberg relaxed visibly. "Thank God," he sighed.

"Your timing could not have been more perfect, Colonel."

"After making radio contact with Major Cleary, we followed your directions through the opening in the ice you smashed with your vehicle." He paused and asked as if in awe, "Did you see the ancient city?"

Pitt smiled. "Yes, we saw it."

"From there it was a routine run with full battle gear," Wittenberg continued, "until we arrived at the hangar and assembled before anyone turned and noticed us."

"It was touch and go, but Major Cleary and I managed to keep everyone's attention focused away from your end of the tunnel until you took up your battle position."

"Is this all of them?" asked Wittenberg.

Pitt nodded. "Except for several of their wounded back at the control center."

Cleary approached, and the two warriors saluted before shaking hands warmly. Cleary's smile was tired, but the teeth showed. "Bob, you don't know how happy I am to see your ugly old face."

"How many times does this make that I saved your tail?" Wittenberg said, humor in his eyes.

"Twice, and I'm not ashamed to admit it."

"You didn't leave much for me to do."

"True, but if you and your men hadn't shown up when you did, you'd have found half an acre of dead bodies."

Wittenberg stared at Cleary's men, who stood gaunt and weary but still vigilant, watching every move made by the Wolf personnel as they dropped their rifles on the ice floor and gathered in hushed groups near the wrecked aircraft. "It looks like they whittled you down some."

"I lost too many good men," Cleary admitted grimly.

Pitt gestured to the Wolfs. "Colonel Wittenberg, may I introduce Karl Wolf and his sisters Elsie and . . ." Not knowing Blondi, he paused.

"My sister Blondi," Karl intervened. He was a man in the middle of a nightmare. "What do you intend to do with us, Colonel?"

"If it was up to me," growled Cleary, "I'd shoot the whole lot of you."

"Were you given orders concerning the Wolfs after you captured them?" Pitt asked Wittenberg.

The colonel shook his head. "There was no time to discuss political policy regarding prisoners."

"In that case, may I ask a favor?"

"After all you and your friend have done," replied Cleary, "you have but to name it."

"I'd like temporary custody of the Wolfs."

Wittenberg gazed into Pitt's eyes, as if trying to read the mind behind. "I don't quite understand."

But Cleary did. "Since you were given no orders concerning the disposition of prisoners," he said to the colonel, "I think it only fitting and proper that the man who saved us from unimaginable horror have his request honored."

Wittenberg thought a moment before nodding. "I quite agree. The spoils of war. You have custody of the Wolfs until such time as they can be transported under guard to Washington."

"No one government has legal jurisdiction over any individual in Antarctica," said Karl arrogantly. "It is unlawful for you to hold us as hostages."

"I'm only a simple soldier," said Wittenberg, with an indifferent shrug. "I'll leave it for the lawyers and politicians to decide your fate after you're in *their* hands."

WHILE the newly combined Special Force teams secured the mining facility and rounded up the captives, eventually placing them in confinement in a workers' dormitory, Pitt and Giordino unobtrusively herded Karl, Elsie, and Blondi Wolf along the huge doors that covered one wall of the hangar. Seemingly unnoticed, they suddenly forced the three Wolfs through a small maintenance door that opened onto the aircraft runway outside. The sudden surge of cold air came as a shock after the sixty-degree temperature inside the hangar.

Karl Wolf turned and smiled bleakly at Pitt and Giordino. "Is this where you execute us?"

Blondi seemed as if she were in a trance, but Elsie stared at Pitt scathingly. "Shoot us, if you dare!" she spat savagely.

Pitt's face was masked by disgust. "By all that is holy in this world, you all deserve to die. Your whole despicable family deserves to die. But it won't be me or my friend here who will do the honors. I'll leave that to natural causes."

The revelation suddenly struck Wolf. "You're allowing us to escape?"

Pitt nodded. "Yes."

"Then you don't see my sisters and me standing trial and going to jail."

"A family of your wealth and power will never step into a courtroom. You will use every means at your command to cheat the gallows or a life behind bars and go free in the end."

"What you say is true," said Karl contemptuously. "No head of government would dare risk the consequences of indicting the Wolf family."

"Nor incur our wrath," added Elsie. "There isn't a high official or national leader who doesn't owe our family. Our exposure will be their exposure."

"We cannot be imprisoned like common rabble," said Blondi, her voice having regained a measure of insolence. "The family is too spirited, too strong-willed. We will rise again, and next time we will not fail."

"I, for one," said Giordino, his black eyes filled with scorn, "think *that* is a bad idea."

"We'll all rest easier knowing you won't be around to have a hand in it," said Pitt coldly.

Karl Wolf's eyes narrowed, and then he stared out over the icy landscape. "I believe I see your motive," he murmured in subdued tones. "You are turning us loose to die out on the ice floe."

"Yes." Pitt nodded his head slightly.

"Not dressed for frigid temperatures, we won't last an hour."

"My guess is twenty minutes."

"It seems I underestimated you as an opponent, Mr. Pitt."

"I have this theory that the world can get along just fine without the chief director of Destiny Enterprises and the family empire."

"Why don't you simply shoot us and get it over with?"

Pitt gazed at Wolf with the briefest of pleasure in his green eyes. "That would be too quick. This way you'll have time to reflect on the horror you attempted to inflict on billions of innocent people."

There was a slight flush on Wolf's temples. In a supportive gesture, he put his arms around his sister's shoulders. "Your lecture bores me, Mr. Pitt. I'd rather meet death by freezing than listen to more of your philosophic drivel."

Pitt looked thoughtfully at Karl Wolf and his sisters. He wondered if it was possible to make a dent in this incorrigible family. The loss of their empire shook them, but the threat of death didn't unnerve them in the least. If anything, it maddened them. He looked from one face to the other. "A word of warning. Don't bother attempting to double back into the tunnels or the mining facility. All entrances and exits will be guarded." Then he made a gesture with his old Colt. "Start walking."

Blondi looked resigned to her fate, as did Karl. Already she was shivering violently from the biting cold. Not Elsie. She lunged at Pitt, only to receive a backhand from Giordino that knocked her to her knees. As she struggled to her feet, helped by Karl, Pitt had rarely seen such a look of pure malevolence on a woman's face.

"I swear, I'll kill you," she snarled through bloody lips.

Pitt smiled ruthlessly. "Goodbye, Elsie, have a nice day."

"If you walk fast," said Giordino cynically, "you'll stay warmer."

Then he slammed and locked the door.

47

Forty-eight hours later, the mining facility was crawling with scientists and engineers, who began studying the Wolfs' nanotechnology systems while making dead certain the network to break off the ice shelf could not be reactivated. They were followed by an army of anthropologists and archaeologists, who descended on the ancient city of the Amenes. Almost all were former skeptics who denied the existence of an Atlantis-type culture before 4000 B.C. Now they stood and walked amid the ancient ruins in reverent awe, gazing at the grotesque shape of the pillars under ice, unable to believe what they were truly encountering. Soon they were cataloging the artifacts found in the damaged aircraft and the storage rooms in the tunnels spreading from the hangar. After being carefully crated, the artifacts were flown to the United States for conservation and in-depth study before being placed on public display.

Every university in every country with a dedicated archaeology department sent teams to study the city and begin removing the ice that had shrouded it for nine millennia. It would be a massive project that would continue for nearly fifty years and would lead to other undiscovered Amenes sites; the incredible magnitude of artifacts would eventually fill museums in every major city of the world.

His face repaired by a medical team flown in to tend and evacuate the wounded, Pitt, along with Giordino, greeted Dad Cussler when he and his crew arrived to disassemble the remains of the Snow Cruiser for shipment back to a restoration shop in the States. They accompanied him to the control center and then stood back with heavy misgivings as he examined the vehicle for the first time since it had left Little America VI.

The old man stared solemnly and sadly at the great red vehicle that was battered to a pulp, riddled with bullet holes, tires shredded and flat, the windows in the control cabin shot to shards. Nearly three full minutes passed as he walked around the wreckage, examining the damage. Finally, he looked up and made a crooked grin.

"Nothing that can't be fixed," he said, pulling at his gray beard.

Pitt stared at him bleakly. "You really believe it can be rebuilt?"

"I know so. Might take a couple of years, but I think we can put her back together as good as new."

"It doesn't seem possible," said Giordino, shaking his head.

"You and I aren't seeing the same thing," said Cussler. "You see a pile of junk. I see a magnificent machine that will one day be admired by millions of people at the Smithsonian." His blue-green eyes gleamed as he spoke. "What you don't realize is that you took a mechanical failure and turned it into an astonishing success. Before, the Snow Cruiser's only distinction was that it was a fiasco and didn't come close to achieving what it was designed to do. And that was to carry a crew in comfort five thousand miles over the ice of the Antarctic. It floundered almost immediately after coming off the boat in 1930 and lay buried for seventy years. You two not only proved her a triumph of early-twentieth-century engineering by driving her sixty miles across the ice shelf in the middle of a blizzard, but you used her brute size and power to prevent a worldwide cataclysm. Now, thanks to you, she's a priceless and treasured piece of history."

Pitt gazed at the huge mutilated vehicle as if it were a wounded animal. "But for her, none of us would be standing here."

"Someday, I hope you'll tell me the entire story."

Giordino looked at the old man oddly. "Somehow, I think you already know it."

"When she's put on display," said Dad, slapping Pitt on the back, "I'll send you both invitations to the ceremony."

"Al and I will look forward to it."

"That reminds me. Could you point out whoever is in charge here. During our crossing from the ice station, my crew and I ran across three frozen bodies about a half a mile from the runway. It looked like they were trying to cross over the security fence before the cold caught up with them. I'd better report it so the remains can be recovered."

"A man and two women?" Pitt asked innocently.

Dad nodded. "Funny thing. They were dressed more like they were going to a football game in Philadelphia than to survive the Antarctic."

"Some people just don't respect the hazards of frigid climates."

Dad lifted an eyebrow, then reached in his pocket and pulled out a red bandanna half the size of a pup tent and blew his nose. "Yeah, ain't it the truth."

AIRCRAFT were landing with frequency, unloading scientists and military personnel, then loading Cleary's wounded along with the injured Wolf security guards and airlifting them to hospitals in the United States. Not to be left out, the nuclear submarine *Tucson* navigated her way through the cavern into the ice-enclosed harbor and moored next to the old Nazi U-boats.

Captain Evan Cunningham was a bantam cock of a man, short and wiry, who moved his arms and legs as if jerked on strings. He had a smooth face with a sharp chin and Prussian blue eyes that seemed constantly in motion. He met with Colonel Wittenberg and General Bill Guerro, who had been sent to Okuma Bay from Washington to take command from Wittenberg and oversee the growing complexity of the discovery. Cunningham offered the services of his ship and crew as authorized by the naval chief of staff.

Wittenberg had described Pitt to Cunningham, and the commander had sought out the man from NUMA. He approached and introduced himself. "Mr. Pitt, we've talked over the radio, but haven't actually met. I'm Evan Cunningham, captain of the *Tucson.*"

"A privilege to meet you, Captain. Now I can properly express my thanks for your timely rescue of the *Polar Storm* and everyone on board."

"A lucky case of being in the right place at the right time." He grinned broadly. "Not every sub commander in today's navy can say he sank a U-boat."

"Certainly not unless they've retired to a nursing home."

"Speaking of U-boats, did you know there are four more docked in the ice harbor?"

Pitt nodded. "I took a quick look at them this morning. They're as pristine as the day they came out of the factory."

"My engine-room crew went on board to study them. They were mighty impressed with the high quality of engineering created when their grandparents were still in junior high school."

"To anyone born after 1980, World War Two must seem as distant as the Civil War was to our parents."

Pitt excused himself as he glanced at the passengers stepping down the boarding ladder of a Boeing 737 that had taxied up to the hangar. A woman wearing a knit cap with red hair flowing from under it like a fiery waterfall stopped for a moment and looked around the hangar, marveling at the busy activity. Then she looked in his direction and her face lit up.

Pitt began to walk toward her, but was overtaken by Giordino, who ran past him, took Pat O'Connell in his muscular arms, lifted her off the ground as easily as if she were a down pillow, and swung her around in a circle. Then they kissed passionately.

Pitt watched them, mystified. When Giordino set Pat on her feet again, she looked over and waved. Pitt kissed her lightly on one cheek, stood back, and said, "Have I been missing something or do you two have a thing for each other?"

Pat laughed gaily. "Al and I looked into each other's eyes when we were in Buenos Aires and something beautiful happened between us."

He looked at Giordino dryly. "Like what?"

"Like we fell in love."

Pitt was no longer mystified. He was dumbfounded. "You fell in love?"

Giordino shrugged and smiled. "I can't explain it. I've never felt this way before."

"Does this mean you're breaking up the act?"

"My friend, you and I have been through a lot together, more wild ventures than I care to remember. It's a miracle we're still alive, and we have more than our share of scars to prove it. We have to face reality. We're not getting any younger. My joints are beginning to creak when I get up in the morning. We've got to think about slowing down." He paused and grinned. "And then, of course, there's Mama Giordino to consider."

"You have a mother?" asked Pat, teasing.

"You and Mama will get along famously," Giordino said approvingly. "Mama said I can't remain a bachelor forever if I want to give her little Giordinos to fatten with her celebrated lasagna."

"We'd better hurry." Pat laughed. "At thirty-five, I don't have much time left to produce a new brood."

"You have Megan," Pitt said.

"Yes, and she adores Al."

Pitt shook his head in wonder. "Megan approves of this alien character?"

"Why shouldn't she?" Pat said. "He saved her life."

Pitt didn't mention that he had a hand in saving mother and daughter, too. Nor did he let on that he had a fondness for Pat that went beyond mere friendship. "Well, I guess there's nothing left for me to do but give my blessing and insist on being the best man at your wedding."

Giordino put his arm around Pitt's shoulder and said wistfully, "I can't think of another mortal I'd rather have stand up for me."

"Have you set a date?"

"Not before six months," answered Pat. "Admiral Sandecker arranged for me to direct the project to decipher and translate the Amenes inscriptions found in the lost city. It will actually take years, but

I don't think he'll hold it against me if I go home early for a wedding with Al."

"No," Pitt said, trying to absorb the unexpected promise of Al becoming married. "I don't guess he will."

Lieutenant Miles Jacobs came up and threw a casual salute. "Mr. Pitt? Major Wittenberg would like a word with you."

"Where can I find him?"

"He and General Guerro have set up a command post in one of the aircraft maintenance offices on the far end of the hangar."

"I'm on my way, thank you." Pitt turned and looked at Giordino. "You'd better get Pat situated in one of the empty storerooms—she can use it for living quarters and a base for her inscription project." Then he turned and strode through the turmoil of activity to the military command post.

Wittenberg sat at his desk and gestured to a chair, as Pitt entered one of the offices the Russians slaves had carved out of the ice nearly six decades previously. A communications center had been set up, manned by two operators. The place was a madhouse, with civilians and military personnel rushing in and out. General Guerro sat behind a large metal desk in one corner, surrounded by scientists who were requesting the military rush in special excavation equipment so they could begin removing the ice shroud from the ancient city. He did not look happy as he made excuses for the delay.

"Have you found the relics yet?"

"We've been too busy to search," answered Wittenberg. "I thought I'd pass the buck to you. If you're successful, let me know and I'll schedule a military transport to fly you back to the States."

"I'll get back to you shortly," said Pitt, rising to his feet. "I think I know where the Wolfs put them."

"One more thing, Mr. Pitt," said Wittenberg seriously. "Do not say anything to anyone. It's best the relics are removed quietly, before a lot of crazies get wind of their existence and move heaven and earth to lay their hands on them."

"Why not destroy them and be done with it?"

"Not our call. The President personally ordered them brought to the White House."

"I think I understand," Pitt assured him.

As he walked across the hangar floor, the weight of his responsibility fell over him like a black cloud. Uneasily, he approached the Wolfs' deserted executive jet and studied the mutilated tail section that he had crushed with the Snow Cruiser, before stepping around to the entrance door and entering the darkened interior. In what little light filtered in through the smashed opening and the windows, he could discern an interior luxuriously appointed with leather chairs and sofas. He pulled his flashlight from a pocket and swept its beam around the cabin. There was a bar and credenza with a large TV. The rear compartment of the cabin held a king-size bed in anticipation of its owner's getting a few hours' sleep while the plane was in flight. The bathroom had gold-plated fixtures and a small shower. Forward, just behind the cockpit, he could see a small galley, complete with oven, microwave, sink, and cabinets that held crystal glasses and china.

His eyes fell on a long box that was tied to the floor beside the bed. Pitt knelt and ran his hands over the surface. He tried to lift one end, but found it was made out of bronze and extremely heavy. There was a brass plaque embedded in the lid. He shined the light on the lettering and leaned closer. The inscription was in German, but relying on the few words he'd learned, he loosely translated the message as "Here lie the treasures of the ages awaiting resurrection."

He twisted the pins from their hasps and removed them. Then, taking a deep breath, he took both hands and lifted the lid.

There were four objects inside the bronze box, all contained in leather cases and neatly wrapped in heavy linen. He carefully opened the first case and unwrapped the smallest object. It held a small bronze plaque with a crack running through it. The sculptured front side displayed a holy knight killing a dragonlike monster. Pitt would learn later that it was considered a sacred Nazi relic because Hitler had had it in a breast pocket of his uniform during the assassination attempt, when German army dissenters had set off a bomb in his forest headquarters.

The next case held the sacred Nazi flag earlier described by Admiral Sandecker as having been smeared with the blood of a fallen supporter of Hitler who'd been killed when the Bavarian police fired on the fledgling Nazi party members during the Munich Putsch in November of

1923. The bloodstain could easily be seen under the beam of the flashlight. He placed it back inside the linen and the leather case.

Then he opened a long mahogany chest and stared in rapt fascination at the Holy Lance, the lance allegedly used by a Roman centurion to pierce the body of Jesus Christ, the lance Hitler believed would give him control over the destiny of the world. The image of the lance being used to kill Christ on the cross was too overwhelming for Pitt to envision. He gently laid the most sacred relic in Christendom back in the mahogany chest and turned to the largest of the leather cases.

After unwrapping the linen, he discovered that he was holding a heavy urn of solid silver a few inches less than two feet high. The top of the lid was decorated with a black eagle that stood on a gold wreath surrounding an onyx swastika. Just below the lid were inscribed the words *Der Führer.* Directly beneath were the dates 1889 and 1945 over the runic symbols for the SS. On the base above a ring of swastikas were the names Adolf Hitler and Eva Hitler.

The horror struck Pitt like a blow to the face. The sheer immensity of what he was staring at sent shivers up his spine and a knot twisting inside his stomach, as his face drained of all color. It didn't seem possible that in his hands he was holding the ashes of Adolf Hitler and his mistress/wife, Eva Braun.

PART FIVE

ASHES, ASHES, ALL FALL DOWN

WHEN THE MILITARY PASSENGER aircraft sent to bring Pitt, Giordino, and the relics from Okuma Bay to Washington landed at the airport in Veracruz, Mexico, Pitt questioned the pilot and was told that Admiral Sandecker had sent a NUMA executive jet to carry them the rest of the way. Sweating in the heat and humidity, they hauled the bronze box to the turquoise aircraft with the big NUMA letters on the fuselage that was parked a good hundred yards away.

Except for the pilot and copilot in the cockpit, the plane was deserted. After loading the box and tying it down to the floor, Pitt tried to open the cockpit door, but it was locked. He knocked and waited until a voice came over the cabin speaker.

"I'm sorry, Mr. Pitt, but my orders are to keep the cabin door locked and permit no exit or entry of the cockpit until the relics are safely loaded in an armored truck at Andrews Air Force Base."

A security overkill, Pitt thought. He turned to Giordino, who was holding up a green hand. "Where did you get the green palm?"

"From the paint on the door hinge. I grabbed it for support when we loaded the box." He rubbed a finger over the stain. "Not green, turquoise. The paint on this plane isn't dry."

"Looks as if the turquoise paint was sprayed on less than eight hours ago," observed Pitt.

"Could it be we're being hijacked?" asked Giordino.

"Maybe, but we might as well enjoy the scenery below until we can determine we're on the right course for Washington."

The plane taxied for a few minutes before taking off over the sea under a cloud-free radiant blue sky. For the next few hours, Pitt and Giordino relaxed and took turns keeping watch through the windows at the water below. The plane flew across the Gulf of Mexico and crossed into the States at Pensacola, Florida. From there it appeared to be on a direct course for Washington. When Giordino recognized the nation's capital in the distance, he turned to Pitt.

"Could it be we're like a pair of suspicious old women?"

"I'll reserve judgment until I see a red carpet leading to an armored car."

In another fifteen minutes, the pilot banked the aircraft and headed onto the flight path for Andrews Air Force Base. Only two miles from the end of the runway, the plane made a barely perceptible sideways motion. Pitt and Giordino, themselves pilots with many hours in the cockpit, immediately sensed the slight course deviation.

"He's not landing at Andrews," Giordino announced calmly.

"No, he's lining up to come into a small private airport just north of Andrews in a residential area called Gordons Corner."

"I have this odd feeling that we're not getting red-carpet, VIP treatment."

"So it would appear."

Giordino gazed at Pitt through squinted eyes. "The Wolfs?"

"Who else?"

"They must want the relics badly."

"Without them, they have no hallowed symbols to rally around."

"Not like them to play games. They could have just as well put down anywhere between Mexico and Virginia."

"Without Karl and Hugo at the family helm," said Pitt, "they either got sloppy or else they knew they'd be tracked all the way from Veracruz and chased by Air Force fighters if they attempted to deviate from the flight plan."

"Should we take over the controls and head for Andrews?" Giordino asked.

"Better to wait until we're on the ground," said Pitt. "Busting into the cockpit while the pilot is flared for touchdown might cause bad things to happen."

"You mean a crash?"

"Something like that."

"That's life," mused Giordino. "I had my heart set on a marching band and a parade through the city."

Seconds later, the wheels gave a brief screech as they smacked the asphalt of the landing strip. Staring through one of the windows, Pitt saw an armored truck and a pair of ML430 Mercedes-Benz suburban utility vehicles converge and follow in the wake of the aircraft. Quick sprinters with 268-horsepower V-8 engines, they were about as close to European sports sedans as a four-wheeler could get.

"Now's the time," he said briefly. He pulled his Colt from the duffel bag as Giordino retrieved his P-10. Then Giordino effortlessly kicked open the cockpit door and they rushed inside. The pilot and copilot automatically raised their hands without turning.

"We were expecting you, gentlemen," said the pilot, as if reading from some script. "Please do not attempt to take control of the aircraft. We cut the control cables immediately after touchdown. This aircraft is inoperable and cannot fly."

Pitt stared over the console between the pilots and saw that the cables to the control column and foot pedals were indeed sliced where they disappeared into the flight deck. "Both of you, out!" he snapped, as he dragged them out of their seats by the collars. "Al, throw their butts off the plane!"

The aircraft was still moving at twenty-five miles an hour when Giordino ejected the pilot and copilot through the passenger door onto the asphalt, taking satisfaction in seeing them bounce and roll like rag dolls. "What now?" he asked, as he reentered the cockpit. "Those tough-looking Mercedes SUVs are only a hundred yards behind our tail and coming fast."

"We may not have flight controls," replied Pitt, "but we still have brakes and engines."

Giordino looked dubious. "You don't expect to drive this thing down Pennsylvania Avenue to the White House?"

"Why not?" Pitt said, as he pushed the throttle forward and sent the aircraft speeding across the taxiway and onto the road leading from the airport. "We'll go as far as we can and hopefully reach heavy traffic where they wouldn't dare attack."

"You're why cynics outlive optimists," said Giordino. "The Wolfs are so desperate for the relics, they'd shoot down a stadium full of women and children to get them back in their dirty hands."

"I'm open for suggestions—"

Pitt broke off as the thump of bullets into the aluminum-skin aircraft sounded inside the cockpit. He began hitting the right brake and then the left, sending the plane zigzagging down the road to throw off the aim of the gunners in the Mercedes.

"Time for me to play Wild Bill Hickok," said Giordino.

Pitt handed him his .45. "You'll need all the firepower you can get. There are extra clips in my duffel bag."

Giordino lay down beside the open passenger door with his feet toward the rear of the aircraft and sighted over the tail section at the pursuing SUVs. Out of the corner of his eye, he saw bullets stitch through the port wing and open the fuel tank. Luckily there was no fire, but it was only a question of time before an engine was struck and flamed. He took careful aim and fired when Pitt turned from zig to zag.

Pitt literally threw the plane up the on-ramp leading to the Branch Avenue Highway that ran into the city. With both jet engines screaming, he soon had the airplane hurtling nearly a hundred miles an hour down the right lane and shoulder of the highway. Startled drivers gaped openmouthed as the plane shot by them, then watched, stunned, the gun battle between a man shooting out the passenger door of the aircraft and two Mercedes-Benz SUVs that chased in and out of traffic from behind.

Pitt knew the aircraft easily had the power to outrun the Mercedes, but he had a great disadvantage because of the forty-two-foot wingspan. It was only a matter of time before he clipped a car, a truck, or a light pole. His only advantage was that the engines were mounted on the fuselage. But they wouldn't turn over long if one or both wings containing the fuel tanks were torn away. As it was, he noticed that the gauge that registered the fuel on the port tank was dropping at an alarming rate. He took a quick glance out his side window and saw the wing shredded by bullets and the fuel spraying out under the head wind.

He steered by the brakes, moving in and out of the light traffic that he knew would become heavier as he neared the city. When possible, he tried to pass and move in ahead of trucks, using them as a shield against the gunfire from the men in the SUVs. He could hear Giordino's gun shooting from the main cabin, but he couldn't see the results, nor could he tell how close his pursuers were behind the aircraft's rudder.

With both feet on the brakes and his right hand on the throttles, he used his left to call a Mayday over the radio. The control tower operator at Andrews Air Force Base replied and asked for his location, as they did not have him on radar. When told he was on Branch Avenue approaching the Suitland Parkway, the controllers thought he was a nutcase and ordered him sharply to get off the radio. But Pitt persisted and demanded they call the nearest police unit, a request they were more than happy to grant.

Back in the cabin, Giordino's slow, methodically aimed fire finally paid off. He shot out the right front tire of the lead Mercedes, sending it into an uncontrollable skid across the highway, where it flew into a drainage ditch and rolled over three times before coming to rest upside down in a cloud of dust. The other Mercedes came on without hesitation and was gaining due to the increased traffic that was slowing Pitt. He needed two lanes and the shoulder to cut past cars and trucks looming ahead.

Sirens screamed in the distance, and soon red-and-blue flashing lights were seen coming from the opposite direction. The police cars cut across the grassy strip between the divided highway and picked up the chase almost on the rear bumper of the Mercedes, passing around it and rushing toward the aircraft the officers thought was in the hands of either a drug addict or a drunk.

For perhaps ten seconds, the police officers were not aware of the bullets coming out of the automatic rifles fired by the two men out the rear side-door windows of the lone Mercedes, but then the bullets ripped through the hoods of the police cars and mauled the engines, causing them to stop dead. The officers, surprised and bewildered, coasted their cars off the highway onto the shoulder as smoke rolled from beneath their hoods.

"They stopped the cops!" Giordino shouted through the cockpit door.

They *are* desperate to retrieve the sacred relics, Pitt thought, as the Mercedes pulled even and the gunners unleashed a gale of bullets that smashed into the cowl of the nose in front of him. But coming too close to the aircraft was a mistake. Giordino held both automatics in his hands and pumped both magazines into the Mercedes, striking the driver, who slumped over the wheel. The SUV then drifted out of its lane and crashed into the side of a giant truck and trailer hauling milk. The rear wheels of the heavy trailer smashed into and over the Mercedes, flattening the occupants and bouncing wildly over the wreckage before leaving it scattered in jagged pieces across the concrete.

"You can slow down now," announced an exultant Giordino. "The posse is no more."

"You're a better shot than I gave you credit for," said Pitt, easing back on the throttles, but still keeping the aircraft moving down the highway. When he was absolutely sure there was no more pursuit, he eased the aircraft onto a wide grassy area of Fort Davis Park and killed the engines.

Within minutes, they were surrounded by nearly ten District of Columbia police cars and forced to lie on the ground with their wrists handcuffed behind them. Later, after they were taken to the nearest station and questioned by two detectives, who thought their story of being chased from the airport for sacred Nazi relics belonged in *Alice in Wonderland,* Pitt convinced them to make a phone call.

"You're entitled to your one call," said Detective Lieutenant Richard Scott, a gray-haired veteran of the force.

"I'd be grateful if you made it for me," said Pitt.

The detective plugged a phone into a jack inside the interrogation room and looked up. "The number?"

"I've never memorized it, but information can give you the phone number for the White House."

"I'm tired of your nonsense," said Scott wearily. "What number do you want to reach?"

Pitt pierced the detective with a cold stare. "I'm dead serious. Call the White House, ask for the President's chief of staff. Tell him we, along with the sacred relics, are languishing in a police station on Potomac Avenue."

"You're joking."

"You must have checked us out and found we're ranking officials of NUMA and not wanted criminals."

"Then how do you explain shooting up the highway with guns that aren't registered?"

"Please," Pitt coaxed. "Just make the call."

Looking up the White House number, Scott followed Pitt's instructions. Slowly, his face changed expressions like a comic actor's. From suspicion to curiosity to downright bafflement. When he set down the receiver, he stared with newfound respect.

"Well?" asked Giordino.

"President Wallace himself came on the line and directed me to get you and your relics to the White House in the next ten minutes or he'd have my badge."

"Don't fret, Lieutenant," Giordino said congenially. "We won't time you."

WITH sirens blaring and lights flashing, Pitt and Giordino and the bronze box were rushed to the northwest gate of the White House. Once inside, the bronze box was opened and searched under the watchful eyes of the Secret Service for weapons or explosive devices. The Nazi relics were removed from their leather cases and unwrapped from the linen and examined. Then, rather than go through the trouble of replacing and rewrapping again, Giordino simply took the sacred lance and carried it in one hand. Pitt kept the little bronze plaque and gave the sacred bloodstained flag to an agent. The silver urn he kept in his possession, firmly gripped with both hands.

The President's secretary stood as she saw them approaching, sur-rounded by no fewer than four Secret Service agents. She smiled and greeted Pitt and Giordino. "The President and quite a few high-ranking people have been patiently waiting for you in his office."

"We look pretty shabby for a reception," said Giordino, surveying his rumpled clothing.

"If I may have a moment," asked Pitt. "Could you direct me to the nearest bathroom?"

"Why, certainly," she said sweetly. "The men's room is just behind you to your right."

In a few minutes, Pitt and Giordino entered the Oval Office. They were stunned to find the room crowded: the Joint Chiefs of Staff, the President's cabinet and top aides, Admiral Sandecker with Hiram Yaeger and Rudi Gunn, several congressional leaders, and Loren Smith, who showed no fear or embarrassment by coming over and kissing Pitt square on the lips. There was a solid round of applause as Pitt and Giordino stood stunned with astonishment.

When the sounds of clapping hands and voices quieted, Pitt could not refrain from saying, "This is certainly a better reception than we got at the Gordons Corner airport."

"Gordons Corner?" blurted Sandecker. "You were supposed to land at Andrews Air Force Base, where a reception committee was still wait-ing for you."

"Yes," said the secretary of state, Paul Reed. "What's this about you being arrested and held by the police?"

"The Wolf family made an attempt to retrieve the relics," answered Pitt.

"They tried to hijack the relics?" asked General Amos South of the Joint Chiefs of Staff. "I certainly hope they failed."

"They failed," Pitt assured him. "We have the relics."

President Dean Cooper Wallace walked up to them. "Gentlemen, the nation, no, the world, owes you a debt of gratitude that can never be re-paid. Unfortunately, only a select few will ever learn how close the world came to chaos and what you did to prevent it."

Vice President Brian Kingman stood beside the President. "It's an in-justice for you not to receive proper acclaim for your tremendous achievements, but if the story of how the world's population came within minutes of being obliterated became known, there would be total chaos. The media would go ballistic, and despite the danger having passed, fear and terror would last for years to come."

"Brian is right," said the President. "Knowing Earth is susceptible to being struck by a comet or asteroid, or experiencing an earthquake, is hardly a concern of the public during their day-to-day existence. But they could never shrug off the thought of another madman like Karl Wolf and his family attempting to annihilate billions of people to fulfill a compulsion for world domination. Fear would run rampant, a situation we cannot allow to happen."

"I don't mind, Mr. President," Giordino said, cheerfully brazen. "I've always hated the thought of people coming up and demanding my autograph while I was dining in a restaurant."

Pitt turned away to suppress his laughter. Sandecker rolled his eyes toward the ceiling. The President looked blank, not knowing if the little Italian was joking or serious.

"I think what my friend is trying to get across," said Pitt, "is that he and I are quite content to remain anonymous."

At that point, everyone in the room began asking questions, mostly about how they had crossed the ice in the Snow Cruiser and saved the Special Forces teams. Then the President stared down and saw the spear in Giordino's hand.

"Is that the Holy Lance I've heard so much about?" he asked.

Giordino nonchalantly laid the lance in the President's hands. "Yes, sir, it is."

Wallace held the lance over his head, as everyone in the room stared in awe.

"The most sacred relic in all of Christendom," proclaimed Pitt. "It's said the man who wields it can command the destiny of the world for good or evil."

"Obviously, Hitler chose the latter," said Admiral Sandecker.

"Is it truly the spear that pieced Christ's body on the cross?" Wallace asked reverently, gazing at the spear point as if expecting to see a hint of dried blood.

"So says the legend," said Pitt.

The President handed the lance to Secretary of State Reed. "You'd better take it, Paul."

"What do you intend to do with it, Mr. President?" asked General South.

Cooper lightly touched the ancient spearhead. "I'm told the lance belongs in the treasure room of the Royal Palace in Vienna, from which Hitler stole it in 1938."

Reed shook his head. "Never," he said emphatically. "I'm sorry, Mr. President, but it must be hidden away, never to fall into malignant hands again and be used as a symbol for tyranny."

After they had all examined the Blood Flag and the small bronze plaque thought to have saved Hitler's life, Pitt went out to the desk of the President's secretary, where he'd left the urn, and carried it into the Oval Office. He set it on the table before the fireplace. "The ashes of Hitler and Eva Braun."

Then he stood back as the crowd in the Oval Office moved in closer to inspect the words etched in the silver. Their voices soon hushed and became quiet murmurs as they examined the container of the accursed remains of history's most infamous despot.

"It makes me shudder simply to look at it," said Loren, clutching Pitt's arm.

Pitt gripped her around the waist. "I'm sure you're not alone."

"Too abhorrent to contemplate," muttered the President.

General South looked at the President and said, "Sir, I think we should inspect the interior of the urn to make absolutely certain that ashes are truly inside."

President Wallace looked around the office. "Does anyone object?"

"I also think it wise," said Secretary of State Reed, "that the FBI labs do a thorough examination to prove they're human."

"Will you please remove the lid, General?" the President asked South.

Even the tough old soldier found it repulsive to touch the urn. Very reluctantly, he gently placed his fingers around the black eagle atop the urn and twisted it cautiously as he lifted. The lid came free and he set it on the desk as if it were tainted with a virus.

Everyone stood back whisper-silent as the President warily peered into the urn. His face took on a puzzled expression, and he looked up into a sea of grim, expectant faces.

"It's empty," he said vaguely. "There are no ashes inside."

The word "empty" was repeated throughout the room. "This certainly is a twist no one counted on," said Vice President Kingman, equally mystified.

"Is it possible the Wolfs took the ashes and rehid them?" General South said, voicing the thoughts of everyone present.

Only Giordino looked strangely contemplative. Then his face brightened as if he had suddenly witnessed a revelation. He turned and looked at Pitt queerly. *"Oh no!"* he muttered softly. *"You didn't?"*

"I did," Pitt answered honestly.

"What are you talking about?" asked Loren. "Do you know who took the ashes?"

"I do."

"Then who?"

"Me," Pitt replied, his opaline green eyes reflecting fiendish mirth. "I flushed them down the toilet in the White House men's room."

PART SIX

FINAL
BLESSING

THE DAY WAS TYPICAL for the nation's capital, the climate hot and sultry. The leaves hung green on their branches and the cool breeze of the coming fall was nowhere to be felt. Crowds of people were standing in long lines to view the recently opened wing of the Natural History Museum, which housed more than three thousand Amenes treasures and artifacts that had been recovered from St. Paul Island, the *Ulrich Wolf,* and the ongoing excavation of the lost city in the Antarctic.

Members of the Wolf family, as expected, walked free from the courts. But an international investigative force was formed for no other purpose than to keep all family members under strict surveillance. There was no way the Wolfs would be allowed to attempt another world-domination scheme without being discovered and stopped dead in their tracks. Destiny Enterprises was no more, and with the death of Karl, the family was rudderless. And without their enormous hoard of wealth and assets, most were forced to endure a far less luxurious lifestyle.

The Chilean government had promptly appropriated the four gigantic Destiny Enterprises ships. After the fjord was extensively dredged to allow their access to open water, the giant superships began sailing the seven seas, carrying vast numbers of passengers and gargantuan cargos that had been thought inconceivable a few short years before. The *Ulrich Wolf* was sold to a conglomerate of shipping lines for a reported three billion dollars. With minor modifications, she was put into service as a round-the-world cruise city with short-term staterooms and privately owned apartments and condominiums. She was renamed the *Ocean Paradise,* and proved extremely popular because international flights could land and take off on her long upper deck runway while she was cruising far offshore.

The other three gigantic ships were purchased by cargo transport lines and oil companies and soon became familiar sights in the few major port facilities that could receive them. Because they showed that leviathan superships could be profitable, it was not long before six other ships of comparable size were under construction.

Admiral Sandecker, along with Pitt, Loren Smith, Giordino, and Pat, who had flown in to help set up the display of Amenes descriptions, were members of a party of VIPs who were invited to preview the exhibits before they were open to the general public. No matter how many times they had seen them, Pitt and Giordino were still amazed at the magnitude of the treasures on display. No one who beheld them could believe they came from a race of people who vanished nine thousand years ago, long before most prehistoric civilizations had emerged from the stone age.

The centerpiece under a spacious stained-glass rotunda was a grouping of the beautifully preserved mummies of the Amenes rulers found on St. Paul Island by Giordino and Rudi Gunn. Everyone stood in awe in the presence of those who had lived and died so far in the past. Pitt found himself wondering if one of these ancient people might have been his direct ancestor.

Nearly five hours later, they exited the exhibit through a side door held open by a guard and began walking across the mall toward the newly built Smithsonian Transportation Museum. Loren looked dazzling, her cinnamon hair falling to her shoulders and accented by the sun. She was dressed comfortably in a light blue sleeveless silk dress that was cut short, revealing a shapely pair of tanned legs. Pitt wore a green golf shirt and light-tan slacks. Al and Pat, shunning any formal look in the heat, both wore light T-shirts and shorts. Like a pair of young lovers, they held hands as they walked across Madison Drive and took the pathway across the Mall, with Sandecker in the lead, puffing on one of his elephantine cigars.

"When are your returning to Okuma Bay?" Loren asked Pat.

"Next week."

Loren smiled at Giordino. "There goes your love life."

"Haven't you heard? The admiral is sending me back to the ancient city on a sabbatical. He's directed me to study and record the seafaring activities of the Amenes for Hiram Yaeger's computer archives. Pat and I will be working together for the next six months."

"That leaves just you and me," said Loren, squeezing Pitt's hand.

"Not for long." Pitt brushed his lips against her hair. "I'm leaving in two weeks to head up a research project on an underwater volcano that's rising toward the water surface southeast of Hawaii."

"How long will you be?"

"No more than three weeks."

"I guess I can endure three weeks without you," Loren said, with a faint little grin.

They crossed Jefferson Drive between the traffic and walked through the entrance of the Transportation Museum. Inside, on four acres of open space, were displayed hundreds of vehicles dating back to the late 1890s. They were laid out in chronological order from the early brass cars to the latest-concept cars from the auto manufacturers. Besides automobiles, every kind of conceivable vehicle was represented from manufacturers of trucks, farm tractors, motorcycles, and bicycles.

The gem of the collection was Admiral Byrd's Snow Cruiser. She sat in a gallery five feet below the main floor so the public could peer through the windows and open doors at eye level. Her new red paint and orange stripe gleamed under overhead lights, revealing the great machine in all her glory.

"They certainly did a masterful job restoring her," said Pitt quietly.

"Hard to believe," murmured Giordino, "considering how we left her."

Sandecker's gaze traveled from one end of the Snow Cruiser to the other. "A majestic piece of machinery. Remarkably modern lines for a vehicle designed nearly sixty-four years ago."

"I can't help wondering what she could do with a pair of new six-hundred-horsepower turbodiesels in her gut," Giordino speculated.

"I'd have given my right arm to put her in my collection," said Pitt wistfully.

Loren looked at him. "This has to be the only time I can remember when you couldn't take home a souvenir with wheels on it from your adventures."

He gave a helpless shrug. "It belongs to the people."

They stood around for several minutes gazing at the Snow Cruiser, while Pitt and Giordino reminisced about their wild ride over the Antarctic wasteland. Then, reluctantly, they left the great vehicle and walked through the aisles, viewing the other exhibits until they reached the main entrance again.

Sandecker bent his wrist and glanced at his watch. "Well, I have to be running along."

"A hot date?" asked Giordino. It was well known that since his divorce many years before, the admiral was one of the most sought-after bachelors in town by the city's eligible ladies. Never making a commitment, he managed to adroitly keep his feminine friends happy without angering or disillusioning them.

"I'm dining with Senator Mary Conrow, and I'd hardly consider her a hot date."

"You old dog," said Loren. "Mary is a ranking member of the budget committee. You're getting cozy so you can sweet-talk her into voting an increase in NUMA's budget."

"It's called mixing business with pleasure." He gave the women a kiss on their cheeks, but didn't shake the hands of the men. He saw them on a daily basis and felt there was no call to act chummy, despite the fact that Pitt and Giordino were like sons to him.

"We're off, too," said Pat. "We promised Megan to take her out for a hamburger and a movie."

"How about dinner at my place on Friday?" Loren said, with her arm around Pat's waist.

"You're on." She turned to Giordino. "All right with you, lover?"

Giordino nodded. "Loren makes a to-die-for meat loaf."

"Meat loaf it shall be." Loren laughed.

THE sun was setting toward the horizon, growing from a small golden ball into a vast orange sphere as Pitt and Loren sat in the apartment of his hangar and enjoyed a glass of Don Julio silver tequila on the rocks while listening to music. She was nestled on the couch, leaning against him, legs curled under her.

"I never understood how women can do that," he said, between sips of his tequila.

"Do what?"

"Sit on their legs. I can't bend mine that far, and if I could, they'd lose circulation and go numb."

"Men are like dogs, women like cats. Our joints are more limber than yours."

Pitt raised his hands languidly in the air and stretched. "So much for Sunday. Tomorrow it's back to studying oceanographic project reports for me and making trivial speeches in Congress for you."

"My term is up next year," she said slowly. "I'm thinking of not running for reelection."

He looked at her curiously. "I thought you said you were going to grow old in Congress?"

"I changed my mind. After seeing how happy Pat and Al are, I realized that if I ever want to have babies while I'm still able, I'd better find a good man and settle down."

"I can't believe I'm hearing this."

She threw him a mock, inquiring look. "Don't you want to marry me?"

It took a few moments for Pitt to absorb her words. "As I recall, I proposed marriage in the Sonoran Desert after the Inca Gold affair and you turned me down."

"That was then," she said airily.

"I never asked you again. How do you know I haven't had second thoughts?"

She stared into his eyes, not certain whether he was serious or simply being funny. "You've gotten cold feet?"

"Can we both really change our lifestyles?" he asked with a straight face. "You still have your seat in the House of Representatives and a luxurious town house in Alexandria. I have my apartment and car collection in an old rusty hangar with noisy aircraft taking off and landing overhead. How can we possibly work it out?"

She put her arms around him and stared at him through eyes misty with love. "I've had my day playing the independent, individualist woman. I enjoyed it. But now it's time to get practical. There are other projects I'd like to take on."

"Such as?"

"I've been asked to take over the directorship of the National Child Abuse Foundation."

"That takes care of the career. What about the lifestyle?"

"We can alternate—one week here, one week in my town house."

"You call that practical?"

She suddenly became flippant. "I don't know what your problem is. We spend most of our free time together anyway."

He pulled her close and kissed her. "Okay, since you begged me nicely, I'll give some thought to marrying you."

She pushed him away and acted as if she were pouting, knowing full well he was teasing her. "On the other hand, I just may look around. There must be hundreds of men out there who would appreciate me. I'm sure I can do better than Mister High-and-Mighty Dirk Pitt."

Pitt pressed her body against his tightly, stared into her violet eyes, and said softly, "Why waste your time? You know that's impossible."

"You're incorrigible."

"A lot can happen in the next year."

Loren curled her arms around his neck. "That's true, but the fun is in making it happen."

POSTSCRIPT

In 1960, ARCHAEOLOGISTS DISCOVERED the ancient bones of a woman on Santa Rosa, one of the channel islands off California. After she lay in the basement of the Santa Barbara museum for forty years, a team of scientists conducted sophisticated DNA and radiocarbon tests on the skeletal remains. Results revealed the bones to be as old as thirteen thousand years, making the lady the oldest known human skeleton found in North America.

During the era in which she lived, the lady would have seen glaciers the size of Australia, woolly mammoths, and saber-toothed tigers, and she could have walked from island to island, since the sea level was 360 feet lower than it is today. Her discovery challenged traditional theories that the first people to live in the Americas came across the land bridge over what is now the Bering Sea between Siberia and Alaska.

The Spirit Caveman, as another human relic is called, lived more than 9,400 years ago in Western Nevada and has a cranial profile that suggests his origins are Japanese or East Asian. The Wizard's Beach Man, whose skull was also found in Nevada, closely resembles both the Norse and the Polynesians. Other skulls found in Nebraska and Minnesota, all at least eight thousand years old, resemble both Europeans and South Asians.

New evidence suggests that the first settlers might have been Polynesians and Asians who inhabited the western end of North and South America while the eastern seaboard was settled by Europeans who arrived by boat, navigating along the ice pack that spanned the North Atlantic during the ice age and following the migratory birds that flew west.

It is known that people traveled by boats from southern Asia to Australia more than forty thousand years ago, so sea travel is hardly an invention of civilizations around the Mediterranean. The seas beckoned ancient mariners, who explored and discovered far more of the world than they were given credit for, and whose history is only now being written.